SELECTED WRITINGS OF ANDRÉS BELLO

SELECTED
WRITINGS OF
ANDRÉS BELLO

Andrés Bello

Translated from the Spanish by

FRANCES M. LÓPEZ-MORILLAS

EDITED, WITH AN INTRODUCTION AND NOTES
BY IVÁN JAKSIĆ

New York   Oxford
Oxford University Press
1997

Oxford University Press

Oxford   New York
Athens   Auckland   Bangkok   Bogotá   Bombay
Buenos Aires   Calcutta   Cape Town   Dar es Salaam
Delhi   Florence   Hong Kong   Istanbul   Karachi
Kuala Lumpur   Madras   Madrid   Melbourne
Mexico City   Nairobi   Paris   Singapore
Taipei   Tokyo   Toronto   Warsaw

and associated companies in
Berlin   Ibadan

Copyright © 1997 by Oxford University Press, Inc.

Published by Oxford University Press, Inc.
198 Madison Avenue, New York, New York 10016

Oxford is a registered trademark of Oxford University Press

Library of Congress Cataloging-in-Publication Data

Bello, Andrés, 1781-1865.
Selected writings of Andrés Bello / by Andrés Bello;
translated by Frances M. López-Morillas ; edited, with an
introduction and notes by Iván Jaksić.
p.   cm. — (Library of Latin America)
Includes bibliographical references and index.
ISBN 0-19-510545-1
I. Jaksic, Ivan, 1954-   .   II. Title.   III. Series.
PQ8549.B3A6   1997
868—dc20   96-44127

1 3 5 7 9 8 6 4 2

Printed in the United States of America
on acid-free paper

Dedicated to Don Pedro Grases,
Bellista infatigable

Contents

II EDUCATION AND HISTORY

Series Editors'
General Introduction

The Library of Latin America series makes available in translation major nineteenth-century authors whose work has been neglected in the English-speaking world. The titles for the translations from the Spanish and Portuguese were suggested by an editorial committee that included Jean Franco (general editor responsible for works in Spanish), Richard Graham (series editor responsible for works in Portuguese), Tulio Halperín Donghi (at the University of California, Berkeley), Iván Jaksić (at the University of Notre Dame), Naomi Lindstrom (at the University of Texas at Austin), Francine Masiello (at the University of California, Berkeley), and Eduardo Lozano of the Library at the University of Pittsburgh. The late Antonio Cornejo Polar of the University of California, Berkeley, was also one of the founding members of the committee. The translations have been funded thanks to the generosity of the Lampadia Foundation and the Andrew W. Mellon Foundation.

During the period of national formation between 1810 and into the early years of the twentieth century, the new nations of Latin America fashioned their identities, drew up constitutions, engaged in bitter struggles over territory, and debated questions of education, government, ethnicity, and culture. This was a unique period unlike the process of nation formation in Europe and one which should be more familiar than it is to students of comparative politics, history, and literature.

The image of the nation was envisioned by the lettered classes—a minority in countries in which indigenous, mestizo, black, or mulatto peasants and slaves predominated—although there were also alternative nationalisms at the grassroots level. The cultural elite were well educated in European thought and letters, but as statesmen, journalists, poets, and academics, they confronted the problem of the racial and linguistic heterogeneity of the continent and the difficulties of integrating the population into a modern nation-state. Some of the writers whose works will be translated in the Library of Latin America series played leading roles in politics. Fray Servando Teresa de Mier, a friar who translated Rousseau's *The Social Contract* and was one of the most colorful characters of the independence period, was faced with imprisonment and expulsion from Mexico for his heterodox beliefs; on his return, after independence, he was elected to the congress. Domingo Sarmiento, exiled from his native Argentina under the presidency of Rosas, wrote *Facundo: Civilización o barbarie,* a stinging denunciation of that government. He returned after Rosas' death and was elected president in 1868. Andrés Bello was born in Venezuela, lived in London where he published poetry during the independence period, settled in Chile where he founded the University, wrote his grammar of the Spanish language, and drew up the country's legal code.

These post-independence intelligentsia were not simply dreaming castles in the air, but vitally contributed to the founding of nations and the shaping of culture. The advantage of hindsight may make us aware of problems they themselves did not foresee but this should not affect our assessment of their truly astonishing energies and achievements. It is still surprising that the writing of Andrés Bello, who contributed fundamental works to so many different fields, has never been translated into English. Although there is a recent translation of Sarmiento's celebrated *Facundo,* there is no translation of his memoirs, *Recuerdos de provincia (Provincial Recollections).* The predominance of memoirs in the Library of Latin America Series is no accident—many of these offer entertaining insights into a vast and complex continent.

Nor have we neglected the novel. The Series includes new translations of the outstanding Brazilian writer Machado de Assis' work, including *Dom Casmurro* and *The Posthumous Memoirs of Brás Cubas.* There is no reason why other novels and writers that are not so well known outside Latin America—the Peruvian novelist Clorinda Matto de Turner's *Aves sin Nido,* Nataniel Aguirre's *Juan de la Rosa,* José de Alencar's *Iracema,* Juana Manuel Gorrit's short stories—should not be read with as much interest as the political novels of Anthony Trollope.

A series on nineteenth-century Latin America cannot, however, be limited to literary genres such as the novel, the poem, and the short story. The literature of independent Latin America was eclectic and strongly influenced by the periodical press newly liberated from scrutiny by colonial authorities and the Inquisition. Newspapers were miscellanies of fiction, essays, poems, and translations from all manner of European writing. The novels written on the eve of Mexican Independence by José Joaquín Fernandez Lizardi, included disquisitions on secular education and law, and denunciations of the evils of gaming and idleness. Other works, such as a well-known poem by Andrés Bello, "Agriculture in the Torrid Zone," and novels such as *Amilia* by José Marmol and the Bolivian Nataniel Aguirre's *Juan de la Rosa*, were openly partisan. By the end of the century, sophisticated scholars were beginning to address the history of their countries, as did João Capistrano de Abreu in his *Capítulos de história colonial.*

It is often in memoirs such as those by Fray Servando Teresa de Mier or Sarmiento that we find the descriptions of everyday life that in Europe were incorporated into the realist novel. Latin American literature at this time was seen largely as a pedagogical tool, a "light" alternative to speeches, sermons, and philosophical tracts—though, in fact, especially in the early part of the century, even the readership for novels was quite small because of the high rate of illiteracy. Nevertheless the vigorous orally transmitted culture of the gaucho and the urban underclasses became the linguistic repertoire of some of the most interesting nineteenth-century writers—most notably José Hernandez, author of the "gauchesque" poem "Martín Fiero" which enjoyed an unparalleled popularity. But for many writers the task was not to appropriate popular language but to civilize, and their literary works were strongly influenced by the high style of political oratory.

The editorial committee has not attempted to limit its selection to the better-known writers such as Machado de Assis; it has also selected many works that have never appeared in translation or whose work has not been translated recently. The Series now makes these works available to the English-speaking public.

Because of the preferences of funding organizations, the series initially focuses on writing from Brazil, the Southern Cone, the Andean Region, and Mexico. Each of our editions will have an introduction that places the work in its appropriate context and includes explanatory notes.

We owe special thanks to Robert Glynn of the Lampadia Foundation, whose initiative gave the project a jump-start, and to Richard Ekman of the Andrew W. Mellon Foundation which also generously supported the project. We also thank the Rockefeller Foundation for funding the 1996 symposium, "Culture and Nation in Iberoamerica," organized by the editorial board of the Library of Latin America. The support of Edward Barry of Oxford University Press has been crucial as has the advice and help of Ellen Chodosh of Oxford University Press. The first volumes of the series were published after the untimely death, on July 3, 1997, of Maria C. Bulle who, as an associate of the Lampadia Foundation, supported the idea from its beginning.

—*Jean Franco*
—*Richard Graham*

Note on the Author and the Editor

Andrés Bello (1781–1865) was perhaps the most significant and influential political and intellectual figure in nineteenth-century Latin America. In the aftermath of independence, Bello provided the most successful blueprint for nation building by emphasizing legal, social, and cultural elements in addition to the requisite political stability and economic viability. Born in the late colonial period, Bello was a minor but competent government official who nevertheless provided loyal service to the Spanish American revolutions. He was a tutor and friend of the famed liberator Simón Bolívar. In England, where he was to spend nineteen years, he advanced the cause of Spanish American independence and produced some notable writings that planted the seeds of cultural independence. In Chile, where he spent his last thirty-six years, he edited the official government paper, founded the University of Chile, wrote the Civil Code, and produced internationally influential treatises on legal topics, philosophy, and Spanish grammar. In the press, he wrote eloquent pieces intended to build consensus on the reforms needed for national development. In the educational system, Bello launched an ambitious literacy program that was at once universal and national. The university under his leadership became a vehicle for national unity. At the legislature, Bello contributed laws that brought Chile into a position of enviable stability in the context of nineteenth-century Latin America. Andrés Bello provides an indispensable example of how intellectuals educated in a humanistic tradition contributed to the creation and consolidation of the new Latin American republics.

Note on the Editor

Iván Jaksić is Associate Professor of History and Fellow of the Kellogg Institute for International Studies at the University of Notre Dame. He is the author of *Academic Rebels in Chile: The Role of Philosophy in Higher Education and Politics* (1989), and co-editor of *Filosofia e Identidad Cultural en América Latina* (1988), *The Struggle for Democracy in Chile* (1991, 1995), and *Sarmiento: Author of a Nation* (1994).

Chronology of Andrés Bello

1781   November 29. Andrés Bello is born in Caracas, Venezuela, the eldest of eight brothers and sisters. Both parents were of Canary Islands descent, and belonged to the middling sectors of society.

1793   Begins studies of Latin language and grammar at the Mercederian convent under the direction of Fr. Cristóbal de Quesada.

1797   Initiates philosophy studies at the Royal and Pontifical University of Caracas under the direction of Fr. Rafael Escalona. His studies include logic, mathematics, and physics. He teaches private lessons on geography and literary subjects to Simón Bolívar.

1800   Joins Alexander von Humboldt's research expedition in Caracas. Receives the degree of Bachelor of Arts and begins studies of law and medicine.

1802   Appointed secretary [*Oficial Segundo*] of the Captaincy General of Venezuela. His family's economic situation deteriorates when his father dies in 1804.

1807   Receives two important administrative appointments: Secretary of War [*Comisario de Guerra*], and interim secretary of the Central Vaccination Board.

1808   Translates an article with the first news to arrive of the French occupation of Spain, which forever changes the life of Venezuela and the rest of Spanish America. Becomes chief writer of the *Gaceta de Caracas*.

1810   Caracas residents form their own government in response to the flux of events in Spain. Bello is appointed *Oficial Primero* of the Ministry of Foreign Relations. He joins Simón Bolívar and Luis López Méndez on a diplomatic mission to England. They meet with Lord Richard Wellesley, but fail to obtain the recognition of the British government. Bello meets Francisco Miranda, and stays in his house when Bolívar and Miranda return to Venezuela. The vicissitudes of independence, including the collapse of the first patriot government in July 1812, force Bello to stay in London.

1814   Marries Mary Ann Boyland (1794–1821) who dies seven years after their marriage. Although rich intellectually, this is a period of enormous hardship for Bello and his family. Various attempts to return to Spanish America fail. Remains active in support of the independence movement.

1822   Joins the diplomatic service as secretary to the Chilean legation in London.

1824   Marries Isabel Dunn (1804–1873). Becomes secretary to the Colombian legation in London. The deterioration of the political situation in Colombia, the collapse of its credit, and strained relations with diplomatic officials and with Simón Bolívar compel Bello to leave for Chile.

1829   Arrives in Chile June 25. The following month he is appointed *Oficial Mayor* of the Ministry of Finance.

1830   Becomes Rector of the Colegio de Santiago. He also joins the paper *El Araucano* as director of the foreign affairs, and letters and science sections. Many of his key writings will appear in this paper.

1832   The Chilean Congress declares Bello a Chilean citizen. This year he publishes the first edition of the *Principios de derecho internacional*.

1834   Appointed *Oficial Mayor* of the Ministry of Foreign Relations.

1837   Elected Senator. He will be reelected in 1846 and 1855. Forms part of numerous commissions, but most importantly those concerning the codification of the laws. Also noteworthy are his contributions to the adoption of the metric system (1848) and the abolition of the *mayorazgos* [entail system] in 1852.

1842   Becomes founder and Rector of the University of Chile, a post he will retain until his death. He becomes a member of the Faculties of Philosophy and Humanities, and Law and Political Science.

1847   Publishes the *Gramática de la lengua castellana destinada al uso de los Americanos*.

1851   Named Honorary Member, and later Corresponding Member (1861), of the Spanish Royal Academy.

1855   Bello's *Código Civil* is promulgated into law.

1857–65   Although his health deteriorates, he engages in a number of intellectual and creative endeavors, especially poetry and Spanish medieval literature, and maintains an active correspondence. He declines, however, various invitations to participate in international diplomatic negotiations.

1865   October 15. He dies at the age of 84, at his home in Santiago.

Preface

The following selection of texts by Andrés Bello attempts to answer a puzzling question: How is it possible that a person who was so central to the major events of the nineteenth century in Latin America, who was one of the most complex, learned and prolific intellectuals of the century, and who was associated at various times with such towering figures as Simón Bolívar, Francisco Miranda, James Mill, Jeremy Bentham, Diego Portales, Manuel Montt, Domingo Faustino Sarmiento, Juan Bautista Alberdi, José Victorino Lastarria, Francisco Bilbao and many others, is virtually unknown in the English-speaking world?

Curiously, this lack of knowledge is shared by many who have been exposed to Andrés Bello since their earliest years. Almost no major city of Latin America lacks its Andrés Bello Avenue, its Andrés Bello statues, prizes and landmarks, even its Andrés Bello university, academy, or major publishing house. In the worlds of politics, diplomacy, and especially education, references to the name are obligatory, to the point that most Spanish Americans can show a flash of recognition, a knowing smile, or a learned nod when the name is mentioned. But discussions of the particulars of his life, the nature of his relationship to various events and peoples of the century, or his thoughts on grammar, law, and international relations, fail to benefit from direct exposure to readings of either his work or his major biographies.

I can venture a somewhat weary interpretation of the reasons for the

lack of familiarity in the English speaking world: except for a few frag-
mentary pieces, and the recent notable exception of the publication of
Philosophy of the Understanding (1984) by the Organization of American
States, the most important works of Andrés Bello—or even the lesser
ones—have not been translated into English. If one adds to this—again
with some notable exceptions—that the study of Latin America has
rarely focused on intellectual developments and their relationship to
nation building, one can begin to understand the gap in our knowledge
of Bello in particular, and of Latin America's intellectual history generally.

It is more difficult to attempt to answer the question about the familiarity of the name without a concurrent knowledge of his works in
the Spanish-speaking world. One might suggest that when a name
becomes familiar, the incentives for finding anything new about a person and his work diminish. One might also point out that, even in
Spanish America, the sources are not readily available, are cumbersome
to read, or are expensive; that there are few venues for the ongoing
discussion of the work of the nation builders; and that many of the
names, including that of Bello, have been associated, utilized, or ma-
nipulated by partisan groups. Yet the fact remains that Andrés Bello
has not occupied the central position that his contributions warrant.

In either case, there is no substitute for the availability of the texts,
which Oxford University Press is publishing in its Library of Latin
America series, and which it plans to publish in Spanish and Portuguese. It is also necessary to provide not just a representative sample of
writings, but a selection with a theme that both respects the internal
coherence of Bello's ideas, and that suggests new paradigms for the
interpretation of Latin American history. I have tried in this collection
to meet both conditions by organizing Bello's key writings around the
theme of the search for order in nineteenth-century Latin America.
Precisely because we have traditionally paid little attention to the world
of ideas, we have failed to understand the magnitude of the tasks confronting those who witnessed—and even contributed to—the collapse
of the Spanish Empire, and who then attempted to build viable political, social, and cultural institutions. What instruments did they have,
what models, which proposals? Bello's writings offer a plethora of answers to these questions.

My interest in Bello comes from having been awakened from my own complacency by the work of various scholars at the La Casa de Bello Foundation in Caracas. A search for very specific aspects of Bello's work led me there in 1988, and planted the idea of some day working exclusively on Bello. Needless to say, I owe an enormous debt to those who have aided me over the years, especially Pedro Grases, Edgar Páez, Rafael Di Prisco, and Oscar Sambrano Urdaneta. Dr. Rafael Caldera took personal interest in my work and for that I am very grateful. I was introduced to the Venezuelan *Bellistas* by Dr. Gonzalo Palacios of the Embassy of Venezuela in Washington, D.C., who has been a consistent friend and critic ever since, and whose own knowledge of Bello has been enormously helpful. This selection is based on La Casa de Bello's 1981 edition of the *Obras Completas*, and I gratefully acknowledge its permission to publish a translation based on that source.

Research on Bello has taken me to various places in Caracas, Santiago, and England. It would be difficult to name all the scholars, librarians, and archivists who have shared their knowledge and facilitated my access to various materials, but I cannot fail to mention Sofía Correa Sutil, Sol Serrano, and the staff of the Biblioteca Central at the University of Chile, especially Darío Oses and Gladys Sanhueza. In London, I benefited enormously from discussions with Malcolm Deas, Eduardo Posada-Carbó, and their students at St. Antony's College, Oxford, and the University of London, respectively. Gloria Carnevali at the Venezuelan Embassy in London was also extremely helpful. In the United States, I have been fortunate to count on the continuous encouragement and valuable comments of Jaime Concha, Angel Delgado-Gómez, Tulio Halperín-Donghi, Gwen Kirkpatrick, Julio Ramos, Timothy R. Scully C.S.C., Juan Carlos Torchia Estrada, James Twiner, and Samuel Valenzuela. To Simon Collier I owe the encouragement, when I was between projects, to work on Andrés Bello. His own knowledge of Bello has been a constant inspiration.

At Oxford University Press, I wish to thank Ellen Chodosh for her patience and support. Dr. Jean Franco, who chairs the Library of Latin America Committee at OUP, has been enormously influential in my understanding of the significance of Bello in nineteenth-century Latin America. Frances M. López-Morillas' expert translation offered additional insights into Bello's thought. Esteban Montes and Juan Carlos Helmstedt generously helped me clarify some concepts of civil law in part three. Finally, I gratefully acknowledge the financial support of the Institute for Scholarship in the Liberal Arts at the University of Notre Dame for a grant that allowed me to search for and consult materials by Andrés Bello.

Notes on the Sources and the Translation

The following selections have been extracted from the recent edition of Andrés Bello's *Obras Completas*, 26 vols. (Caracas: Fundación la Casa de Bello, 1981–86), by far the most complete of all of Bello's collected works to date. The English translation that follows relies heavily on the expert work and annotations of the multinational team of distinguished scholars who collected Bello's work. Because many selections have been published in Spanish in numerous formats, in this selection I provide the original venue and date of publication, followed by the citation in the latest edition of the *Obras Completas*, and a brief explanation of the context in which it appeared.

Most selections have been translated in their entirety, but a few have been edited for the purposes of this collection. Generally, the material that has been omitted involves long quotations or detailed statistical information, as in the case of the report on educational developments in Part Two. Most notes and references by Bello have also been omitted in order to facilitate reading and economize on length were it does not affect understanding of the contents. In cases where quotations are crucial for the development of an argument, but where Bello does not precisely identify the source, the translation is based on the Spanish version provided by Bello even if the quote comes from an English-language source. Fortunately, those cases are rare.

The Bello selections have been translated in their entirety by Frances

M. López-Morillas, except for the quotations from Latin, which were provided by Professor Daniel J. Sheerin of the University of Notre Dame. I gratefully acknowledge his assistance.

The editor and the translator have decided to respect the original reference to the former colonies of the Iberian empires as "America." There was no concept of "Latin" America at the time of Bello's writings, and, from his standpoint as well as that of other writers, the United States was still a confederation of states more frequenty known and referred to as "North America." There was also a revolutionary aspect as well as a poetic resonance to the use of the word "America" to refer to the former provinces of the Spanish empire. It involved an assertion of identity vis-à-vis the peninsula, which had significant meaning at the time, and well into the twentieth century.

Finally, all materials in square brackets are clarifications, definitions, or identifications of authors, places, and events, by either the translator or the editor.

Introduction

Andrés Bello was a central figure in the construction of a new political order in post-independence Latin America. A quiet, unassuming, self-effacing man, Andrés Bello was nevertheless a person of enormous influence, a mentor to generations, an advisor to powerful political figures, and a builder of institutions. Andrés Bello was also a product of his times, a man whose long life straddled the eighteenth and the nineteenth centuries; who lived long enough to have known and participated as an official in the Spanish imperial bureaucracy; who was an actor in the independence process, a friend and interlocutor of many of the leaders of emancipation; who represented several Latin American nations before England, a country where he also worked with some of the most influential intellectuals of the Spanish and English-speaking worlds; who steered a nascent Latin American republic into a model of stability and prosperity; and who wrote some of the most enduring and influential pieces of scholarship and policy in nineteenth-century Latin America.

Andrés Bello was also a bridge between religious and secular traditions, a scholar who responded to the dissolution of the Spanish empire with a rationale for the construction of a new order which was rooted in a humanistic tradition. Bello bridged the ancient and the modern, the neoclassic and the romantic, the scientific and the humanistic worlds, and brought Europe and Latin America into closer contact. Bello was a person who balanced disparate traditions and interests for the sake of constructing new nations.

As might be expected, Bello has been celebrated to the point of sycophancy, and vilified to the point of slander, by a large contingent of contemporaries and subsequent historians who have struggled to understand his role, often from the standpoint of their own partisan positions. Somehow, the Bello that bears witness to the dramatic creation of new nations in the nineteenth century has been obscured, his record distorted, and his ultimate objectives misunderstood. With significant exceptions, it is only with the research of the last few decades, culminating with the newest edition of Bello's complete works in 1981–86, that the proper assessment of his role in a variety of areas is beginning to emerge. And yet he remains virtually unknown in the English-speaking world, despite his centrality for understanding key nineteenth-century issues in Latin America and beyond.

Part of the difficulty in understanding Bello comes from the variety, complexity, and enormity of his intellectual production. His writings range from poetry to philosophy, from philology to civil law, from education to history, from international relations to literary criticism. Two recent tomes of correspondence complete the twenty-six volumes of Bello's collected works. This astonishing variety has led to much learned, but generally field-specific, commentary, often bearing little relationship to the larger body of his work. The task of the contemporary scholar is to identify the inner dynamics of Bello's work; probe the relationship between his various areas of concern and the larger social, cultural, and political issues of the period; and attempt to analyze his significance vis-à-vis the national and international contexts in which he operated. My own view is that Bello's fundamental, life-long concern was the problem of order, a problem of particular urgency for a region struggling to build durable social and political arrangements in the wake of the collapse of the Spanish empire. Bello advanced a view of order that rested on three interrelated spheres: the ordering of thought via language, literature, and philosophy; the ordering of national affairs via civil law, education, and history; and the participation of the new nations in the world order of the nineteenth century via international law and diplomacy. The persistence of Bello's interest in order reflects, I believe, not only his informed reading of nineteenth-century needs for national development, but also a deep and very personal search that was motivated by the dramatic events that he witnessed and experienced. Certainly the most dramatic of all was the disintegration of the imperial order, which opened some hopeful possibilities, but which in the beginning offered a nightmarish picture of blood, chaos, and confusion.

Bello's contribution to the history of nineteenth-century Latin America, in short, consisted of the elaboration of a rationale for order that looked past the initial chaos of the aftermath of war in order to build the new republics on solid ground. Just as nations struggled, and often failed, to establish order via political experimentation or force, Bello concentrated on the quieter, but deeper and ultimately more successful, development of an agenda for order that emphasized the rule of law—both domestic and international—and sought unity via education and a concept of language that served as the basis for the structuring of nationhood. Although not applied, or even applicable, in every country of Latin America (due to myriad historical factors) Bello's rationale for order remains the most important nineteenth-century contribution to the complex and still relevant issues of nation-building.

Three Biographical Periods: Venezuela, England, and Chile[1]

Andrés Bello was born in Caracas, Venezuela, on 29 November, 1781. The eldest son of a minor official in the Spanish colonial bureaucracy, Bello grew up during a period of significant economic growth and political importance resulting from the upgrading of the Captaincy General of Venezuela.[2] He received an extraordinary education by the standards of the time, one which he would remember with fondness. He studied Latin and philosophy, receiving a Bachelor's degree from the University of Caracas in 1800, at which time he could translate texts in Latin and impress mentors and classmates with his scholastic abilities.[3] By this time, he had instructed Simón Bolívar on literature and geography, and had assisted Alexander von Humboldt during the latter's research in Venezuela. The anecdote is often told of the time when an enthusiastic, if out of breath, young Bello accompanied Humboldt on his ascent to Mount Avila. Although they did not reach the top together, Bello followed Humbolt's scientific interests. He may well have learned from Humbolt about the linguistic theories of Humbolt's younger brother, Karl Wilhelm. Bello continued, but did not complete, studies in law and medicine. Economic necessity prompted him to go to work for the colonial government in 1802. He launched a successful career in administration without abandoning his literary interests, especially in poetry and linguistics. Bello's colonial position allowed him to participate in projects of national scope, such as smallpox innoculation, a major development that probably contributed to his positive view of the enlightened reforms and scientific emphasis of the late colonial period. In 1808, he was entrusted with the major responsibility for editing the *Gaceta de Caracas*, the first newspaper of Venezuela, and among the first on the South American continent.

It was in that year that the fate of the Spanish empire, and his own, changed forever with the French invasion of the Iberian peninsula. Bello remained with the colonial government, navigating the increasingly difficult waters of international politics as the Spanish Juntas came and went, and as conflicting reports about lines of authority confused the local population. It was probably due to Bello's competence in matters of government, plus his language ability (in English and French, in addition to Latin), that the creole Junta that overthrew the Captain General invited him to join the revolutionary government as first officer in the ministry of foreign relations in April 1810. Soon after, in June 1810, he set sail for England with Colonel Simón Bolívar and government representative Luis López Méndez, to seek the protection of Great Britain in the event of either Spanish retaliation or French invasion.

Andrés Bello was to remain in England for nineteen years, a rich period for his intellectual development, but at times a period of economic hardship, frustration, and personal tragedy.[4] In London, he met and admired Francisco Miranda, his compatriot and early advocate of independence, lived in his house at Grafton Street, and benefited from Miranda's substantial library. By 1812, with the collapse of the revolutionary government, Bello was forced to seek a variety of employments, and even attempted to return to the service of Spain during a desperate moment in 1813. During the 1812–1822 period he worked in various temporary jobs that were always insufficient for sustaining his growing family, and received some temporary assistance from the British government. He tutored English children, he translated or proofread various works, and also worked with James Mill in attempting to decipher

Jeremy Bentham's handwriting. This appears to have been a miserable period for Bello; he could not find the means to return to Venezuela, he could not find stable employment, and his first wife and youngest child died in 1821. It was only in 1822 that he achieved some relative security when he returned to the diplomatic service, this time for the government of Chile. Soon thereafter, in collaboration with Juan García de Río, he launched two extremely significant publications, the *Biblioteca Americana* (1823), and the *Repertorio Americano* (1826–27). These two journals addressed to a Spanish American audience reveal, on the one hand, the substantial amount of research work that Bello had carried out at the library of the British Museum, and, on the other, Bello's by now clear and public effort to build a Spanish American culture that would serve as a vehicle for continental unity.

Although he worked in a variety of positions at the legations of Chile and Gran Colombia from 1822 until 1829, this work was not stable, and led to his permanent alienation from Simón Bolívar and other members of the government of Gran Colombia. Bello had been suspected of monarchical leanings, was rumored to have betrayed the revolution, and had shown less than energetic enthusiasm for a Bolívar who in the late 1820s had a few problems of his own. Despite increasingly urgent requests from Bello to improve his situation in England, Bolívar could not or would not give him assistance until it was too late.[5] Bello left England for Chile, and would never return to his homeland. Negative rumors about Bello were only slowly proven false, and may have contributed to his decision not to return to Venezuela, even after Bolívar's death.

Chile proved to be, in most respects, a congenial place for Bello. In Santiago, he quickly became a respected public and intellectual figure. Arriving in 1829 at the age of forty-seven, Bello brought with him enormous experience as government official in Caracas, diplomat, publisher, and scholar-at-large in England, and had matured into a cautious and moderate political thinker who had a unique perspective on both the functioning of government institutions in Europe, and the potential of the new republics for a role in the larger community of nations. Bello was, from the beginning, very close to Chilean government circles. He became Undersecretary of Finance and then Foreign Relations from his arrival until his retirement in 1852. He became the editor of the government newspaper, *El Araucano*, from its inception in 1830 until his retirement in 1853. He was elected senator in 1837 and was reelected in 1846 and 1855, a position he held until his death. He wrote most official Chilean documents concerning foreign relations, and also wrote presidential messages and congressional responses. He contributed to the discussions on the constitution of 1833 and wrote Chile's Civil Code, promulgated into law in 1855. All along, he was a respected voice in government circles in Chile and abroad, and he was frequently asked to chair government commissions and preside over diplomatic negotiations.[6]

Andrés Bello was also a successful educator. His first position in education in Chile was as Director of the Colegio de Santiago, a short-lived school that was nevertheless at the center of some of the first significant intellectual debates of the period. He was part of several commissions reviewing educational developments in Chile beginning in the 1830s. He tutored students privately in his house, including many who would become leading intellectual and political figures, and became the creator and first Rector of the University of Chile in 1843, a position for which he was reelected by the faculty four times (1848, 1853, 1858, and 1863) and that he held until his death. The University of Chile, which became known as *La Casa de Bello*, successfully concentrated the supervision of national education, and served as the center for research activities with a national focus.[7]

Despite his multiple public activities, Bello maintained an astonishing level of intellectual production. Although the origin of his many intellectual concerns goes back to his Caracas and London years, it was in Chile that he wrote all of his major works, including the *Gramática de la Lengua Castellana* (1847), the *Principios de Derecho Internacional* (1832, 1844, and 1864), and the *Código Civil* (1855). He also wrote poetry, reviewed books and theatrical productions, engaged in scholarly debates, and even wrote on astronomy, one among many other scientific interests. The first edition of his posthumous collected works published in Santiago in 1881–86, comprising what was then known about the extent of his intellectual production, included fifteen volumes.

In spite of his multiple public activities and the forceful and authoritative tenor of his writings, Bello was an intensely shy and sensitive man. Reports from his closest friends and the letters to and from his family show him to have been loyal, patient, and caring. He exhibited the sadness of an exile who was never able to return to his native land, never saw his Caracas family again, and mourned the loss of nine of his fifteen children. He was, however, capable of good humor, as shown by several of his poems and some of his letters, and was also a good conversationalist. He lived a long life, but was plagued by headaches, poor eyesight, and was severely impaired in the last eight years of his life. Although almost blind and confined to a wheelchair, he worked on various projects, but most consistently on poetry and the revision of his publications until he was bedridden in September of 1865. He died on October 15 of that year, reportedly struggling to read passages of Latin and Greek poetry.

In view of Bello's personal qualities and intellectual achievements, it is perhaps not surprising that a literature of celebration should have developed, some of it written by his descendants and perpetuated by his admirers. But this should not obscure the magnitude of the criticisms, both fair and unfair, directed against Bello's personality and larger role in the politics of the period. He was accused of betraying the revolutionary movement in Caracas, and was suspected of complicity with writer and diplomat Antonio José de Irisarri in the latter's dubious financial dealings in London. Ventura Marín, a Chilean philosopher in the 1830s, denounced him as a corruptor of youth while José Miguel Infante, the Chilean advocate of federalism, frequently denounced him in the press as a monarchist and a reactionary. Bello's friendship with Diego Portales, the power behind the throne in the Chile of the 1830s, made him anathema to the liberals who had suffered Portales' heavy-handedness. Other contemporaries—including the Chilean writer and politician José Victorino Lastarria and the Argentine educator, journalist, and later president Domingo Faustino Sarmiento— attempted for various reasons to present Bello as an authoritarian, somewhat passé old man. If the all-too-human jealousies are discounted, it appears that Bello's austere and serious demeanor, combined with a clear commitment to the conservative (but liberalizing) side of the Chilean political spectrum, generated genuine opposition to his influence. The challenge for the contemporary scholar is not to defend him—in fact, Bello sometimes needs to be defended from his defenders—but to clearly understand his intellectual and political positions.

To begin an assessment of Bello's thought and his contributions to the process of nation-building in the nineteenth century, one must recall the difficulties of transferring the solid legitimacy of monarchical rule claiming divine origin to the untested and fragile institutions of representative government.[8] In addition, the devastation of the wars of independence and the disappointing economic performance of the new nations provided fertile ground for social and political tensions that often exploded in civil wars in an ever-increasing spiral of violence and instability. Much intellectual energy was devoted to defending various political models, but they often degenerated into partisan bickering that only compounded the difficulties of the new nations. It is in this context that Bello identified the issue of order as central to the consolidation of the new states, and approached it from a variety of perspectives. He posited that without internal order there would be little hope for the trade and exchange that could come from, and contribute to, the external world. In turn, the domestic order could only be achieved if individuals developed the civic virtues essential to the functioning of republican institutions.

Bello's extensive production can be divided in three major clusters of concerns: language and literature; education and history; and government, law, and international relations. They represent Bello's key intellectual interests, but they also represent key vehicles for the establishment and consolidation of nationhood.

Language and Literature

Although Bello became proficient, and indeed an expert, in a wide variety of fields, language was perhaps his most central and sustained concern. Language, in the context of Bello's intellectual interests, translated into at least three major areas of activity: grammatical studies; poetry; and literary history. His most consistent efforts, and probably his most successful, were devoted to the first, although the second and third were also important ingredients in his larger plans for language and national development.

Language, for Bello, was the key vehicle for the construction of a new political order in post-colonial Latin America. The potentialities of language, in this respect, were not immediately apparent to Bello; in fact, it took him years of study and experience before he could make a connection between the two. But once he made it, in the 1820s, he pursued the relationship between language and nationhood with a tenacity that was paralleled only by his work on the Chilean civil code.

And even in this latter activity, the connection that Bello established between language and the law is strong.

Just as there are three clearly discernible periods in Bello's life, there are three periods in his approach to language issues. During his years in Caracas he devoted considerable time to the study of Latin, which he pursued at the University of Caracas under the direction of the preeminent scholars of his day. He also devoted considerable energy to the philosophical study of language, particularly through the works of Etienne Bonnot de Condillac. It is widely believed—and indeed Bello himself implied so—that his famous work on the tenses of the Spanish verb, which first saw the light in Santiago in 1841, had originally been prepared in Caracas. Lastly, during the Caracas years he also read and wrote poetry, some of it imitative of Vergil, but some of it original work designed to aesthetically probe into the possibilities of the Spanish language, as well as to celebrate such events as the introduction of the smallpox vaccine in Venezuela and the victory of the Spanish resistance at Bailén.

Through his position in the colonial government, Bello also had two other important contacts with language-related matters: one was his experience with the English language, which he used for reading London newspapers, for communicating with English officials in Curaçao, and for translating various documents. English-language newspapers had become extremely important to Caracas officials, especially as the Napoleonic invasion of the Iberian peninsula unfolded. Bello emerged as the key person in government who could converse in the language, and this was probably one of the major reasons why he was appointed secretary of the first diplomatic mission to England after the creation of the first independent government in Caracas.

The other important experience related to language involves the dissemination of information through the medium of print. Bello became the chief writer for the first paper printed in Caracas, the *Gaceta de Caracas*, founded in 1808.[9] His role in the *Gaceta* is probably among the least studied, but it was substantial enough to provide him with an understanding of, and experience with, the significant possibilities of print. The periodical press was a rarity in Spanish America at the time, a medium that was closely controlled by government. Bello became the chief writer of this first newspaper at a time when political flux in the peninsula provided him with an opportunity to select and present information that was enormously influential in the process of independence. His knowledge of English allowed him to publish information about Spain that was almost contemporary with events in the peninsula. Because England had become an ally of Spain against Napoleon, Bello was in a position to convey relevant British information and to offer several of the first defenses of the Spanish resistance. This experience would serve him well: he became the principal writer and editor of several other periodicals in his career, most notably the *Biblioteca Americana* and the *Repertorio Americano*—both published in London—and *El Araucano*, the official newspaper of independent Chile.

It was in London, however, that he devoted concentrated attention to the scholarly study of language. He had an important early exposure to philological studies at the impressive library in Miranda's house.[10] Bello taught himself Greek during his residence there between 1810–12, and there is some speculation that he might have begun his study of medieval literature at Miranda's library as well. But unquestionably, it was at the library of the British Museum, which he began to consult in 1814, that he found the materials and the inspiration for the work that would occupy him the rest of his life. Although he did not publish some of the results of his work at the British Museum until the 1820s, the general direction of his language concerns becomes clear from an examination of the notebooks he kept during the 1810s. He first concentrated on medieval literature, especially the *Cantar de Mío Cid*, but also on such specialized matters as the origins of meter, rhyme, and the use of assonance. In retrospect, it can be said without any doubt that he was actively investigating the origins of vernacular literature after the decline of Latin as the language of educated Europe. He was also looking into the emergence of national languages, their sources and their influences. He was especially interested in chronicles and romances as foundations for national myths.[11]

There is probably a more personal reason for Bello's language concerns. Though he had become conversant in Latin and English prior to his departure for England, extended exposure to the latter language—he lived in England for nineteen years and was twice married to British women—might have made him sensitive to the need of studying and keeping his Spanish. He was also in contact with several peninsular Spanish scholars, including such accomplished linguists as Bartolomé José Gallardo and Antonio Puigblanch, who surely encouraged, even if they were puzzled by, his interests in the origins of romance languages.[12] Some of the extant correspondence indicates that he communicated frequently with these and other scholars on matters of philology. One might also speculate that the vagaries of the early independence period, which had catastrophic implications for his personal situation, may have inspired him to look into the processes of social dissolution and subsequent creation of geographic-linguistic entities in medieval Europe. After all, the emergence of ten new nations out of the ruins of the Spanish empire had few precedents in history, and posed startling questions about their future. Intellectually and personally, the London years are probably the source of Bello's most enduring philological, grammatical, and literary interests.

Four of the pieces included in the language section of this collection were written during Bello's London years. Though on the surface some of them appear to be quite specialized, they are animated by two central concerns, which can only be understood fully in the context of historical developments resulting from the breakdown of the Spanish empire: Bello may have had some doubts about the fate of the independence movements in the 1810s, but by the early 1820s he was convinced that the revolutions had succeeded or were about to succeed in most places in the continent. One of Bello's central objectives was to provide a document, both aesthetic and political, about the meaning of independence, and the tasks that lie ahead. As early as 1823, with his "Allocution to Poetry," he launched perhaps the first overview of independence as a continental phenomenon. From Mexico to Chile, Bello described the various movements as heroic Latin American responses to the desire for independent nationhood. In Bello's poem, political differences, civil war, and the agonizing confusion of the early independence period gave way to a foundational myth that celebrated the deeds of selfless patriots. In his "Allocution," Bello provided the language and the events that served as the basis for the myth and aesthetics of independence. The "Allocution" is also a document for considering a less fortunate event in Bello's life. His inclusion of Francisco Miranda in the pantheon of Latin American heroes, and his rather lukewarm celebration of the deeds of Simón Bolívar, may have caused his downfall in the eyes of the Liberator and some of his followers. As indicated above, it may also have influenced Bello's decision not to return to his native Venezuela.[13]

The other central matter to be addressed was the political organization of the new republics. Independence could be a fact, but the biggest challenge in Bello's eyes was the construction of a new political order. In this respect, he was confident that there was something that he could contribute from London, and from his unique perspective concerning matters of language. London, as he presents it in the prospectus of the first *Repertorio* issue, was well positioned to serve as the center for the dissemination of useful information to the new nations. Not only did England provide an example of political freedoms at work, but it was also the center of much needed trade. Bello was clearly proposing a new order for Latin America that would have England as its most important partner, if not model. As for Latin America itself, he envisioned an agricultural society of farmer-citizens who would alternate vigorous physical labor with the tasks of government. As presented in his justly famous "Ode to Tropical Agriculture," Latin America would exploit its natural endowments for the ultimate aim of good government.

From a language perspective, and informed to a large extent by his research in medieval languages and literatures, Bello also articulated a rationale for the defense of a Spanish language that would be uniquely Latin American, and that would undergird the new political order. Bello understood quite early that such a new arrangement could succeed only to the extent that Spanish America became united in terms of purpose and language. Unity in commercial and political terms was essential to the success of the post-colonial order, and England appeared to be ready to support such a process. But more problematic was the unity of language now that the peninsular Spanish center no longer held. It was essential, in Bello's view, to strengthen unity by producing a language that was more responsive to Spanish American needs. In essence, as illustrated by his first article on orthography published in London in 1823, he sought a simplicity of rules that would make the acquisition of educated Spanish easier for the larger, mostly illiterate or semi-literate, population. Spanish Americans would, in his view, have an easier learning experience if they could establish a closer correspondence between speech and the alphabet. In terms of ultimate objectives, Bello believed that only an educated population, steeped in a common language, could ensure the stability of the new political order.

Long after the new order had been secured, Bello insisted on the necessity of clear rules not only for the writing of Spanish, as can be seen in his second major defense of a Spanish American orthography in 1843, but for general grammar. Even from the most stable of nations—at least by nineteenth-century standards—Bello often expressed his concern about the dissolution of core languages and their fragmentation into incommunicable dialects. His response was a rationale for the predominance of the written word over a primarily oral culture. This predominance would have to be established by a grammar specifically designed for the use of Spanish Americans, and promoted at the highest levels of state. Nothing else—education and the law in particular—could succeed if the fundamental basis of language was not firmly established. This central concern initially developed in London, with the publication of his essay on "The Origin and Progress of the Art of Writing," which was primarily a rationale for viewing the written word as the culmination of civilized order.

Just as the recognition of independence led to questions about the political order that would follow, Bello's early language concerns evolved from foundational myths, in the form of poems, to reform proposals for specific aspects of the Spanish language, to the ultimate adoption of a grammar. Bello did not succeed in each of his proposals, but his *Gramática de la Lengua Castellana destinada al uso de los Americanos* did, providing him not only with the rare recognition—indeed the first for a former subject of the Spanish empire—of the Royal Academy but also with the publication of more than seventy editions of his work in such countries as Chile, Venezuela, Colombia, Peru, Argentina, and Spain itself. This single work continues to be studied and reprinted, undoubtedly because of its inherent qualities, but also because it contained a most practical response to the complexities of establishing a new political order in Spanish America.[14]

What was Bello's blueprint, from the unlikely field of grammatical studies, for addressing the central issues of nation-building in nineteenth-century Latin America? Quite simply, to reform and adjust the institutions of Spain to the new realities of the Spanish American nations; to establish needed continuities between past and present, especially at the level of literature and culture; and to establish a well-regulated language firmly rooted in the ancient traditions of Spain, yet responsive to changing Spanish American realities. When placed in the context of the more radical solutions offered by Domingo Faustino Sarmiento, Francisco Bilbao, José Victorino Lastarria, and many others around the continent who wanted a cleaner break with the Hispanic past, Bello's blueprint appeared hopelessly conservative. But it was successful precisely because it was moderate: it offered a rationale for the reconciliation of tradition and change, past and present, that a war-torn region eager to achieve stability, prosperity—or both—could understand. And it offered more than a solution to contemporary issues and debates; it offered a long-term plan for the education of the new generations that would make independence, both cultural and political, a reality.

Three of the selections in the language section illustrate Bello's fundamental views on grammar. The earliest is his *Ideological Analysis of the Tenses of the Spanish Conjugation*, published in 1841, but probably prepared in Caracas before 1810. In it, he shows an early concern for the need to systematize verb tenses (in disarray on both sides of the Atlantic) without postulating the existence of a universal grammar for all languages, as more optimistic eighteenth-century logicians had proposed. This early statement would serve as the basis for his fuller argumentation in favor of a national grammar. By "national," however, Bello did not mean a grammar for each of the nations of Latin America. That is precisely what he most vehemently tried to avoid. "National" was meant as a geographic-linguistic category, as a grammar of the Spanish language. The title of his grammatical masterwork, however, adds the telling subtitle of "for the use of Spanish Americans." This is on the surface a problematic subtitle, but key to understanding his grammatical position and the reasons for his success. Bello differed sharply from other Spanish Americans who understood the direct relationship between language and nationhood just as he did, but who wanted local usage to be the means for the assertion of independence and national identity. Bello, for his part, did not seek to separate peninsular from Latin American Spanish, but rather to organize the Spanish language as spoken in Latin America on the basis of categories that responded directly to the linguistic practices of the continent. He was not seeking new languages, separate from one another and from their linguistic source. Rather, he insisted on a point that is particularly poignant in both the grammar article of 1832 and the prologue of the *Gramática* in 1847, both included in this section: The Spanish Royal

Academy could not serve as a useful model for contemporary Spanish on either side of the Atlantic because of its insistence on basing grammar on the model of the Latin language. Bello demonstrated that Latin grammatical categories not only did not conform to, but in fact obscured, an understanding of the grammatical workings of Spanish. Latin categories constrained the verb, and, as shown by various examples of peninsular orthography, they also imposed etymology as a criterion for spelling, a practice that made the acquisition of literate Spanish difficult for people just making the transition from oral to written language. Bello's grammar was thus an argument for systematization within the parameters of the Spanish language, independent from other languages or from abstract logical categories.[15] This search for uniqueness and balance is, in many ways, a linguistic counterpart to Bello's hopes for the larger process of Latin American nation-building.

Although Bello's key writings on language were published between the 1820s and 1840s, they reflect much longer and more central concerns than this relatively short period would suggest. They speak of Bello's unique contribution to political developments in nineteenth-century Latin America. On the basis of his early education, combined with his London experience, Bello understood that it was in the area of language that he could effect the most profound changes in Latin American society. Language rooted him firmly in ancient tradition and a community of nations. The study of language provided him with a sense of how reform could be accomplished within tradition, and how language could provide the sort of unity that was essential for post-colonial Latin America. In a region divided by numerous cleavages (economic, social, and cultural, among others), language could serve an important integrating role in that it could not only provide a bridge between literate groups and the larger population, but also cement the sense of nationhood so vital for order and stability.

Education and History

An examination of his major activities in Chile, beginning with the creation of an educational system and the development of the field of history, demonstrate that Bello's philosophy of language informed these two key areas of nation-building: his experience with language studies allowed him to develop views of education and history as sources of national unity. In each of these areas, one can see the same principles at work: Bello tried to reconcile tradition and change; use rather than reject the Hispanic past; and build a sense of nationhood that was not separate from the larger community of nations. Both areas, in addition, required the firm establishment of a culture based on the written word. Indeed, his view of a community of nations depended heavily on the extent that they shared a written language that could bring the past into the present, benefit from the same sources of knowledge, and be easily and massively disseminated.

Upon his arrival in Chile in 1829, Bello was soon seen as a major intellectual force who could develop Chile's fledgling educational system. Education had been a long-term concern (sometimes a necessity) of his, as seen in his teaching and tutoring activities in Caracas and London. In the latter city, he studied the teaching techniques of Joseph Lancaster with a view to its possible application in Latin America (he was not convinced). But it was in Chile that he devoted concentrated attention to educational matters. His views on education were usually articulated in the context of specific reforms or institutional obligations, or sometimes in the heat of debate, but in all cases one can see important connections to the building of a new political order.[16]

The study of the evolution of Bello's thinking on education can be framed in the context of a search for the means to spread literacy in order to make the concept of citizenship—and therefore nationhood—a reality. Once Bello understood that the change in political regime from monarchy to republic called for the authority of the law and the institutions of representative government, he viewed education as the principal means for the introduction of civic values into the larger population. Bello's writing style sometimes makes it difficult to discern what was most important to him: education of the larger population or education of the elite; religious education or secular education; humanities or sciences. But this difficulty can be easily overcome once one understands that at different times he was emphasizing different aspects of the same overall project: there must be a national system of education, closely supervised and supported by the state, in order to bring literacy to the larger population so that citizens could contribute and become loyal to the workings of representative government. That education should also bring in several other elements: religion, which he viewed as indispensable for public and private morality; respect for Hispanic traditions stretching back to Roman origins; and a practical emphasis that would provide the citizenry with the instruments to benefit from the scientific and technological advances of the contemporary world. Bello was very (perhaps overly) confident that all of these disparate elements could be reconciled. Such confidence depended on the ability of the state to provide a space for education to flourish despite increasingly divisive partisan politics. That ability was eroding even during Bello's lifetime. But for as long as he was an actor on the educational stage, he operated as if education could create a sense of citizenship that was at once socially constructive and privately liberating.

One of the selections in this collection speaks directly to the centrality of primary education as the vehicle for the construction of citizenship. Bello's "The Aims of Education," published in 1836, makes a case for the necessity of universal primary education in political, economic, and moral terms. A republic, Bello argued, cannot survive without an educated citizenry aware of its rights and responsibilities. At this early date, he proposed some practical solutions that would guide the successful development of national education in subsequent years: the establishment of a strong tutelary role for the state in education; and the creation of teacher-training schools. As a more subtle, but no less important point in this essay, Bello established a rationale for education as a means to instill civic values strongly informed by religion.

This is, in fact, the thread that ties all of his educational writings, be they of a more philosophical or a more practical hue: there must be an institutional machinery that links individual and society in a series of interlocking mechanisms; and there must be a strong philosophical principle that guides the system by reconciling the religious and secular worlds, and by bringing Chileans close to the spiritual and intellectual accomplishments of humanity.[17] It is in this context that one can understand his eloquent and insistent defense of the need for constantly expanding the moral and intellectual horizons of the population. While government institutions were necessary, it was also important to bring the population to a stage of self-imposed civic virtue.

Perhaps no work of Bello summarizes these views better than his inaugural speech at the University of Chile in 1843. It is a carefully crafted presentation that, in addition to placing the university at the center of national education, establishes a key political and educational principle, one that comes closest to defining his intellectual outlook, and the most important challenge for independent nations in nineteenth-century Latin America: the extent and meaning of the concept of freedom. Freedom may have meant military victory and political emancipation from Spain. To some, it continued to mean the destruction of the Hispanic legacy. But in a context of nation building, freedom must be closely connected with, perhaps even subordinated to, the concept of order. Bello did not think that one concept contradicted the other. Quite to the contrary, it was Bello's conviction that there could be no true freedom without restraints on personal and political passions. Order, therefore, had political and moral connotations. The challenge was to move nations from the external imposition of order to an internalized self-discipline that achieved social and political stability while ensuring civic and personal freedoms.

How to achieve such an aspect of the concept of order? Bello's unequivocal answer was: through the cultivation of reason understood in moral and intellectual terms, and disseminated through appropriate educational institutions. This required a humanistic culture in which religious and secular traditions were reconciled and encouraged. That is the reason he defended the study of Latin and advocated an approach to jurisprudence that transcended legal practice; both could connect Latin Americans to a long humanistic tradition as well as a sense of the historical search for social and political order. It is in this context that one can understand Bello's appeal to the religious community not merely to join in the educational efforts of the government, but to understand the benefits to be accrued by exposure to secular traditions. It is in this context, finally, that Bello's elaborate construction of a national educational machinery can be understood: order would come from widely shared values based on a humanistic tradition that also encouraged participation in the political and economic life of the nation.

Underlying Bello's educational views was his determination to separate all levels of education from the political divisiveness that was all too present as Latin American nations, Chile included, experimented with new political systems. One key area where education was likely to be politicized was history, for its study involved competing interpretations of the past and disparate political proposals for the future. At the same time, it could be a significant instrument for building a sense of nationhood, and thus he encouraged its cultivation at the university. As a result, in the 1840s Bello wrote a series of articles on history that provides significant insights into his views not just on the discipline, but on the task of defining a past that was consistent with his larger vision of order.

The occasion for Bello's reflections on history was provided by José Victorino Lastarria's essay on the colonial legacy of Spain, presented in 1844.[18] In this essay, Lastarria invited the rejection of the Iberian past in order to build a truly free and independent future, and claimed that his conclusions were based on the impartial and objective examination of historical facts. He also claimed that it was his search for objectivity that prevented him from writing about the more recent events of independence, where impartiality was nearly impossible. Bello replied by contesting both the interpretation of the past and Lastarria's historiographical choices and assumptions. In the process, he produced a rationale for an approach to history that could serve both the advancement of the field and the larger process of nation building.[19]

An important element in this discussion was treatment of the delicate issue of how Chile was to view itself vis-à-vis its colonial past. It was at this time, in the 1830s and 1840s, that Chile was negotiating the reestablishment of relations with Spain. All of this called for reflection on matters that went far beyond historical scholarship. Bello's position, as indicated above, was informed by his experience with language studies, which was in turn the product of a search for the rise of national identities and their linkages to previous traditions. The history of Chile included the Spanish imperial past, and both history and the country would be ill-served by summarily rejecting it. Spain was the bridge to a Roman past as well as to legal and literary traditions that Chile could not afford to do without. But more than an argument for utility, in Bello's response there was a statement about the historical development of nations: empires dissolved and new national configurations emerged. Traditions meshed (though some predominated, like Roman traditions in Spain, and Iberian traditions in Latin America), and they called for study and reflection rather than rejection in the name of emancipation and freedom.

Bello could not be comfortable with Lastarria's interpretation of the past, which was more of a call to destroy the persistence of Spanish institutions in independent Chile. This call depended on the assessment of historical events, and therefore questions had to be asked about historical scholarship *the craft itself*. Beginning with his comments on the "Investigations," but especially in the "Historical Sketch" and "The Craft of History," Bello rejected, though not as completely as claimed by Jacinto Chacón—a history teacher friendly to Lastarria's views—the vogue of a "philosophical" approach to history that dispensed with the cumbersome establishment and description of historical facts.[20] What was important to the propounders of the "philosophy of history" was to determine the general direction of historical developments, which in the case of Chile called for a radical break with the past. In the essay on historical scholarship "The Craft of History" included in Part Two, Bello presented a case for the need to work on original documents and manuscripts, for the need to carefully establish evidence and context before interpretations, philosophical or otherwise, could be produced. Although this was not known in detail until recently, Bello was speaking from actual experience working with medieval manuscripts at the British Museum.[21] His reconstruction of the origins and development of vernacular Spanish had given him a sense of the importance of documentation, and explains the insistence with which he drove home this point. A history that did not carefully and thoughtfully establish its evidence was likely to lead to misinterpretation and political manipulation. Chile could ill afford the prospect of political divisiveness resulting from a misunderstanding of the past.

An interesting aspect of the debate is that many if not most of Bello's references to historical works were of European origin. But it would be mistaken to conclude from this use of illustrations that he advocated a "European" model. On the contrary, it is in his historical reflections that we find the most explicit arguments in favor of a scholarship using Chilean sources, and written with due consideration to the Chilean peculiarities of geography, economics, and social development. As in his grammatical pieces, Bello took into consideration other models (like Latin and some aspects of the "universal" grammar of eighteenth-century thinkers) but was decidedly in favor of a history that emerged from, and developed its own categories to interpret, Chilean events. If there was anything to imitate from European models, it was "independence of thought." A corollary of this emphasis was, in disagreement with Lastarria's protests of objectivity, that no aspect of Chilean history was closed to scrutiny as long as it combined factual accuracy, judgment, and accountability. In particular, Bello advocated research on Chilean events since independence and, in his capacity as Rector of the University of Chile, commissioned several works on the subject that provided the basis for Chilean historiography.

Bello spoke on historical matters on the basis of his own experience with the field, and on the basis of his assessment of how history could either be a divisive element or an important vehicle for the construction of national unity. In both cases, it is the larger project of nation building that informed his historical interests. Language, education, and history were all significant elements in Bello's search for national unity. With different degrees of emphasis, these were his fundamental intellectual concerns. But there is still an important part of his work, and an important ingredient in the construction of a new political order, that needs to be addressed and which is perhaps the most difficult: the establishment of the rule of law in a context of political freedom.

Law, Politics, and International Relations

First, it is important to establish the vicissitudes of Bello's own political development. He was, after all, a faithful servant of the colonial regime who found himself in the midst of the whirlwind of independence, pronounced himself at one point in favor of a limited monarchy, and eventually embraced the republican system with conviction. There is no sharp break or transition from one political advocacy to the other, and in effect there is a clear thread uniting the two. Bello's fundamental concern was social and political order; the form of government, although by no means unimportant, was subordinated to the larger project of achieving functioning institutions that responded to local conditions without being separate, or militantly distinct, from the rest of the world.

Bello's experience of nineteen years in England, where he examined first hand the emergence of a new world order in the post-Waterloo years, but most importantly where he saw the political system of England at work, inclined him in favor of a constitutional monarchy. Perhaps the key distinction—not always understood by Bello's critics—between traditional monarchy (as exemplified by Ferdinand VII in Spain in the 1820s) and constitutional monarchy is the legitimacy of popular sovereignty recognized by the latter. In the post-independence period, Bello defended constitutional monarchy precisely because of its recognition of popular sovereignty, which reflected his own evolving political views. As it is clarified in his letter to the Mexican advocate of independence, Servando Teresa de Mier (included in this collection) Bello's recommendation for a constitutional monarchy was qualified and mild, but brought him both short and long term problems. His letter was intercepted and played a role in his isolation from his country in the 1820s, and perhaps contributed to his decision to serve the Chilean legation in London and to eventually move to Chile. Since Bello never disclaimed his inclination, and even continued to affirm that monarchy was not intrinsically a bad political system, he was continually under attack for his allegedly conservative views.

In practice, Bello did not advocate monarchy as *the* political system for Latin America. He wanted to achieve order at a time when examples of good government could more often come from constitutional monarchies than from fledgling republics. His own arrival in Chile was punctuated by a civil war resulting from political experimentation along republican lines in the 1820s. Order, it appeared to him and others in Chile, could only be ensured by a political system that provided for strong executive powers, limited the number of elected offices, especially at the provincial level, and discouraged popular mobilization. The issue was not finding the most perfect political system, but simply one that would work given the peculiar conditions and challenges of the post-independence period. The result was, in the case of Chile (where Bello had influential supporters) a strong, even authoritarian, centralized government that also contained the potential for subsequent liberalization. Bello's support for the 1833 constitution, which he may have helped craft, is made clear in his "Reforms of the Constitution" essay included in this section.[22] This is the constitution that would prove to be one of the most durable in Latin America, lasting until 1925. But more than for its longevity, this constitution is significant for the institutional framework that it provided to establish and consolidate the republic.

Bello's fundamental concern about order had both internal and external aspects. Bello's work in these two areas translated into two masterpieces, the *Principios de Derecho Internacional* and the *Código Civil*. Both were enormously influential works that were repeatedly edited, printed, and even plagiarized. The first guided the external relations of the Spanish American nations and informed the principles that culminated in the creation of the Organization of American States. The second, which is still in use, was adopted by several nations in the region, including Colombia, Ecuador, and Nicaragua. Understandably, both works have invited enormous amounts of commentary, much of it extremely specialized and confined to the fields of international and civil law. But they have a larger significance in the context of the emergence of Latin American nations as independent republics and the construction of a domestic blueprint for order that was not simply a copy of European models (the French civil code most often comes to mind).[23]

Both the *Principios* and the *Código Civil* have their own intellectual history, and the contents of both are illustrated in this section by related essays and selections from the volumes themselves. The *Principios*, as already indicated, was the product of a search for Latin America's position in the new international order. The literature on international law available in the 1820s and 1830s did not take into consideration the emergence of the new Latin American nations. Its limited focus on non-European areas was insufficient for guiding the international relations of nations that viewed themselves as independent and sovereign. Bello's major concern was, on the one hand, to provide an adaptation of the existing literature to the new phenomenon of independence, and, on the other, to work toward the recognition of nationhood by other countries from his position as a high official in the ministry of foreign relations. One of the fundamental elements of the *Principios* is its emphasis on the equality of nations, regardless of their political system or the way in which they originated as countries. In a new world order that included the nations of Latin America, countries were only required to exercise their sovereignty by providing for internal order and by appointing representative officials for the conduct of affairs that concerned relations with other nations.[24]

From the more practical standpoint, Bello was centrally involved in the search for the recognition of independence and nationhood on the part of Spain. This was an extremely delicate political issue that had implications for national unity and identity, as indicated in my previous comments on national language, education, and history. But Bello was able to demonstrate that there was little to lose, and much to gain, from the recognition of independent nationhood by the former empire. For one thing, Latin America was still outside the pale of international law, and other European nations could support Spain, as in fact they did, in its search for what it considered legitimate claims. Achieving the recognition of Spain itself would substantially reduce that threat. There was also the matter of the benefits to be accrued by trade and other exchanges in a context of peace. At any rate, the very rationale for reestablishing relations between Chile and Spain, which materialized in 1844, (Mexico and Spain reestablished relations earlier, in 1836) was part of the larger project of securing the position of the Latin American republics on a firm international legal basis. His thoughts on the desirability of a Latin American congress—although partly dismissed later as experience proved the difficulties of balancing national and supra-national interests—also reveal Bello's emphasis on the search for international arrangements sustained by the rule of law.

The search for this legitimate international position was not unrelated to internal order. Countries would not be able to deal with other nations without a political system that was legitimate and ensured accountability. Bello's view of internal order, however, went beyond the achievement of a strong government able to impose its will on the citizenry. Bello hoped that order would be internalized in the form of civic virtue and practice. Order could not be achieved if the laws were not seen as just and beneficial, and were consequently not observed, or if governments were expected to move the country forward without the understanding and support of the larger society.

Bello's *Código Civil* was prepared with the aim of reducing the areas of conflict most likely to engage the citizenry and therefore threaten both the internal and external components of the larger vision. The very structure of the work, which occupied him for more than twenty years, reveals a search for clear rules and regulations to guide the conduct of complex, yet central, human affairs. The major areas covered in the 2,525 articles of the Civil Code include (1) definitions of personal status (marital, national, residential, juridical, etc.); (2) control, possession, and use of assets; (3) matters of inheritance and donations; and (4) contracts and other obligations. That is, the multiplicity of daily human affairs whose lack of attention had led either to litigation without uniform results, or simply neglect and abuse. Latin American nations up to the promulgation of the civil code only had the old imperial legislation to deal with the changing realities of independent nations that were in addition more complex and more a part of the larger world. Bello's work provided a precedent and a model for other nations to follow.

Bello's *Código Civil* is justly considered a masterpiece because it involved a compilation and elaboration of numerous sources, from modern legislation to traditional Hispanic documents, in order to respond to peculiar national conditions. While the work called for civil legislation covering a number of private issues, it still provided recognition to the Church on matters of marriage. A union that was acceptable to the Church was also legitimate for civil law. Just as in his other intellectual endeavors, Bello made sure that tradition and change would be reconciled, that the guiding elements of the new political order would combine the best civil legislation of the past with the best of the present, and that there would be a role for religion. Bello's civil code was promulgated into law in 1855, and although modified in several parts, it continues to be used today, in Chile and elsewhere, a testimony to the applicability of its central principles.

Conclusion

The massive extent and variety of Bello's writings are only superficially difficult to assess. The fundamental motive for Bello's intellectual activity was the achievement of order, which he explored from at least three angles: individual, national, and international. In the process, he invited the reconciliation of ancient and modern traditions, religious and secular thought, and argued in favor of a strong yet liberalizing state that instilled civic virtues through education in the larger population so that representative government could be predictable and self-sustaining.

Bello's position in the history of Latin America is strong and secure, but unfortunately misunderstood. There are numerous examples of esteem for Bello's contributions. There are also deserved tributes to his scholarly stature and his poetic achievements. But there is little reflection, especially in English, about the relationship between Bello's intellectual production and the fundamental issues of that critical period in Latin American history: the creation and consolidation of nationhood. This is certainly a historical concern: we need to better understand Bello, and we need to better understand the intellectual and political history of Latin America. But the issue of how to respond to change and construct appropriate institutions and arrangements goes beyond the field of history; it relates to the resources that intellectuals at all times have mustered, often in very creative ways, to offer solutions to contemporary problems. Bello witnessed the dissolution of the Spanish empire in America, and contemplated with no small concern the

available options. That he would go back to the medieval chronicles—
and even farther back to Roman law—to construct one of the most
enduring blueprints for order and stability in the nineteenth century,
reveals a great deal about the ingenuity of Bello and the resources offered to him by a humanistic tradition. The following selection will
illustrate both the richness and variety of Bello's thought, as well as the
complexity of the issues involving the process of national consolidation
in Latin America.

NOTES

1. The best comprehensive biographies of Andrés Bello's life and works
include Miguel Luis Amunátegui, *Vida de don Andrés Bello* (Santiago: Imprenta
Pedro G. Ramírez, 1882); Rafael Caldera, *Andrés Bello* 7th ed. (Caracas: Editorial Dimensiones, 1981). First published in 1935, Caldera's book has been
translated into English as *Andrés Bello: Philosopher, Poet, Philologist, Educator,
Legislator, Statesman*, trans. by John Street (Caracas: La Casa de Bello, 1994);
Emir Rodríguez Monegal, *El Otro Andrés Bello* (Caracas: Monte-Avila Editores, 1969); and Fernando Murillo Rubiera, *Andrés Bello: Historia de una Vida
y de una Obra* (Caracas: La Casa de Bello, 1986). Among the most lucid studies
of Bello's various intellectual endeavors is Pedro Grases, *Estudios sobre Andrés
Bello*, 2 vols. (Barcelona: Editorial Seix Barral, 1981).

2. An important collection of essays on Bello's life in Caracas, where he
lived from 1781 to 1810 is La Casa de Bello, *Bello y Caracas* (Caracas: La Casa
de Bello, 1979). See also John V. Lombardi, *Venezuela: The Search for Order,
the Dream of Progress* (New York: Oxford University Press, 1982), and Caracciolo
Parra-Pérez, *Historia de la Primera República de Venezuela* (Caracas: Biblioteca
Ayacucho, 1992).

3. For a description of higher education in Venezuela at the time of Bello's
life in Caracas see Caracciolo Parra-León, *Filosofía Universitaria Venezolana*, in
Obras (Madrid: Editorial J. B., 1954).

4. The England that Bello encountered upon arrival in London, and much
of the background to independence as well as British policy to it, has been
described by William Spence Robertson, *The Life of Miranda*, 2 vols. (New
York: Cooper Square Publishers, 1969). On the various facets of Bello's life in
London, see the essays collected in La Casa de Bello, *Bello y Londres*, 2 vols.
(Caracas: La Casa de Bello, 1981). See also John Lynch, ed., *Bello: The London
Years* (Richmond, Surrey: The Richmond Publishing Co., 1982), and Karen L.
Racine, "Imagining Independence: London's Spanish American Community,
1790–1830," (Ph.D. Dissertation, Tulane? University, 1996).

5. Simón Bolívar and Andrés Bello exchanged twelve letters between 1826

and 1828. They have been collected in vol. 25 of Bello's *Obras Completas*, 26 vols. (Caracas: La Casa de Bello, 1981–86). Bolívar's frustration at the imminent departure of Bello can be seen in his letter to José Fernández Madrid dated April 29, 1829, included in Bello, *Obras*, vol. 26, p. 9.

6. A collection of essays on the various activities of Bello in Chile is *La Casa de Bello*, *Bello y Chile*, 2 vols. (Caracas: La Casa de Bello, 1981). See also Guillermo Feliú Cruz, *Andrés Bello y la Redacción de los Documentos Oficiales Administrativos, Internacionales y Legislativos de Chile* (Caracas: Biblioteca de los Tribunales del Distrito Federal, Fundación Rojas Astudillo, 1957), and Simon Collier, *Ideas and Politics of Chilean Independence, 1808–1833* (Cambridge: Cambridge University Press, 1967).

7. See Sol Serrano, *Universidad y Nación: Chile en el Siglo XIX* (Santiago: Editorial Universitaria, 1994), and Iván Jaksić and Sol Serrano, "In the Service of the Nation: The Establishment and Consolidation of the Universidad de Chile, 1842–1879," *Hispanic American Historical Review* 70, No. 1 (1990) : 139–171.

8. The complexities of this transition have been discussed by Tulio Halperín-Donghi, *Reforma y Disolución de los Imperios Ibéricos, 1750–1850* (Madrid: Alianza Editorial, 1985). See also David Bushnell and Neill Macauley, *The Emergence of Latin America in the Nineteenth Century*, 2nd ed. (New York: Oxford University Press, 1994); and Frank Safford, "Politics, Ideology and Society," in Leslie Bethell, ed., *Spanish America After Independence, c. 1820–c. 1870* (Cambridge: Cambridge University Press), 48–122.

9. Bello carried the primary responsibility for writing the articles of the *Gaceta* between 1808 and 1810; that is, the period from the Napoleonic invasion of the Iberian peninsula to the establishment of local governments in the colonies. There is a facsimile edition of the *Gaceta de Caracas, 1808–1810* (Paris: Établissements H. Dupuy, 1939).

10. A listing of the books in Miranda's library is in Arturo Uslar Pietri, *Los libros de Miranda* (Caracas: La Casa de Bello, 1979).

11. Bello's fourteen London notebooks are deposited in Box 94 of the Archivo Central Andrés Bello at the Biblioteca de la Universidad de Chile in Santiago, Chile. Marcelino Menéndez y Pelayo did not consult these notebooks, but learned about Bello's scholarship on Spanish medieval literature through Miguel Luis Amunátegui. It was Menéndez y Pelayo's impression that Bello had anticipated much of the research that would be conducted later in the Spanish peninsula. See his letters of 25 August 1885 and 26 February 1886 in Domingo Amunátegui Solar, *Archivo Epistolar de Don Miguel Luis Amunátegui*, vol. 2 (Santiago: Ediciones de la Universidad de Chile, 1942), pp. 678–681.

12. An important study of the Spanish exile community in London in the 1820s is by Vicente Lloréns, *Liberales y Románticos: Una Emigración Española*

en Inglaterra, 1823–1834, 3d ed. (Madrid: Editorial Castalia, 1979). See also Diego Martínez Torrón, *Los Liberales Románticos Españoles ante la Descolonización Americana* (Madrid: Editorial MAPFRE, 1992).

13. Antonio Cussen, *Bello y Bolívar: Poetry and Politics in the Spanish American Revolution* (Cambridge: Cambridge University Press, 1992). See also the important discussion of Bello's poetry by Marcelino Menéndez y Pelayo in *Historia de la Poesía Hispano-Americana*, 2 vols. (Madrid: Librería General de Victoriano Suárez, 1911), I: 353–416.

14. An important study of the political uses of grammar in nineteenth-century Latin America is by Malcolm Deas, "Miguel Antonio Caro y Amigos: Gramática y Poder en Colombia," in Deas, *Del Poder y la Gramática (y Otros Ensayos sobre Historia, Política y Literatura Colombiana)* (Bogotá: Tercer Mundo Editores, 1993), pp. 25–60.

15. See the important study by Amado Alonso, "Introducción a los Estudios Gramaticales de Andrés Bello," in Bello, *Obras Completas*, vol. 4, pp. ix–lxxxvi, and his *Castellano, Español, Idioma Nacional: Historia Espiritual de Tres Nombres* 2nd. ed. (Buenos Aires: Editorial Losada, 1949). See also Lidia Contreras, *Historia de las Ideas Ortográficas en Chile* (Santiago: Centro de Investigaciones Diego Barros Arana, Biblioteca Nacional, 1993), and Barry L. Vellerman, "The *Gramiatica* of Andrés Bello: Source and methods" (Ph.D. Dissertation, University of Wiscousin-Madison, 1974).

16. Volumes 21 and 22 of Bello's *Obras Completas* compile Bello's writings on education. For an interpretation, see Julio César Jobet, *Doctrina y Praxis de los Educadores Representativos Chilenos* (Santiago: Editorial Andrés Bello, 1970), especially chapter 4: "Don Andrés Bello, Orientador de la Enseñanza de su Epoca," pp. 155–279.

17. On Bello's philosophy and its connection to education and politics, see Iván Jaksić, "Racionalismo y Fe: La Filosofía Chilena en la Epoca de Andrés Bello," *Historia*, Vol. 29 (1995–96): 89–123. See also O. Carlos Stoetzer, "The Political Ideas of Andrés Bello," *International Philosophical Quarterly* 23, No. 4 (December 1983): 395–406; and Antonio Scocozza, *Filosofía, Política y Derecho en Andrés Bello* (Caracas: La Casa de Bello, 1989).

18. The "Investigaciones Sobre la Influencia Social de la Conquista i del Sistema Colonial de los Españoles de Chile" by Lastarria first appeared in *Anales de la Universidad de Chile* No. 1 (1843–44): 199–271. It was reprinted in his *Miscelánea Histórica y Literaria*, vol. 1 (Valparaíso: Imprenta de la Patria, 1868), 3–136.

19. The historiographical implications of this debate have been amply covered by Allen L. Woll, *A Functional Past: The Uses of History in Nineteenth-Century Chile* (Baton Rouge and London: Louisiana State University Press, 1982).

20. See Jacinto Chacón's prologue to José Victorino Lastarria, *Bosquejo Histórico de la Constitución del Gobierno de Chile* (Santiago: Imprenta Chilena, 1847),

pp. v–xxiv. For an examination of Lastarria's significance in nineteenth-century Chile, see Bernardo Subercaseaux, *Cultura y Sociedad Liberal en el Siglo XIX (Lastarria, Ideología y Literatura)* (Santiago: Editorial Aconcagua, 1981).

21. Pedro Grases points out that in addition to his studies in medieval literature, Bello produced an important historical piece, the *Resumen de la Historia de Venezuela* (1810). See his discussion of this work in his *Estudios sobre Andrés Bello*, vol. i, pp. 109–277. Bello's historical works have been included in vol. 22 of his *Obras Completas*.

22. Bello's involvement in the writing of the 1833 constitution is suggested by Diego Portales, who was well positioned to know, in a letter to Antonio Garfias dated 3 August 1833. The relevant passage is cited in Feliú Cruz, *Andrés Bello y la Redacción*, pp. 310–311.

23. Bernardino Bravo Lira, "Difusión del Código Civil de Bello en los Países de Derecho Castellano y Portugués," in La Casa de Bello, *Andrés Bello y el Derecho Latinoamericano* (Caracas: La Casa de Bello, 1987), 343–373. See also John Henry Merryman, *The Civil Law Tradition*, 2nd ed. (Stanford: Stanford University Press, 1985), 58.

24. See Frank Griffith Dawson, "The Influence of Andrés Bello on Latin American Perceptions of Non-Intervention and State Responsibility," *The British Yearbook of International Law, 1986* (Oxford: The Clarendon Press, 1987), 253–315.

BIBLIOGRAPHY

Amunátegui, Miguel Luis. *Vida de don Andrés Bello*. Santiago de Chile: Imprenta Pedro G. Ramírez, 1882.

Barros Arana, Diego. *Un decenio de la historia de Chile, 1841–1851*. 2 vols. Santiago: Imprenta, Litografía y Encuadernación Barcelona, 1913.

Bello, Andrés. *Obras completas de Andrés Bello*. 26 vols. Caracas: Fundación La Casa de Bello, 1981–86.

Bethell, Leslie, ed. *Spanish America After Independence, 1820–1870*. Cambridge: Cambridge University Press, 1987.

Bushnell, David, and Macauley, Neill. *The Emergence of Latin America in the Nineteenth Century*. 2nd ed. New York: Oxford University Press, 1994.

Caldera, Rafael. *Andrés Bello*. 7th ed. Caracas: Editorial Dimensiones, 1981. English translation of the fifth edition, *Andrés Bello: Philosopher, Poet, Philologist, Educator, Legislator, Statesman*. Trans. by John Street. Caracas: La Casa de Bello, 1994.

Collier, Simon. *Ideas and Politics of Chilean Independence, 1808–1833*. Cambridge: Cambridge University Press, 1967.

Cussen, Antonio. *Bello and Bolívar: Poetry and Politics in the Spanish American Revolution*. New York: Cambridge University Press, 1992.

Dawson, Frank Griffith. "The Influence of Andrés Bello on Latin American Perceptions of Non-Intervention and State Responsibility," in *The British Yearbook of International Law* (Oxford: Clarendon Press, 1986), 253–315.

Feliú Cruz, Guillermo. *Andrés Bello y la Redacción de los Documentos Oficiales Administrativos, Internacionales y Legislativos de Chile.* Caracas: Biblioteca de los Tribunales del Distrito Federal, Fundación Rojas Astudillo, 1957.

——, ed. *Estudios sobre Andrés Bello.* Santiago: Fondo Andrés Bello, 1966.

Fundación La Casa de Bello. *Bello y Caracas.* Caracas: Fundación La Casa de Bello, 1979.

——. *Bello y Londres.* 2 vols. Caracas: Fundación La Casa de Bello, 1980.

——. *Bello y Chile.* 2 vols. Caracas: Fundación La Casa de Bello, 1981.

——. *Bello y la América Latina.* Caracas: Fundación La Casa de Bello, 1982.

Grases, Pedro. *Estudios sobre Andrés Bello.* 2 vols. Caracas, Barcelona and Mexico: Editorial Seix Barral, 1981.

Lastarria, José Victorino. *Recuerdos literarios: Datos para la historia literaria de la América española i del progreso intelectual en Chile.* 2nd ed. Santiago: Librería de M. Servat, 1885.

Lira Urquieta, Pedro. *Andrés Bello.* Mexico: Fondo de Cultura Económica, 1948.

Lynch, John. *Andrés Bello: The London Years.* London: The Richmond Publishing Co., 1982.

——. *The Spanish American Revolutions, 1808–1826.* New York: W. W. Norton, 1973.

Murillo Rubiera, Fernando. *Andrés Bello: Historia de una vida y de una obra.* Caracas: La Casa de Bello, 1986.

Orrego Vicuña, Eugenio. *Don Andrés Bello.* 4th ed. Santiago: Editorial Zig-Zag, 1953.

Ramos, Julio. *Desencuentros de la modernidad en América Latina: Literatura y política en el siglo XIX.* Mexico: Fondo de Cultura Económica, 1989.

Robertson, William Spence. *The Life of Miranda.* 2 vols. New York: Cooper Square Publishers, 1969.

Rodríguez Monegal, Emir. *El otro Andrés Bello.* Caracas: Monte-Avila Editores, 1969.

Silva Castro, Raúl. *Don Andrés Bello, 1781–1865.* Santiago: Editorial Andrés Bello, 1965.

Serrano, Sol. *Universidad y nación. Chile en el siglo XIX.* Santiago: Editorial Universitaria, 1994.

Woll, Allen. *A Functional Past: The Uses of History in Nineteenth-Century Chile.* Baton Rouge and London: Louisiana State University Press, 1982.

I

Language and Literature

El Repertorio Americano

PROSPECTUS

(1826)

For some years now, advocates of American civilization have wanted to publish a periodical that would defend, as a cause close to its heart, the independence and freedom of the new nations that have emerged in the New World, upon the ruins of Spanish domination; a periodical which, in addition to dealing with the literary subjects most likely to attract the attention of Americans, would give special attention to America's geography, population, history, agriculture, commerce, and laws.[1] It would summarize the best works written on these subjects by both native and foreign writers, and also collect unpublished works. How many of these lie buried in the coffers of collectors for lack of resources to publish them in America? How many perish in the hands of ignorance and apathy, defrauding their countries of useful information and their authors of public praise and gratitude? A publication such as we have described, by preserving these interesting productions, would probably contribute to an increase in their number, and even though no other result could be expected, this alone would recommend them to all enlightened Americans who care about the renown and advancement of their countries.

Given the present state of America and Europe, London is perhaps the best place to publish this periodical. Its commercial relations with the countries on the other side of the Atlantic make it, in a sense, the center of them all, and the aid given to literary circulation by industrial circulation is too obvious to need description. But London is not only the metropolis of trade; in no part of the globe are the causes that vivify and nourish the human spirit as active as they are in Great Britain. Nowhere are researches bolder, the flight of genius freer, scientific speculations more profound, experiments in the arts more spirited. Rich in herself, Great Britain draws to herself the riches of her neighbors; and if she cedes to one of them the primacy of invention or perfection in some branch of the natural sciences, she is far ahead of them in cultivating the most essential knowledge that is useful to man, and that must be promoted in America.

We also doubt whether a project of this kind could be brought to birth with equal freedom in any other part of Europe; and the state of the typographical art in America would make extremely difficult the printing of a periodical on a scale adequate to the requirements I have indicated above.

Such were the considerations that we had in mind for publication of the *Biblioteca Americana*, which began to appear in London in 1823. We were not unaware of the inadequacy of our resources to carry out such a task, but believed that merely by opening the road we were doing an important service to our compatriots. And we flattered ourselves that, once the usefulness of the project and the difficulty of achieving it were recognized, we would be aided by other minds and new materials, and that the defects of its performance, especially during its first attempts, would be regarded with indulgence. We were not mistaken in this idea. The favor with which the first volume of the *Biblioteca* was received in America surpassed our fondest hopes. The number of copies printed, though considerable, was insufficient to satisfy the demand, and supportive comments were received from many sources, which encouraged us to continue the task and offered aid in carrying it out.

Obstacles impossible for us to foresee or overcome had already suspended publication of the second volume. Fortunately, participation in this periodical by Messrs. Bossange, Barthés, and Lowell, booksellers in London; and M. Bossange, senior, in Paris, have made it possible for us to take up the work again, with the prospect that its continuation will not depend on contingencies like those that interrupted it the first time. A better organized system in the distribution and circulation of the journal will bring it into the hands of transatlantic readers as rapidly as possible, by consistently taking advantage of the first occasions that present themselves in British ports. And, in the ever more prosperous economic condition of the new nations, the persistence of our efforts to merit the approval of their enlightened citizens, and our acceptance of the suggestions that they make to us, in the material order as well as in the method of dealing with them, will assure us of their favorable reception and will inspire them to favor us with submissions and communications.

From the outset we have decided to make the periodical even more specifically American than when we conceived it and stated our aims in our prospectus of 16 April 1823; and with this in mind we will reduce considerably the section on the natural and physical sciences, restricting it to points that apply most directly and immediately to America, and in other respects will limit ourselves to giving short notices of the best books published in that field.

In the other two sections, those of the humanities and intellectual and moral sciences, we also intend to omit everything that we believe is not in conformity with the present state of American culture. To these variations in content other changes in form will be added, intended to lower the cost and make the price of the work more moderate. It will have a single printing, of about 300 to 320 printed pages; but in neatness and typographical accuracy, it will not be inferior to the *Biblioteca*.

Hence our journal, already different in some respects from the one we published in 1823, will bear a different title.

However, *El Repertorio Americano* (for that is the name we intend to give it) will closely follow the plan of the *Biblioteca*, insofar as it gives preference to everything related to America, especially the productions of America's children, and to its history. We will deal (as we announced in the previous work) with the biographies of the heroes and other notable men who have adorned our countries, accompanying them, as often as possible, with illustrations of their venerable faces. Through original essays and historical documents, we propose to illustrate some of the most interesting events of our revolution, unknown to much of the world and even to Americans themselves. We also wish to bring to the light of day any number of interesting anecdotes in which the talents and virtues of our immortal leaders stand revealed, as well as the sufferings and sacrifices of a heroic people who have purchased their liberty at a higher price than that of any other nation that celebrates its history: the clemency of some, the generosity of others, and the patriotism of almost all. Borrowing in this regard the opinion of a distinguished writer, "we believe that the heritage of every free country lies in the glory of its great men."

In a word, we mean to examine, under their different aspects, ways of helping arts and sciences to develop in the New World, and of completing its process of civilization; to make it aware of useful inventions, so that it may adopt new methods, perfect its industry, trade, and navigation, open new channels of communication, and broaden and improve those that already exist. We mean to make the fruitful seed of freedom flourish, destroying the shameful prejudices that have nourished it since infancy; to establish the cult of morality on the indestructible basis of education; to preserve the names and actions that figure in our history, assigning them a place in the memory of time. This is the noble, but vast and difficult task, that love of country has imposed on us.

We shall take special care to banish from this work favoritism toward any one of our nations or peoples; we will write for all of them, and the *Repertorio*, faithful to its motto, will be truly American.

We will adopt everything that can be useful, and will speak the language of truth. We love freedom, we are writing on freedom's classic ground, and do not feel inclined to flatter power or temporize with prejudices that we consider harmful.

We will be happy indeed if, as a reward for our efforts, we cause the truth to shed its rays everywhere in the New World; if Nature awakes intellect from its long sleep, and talents and arts spring to its voice; if the light of philosophy scatters a thousand wretched errors; if the American people, civilized by letters and science, feel the beneficent influence of the mind's beautiful creations, and hasten with giant steps along the vast path opened throughout the ages by the peoples that have preceded them; until the happy time arrives when America, sheltered by moderate governments and wise social institutions, rich, flourishing, and free, returns to Europe with interest the stream of enlightenment which today she borrows, and, fulfilling her lofty destiny, receives the blessings of posterity!

Allocution to Poetry

(1823)

       Divine poetry, you who dwell in solitude[2]
taught to enwrap your songs
in the shady forest's silence,
you who lived in the green grotto
5   and had for company the mountain's echo;
it is time for you to leave effete Europe,
no lover of your native rustic charms,
and fly to where Columbus's world
opens its great scene before your eyes.
10   There heaven respects the laurel, ever green
with which you crown men's valor.
There too the flowering meadow,
the tangled wood, the twisting river,
offer a thousand colors to your brush,
15   and Zephyr flits among the roses,
and shining stars spangle night's chariot.
The king of heaven rises, among bright curtains
of pearly clouds; and little birds
sweetly sing songs of love in tones unlearned.

20   Oh, sylvan nymph, what have you to do
with pomps of gilded royal palaces?

Will you too go there with the courtesan crowd
to offer the foolish incense of servile flattery?
You were not thus in your most beauteous days,
25   when in the infancy of humankind,
teacher of peoples and of kings,
you sang its first laws to the world.
Oh goddess, do not stay
in that region of wretchedness and light,
30   where your ambitious rival, Philosophy,
subjecting virtue to calculation,
stripped you of mortals' worship,
where the crowned hydra menaces,
bringing anew to enslaved thought
35   the old night of savagery and crime;
where freedom is called vain delirium,
faith servility, and pomp greatness,
and corruption bears the name of culture.
Take from the rotted oak your golden lyre
40   with which you sweetly sang to spellbound men
of meadows and flowers, of the whisper
of the dark forest, the tranquil murmur
of the transparent stream,
and innocent Nature's fresh allure.
45   Spreading your diaphanous wings,
over the vast Atlantic go,
to other heavens, other folk, another world,
where earth still wears its ancient dress,
and man has scarcely conquered it;
50   America, the sun's young bride,
last daughter of old Ocean,
where the riches of all other climes
grow and flourish in her fertile breast.

What abode awaits you? what high peak,
55   what pleasant meadow, what secluded wood,
will be your home? On what happy shore
will your gold sandal first be placed?
By the bright river which first saw

the heroes of Albion humbled?
60 Where the blue flags
of Buenos Aires flutter, and it proudly brings
the tribute of a hundred mighty rivers
to the astonished sea?
Or where the double peak
65 of Avila is wrapped in clouds,
and Losada's city is reborn?
Or will the valleys of fortunate Chile,
smile more upon you, beloved Muse?
They bring forth golden harvests and sweet fruits,
70 where innocence and ingenuous candor dwell
and old-world hospitality combines
with courage and with love of country?
Or shall it be the city that the eagle, perched
upon the cactus, showed the wandering Aztecs,
75 and its rich soil of endless veins of ore
that almost sated Europe's greed?
The southern sea's beautiful queen,
whose daughters Nature gave a dowry
of grace, offers you a home
80 under her mild skies, where rains
do not disturb, nor turbulent winds.
Or will you come to rest in lofty Quito,
seated between the snowy peaks,
hearing the storms rage under your feet,
85 and drinking in clear air to match
your heavenly inspiration?
But listen where the thundering Bogotá,
leaps between sheer rock walls.
Wrapped in a white cloud of vapors
90 shimmering with rainbow tints,
it seeks the valleys of the Magdalena.
There memories of earlier days
await your lyre; when in sweet idleness
and happy, native innocence,
95 Cundinamarca's dwellers lived an easy life,
first children of her fertile breast,

before the curving plow deflowered the ground,
or foreign ship had seen her far-off coasts.
Ambition had not yet honed her horrid knife;
100   and man, not yet degenerate, sought refuge
under the dark roofs of caves and woods
that gave him safe and wholesome shelter.
Land had no master, fields were undivided,
towns had no walls, and without laws
105   freedom thrived, and all
was peace, content, and joy.
Then beautiful Huitaca, goddess of the waters
jealous of so much joy, submerged the valley,
making the Bogotá arise and drown it.
110   A remnant of that unhappy folk
took refuge in the mountains, and the rest
were buried in the ravenous abyss.
You will sing of how the dreadful fate
of his almost extinct race
115   roused Nenqueteba's anger, the Sun's son,
who with his divine scepter broke
the stony mountain, opening
a channel for the waves.
The mighty Bogotá, which once
120   spread its vast lake from peak to peak,
scorning the prison of its narrow banks,
assailed them furiously, and hurled
its waters through the breach.
You will sing how Nenqueteba, tenderly,
125   imparted laws and arts and faith,
and how he changed the wicked nymph
into night's lamp, and how the moon,
her silver coach, first crossed Olympus.

          Then come to celebrate the marvels
130   of the equator; sing of gorgeous sky
made joyous by the chorus of the stars,
where the vast dragon of the North
curls his gold tail around the moveless star

that points the brave sailor's way,
135   and the white dove of Arauco
dips her wing in southern waves.
If you prepare your richest colors,
if you take up your best of brushes,
you can paint climes that keep entire
140   their old primordial vigor at the time
when God's omnipotent voice,
heard in the abyss of chaos,
swelled the earth, newly created
out of the void, and covered it
145   with verdure and with life.
Eternal forests, who presumes to name or number
the vast crowds of your green labyrinths,
whose various forms, and height, and dress
seem to make boast of all their being?
150   Ceibas, acacias, myrtles now entwine,
and reeds and vines and grasses too.
From branch to branch, they all
perpetual warfare make, struggling to reach
the light and sun, and in the ground
155   their roots grow thick and crowded.

       Oh, pleasant Poetry, who would not go
with you to Cauca's banks, to breathe
the soft air of her eternal Spring,
where she has built her kingdom and her court!
160   Or if, once freed from care, I might traverse
Aragua's pleasant banks and wander there,
or maybe recline in the green shade
of a palm tree on the plain, and watch,
oh Southern Cross, your four bright lights,
165   burn in the azure dome, which mark
the errant traveler's nightly hours
through the vast solitude.
Would I could see the firefly's gleam
cutting the dusky air, and from the far-off inn
170   hear the yaravi's amorous cry.

A time will come when by your inspiration,
goddess, an American Vergil will arise
to sing of harvest and of flocks,
the rich soil overcome by man,
175 the thousand gifts with which the Torrid Zone
beloved of Phoebus, crowns its children's toil.
Where sugar cane bears its white honey
and cactus grows its carmine buds,
where cotton nods its snowy head
180 and pineapple ripens its ambrosia.
The palm tree yields its varied fruits;
the plum tree gives its sugared globes,
the avocado butter, indigo its dye.
The banana droops under its sweet burden,
185 and coffee concentrates the odor
of its white blooms, and cocoa
ripens its bean in purple urns.

But ah! do you prefer to sing the horrors
of impious war, and to the beat of drums
190 that fright the maternal breast, depict
armies that hasten to their doom
and soak the soil with mourning?
Would that you offered a less fertile theme
my fatherland, for warlike melodies!
195 What city and what field have not been bathed
with your sons' blood, and Spaniards' too?
What bleak plain has not offered human limbs
to feed the condor, and what rustic homes,
remote enough to escape fierce civil strife,
200 could shun its fury?
But love of country worked no miracle in Rome,
or Sparta the austere, Numancia generous.
Muse, no other page of history gives
more lofty deeds to supply your song.
205 What province will accept your praise,
what man will first receive the prize?

Chile, thankful, lauds Gamero's name,
who, victor in many a bloody fight,

in dying consecrated Talca's soil.
210 She wants eternal memory kept
of those mounted grenadiers whom Necochea
commanded in Chacabuco.
But, Muse, on Maipo's field alone,
what a long list from which to choose,
215 is offered, that you may repeat the songs
of all the champions who wear on their brows
the unfading green of honor!
Where Bueras gained so bright a name,
who with his dauntless knights
220 broke through the enemy's lines,
and where the regiment of Coquimbo
numbered as many heroes as it had soldiers.

Do you not see the gallant people
of Buenos Aires, who request the prize of valor?
225 Brave Castelli, who measured forces
with that monster who hides his face
above the clouds, and tramples men.
Moreno, who with measured speech upheld
the cause of the oppressed;
230 Balcarce, who on Suipacha's plains
predicted victory for your cause.
And you, Belgrano, and a hundred more
who enriched your native soil with glory
by using sword or pen; and if
235 the well-earned prize is given you
fear not to be forgotten.

Nor will the memory of Peace be lost,
Peace, who weeps for so many brave sons,
nor Santa Cruz, nor Chuquisaca,
240 nor Cochabamba, which guards like treasure
memorable examples of patriotic zeal.
Nor Potosí, richer in noble hearts
than in all its mines.
Nor Arequipa, which rightly praises Vizcardo,
245 nor that town where Rimac's waters lave its walls
that once was "of the kings," now owned by none.

Nor the city that gave the Incas cradle,
and laws to the south; if it still groans enslaved
it lacked no virtue, only better fortune.
250   But freedom, underneath the blows
that left her bloody, more courageous grew,
more untamed still, and rose again,
and made the despot drop his club.
Not for long will foreigners from Spain
255   usurp power from the empire of the sun,
nor will the ghost of Manco Cápac
groan for long, to see his throne so scorned.
The ashes of Angulo and Pumacagua
will be avenged by new and happier captains,
260   and the destinies of their people
will open the way, victorious.
Flee, days of conflict, days of mourning,
and bring apace the time that is to come.

        Goddess of memory, hymns are asked of you,
265   by Montezuma's empire too,
which, once Iturbide's yoke was broken,
is numbered now among the free.
Freedom expects, brave Mexican nation,
much of your power and your example.
270   Nor is her expectation vain
if you escape the risks that threaten
and do not set sail upon a sea
already strewn with many wrecks.
When the happy port is reached, some day
275   you will sing the heroes to whom you owe
the first bold deeds of daring,
who faced the veteran ranks with folk
unarmed and poor and ignorant,
lacking everything but courage,
280   and shook the bronze Colossus
that for three centuries had stood
firmly upon its base.
If Heaven gave a happier arm—not more robust—

to topple the Colossus, not for this
285 will oblivion hide the names
of Hidalgo and Morelos,
nor will the triumphs of your heroic fight
obscure the name of Guanajuato, and other cities
which, reduced to sad desert, curse an enemy
290 who, victory won, forgets his promises.
He makes a slaughter and calls it victory.

      Awake, oh Muse, for now it is the time.
Awake some higher genius, that will rise
in flight to such a splendid theme,
295 and sing the deeds done at Popayán,
and Barquisimeto, just as great,
and of the city too, whose homes
the Manzanares sees. Not that Manzanares,
river of feeble stream and dusty verdure,
300 that endures the pomp of the royal court
proud of its servitude,
but the river of abundant, lovely waters,
as its dwellers abound in splendid souls.
In its smooth glass Heaven paints
305 its pure azure, as it runs among the palms
of this and that delicious estate.
Sing too the deeds of Angostura,
home of the firm defense of freedom,
where the devouring storm burst like a fury.
310 And gently tell the world the feats of Bogotá,
of Guayaquil and Maracaibo (which now groans
under barbarous chain), and tell
of all the provinces that Cauca bathes:
Orinoco, Esmeralda, Magdalena, and the streams
315 that in Colombia join in brotherhood.

      Look where Barcelona, city without walls,
resists a thousand obstinate attacks.
A convent is the final refuge,
of the brave but all too meager troop
320 who are defending her; and all around

the enemies, as many as fierce Mars knows,
spread their destruction; a hundred times
the weak wall cedes to battering cannon fire,
and at each breach pours in

325 a legion better armed than they.
All that courage and love of country can,
they spent in patriotism and in valor.
But alas! without result. You will paint
the horror of that scene, you who can give

330 beauty to shadows, and absorb the mind
by representing death.
You will depict the furious victor,
not sparing even tremulous old age,
or innocent youth, and in the very lap

335 of the wronged woman kills her babe.
Few prisoners are taken; the others suffer
the enemy's mad rage, who always knew
how to make victory bloodier than battle.
You will paint the sad but glorious end

340 of Chamberlén. The loving wife
goes to seek her wounded spouse. He leans
his feeble body on his bloody sword,
pressing her to his bosom.
"Only death," he says, "can free me now

345 from the vile scaffold; and this last embrace
will make death sweeter; fare you well!"
As he prepares to strike the blow, she grasps
his hand, already raised, and says,
"Do you abandon me to such dishonor,

350 to ignominious slavery, and to insults
more horrible than death? I have not the courage
to suffer wrong, but more than enough
to imitate you. Let us both perish." Two blades
pierce two breasts together,

355 and they die embraced.

What name can eclipse the name of Margarita,
where even the fairer sex shared with the men

the perils and the dangers of the war;
where the defenders of their country
360 had to seize their enemies' arms
even as they fought; and where their chief,
armed by Fernando with all his strength
and all his forces, to satiate his vengeance
on the untried peasant host
365 that attacked his troops so furiously,
left the field in ignominious flight?

No lesser glory will the time to come
confer on Cartagena's courage.
Valor did not defeat her, hunger make her yield,
370 though hundreds of her warriors starved.
None lent an ear to treacherous talk;
those who retained a bit of vigor
took to the sea, and on their clumsy craft
traversed the enemy fleet.
375 But exile did not cool their constancy,
nor did they bend their necks to woeful fortune;
and though they departed from one shore,
profaned by usurpation, stripped by vengeance,
they returned with banners that forced fortune
380 to crown their patriotism with victory.
And Heaven permitted them to wrest
the prey from those unworthy hands.
Meanwhile, through the silent streets,
leading a soldiers' army, amid rotting corpses
385 and living men on whose faces
the Fates had stamped the sign of death,
the Inquisition now parades its horrid triumph;
making the altars sound with sacrilegious hymns,
it descends, ravenous, to its deep cave,
390 and feeds on the tormented martyrs.

What shall I say of that great city
that gave so many leaders to the sacred fight?
Murky Catuche, among the rubble
how you seem to forget your accustomed bed!

395   Why did the festive noise fall silent
along your banks? Where is the boisterous tower
with torches crowned, that used to greet
the august pomp of your solemn day?
Among the broken cupolas that yesterday
400   held sacred rites, slow serpents nest,
and in the hall that joyful banquets saw,
and loves, grass pushes up today
its wretched spikes.
But in your desolation, still more great
405   and lovely do you shine, oh land of heroes!
You, fighting bravely in the vanguard
of the family of Columbus, gave
example unsurpassed of constant faith.
If on your soil, torn by the shock
410   of constant earthquakes, the tyrant's flag
could flutter for a time, you lived
triumphant in your noble sons,
victorious over men and elements.
Now you will be reborn; peace and abundance
415   will flourish in your devastated fields.
Divine Muses will make their favored dwelling
among you, and heap your ruins with roses.

           Colombia! Ah, what mountain and what shore,
what inhospitable beach, where formerly
420   only the panther's fury could be seen,
or on the ground the caiman's bloody mark.
What jungle can there be in all your country,
what solitary height can still remain,
that does not cause us horror and repugnance
425   so thickly strewn is it with human bones,
hideous model for the bloody instinct
that causes man to turn on man as well?
How dear-bought was your victory!
How devastated was your land!
430   How many families were left shelterless!
But the good attained outweighed the price.

And how many famous names
have you not given to the memory's temple?

Ricaurte's name will live forever,
435   along with those of Codro and Curcio,
as long as the human breast
still beats for freedom. The Aragua
gave luster to its country in bloody battles,
and fear to Spain; despotism doubled its ranks,
440   yet courage did not cede to greater numbers.
A column approaches to surprise the store
that Ricaurte guards, with a meager troop.
He sends them far away,
forgoing his own safety and saving them.
445   He hides his plans with cheerful face. And now
the air is filled with heavy dust, the sound
of empty brass is heard nearby,
amid the unarmed crowd's painful cries,
falling before the victor's blows.
450   But not unchallenged; Ricaurte waits
armed with a torch, and when the post he holds,
surrounded by the enemy host, advancing
drunken with blood upon the easy prey,
when he sees that the fatal time has come,
455   not for vengeance (that he finds unworthy),
but for the lofty sacrifice
with which he yearns to do his honored task,
¡*Viva la patria*! he cries, and then applies
the torch, and blows up the building.

460   Nor will you hide the fame of Ribas,
Victorious at Niquitao, Horcones, Ocumare,
Vigirima, and omitting other names
that Venezuela deems equally worthy.
Urica, which alone could illustrate,
465   where, speared with a heroic lance,
died blood thirsty Boves, monster of atrocity
who out-Spaniarded the other Spaniards.
What of it, if to Ribas's lofty deeds,

fortune at last offered an unjust prize?
470 What if the Spanish captive insulted him?
If he perished under torture in the very sight
of his own men? If his rigid head
was exposed upon a shameful stake?
Tyranny dispenses death at pleasure,
475 but glory goes with the hero in his chains
and bathes his scaffold in divine light.

          Covered with honor, Baraya died there too,
among a thousand victims, at the hands,
of your vile satellites, Morillo. Nor did it serve
480 to temper a harsh sentence when his sad sister,
in mourning, with a hundred ladies more,
implored your pity. You said, "Let the traitor,
Baraya, die, and his family go to exile."
Baraya died, but his example lives.
485 Do you think you can put out with blood
the fire of freedom in such great souls?
As well extinguish the fires of Cotopaxi,
fed in the bosom of the Andes.
Watch the blood of Rovira flow,
490 lamented by Mérida and Pamplona,
and see the blood of Freites shed,
the faithful leader of Barcelona.
Ortiz and García de Toledo perish;
Granados, Amador, Castillo, die.
495 There lies Cabal, mourned in Popayán,
and mourned by science too; a fierce ball
pierces Camilo Torres's breast.
Gutiérrez draws his last breath here;
Pombo dies, who on the fatal bench
500 revealed his country's glorious future
in prophetic tones. Torices was not saved
by his great virtue, nor did modesty
and genius preserve Caldas in the end.
Venezuela is wrapped in mourning,
505 desolate, Cundinamarca groans,

Quito mourns her most illustrious sons.
But what does cruelty come to in the end?
Does Ferdinand rule Colombia again?
Does Mexico, prostrate, worship her vizier?
510 Do you still bear the ancient tribute,
of a whole hemisphere slavishly to Spain?
Does the Inquisition fill its cells
with the Americans, or do Spanish Cortes
give new names to servitude?
515 Does greedy Cádiz watch her ships return
with a hundred cities' spoils?
Colombia triumphs, and liberty
deceives the despots' useless plans;
and your inhuman triumphs, more fecund
520 than gold, are shame for Spain.
The world could pardon a Cortés,
and a Pizarro, for the blood they shed;
they conquered empires with a sword.
But you possess no vain, illusory shadow
525 of what the crowd, adorers of fortune,
calls glory; that fleeting victory
that made you master of unarmed provinces,
vanished like the airy fabric of a dream,
and nothing left behind, nothing for your nation
530 except for shame, shame for the sins
with which the victory was bought.
Whoever compares you with Alba,
Oh, how he errs! Philip's great minister
bathed Batavia's soil in blood.
535 But cruel and bloody as he was,
base he was not; he did not change
his face to fit the changing times,
deserting one side, then the other;
only his self-concern was constant.
540 He did not change from fierce soldier
to false patriot; he did not give
a sword to the Inquisition on one day
and fight for freedom on the morrow;

nor did he sell pardons, vilely profiting
545 from the very scaffold.

        Muse, when you recall to future times,
the Spanish arts that left
thousands of victims dead,
cities turned into solitudes; the altars
550 and the hospitable table stained
with brothers' blood; the plazas
adorned with lifeless heads, even the tombs
desecrated; wherever swords were drawn
the tribunal of fear reigned supreme.
555 Silence and tears are witnesses
and summon thought into their presence.
The informer is compensated with the prize
of the proscribed family's wealth,
and sells permission to the trembling victim
560 to live, by weight of gold, in Ferdinand's name.
It may be that your truths appear
delirium of depraved fantasy,
delighting in imagined horrors;
but oh, the bloody peace of Quito!
565 Oh, Valencia's abominable oath! Oh Muse,
can your colors paint so frightful a reality?
A witness was the consecrated host,
exposed in sacred solemn rite
to the Iberian chief's deceitful oath.
570 And with devoted prayers, the clergy raised
to heaven, to the author of concord,
in the name of God's presence, in the name
of their monarch and their honor, before
both sides and in the presence of the people,
575 promising brotherhood to those
already on the list of the proscribed.
Peace is hailed with a splendid banquet,
toasts are drunk with smiling face . . .
and in silence is prepared
580 the outcome of this infamous drama.

The same sun that saw the oaths of peace,
Colombia, saw your patriots die.

You too, Javier Ustáriz, had a dreadful end;
pierced by a sword before your spouse's eyes
585 whose weeping could not melt the heart
of your assassin, pity absent from his breast;
your unhappy wife was bathed
in your blood and your children's all at once.
Oh, Maturín! Oh, what a tragic day!
590 Oh, day of sadness for Venezuela
which even today, after so many losses
can scarcely be consoled with glories!
Ustáriz, in the mansion of the just,
surely you enjoy the prize
595 for your efforts and your zeal, devoid
of base self-interest; your soul was clean,
noble, and pure, the model for high minds
even in that dark time when honor's prize
went only to him who vilely sold his honor,
600 and when the blush of virtue was adjudged
to be disdain and treason.
Is music your delight, sweet poetry,
now, as once it was to you?
Or do you think of higher themes,
605 and do you speak with heroes, with great souls
of past and present time, opening the great book
of mankind's fate and of the future times,
when you read of the great fight for freedom,
which now begins, and of its far-off victory?
610 Martyrs who gave their lives for country
in sacred chorus stand around you;
Regulus, Thrasea, Marcus Brutus, Decius,
and all the men free Athens made immortal,
all those of Sparta and of Roman Tiber;
615 and those who died to hallow
Batavian and Helvetian soil, and British too.
Padilla, honor of the Spanish name,

Caupolicán and haughty Guacaipuro,
and daring España; with smiling face
620 Cuauhtémoc shows the burning bed of coals.
Gual shows the poison cup, Luisa the cruel lash
and you, heroic Policarpa, display
the red stain of murderous bullets
on your white breast. You watched your lover die
625 with firm resolve, and gave your life for others
in the first flush of youth, to a savage tyrant.

Miranda! Colombia also glories in your name.
Constant defender of her rights, and lover
of discipline and of sacred laws.
630 To your ashes reverently I offer
this humble tribute, and the holy branch
I place upon your venerable image,
illustrious patriot who, though banned and fleeing
did not forget the tender love
635 of the sweet home that rocked you in your cradle.
Now a target of fortune's blows, now fortunate,
American freedom your first vow and concern.
Alone, you dared to declare war
on the tyrants of your well-loved country,
640 and from the shores of England helped the note
of trumpet that dispelled America's long sleep,
lulled in superstition. Your sword was there
to help the noble causes of your friends.
And yet, plagued by misfortune, no resistance
645 by human means was possible; you had to yield,
and die in chains by perfidy.
Your spirit has not died; the echo of that cry
with which you called to battle still resounds;
you unfurled the flag of that great fight,
650 and now it triumphs, and you share the victory.

Your name, Girardot, also will resound
in the immortal songs of fame,
because you left so many proofs of valor
on Santo Domingo's shores.

655   Why did Fortune give you an early death,
       cut off your exploits' joyous course?
       You fell, but fell a victor; and your flag
       gave you triumphant shadow when you died,
       spread over the conquered batteries
660   that were the usurpers' tomb.
       Puerto Cabello saw your end of days,
       but not your memory, no, for it endures forever.

           Roscio's fame will not be less esteemed
       in the remotest future age. The Senate saw him
665   as wise lawgiver, the people as honest judge.
       Honorable citizen, loving spouse, faithful friend,
       a perfect model of the virtues
       that honor humankind. Among the waves
       of civil strife, his soul was unperturbed;
670   with equal mien he saw the treacherous smile
       of fortune, and himself in chains.
       And when the brutish Canarian made him drink,
       perfidiously, the bitter cup of insult,
       the modest dignity of virtue
675   did not abandon him.
       If of that wreath that Gradivo soaks
       in blood and tears his head is bare,
       what other honor would he not deserve?
       Not only was he budding liberty's defender
680   but was its mentor and its father too.

           Apollo will not deny his divine voice
       to your virtue, oh Piar! his divine voice
       that redeems the memory of brave deeds
       to time and miserly Fate.
685   Maturín well declares your prowess,
       and Cumaná and Güiria and Barcelona,
       and the memorable day of Juncal;
       the field of San Félix proclaims it,
       where they fought the enemy ranks
690   with such fury and courage
       that, even in death, they kept the triple line

in which they marched to battle.
If Fortune had cut short your career
on that day, happy would you be,
695 had not a fatal slip obscured your glory!

But where can we turn our gaze,
and not find monuments to heroism?
I'll speak of the retreat
commanded by MacGregor,
700 and that handful of heroes
who broke so bravely through the very center
of Spanish ranks, and at each step
left trophies of their valor.
Shall I tell the glories
705 that Anzoátegui won in fighting there,
or those in the valleys of Carúpano
or in the campaigns of Apure,
that gave such luster to his name,
either as expert chief or as brave soldier?
710 Shall I speak of the battalion
which in the fierce battle of Bomboná
pierced the steep cliffs with bayonets
and dared to scale the lofty peaks with them,
and took the fortress that defied our arms?
715 Shall I speak of Vargas's famous battle,
where Rondón's thousand mouths spewed death
unceasingly? How he faced the fire,
and took the bridge, guiding his warriors
over bristling peaks that on that day
720 were first to bear the steps of men,
surprised the Spaniard, attacked him and defeated?
Or shall I cite the celebrated day
when Cedeño saw broad Caura,
and his brave companions
725 leading their horses by the reins,
their blades confided to their mouths,
swam the deep current and caused to flee
the frightened Spaniards from their batteries?

As in that garden equally adorned
730   by nature and art in competition,
the busy bee flits vaguely, and drinks in
the subtlest and most delicate perfume
of the most odorous flowers,
he does not touch the rest, although they shine
735   with brilliant colors and with lovely odors.
His wings exhausted, he turns from his sweet task
back to the hive. Just so does one
who tried to measure forces with a theme
so rich that he cannot decide
740   which name to praise before the others,
which virtue, and which deed.
And he who tries his lyre and voice
will only finish a small part
of that attempt.

745   And shall we shrink from praising the idea
of those our country loves, those who still live
(and may it please the Lord
that the day we weep for them is far away),
sing of the man who crossed the Andes' frozen peak
750   and broke the chains of Chile, and freed Lima?

        Or he who from that strong fort, Cartagena,
made it belong to Colombia once again?
Or he who caused the Spaniards fear and fright
a thousand times, with his martial plainsmen.
755   Did he not make even Mars fear?
Or the illustrious hero, laurels on his brow,
turned white before its time,
who tamed the Spaniards' pride in Cúcuta,
San Mateo, and Araure. Will they not give fame
760   that lives forever to the man who won
at Cauca and at the broad Apure;
in Gámeza and Carabobo, and Boyacá,
where a whole empire
was snatched from Spanish despotism?
765   But not by my weak voice the sum

of victories be numbered; the grateful fatherland
deserves a finer mind, a more polished pen
for such a lofty purpose. For like that tree,
centuries old, worshiped by people all about,
770 that saw the forest many times renewed
around its mighty trunk, covering vast space
with its great canopy, victorious
over many winters, thus does your glory rise
to Heaven, Liberator of the Colombian people,
775 worthy to receive sweet rhyme
and history's praise, until the end of ages.

Ode to Tropical Agriculture

(1826)

Hail, fertile zone, that circumscribes[3]
the errant course of your enamored sun,
and, caressed by its light,
brings forth all living things
5   in each of your many climes!
You weave the summer's wreath of golden grain,
and offer grapes to the bubbling pail.
Your glorious groves lack no tone
of purple fruit, or red, or gold. In them the wind
10   imbibes a thousand odors, and innumerable flocks
crop your green meadow, from the plain
bordered by the horizon, to the mountain heights,
ever hoary with inaccessible snow.

You give sweet sugarcane, whose pure sap
15   makes the world disdain the honeycomb.
In coral urns you prepare the beans
that overflow the foaming chocolate cup.
Living red teems on your cactus plants,
outdoing the purple of Tyre.
20   And the splendid dye of your indigo
imitates the sapphire's glow.

Wine is yours, which the pierced agave
pours out for Anahuac's happy brood.
Yours too is the leaf that solaces
25   the tedium of idle hours, when its soft smoke
rises in wandering spirals.
You clothe with jasmine the bush of Sheba,
and give it the perfume that cools
the wild fever of riotous excess.
30   For your children the lofty palm brings forth
its varied products, and the pineapple ripens
its ambrosia. The yucca grows its snowy bread,
and the potato yields its fair fruit,
and cotton opens to the gentle breeze
35   its golden roses and its milk-white fleece.
For you the passion plant displays
its fresh green branches, and sweet globes
and dangling flowers hang from climbing branches.
For you maize, proud chief of the tribe of grains
40   swells its ears; and for you the banana plant
sags under dulcet weight. Banana, first
of all the plants that Providence has offered
to happy tropic's folk with generous hand;
it asks no care by human arts, but freely yields
45   its fruit. It needs no pruning hook or plow.
No care does it require, only such heed
as a slave's hand can steal from daily toil.
It grows with swiftness, and when it is outworn
its full-grown children take its place.

50   But, fertile zone, though rich,
why did not Nature work with equal zeal
to make its indolent dwellers follow her?
Oh, would that they could recognize the joy
that beckons from the simple farmer's home,
55   and spurn vain luxury, false brilliance,
and the city's evil idleness!
What vain illusion has a grip on those
whom Fortune has made masters of this land,

so happy, rich and varied as it is,
60 to make them leave hereditary soil,
forsaking it to mercenary hands?
Shut in blind clamor of the wretched cities,
where sick ambition fans the flames
of civil strife, or indolence exhausts
65 the love of country. There it is
that luxury saps customs, and vices trap
unwary youth in ever stronger bonds.
There, youth does not tire from manly exercise,
but sickens in the arms of treacherous beauty
70 that sells its favors to the highest bidder;
whose pastime is to light the flame of outlaw love
in the chaste bosom of a youth.
Or dawn will find him drunk, perhaps,
at the base, sordid gaming table.

75   Meanwhile the wife lends an eager ear
to the ardent lover's seductive flattery.
The tender virgin grows in her mother's school
of dissipation and flirtation, and that example
spurs her to sin before she wishes to.
80 Is this the way to form the heroic spirits
that bravely found and undergird the state?
How will strong and modest youth emerge,
our country's hope and pride,
from the hubbub of foolish revels
85 or the choruses of lewd dances?
Can the man who even in the cradle
slept to the murmur of lascivious songs,
a man who curls his hair and scents himself,
and dresses with almost feminine care
90 and spends the day in idleness,
or worse, in criminal lust: can such a man
hold firmly to the reins of law,
or be serene in doubtful combat, or confront
the haughty spirit of a tyrannous leader?
95 Triumphant Rome did not thus view

the arts of peace and war; rather, she gave
the reins of state to the strong hand,
tanned by the sun and hardened by the plow,
who raised his sons under a smoky peasant roof,
100   and made the world submit to Latin valor.

Oh, you who are the fortunate possessors,
born in this beautiful land,
where bountiful Nature parades her gifts
as if to win you and attract you!
105   Break the harsh enchantment
that holds you prisoner within walls.
The common man, working at crafts,
the merchant who loves luxury and must have it,
those who pant after high place and noisy honor,
110   the troop of parasitic flatterers,
live happily in that filthy chaos.
The land is your heritage; enjoy it.
Do you love freedom? Go then to the country,
Not where the rich man lives
115   amid armed satellites, and where
Fashion, that universal dame,
drags reason tied to her triumphal car.
Go not where foolish common folk adore
Fortune, and nobles the adulation of the mob.
120   Or do you love virtue? then the best teacher
is the solitary calm where man's soul,
judge only of itself, displays its actions.
Do you seek lasting joys, and happiness,
as much as is given to man on earth?
125   Where laughter is close to tears, and always,
ah, always, among the flowers pricks the thorn?
Go and enjoy the farmer's life, his lovely peace,
untroubled by bitterness and envy.
His soft bed is prepared for him
130   by labor, purest air, and great content,
and the flavor of food easily won.
He is untouched by wasteful gluttony,

and in the safe haven of his loyal home
is host to health and happiness.
135 Go breathe the mountain air, that gives
lost vigor to the tired body, and retards
fretful old age, and tinges pink
the face of beauty. Is the flame of love,
tempered by modesty, less sweet, perchance?
140 Or is beauty less attractive
without false ornament and lying paint?
Does the heart hear unmoved
the innocent language that expresses love
openly, the intent equal to the promise?
145 No need to rehearse before the mirror
a laugh, a step, a gesture;
no lack there of an honest face
flushed with modesty and health, nor does
the sidelong glance cast by a timid lover
150 lose its way to the soul.
Could you expect a marriage bond to form,
arranged by an alien hand, tyrant of love,
swayed by base interests, for repute or fortune,
happier than one where taste and age agree,
155 and free choice reigns, and mutual ardor?

There too are duties to perform: heal, oh heal
the bitter wounds of war; place the fertile soil,
now harsh and wild, under the unaccustomed yoke
of human skill, and conquer it.
160 Let pent-up pond and water mill
remember where their waters flowed,
let the axe break the matted trees
and fire burn the forest; in its barren splendor
let a long gash be cut.
165 Give shelter in the valleys
to thirsty sugarcane; in the cool mountains make
pear trees and apples forget their mother, Spain.
Make coffee trees adorn the slopes;
on river banks, let the maternal shade

170   of the *bucare* tree guard the tender cacao plants.
       Let gardens flourish, orchards laugh with joy.
       Is this blind error, foolish fantasy?
       Oh agriculture, wetnurse of mankind,
       heeding your voice, now comes the servile crowd
175   with curving sickles armed.
       It bursts into the dark wood's tangled growth.
       I hear voices and distant sounds, the axe's noise.
       Far off, echo repeats its blows; the ancient tree
       for long the challenge of the laboring crowd,
180   groans, and trembles from a hundred axes,
       topples at last, and its tall summit falls.
       The wild beast flees; the doleful bird
       leaves its sweet nest, its fledgling brood,
       seeking a wood unknown to humankind.
185   What do I see? a tall and crackling flame
       spills over the dry ruins of the conquered forest.
       The roaring fire is heard afar,
       black smoke eddies upward, piling cloud on cloud.
       And only dead trunks, only ashes remain
190   of what before was lovely green and freshness,
       the tomb of mortal joy, plaything of the wind.
       But the wild growth of savage, tangled plants
       gives way to fruitful plantings, that display
       their proud rows and orderly design.
195   Branch touches branch, and steals
       the light of day from sturdy shoots.
       Now the first flower displays its buds,
       lovely to see and breathing joyful hope.
       Hope, that laughing mops the tired farmer's brow,
200   Hope, that from afar
       paints the rich fruit, the harvest's bounty
       that carries off the tribute of the fields
       in heaping baskets and in billowing skirts,
       and under the weight of plenty, the farmer's due,
205   makes vast storehouses creak and groan.

Dear God! let not the Equator's farming folk
sweat vainly; be moved to pity and compassion.
Let them return now from their sad despair
with renewed spirit, and after such alarms,
210   anxiety and turmoil, and so many years
of fierce destruction and of military crimes,
may beg your mercy more than in the past.
May rustic piety, but no less sincere
find favor in your eyes. Let them not weep
215   for a vanished golden dream, a lying vision,
a future without tears, a smiling future
that lightens all the troubles of today.
Let not unseasonable rains
ruin the tender crops; let not the pitiless tooth
220   of gnawing insects devour them.
Let not the savage storm destroy,
or the tree's maternal sap
dry up in summer's long and heated thirst.
For you, supreme arbiter of fate,
225   were pleased at long last to remove the yoke
of foreign rule, and with your blessing
to raise American man toward heaven,
to make his freedom root and thrive.
Bury accursed war in deep abyss,
230   and, for fear of vengeful sword,
let the distrustful farmer not desist
from noble toil, that nourishes
families and whole countries too.
May anxious worry leave their souls,
235   and plows no longer sadly rust.
We have atoned enough for the savage conquest
of our unhappy fathers.
No matter where we look, do we not see
a stubbled wilderness where once were fields,
240   and cities too? Who can sum up the dreadful count
of deaths, proscriptions, tortures,
and orphans left abandoned?
The ghosts of Montezuma, Atahualpa,

sleep now, glutted with Spanish blood.
245   Ah! from your lofty seat,
where choirs of winged angels veil their faces
in awe before the splendor of your face
(if luckless humankind deserves, perchance,
a single glance from you),
250   send down an angel, angel of peace, to make
the rude Spaniard forget his ancient tyranny,
and, reverent, hear the sacred vow,
the essential law you gave to men;
may he stretch out his unarmed hand,
255   (alas, too stained with blood!)
to his wronged brother.
And if innate gentleness should sleep
make it awake in the American breast.
The brave heart that scorns obscure content,
260   that beats more strongly in the bloody hap
of battle, and greedy for power or fame,
loves noble perils,
deems an insult, worthy of contempt,
and spurns the prize not given by his country.
265   May he find freedom sweeter far than power,
and olive branch more fair than laurel crown.
Let the soldier-citizen put off
the panoply of war; let the victory wreath
hang on his country's altar,
270   and glory be the only prize of merit.
Then may my country see the longed-for day
when peace will triumph:
peace, that fills the world
with joy, serenity, and happiness.
275   Man will return rejoicing to his task;
the ship lifts anchor, and entrusts herself
to friendly winds. Workshops swarm, farms teem,
the scythes to not suffice to cut the grain.

       Oh, youthful nations, with early laurels crowned,
280   who rise before the West's astonished gaze!

Honor the fields, honor the simple life,
and the farmer's frugal simplicity.
Thus freedom will dwell in you forever,
ambition be restrained, law have its temple.
285 Your people will set out bravely
on the hard, steep path of immortality,
always citing your example.
Those who come after you will imitate you eagerly,
adding new names to those whose fame
290 they now acclaim. For they will say, "Sons, sons
are these of men who won the Andes' heights;
those who in Boyacá, and on Maipo's sands,
and in Junín, and Apurima's glorious field,
humbled in victory the lion of Spain."

La Araucana

DON ALONSO DE ERCILLA Y ZÚÑIGA

(1841)

A t the time when letters were unknown, or when writing was not in general use, all of man's knowledge was entrusted to poetry.[4] History, genealogies, laws, religious traditions, moral teachings, were all cast into metrical lines which, by stringing words together, fixed ideas and made them easier to retain and transmit. The first history was in verse. Heroic deeds, military expeditions, and all great events were chanted, not to entertain their hearers' imaginations by warping the truth of events with ingenious fictions, as was done later on, but rather for the same reason that subsequent historians and chroniclers wrote in prose. This was the original epic or narrative poetry: a history in verse, whose purpose was to transmit important events from one generation to another in order to perpetuate their memory.

But in that early stage of societies, ignorance, credulity, and love for the marvelous inevitably adulterated historical truth and plagued it with fabrications which, piled one on another, formed that heap of cosmogonic, mythical, and heroic fables under which we find buried the history of a people when we trace that history to its sources. Of course the Greek rhapsodists, the Germanic skalds, the Breton bards, the French *trouvères*, and the old Castilian ballad singers belong to that class of poet-historians who initially only intended to cast history into verse. Subsequently they filled it with wonderful tales and popular traditions, adopted willy-nilly and generally believed. Then, embellishing it with their own inventions, they gradually, and without meaning to do so, created a new genre, that of fictitious history. The historical epic was replaced by the fictitious epic, which borrows its materials from real events and celebrates known persons, but mingles those events with fictions and no longer aspires to capture men's belief, but rather to delight their imagination.

A large number of compositions belonging to the period of the historical epic are preserved in the modern languages. For example, what else are the religious poems of Gonzalo de Berceo but biographies and accounts of miracles, naively composed by the poet and received with implicit faith by his credulous contemporaries?

We do not mean that after this separation, when history became more or less contaminated by apocryphal traditions, it no longer offered material for poetry. We have examples of the opposite in Spain, where there was a long-established custom of putting events that were either real or reputed to be real into verse to make them easier to remember. It can even be said that this custom has lasted up to our day, though with a noticeable difference in subject matter. In their songs the old ballad singers celebrated national glories, the victories of the Peninsula's Christian kings over the Arabs, the legendary exploits of Bernardo del Carpio, the fabulous adventures of members of the House of Lara, the deeds whether real or imagined of Fernán González, Ruy Díaz, and other famous captains. Sometimes they even threw in ancient history, both sacred and profane. In later ages the courage, skill, and tragic deaths of famous bandits, smugglers, and bullfighters have given more frequent exercise to the pens of popular poets and the voices of blind men.

It was in the thirteenth century that the Castilians most successfully cultivated the historical epic. Very few compositions of this kind that appeared in the fourteenth and fifteenth centuries contain the slightest spark of poetry. For they must not be confused, as some critics on the other side of the Pyrenees have done, with certain narratives written in the seventeenth century which imitate the language of the old verse writers. These are fully realized works, whose richness of expression matches the perfection of their style.

There is another group of old ballads which are narrative in style but have no historical content. These celebrate the battles and love affairs of foreign characters, sometimes wholly imaginary ones. To this group belong the ballads of Gawain, Lancelot of the Lake, and other knights of the Round Table; that is, those of the legendary court of Arthur, king of Britain (called Artus in the ballads). There are also ballads of Roland, Oliver, Baldwin, the Marquis of Mantua, Richard of Normandy, Guy of Bologna, and other paladins of Charlemagne. All of them are merely pale and truncated copies of the ballads composed about these knights in France and England, beginning in the twelfth century. The place where the Spaniards' inventive talent began to shine was in the so-called books of chivalry.

As soon as writing became more widely understood it ceased to be necessary for people who enjoyed the pastime of listening to fictitious narratives to hear them from the lips of jongleurs and minstrels who, wandering from castle to castle, town square to town square, and delighting banquets, fairs, and religious pilgrimages, sang of battles, loves, and enchantments to the sound of harp and lute. Works intended as literature and not for singing began to be written in prose; this novelty, I believe, cannot be assigned a date later than 1300. At least, it is certain that prose romances became common in France during the fourteenth century. Generally these continued to deal with the same subjects as before: Alexander of Macedon, Arthur and the Round Table, Tristan and the beautiful Iseult, Lancelot of the Lake, Charlemagne and the Twelve Peers, etc. But once this new fictional form of the epic or history was introduced, new and often entirely imaginary characters soon appeared in them. That was the time when the Amadises, the Belianises, and the Palmerins began to appear, as well as the horde of knights errant whose flamboyant adventures were Europe's chief pastime during the fifteenth and sixteenth centuries. Spaniards were especially devoted to the reading and composition of this type of romance, until the immortal hero of La Mancha held them up to ridicule and left them consigned to permanent oblivion.

The prose form of the epic inevitably became more frequent and more widespread as the cultivation of letters, especially the elementary skills of reading and writing, increased in modern nations. During times when the art of representing words with visible signs was completely unknown, or was available only to a very few, meter was essential to fix them in remembrance, and to transmit memories and all the revelations of human thought from one time and place to another. As intellectual culture spread, not only did this advantage of poetic forms become less important, but, as taste became more refined, it imposed fixed laws on rhyme and demanded polished and finished compositions from poets. The verse epic simultaneously became less necessary and more difficult; and both these factors made increasingly widespread the use of prose in fictional tales. Intended for general entertainment, they grew in number and became infinitely varied, drawing their material from fables, from allegory, from knightly adventures, from a pastoral world no less ideal than that of the knights errant, and from prevailing customs. In this latter genre they covered all classes of society and all the settings of life, from the court to the village, from the salons of the rich to the haunts of poverty and even the most unsavory dens of crime.

These descriptions of social life, which in Spanish were called *novelas* (though at first this name was given only to shorter pieces such as Cervantes's *Novelas ejemplares*), constitute the preferred epic of modern times, and correspond, in the present state of society, to the rhapsodies of Homer's time and the rhymed ballads of the Middle Ages. A particular form of fictional writing is characteristic of each social period, each cultural change, each new intellectual development. In our day that form is the novel. Enthusiasm for positive realities has become so great that even the verse epic has had to sink to describing them, abandoning its fairies and wizards, its enchanted gardens and islands, in order to describe scenes, customs, and characters whose originals either have existed or could have existed. The chief characteristic of the fiction that is read today with the most enjoyment, whether written in prose or in verse, is the depiction of physical and moral nature brought within its real limits. In the Greek and romantic epic, and in the fictional tales of the Orient, we observe with pleasure the marvels wrought by supernatural beings. But either because this sort of fiction, though it seems rich, is in fact exhausted, or because we find its fabrications cloying, we are soon sated with them. Perhaps when we read the productions of faraway ages and lands, we adopt almost by tacit convention the principles, tastes, and concerns under whose influence they were written, while we expect other productions to conform to the criterion of our usual beliefs and feelings. The truth is that nowadays we seek, in the works of imagination produced by the European languages, a different kind of actors and settings, characters we can understand, convincing plots, happenings that do not go beyond what is natural and probable. Nowadays the poet who used the style of *Gerusalemme liberata* in an epic poem would certainly risk displeasing his readers.

Yet we need not believe that the epic muse has a narrower field in which to operate. Quite the opposite: she has never had available so many eminently poetic and picturesque objects. Human society regarded in the light of history's constant changes, and the varied phases that history offers us in the waves of religious and political revolutions, are an inexhaustible vein of material for the labors of novelist and poet. Sir Walter Scott and Lord Byron have demonstrated the enhancement that the spirit of faction and sect can give to moral traits, and the profound interest that disturbances in social equilibrium can shed on domestic life. Even in viewing the physical world, how many new resources are not opened to the poet's brush now that the earth, explored to its uttermost corners, presents us with an infinite number of local shadings to improve the scenes of this drama of real life, so varied and so abundant in emotions? Add to this the conquests of the arts, the prodigies wrought by industry, the secrets of nature revealed to science. Then you may tell us whether, having abandoned the agency of supernatural beings and magic, we possess a rich stream of epic and poetic materials not only greater in number and variety but better in quality than those employed by Ariosto and Tasso. For how many centuries have navigation and war offered powerful stimuli for fiction! And yet Lord Byron has proved in practice that travels and feats of arms in modern forms are as adaptable to the epic as they were in their old ones. He has shown that it is possible to bring them vividly to life without translating Homer, and that war as it is waged today, with modern battles, sieges, and attacks, is susceptible of poetic nuances that are as brilliant as the combats of Greeks and Trojans and the sack and destruction of Ilium.

> *Nec minimum meruere decus uestigia Graeca*
> *ausi deserere et celebrare domestica facta.*
> —HORACE, *Ars poetica*

[No little glory have they obtained who dared to forsake Greek models and celebrate the exploits of countrymen.]

In the sixteenth century the metrical romance reached its apogee in Ariosto's immortal poem, and from that point began to decline until it entirely disappeared among the ruins of knight erranthood, which lived out its last days in the following century. In Spain the exemplar of the Italian form of metrical romance is Bishop [Bernardo ole] Balbuena's *El Bernardo*, a work praised out of all proportion to its merits by one literary faction and belittled with equal exaggeration and unfairness by another. It must be admitted that in this long poem there are some excellent touches, a palette rich in colors, a large number of adventures and incidents, beautiful comparisons, and happy turns of verse. But these hardly make up for the intolerable prolixity of the descriptions and stories, the inappropriate and exaggerated language of the love passages, and the almost constant sacrifice of reason to rhyme, which, far from being Valbuena's slave (as one elegant Spanish critic avers) tyrannically and violently shoves him hither and yon and is the chief reason why his narrative style seems so cluttered and tortuous.

The metrical romance left the scene to be succeeded by the classical epic, whose representative is Tasso. It has been cultivated more or less successfully in all the European countries up to the present day, and is notable in Spain for its sheer volume, though its artistic quality is generally quite low. *La Austriada*, *El Monserrate*, and *La Araucana* are considered to be the best poems of this genre written in the Spanish language; but the former two are scarcely read today except by professional men of letters, and the third might be said to belong to a sort of middle species. That is, as far as its events are concerned it leans more in the direction of the historical and positive, yet its manner is closer to the simple and familiar tone of the ballad.

Even if we take *La Araucana* into account—were we to agree with the judgment made of it by some Spanish and other critics—we would have to say that in this regard the Spanish language does not have much to boast about. But this opinion has always struck me as excessively severe. Ercilla's poem can be read with pleasure, not only in Spain and the Spanish American nations but in other countries. This gives us the right to protest against Voltaire's hasty decision, and even against [Friedrich] Bouterweck's faint praise. Of all the critics that I have read, Martínez de la Rosa has been the first to judge *La Araucana* with discernment. However, though generally speaking he has done justice to its extraordinary excellences, I believe that the inflexibility of his literary principles has misled his judgment at times. As to what he says about "the mistaken choice of subject," I beg to differ with his opinion. I am not ready to admit that to be worthy of epic poetry an undertaking has to be great, in the sense given this word by critics of the classical school. For I do not believe that the interest with which we read an epic can be measured by the square leagues covered by the scene, or the number of chieftains and nations that appear in it. Any action capable of arousing vivid emotions, and of holding the reader enthralled, is worthy of the epic. Or, not to dispute about words, it can be the subject of an interesting poetic narrative. Is the subject of the *Odyssey*, perchance, larger than that chosen by Ercilla? And is not the *Odyssey* a splendid epic poem? What does the subject of the *Iliad* itself come down to, stripped of the splendor with which Homer's genius clothed it? What is so important and grandiose in the determination of a minor king of Mycenae who, as leader of other minor kings of Greece, besieged for ten years the little city of Ilium, head of a small district whose extremely doubtful geography has given rise—and still gives rise today—to so much debate among scholars? All that is great, splendid, and magnificent in the *Iliad* is the work of Homer.

There is another viewpoint from which this subject might seem ill-chosen. Ercilla, in describing the events in which he himself participated and the deeds of his companions in arms, facts known to so many, was forced to stick somewhat slavishly to historical truth. His contemporaries would not have forgiven him for inserting into those events the gaudy fantasies with which Tasso adorned the times of the First Crusade and Balbuena the legend of Bernardo del Carpio. This clothing of the narrative in marvels, to which sixteenth-century taste was not averse, required even at the time, in order to be appropriately used and to cause its effect, an event which in the course of centuries had acquired the mysterious obscurity that predisposes the imagination to meekly accept wonders: *Datur haec uenia antiquitati ut miscendo humana diuinis primordia urbium augustiora faciat* ... [This indulgence is granted to antiquity, to make the origins of cities more impressive by mingling the human with the divine ... —Livy, *Ab urbe condita*] Thus, the artificial episode of the wizard Fitón is one of the least appealing passages in *La Araucana*. Since we agree that this poem must deal with its material in such a way that, in large part and especially with regard to the Spaniards' deeds, it does not depart from historical truth, was it such a bad mistake for Ercilla to include it? Certainly the theme does not permit the splendid artifices of *Gerusalemme* or *El Bernardo*. But does art's only method of attracting attention lie in this? There is also depiction of living customs and characters, copied from nature not with the rigidity of history, but rather with the coloring and small imaginative touches that are the essence of all graphic narration, in which Ercilla could give free rein to his own imagination without causing the imaginations of his readers to rise up against him, and without departing from the accuracy of the historian much more than Livy did in his annals of Rome's early centuries. A portrait painted in this way, I repeat, could include embellishments and extra details that did not betray the nature of the ancient epic, and were more consistent with the philosophical era that was about to begin in Europe. Our present century no longer recognizes the authority of those conventional laws that have attempted to force the intellect to follow forever the iron rails of Greek and Latin poetry. The vain efforts made since Tasso's time to compose interesting epics, cast in the mold of Homer and the Aristotelian rules, have made us realize that it was time to follow another path. Ercilla had the first inspiration of this sort, and if he can be blamed for anything it is for not being consistently faithful to it.

If we are to judge him we must also keep in mind that his protagonist is Caupolicán, and that the concepts on which he dwells most lovingly are those of Araucanian heroism. Unlike Vergil, Ercilla did not set out to flatter the national pride of his countrymen. The ruling emotion of *La Araucana* is of a nobler kind: love for humanity, the cult of justice, and a generous admiration for the patriotism and bravery of the conquered people. Though offering ample praise for the Spaniards' courage and constancy, he condemns their greed and cruelty. Was it more worthy of the poet to flatter his native land than to give it a lesson in morality? Among all the other epic poems, *La Araucana* has the peculiar feature that the poet is a participant in it. But he is an actor who does not boast about himself, and when he reveals as if unwittingly what is going on in his soul amid the events to which he is a witness, he places before our eyes, along with the military and knightly dignity of his nation, pure and righteous feelings that were characteristic neither of the army nor Spain nor the century.

Though Ercilla had less reason to complain of his countrymen as a poet than as a soldier, it is undeniable that Spaniards have so far failed to appreciate his work as it deserves. But posterity is beginning to view it more fairly. We will not pause to enumerate the excellences and beauties that adorn it, in addition to those already mentioned: first, because Martínez de la Rosa has vindicated the singer of Caupolicán in this regard; and second, because we assume that *La Araucana*, their *Aeneid*, is familiar to the people of Chile, the first modern nation whose foundation has so far been immortalized in an epic poem.

But before leaving the subject of *La Araucana*, it would not be amiss to say something about Ercilla's particular tone and style, which, like his partiality toward the Indians, has been so great a factor in the disfavor with which the poem has for long been viewed in Spain. Ercilla's style is plain, moderate, and natural; without emphasis, without rhetorical frills, without archaisms, without artificial transpositions. Nothing could be more fluid, laconic, and crystal clear. When he describes things he does so with appropriate words. If he makes his characters speak, it is in ordinary language, in which they would naturally express the passion that imbues them. And yet his narrative is lively and his speeches eloquent. In them he can be compared to Homer, and sometimes betters him. In narration, we know that the model he set himself to imitate was Ariosto, and though he is certainly inferior to him in that graceful artlessness that is the rarest of artistic gifts, he still occupies (insofar as execution is concerned, and that is what we are discussing) a respectable place, perhaps the first place—after Ariosto and Tasso—among modern epics.

The epic is susceptible of different tones, and the poet is free to choose among them the tone most appropriate to his genius and the subject with which he is going to deal. Is there not a difference, in the historical-mythological epic, between Homer's tone and that of Vergil? In the knightly epic the contrast is between the easy, mischievous, and festive, sometimes jesting, style of Ariosto, and Tasso's grave meter, deliberate movements, and artificial symmetry. Ercilla chose the style best suited to his narrative talent. All those who, like him, have tried to tell a tale in a individual voice, have avoided the bombastic loftiness of tone which seems to scorn descending to the small details that are so useful, when well chosen, in conferring life and color on poetic scenes.

But this calm and familiar tone of Ercilla's, which sometimes (we must admit) degenerates into the dull and trite, inevitably diminished the merit of his poem in the eyes of Spaniards during the age of refined elegance and pompous grandiloquence that followed the healthier and purer taste of poets like Garcilasso and Fray Luis de León. Spaniards abandoned the simple and expressive naturalness of their older poetry only to assume, in almost all serious compositions, a majestic tone that avoided the idiomatic, familiar phrases so intimately linked with the emotions and so powerful in arousing them. Thus it was that, with the exception of lyrical ballads and some scenes in the comedies, passages that speak the human spirit's native tongue have been rare ever since the seventeenth century. There is enthusiasm, there is warmth, but naturalness is not their chief characteristic. The style of serious poetry became too artificial, and out of sheer elegance and loftiness lost much of its former ease and fluidity, and rarely succeeded in expressing the soul's emotions with vigor and purity. Corneille and Pope might be translated into Castilian with fair accuracy; but how to translate into this language the most beautiful passages from Shakespeare's tragedies or Byron's poems? We rejoice to see the rights of naturalness and freedom of genius vindicated at last. A new era is dawning for Castilian letters. Writers of great talent, by humanizing poetry and bringing it down from the stilts on which it took pleasure in climbing, are making efforts to restore its original and irreplaceable purity and ingenuous graces, for whose lack nothing can compensate.

A Short Essay on the Origin
and Progress of the
Art of Writing

(1827)

The invention of the alphabet—the idea of breaking down all the words in a language into a small number of elements and furnishing each element with a sign, thus fixing the most elusive of the accidents of matter and binding thought itself—supplied to every man the means to communicate with every place on the globe and with all the generations to come after him.[5] If this grandiose idea had been conceived and carried out by a single man, what glory would we have thought adequate to the merit of such a discovery, whether we consider the importance of the object or appreciate the degree of ingenuity needed to bring it into being? But in the age that preceded writing no single intellect would have been capable of so sublime an accomplishment. Writing could only be the result of a multitude of small and gradual inventions to which many centuries and probably many peoples contributed, and which will not be entirely complete unless we achieve a perfect alphabet, something that no nation possesses or perhaps has ever possessed.

What we propose to do here is to trace the progressive steps of this invention by examining the few landmarks that have come down to us from its earliest periods in different parts of the world. To be sure, we are far from possessing enough of these to record each century, each people, each individual among those that have contributed to its development. But we need not indulge in flights of fancy to indicate the route and recount the most important steps that have been taken to achieve this undertaking, if something that began without a plan and as a sort of instinct can be called an undertaking. Nor could the process be seen in all its dimensions and importance until it was finished.

What, then, was the starting point for discovery of this wonderful art? Undoubtedly it was painting. The art of representing objects by means of lines and colors has been cultivated with more or less taste and skill by all human races, ever since the first glimmerings of civilization. The need to commit to memory great events, religious and civic laws, and the first discoveries in the arts and sciences must inevitably have been felt very early. To satisfy it, man had recourse to two means: that of oral tradition, which speaks to the ear; and that of painting, whose message is aimed at the eye. The obviousness, ease, and completeness of the first means was no doubt the chief reason why the second means made such slow progress, and why perfect acquisition of it has been limited to so few countries. But painting has peculiar advantages. Though it speaks an unspecific and hence obscure language, it often succeeds in surviving oral tradition, and in many cases has served to perpetuate it. A picture is constantly in view, and over time causes a profound impression. This is the reason why, among most peoples, painting has been recognized as a powerful instrument for engraving on the mind past events, the teachings of experience, and the consoling promises—as well as the frightening hints—of religion.

But equal use of painting as a monumental art has not been made in the same way everywhere, nor is it easy to say why some nations paid little attention to this means of enriching memory, while in others not only were temples and other public buildings covered with historical paintings, but vast collections of canvases and painted paper were kept even by private citizens, with the same curiosity and for the same reasons that diplomas, edicts, titles to property, and other documents are preserved in our archives today. And perhaps it is not mere coincidence that the two peoples who have cultivated painting most assiduously as a vehicle of tradition and teaching have been equally notable for having made so little use of the epic, or of the creation myths that are so familiar elsewhere for transmitting historical memories and religious dogmas. Perhaps there have never been two nations of equally high culture, like the Egyptians and the Mexicans, who have regarded poetry with such indifference.

Once the art of painting had been used as a means of historical instruction, it was natural for man to try to correct its flaws and make its language more spiritual, emphasizing the eyes less than the mind. Only rarely can painting restrict the actions it describes to particular persons and motifs, times, and places. For instance, when a battle is transferred to canvas it will show the age, weapons, and clothing of the combatants, but it can hardly show us what individuals were in it, what cause they upheld or fought against, not even the place and precise time of the event. These are often important circumstances. Even so, sometimes painting can find ways to indicate more or less clearly even these moral and metaphysical relationships. A pyramid, a mountain or tower of a particular shape, the confluence of two rivers, whatever other detail capable of being presented to the eyes, could have offered a local indication as appropriate as it was intelligible. Could painting undertake to individualize a country? Its natural or industrial products, or some notable physical trait, skillfully introduced, could have made it easily understandable. All painters have taken advantage of the infinite number of characteristics that different seasons and hours can provide. And just as, in paintings intended for teaching purposes, there needed to be no attempt to seek regularity of design or beauty of coloring, or any other among the qualities that make up the existence of a painting whose only aim is to please the eye. The principal figures and especially the secondary indications would be reduced to the number of strokes and lines absolutely necessary to instill the idea of objects. For instance, a gently curving horizontal line would be employed to indicate water; fire could be represented by another wavy line, but vertical this time; a pyramid by a simple triangle; and so on for other objects. And as these alterations in form would not have been produced all at once, it was easy to maintain their significance, and they could be transmitted from one age to another.

Here we have reached the first stage in the transformation of painting into writing. While the main part of the picture retains the character of a real painting, other parts of the objects exhibited by the artist are reduced to simple outlines that retain a less-than-perfect resemblance to their originals. Hence these first letters (if we can call them by this name at such an early stage) were up to a point *mimetic*, or imitative of objects.

It is easy to imagine that the number of mimetic characters continued to increase, and that secondary indications would gain ground over the purely pictorial factor. After these signs, which we could call natural ones, came others in which a conventional and arbitrary factor began to appear. In these signs, taking as a model the processes of speech, an object was recognized by its accompanying sign, the whole by a part, the end by the means, the content by the container, the abstract by the concrete; and in a word, the *tropes* of ordinary language were transferred to painting. A cradle, for instance, would mean birth; a funeral urn, death; a flower, spring; a stalk of grain, summer; a crown, regal dignity; an incense burner, the priesthood; a ring, matrimony; a tongue, speech; a human footprint, a road, as in some Mexican hieroglyphs; an arrow, swiftness; laurel, victory; and an olive tree, peace, as in the emblematic representations of the Romans and of modern nations. These characters are called *tropic* signs, and when the analogy between the sign and what is signified was obscure and known only by initiates into the secrets of the art, they were called *enigmatic* signs. Thus the emblem of eternity was a circle, because it has no beginning and no end.

The introduction of tropic signs marks the second phase of writing. Enigmatic signs could be thought of as a kind of cipher used by those who had an interest in hiding certain kinds of knowledge, or who hoped to gain advantage from exclusive possession of them, or who wanted to gain importance by means of this mysterious device and win respect for something that might be scorned were it to be divulged.

After tropic signs had increased in number, certain conventional rules had to be established to explain them and to represent complex ideas, and it became more and more difficult to understand them. Hence preliminary instruction eventually became necessary, as much to understand the meaning of those characters as to express ideas with them. In other words, an art of reading and writing had come into being. But that sort of writing was notably different from ours. It immediately represented ideas; ours indicates the sounds that we use to express ideas by speaking and is in fact a system of signs into which another system of the same kind was translated.

It was natural for language to exert a certain influence on *ideographic* writing. Once man had achieved the analysis of thought by means of speech, it inevitably served as the basis for the new language, whose purpose was to speak to the eyes, as speech did to the ears. The grammar of both languages—if we may express it like that—was in large part the same, and translation from one to another obvious and easy. However, it was possible for the *optic* kind of language, cultivated for several centuries and applied particularly to science, to acquire an ideographic literature, and not only to become considerably richer in signs, but capable of refinements and elegances of which we can form no idea. Who can say that there is not a kind of visual poetry? The poetry we know is merely the art of arousing a pleasant series of ideas by means of words. Why could there not be an art that employed other kinds of signs for arousing thoughts and fantasies to beguile and delight us? The delicacy, or the energy, with which the concepts of a great poet are transmitted through lines, shapes, and colors, could sometimes be untranslatable into the vernacular, just as we often find it difficult, if not impossible, to pour into one language the grace, sublimity, or delicacy of feeling that we admire in another. And do not think that we are describing a merely possible state of affairs here. Unlikely as it seems, and contrary to our habits, this extraordinary development of ideographic writing has had its effect on a very great people, where the art of communicating thoughts has been cultivated for a long time and is still cultivated, not only as a means of instruction but of pastime and pleasure. The writing of the Chinese is a complete ideographical system, consisting of more than eighty thousand complex characters, connected to two hundred fourteen keys or radical symbols. Poetic compositions do not exist in spoken words, but in these visual signs; and most beautiful passages in Chinese cannot be translated into the vernacular. Their most surprising feature is that these characters can be represented by actions and gesticulations. Chinese philosophers discuss by tracing lines and figures in the air with their folding fans, for often there are no equivalent words in speech.

By simplifying the signs more and more, as naturally happens when such frequent and universal use is made of them, the natural or tropic resemblance to objects that they originally possessed is in the end lost; this is the third stage, and the state in which Chinese writing now exists. The connection between ideas and characters seems totally artificial.

But, no matter how great the perfection which we suppose this system of signs to have achieved, it has no indication of proper names. And without this, how could the reader, in most cases, have identified the individuals symbolized in this language with those represented by names in the vernacular, which is always the most familiar means of communication among people? Hence it became necessary to find a way to express the actual sounds of speech; and just as in our system of writing sounds suggest ideas, it was natural that, in the symbolic writing that preceded it, ideas suggested sounds. If a proper name signified a general idea, or could be broken down into two or more parts that had that meaning, its symbolic expression could serve to indicate the actual composition of that name. Such was the device adopted in Mexican hieroglyphs. For example, to refer to King *Ilhuicamina*, whose name divides into two parts meaning "face" and "water," the painter drew the image of a face and the symbol of water. *Axajacatl* means "arrow that pierces the sky"; the king of this name was represented by the signs that corresponded to these ideas. The city of *Macuilxochitl* ("five flowers") was a flower above the sign for five; that of *Quauhtin-chan* ("house of the eagle"), a house in which the head of this bird appears. The Chinese, the Egyptians, and other nations used this type of characters, which, because they had originally represented the sounds of which their names consisted, were called *ciriological*, from *kyrios*, own, and *logos*, word.

The Mexicans had reached this point, but their writing (if it may be so called) shows that it was still in the infancy of the art. The purely pictorial part, which had disappeared in Chinese and Egyptian writing, occupied considerable space in the Mexican system, which can be looked upon as a series of pictures (though very crudely drawn because they were used exclusively for instruction) with short ideographic and ciriological inscriptions.

Despite this lack of perfection, the Mexican pictures went a long way toward supplying the lack of other, commoner, and easier ways of transmitting ideas. And the zeal with which this embryonic art of writing was cultivated among the inhabitants of that cultured empire would soon have resulted in considerable progress. At the time of the last Aztec king several thousand persons were working on these paintings. Paper, cotton fabrics, and deerskin were the materials used to make them. Though the drawing was crude, as occurs in every nation that uses pictures to provide information rather than entertainment, the colors were strong and beautiful. Each piece was customarily folded o form pleats like those of a fan, and strips of wood were glued to the two ends, so that before it was opened it looked very much like a bound book. These books, when unfolded, were sometimes as much as fifteen and twenty yards long.

Once this method of representing spoken words was introduced into writing, it was easy to extend it from proper names to common and general things, composed of meaningful parts whose symbols were already familiar. Some languages have a large number of these words divisible into other words, and the usefulness of indicating an idea by indicating the name that represented it in ordinary language, together with the intelligibility of this type of indication, must undoubtedly have led men to increase still further the number of *phonetic* characters; that is, characters representative not of thought, but of the voice (*phone*). In any case, the breaking up of words into meaningful elements could be applied only to a comparatively small number of cases. How, then, to represent words that did not allow for this breaking up? Suppose that we had been faced with the problem of indicating this word, *árbol* ("tree"), which in Spanish cannot be broken down into meaningful elements. What would we have done? The stratagem that occurred to several peoples was to divide the word into two or three parts, each of which, since they did not represent any easily symbolized idea, could at least form the beginning of a word whose idea it might be. *Arbol* is divisible into *ár* and *bol*. *Ar* and *bol* respectively begin the words *arco* (bow) and *bola* (ball). Supposing that these ideas were represented by the mimetic symbols U and O, the actual structure of the word *árbol* would be represented thus: UO.

The fourth stage in the art of writing is the analysis of the actual structure of words. This analysis would lead by degrees to monosyllabic writing, in which each syllable would be represented by a simple character such as is used today among the Tartar-Manchus and the inhabitants of Korea. The number of syllables making up all the words of a language, though large in comparison with the number of really elementary vowels and articulations, is not so great that each syllable cannot be symbolized fairly easily with a sign of its own, and hence this constituted a complete system of phonetic writing. The alphabet of the Tartar-Manchus, whose language is especially ingenious and rich, is composed of fifteen hundred characters.

The Spanish tongue has more or less the same number of syllables; and according to this system the syllables *a, ca, o, ra, ser,* could be represented with the ideographic signs that denoted respectively a bird (*ave*), a chain (*cadena*), an oval, a branch (*rama*), and a serpent, objects whose names begin with those syllables. Applying this device to all the syllables that make up the language, we would eventually have had a writing system with fifteen hundred characters more or less, with which we would have been able to represent all the syllables and in consequence all the words in the Spanish language. In this system the characters remind the reader of ideas or objects, these recall their names, and their names recall the respective initials of the syllables. But once the reader had familiarized himself with them, he would soon associate the characters with the syllables without having to think of the objects or their names. By this time ideographic signs have been changed into merely phonetic signs, representative of the sounds of speech: the fifth stage in the art of writing.

Only one step remains, which is to reduce the number of these characters by transferring the breakdown of words to elementary sounds. It is an extremely easy step to take, if (as some peoples in Asia did) the vowels are omitted in writing. In this case the old phonetic characters, reduced to a small number, would in fact be consonants with a simple value, such as our letters b, p, m; others would have double value, as the letters *zeta*, *xi*, and *psi* did in Greek (*ds*, *cs*, and *ps*), and some few would perhaps have more complicated values. To perfect this alphabet it was only necessary to add signs for the vowels, and to replace every double or triple consonant by the signs of the respective simple sounds, as some do in Spanish by substituting *cs* (though in my view improperly) for *x*. To reach perfection the Greeks merely had to complete this analytical procedure by eliminating all the double consonants. The Latins had a somewhat less perfect alphabet. Both, however, possessed the easiest and simplest writing systems known to antiquity. It was an inestimable heritage which they transmitted to the peoples of modern Europe, and which passed with them to the New World.

From this sixth and last stage in the art of writing, let us look back and observe the path that man has followed to reach the system of alphabetic writing. We can imagine the chief stages in this long and sometimes retrograde progress by concentrating on a single letter: *r*.

First stage: the picture of a tree branch (*rama*) is reduced to a summary drawing that retains a remote resemblance to this object.

Second stage: this figure or imperfect sketch of the branch comes to signify, through a sort of trope, the branching of anything; for example, the distribution of water into a series of streams, canals, and ditches, and the abstract idea of the act of distributing.

Third stage: this sketch becomes reduced to a simple letter *r*, which retains no resemblance to the original object and in its natural state means a branch.

Fourth stage: *r* denotes the syllable *ra*, not directly but by suggesting in succession these three ideas: the idea of a branch, the idea of the name by which this object is known in ordinary language (that is, the idea of the word *rama*), and the idea of the syllable *ra* with which this word begins. This marks the transition from ideographic writing to phonetic writing.

Fifth stage: *r* denotes the syllable *ra* exclusively and directly.

Sixth stage: *r* denotes the sound that we give to this letter in Spanish.

Needless to say, this history of the letter *r* is completely imaginary, and by using it we intend only to describe the progress of human intellect in the invention of alphabetic writing.

Among the Egyptians, ideographic writing was mixed with the phonetic writing of this last stage. Recent discoveries in the interpretation of hieroglyphs of that famous people, a source of Greek culture, are so important for the study of antiquity, and have gained so much repute in England, France, and Germany, that we believe our readers would appreciate a short description of their results, and of the ingenious labors that have led up to them.

The ancient Egyptians practiced three methods of writing: popular (demotic); sacred (hieratic); and hieroglyphic properly speaking, which according to Saint Clement of Alexandria took two forms. That is, it consisted of two different kinds of characters, some of them ideographic either by imitation (mimetic) or by tropes and enigmas (tropic and enigmatic), and the others (which this writer calls ciriologic, perhaps because of the use that was always made of them to express proper names) representative of the elementary sounds of words, by virtue of the relationship that they had, or had had originally, to familiar objects whose names began with those sounds.

The word *hieroglyph* means "sacred sculpture," referring to the use made of those characters on the Egyptians' ancient monuments. The study made of them following the French invasion of Egypt has clarified the meaning of the passage referred to in Saint Clement of Alexandria, and has wholly confirmed it. The celebrated pillar of black basalt discovered by the French in Rosetta later fell into the hands of British troops and has recently been deposited in the British Museum; it contains three inscriptions, in large part obliterated and mutilated. The last of these, written in Greek, ends by saying that the decree carved on that pillar (in honor of Ptolemy Epiphanes) had been ordered carved in three kinds of characters: hieroglyphic, demotic, and Greek. Initially these last were compared with those of the demotic inscription. It was observed that in it the repetitions of certain groups of characters corresponded with those of certain words in the Greek inscription. Doctor Thomas Young was thus able to recognize the groups representing the words *Ptolemy, king, Egypt,* and the conjunction *and.* By applying the same procedure to the hieroglyphic inscription, he recognized the groups meaning *Ptolemy, king, God, sanctuary,* and *priest.* We also owe to Dr. Young the discovery that some of the characters on these inscriptions were simply phonetic, and even the discovery of the precise meaning of a few of them.

M. Champollion, junior, followed him in these careful investigations, examining the Rosetta pillar again and comparing its inscriptions with those of other Egyptian monuments. He has established that each phonetic hieroglyph was the picture of a physical object whose name in the vernacular began with the sound that the sign indicated. The picture of an eagle, for example, which in the Egyptian language was called *ahom,* was the sign of the letter *a;* that of an incense-burner, called berbe, stood for *b;* that of a hand, *tot,* for *t;* that of an axe, *kelebin,* for *k;* that of a lion, *labo,* for *l;* that of a flute, *sebiadyo,* for *s,* etc. In this way a hieroglyphic alphabet was formed, and the same procedure was applied to the investigation of the popular or demotic text. It was recognized that not only proper names but appellatives were represented phonetically, and that the characters of this type were more frequent in Egyptian writing than had been thought at the outset. It became apparent that, to distinguish them from ideographs, each group of them was usually enclosed in an oval cartouche. It was observed that the three types of writing mentioned by Saint Clement did not constitute three different systems but only one, more or less abbreviated and more or less elegant in the forming of the characters, which in the hieroglyphic style retained its old forms and in the popular script was reduced to strokes and figures that were easy to draw. In the demotic type the number of ideographic characters was much smaller and the number of phonetic characters proportionally much greater, in which there was hardly any resemblance to the hieroglyphic prototypes from which they were derived. Mr. Salt, consul-general of His Britannic Majesty in Egypt, has contributed no little to the progress of this interesting branch of archeology by confirming Champollion's discoveries and deciphering a long list of proper names related to mythology and to various periods of Egyptian history. The work of both men has proved that the use of hieroglyphic writing goes back, in that nation, to a very remote period.

How is it possible, it will be asked, that writing could remain stationary for so long in a very gifted nation, to which are owed the seeds of Greek civilization and culture, and the birth of our sciences and arts? Why did the Egyptians not rise to the perfection that was almost within their grasp? When they had an alphabet of elementary sounds, why did they retain the symbolic characters, forming with these and with the others a fanciful mixture that must have been as much trouble to write as it was perplexing to read? But we need not be astonished that the Egyptians clung to their ancient writing. The same motives did not operate in us as in them; we do not have pyramids, obelisks, and columns covered with sculptures that a simplified alphabet would render illegible. Reforms of our alphabet would not prevent our understanding anything written since the [thirteenth century's] *Siete Partidas*; and as our writing is perpetuated not by the hardness of the material on which it is written but in the manner of a living species, by the fecundity of its reproduction, each five-year period, each year, will see the editions of elementary and popular books increase in number, with progress in other branches of literature matching those of the first and most essential of the arts. Yet, despite the fact that these advantages can be realized effortlessly and easily, despite the incalculable benefits they would bring by disseminating instruction and making education general among the mass of the people, we do not take the trouble to improve our writing by endowing it with all the simplicity and ease of which it is capable. And in our system of writing we preserve with superstitious veneration the primitive traits that it acquired during the centuries when, from the contact of the North's harsh dialects with the polished languages of the South, new languages of a completely different structure emerged. In these languages, when the Latin alphabet was applied irregularly and capriciously to all of them, new sounds that had been unknown to the Romans and Greeks were represented by the old letters. Words that varied in sound did not vary in letters. The double represented the single and the single the double. There were also letters that eventually signified nothing. And finally, there was no irregularity by which a system of signs can be afflicted that did not plague the alphabet.

Notes on the Advisability
of Simplifying and Standardizing
Orthography in America

(1823)

O ne of the studies most interesting to a man is that of the language spoken in his native land.[6] Its cultivation and improvement form the basis for all intellectual progress. Heads are formed by tongues, says the author of *Emile*, and thoughts are tinged with the color of languages.

Ever since the Spaniards subjugated the New World, the aboriginal tongues gradually have been lost, and though some few are still maintained in all their purity among tribes of independent Indians, and even among those who have begun to be civilized, Spanish is the prevailing tongue in the new states formed by the dismemberment of the Spanish monarchy, and doubtless will gradually cause all the others to disappear.

In Spanish America, cultivation of that language has suffered from all the vices of the educational system followed there. And though it is shameful to admit the fact, it must be confessed that, among the bulk of the inhabitants of America, not five persons in a hundred could be found who had grammatical knowledge of their own language, and hardly one who could write it correctly. This was the result of the plan adopted by the court in Madrid for its colonial possessions, and indeed was the inevitable consequence of Spain's own backwardness.

Among the means available not only to polish the language, but to enlarge all branches of knowledge, few are more important than simplifying its orthography, for upon it depends the more or less easy acquisition of the two primary arts on which the whole edifice of literature and science rests: reading and writing. It is orthography, says the Spanish Academy, which improves languages, preserves their purity, indicates the correct pronunciation and meaning of words, and declares the written text's proper meaning. It makes writing a faithful and dependable expression of laws, arts, and sciences, and of everything discussed by wise and learned men in all professions, and by this means is entrusted to posterity for universal instruction and teaching. The need to simplify orthography arises from its importance, and the plan or method to be followed in the innovations introduced for this necessary purpose will be the subject of the present article.

We do not have the audacity to suppose that the reforms we are about to suggest will be adopted immediately. We know all too well the power of prejudice and habit. But nothing will be lost by pointing out these reforms and placing them under discussion by intelligent people, or by causing them to be modified, if necessary, or by bringing closer the day of their introduction and smoothing the way for the literary bodies that will give a new direction to language studies in America.

To stimulate the reforms that we are going to mention, let us examine, in the latest edition (1820) of the treatise on Spanish orthography, the different systems of various writers and of the Academy itself; and we will deduce our system from all of these.

To regulate orthography, Antonio de Nebrija established the principle that each letter must have a different sound and that each sound must be represented by a single letter. This is the path that all spelling reforms must follow. Carrying forward the idea of that most learned philologist, Mateo Alemán adopted pronunciation as the sole standard for writing, to the exclusion of usage and origin. Juan López de Velasco took another direction. In the belief that pronunciation ought not to dominate exclusively, and following the advice of Quintilian, *[Ego] nisi quod consuetudo obtinuerit, sic scribendum quidque [iudico] quomodo sonat,* [Unless a customary practice obtains [I judge] that everything should be written the way it sounds] he established that language must be written simply and naturally, as it is spoken, but without introducing any offensive novelty. Gonzalo Correas, however, rightly scorned this usurped domination of custom, and attempted to correct one of the Spanish alphabet's most awkward irregularities by replacing hard *c* and *g* by the letter *k*. Other writers both ancient and modern have suggested other reforms. All have agreed on the aim of making writing in Spanish uniform and easy, but there has been a variety of opinions about the method of doing so.

As for the Spanish Academy, I certainly believe that its labors are very praiseworthy. If we compare the state of Spanish writing at the time when the Academy assumed the task of simplifying it with its state today, we do not know which to praise more, the liberal spirit (very different from that usually displayed by such bodies) with which the Academy has sponsored and introduced useful reforms, or the public's docility in accepting them, within the Peninsula as well as outside it.

Its first attempt of this kind, as the Academy itself says, was in the introduction to the first volume of the great *Diccionario*; and since then it has proceeded from step to step, simplifying spelling in the various editions of its *Ortografía*. We do not know whether it would have been preferable to introduce all the changes at once, bringing the alphabet to its greatest possible point of perfection and making it conform perfectly to the principles previously cited, those of Nebrija and Mateo Alemán. It certainly would have been desirable to have caused all these changes to follow a consistent and uniform plan, and to make each change represent an effective step toward the ends desired, without indulging in useless detours. But we must keep in mind that the operations of a body of this kind cannot be as systematic, or its principles as firm, as those of an individual. Thus, though we render to the Academy the thanks it deserves for the good things it has done, and for the general direction of its labors, we must also consider the imperfections of its results, inherent as they are in the nature of a philological society.

In 1754 the Academy added (as it says itself) several letters peculiar to the language, which had been omitted up to that time and were necessary for its perfection. And it made changes in others which it considered appropriate in order to facilitate practice without too much dependence on origins.

In the third edition, of 1763, it established the rules for accents and suppressed duplication of the letter *s*.

In the four subsequent editions of 1770, 1775, 1779, and 1792, it merely expanded the lists of words of doubtful orthography. In 1803 it added to the alphabet the letters *ll* and *ch*, as representative of the sounds used

to pronounce words like *llama* and *chopo*, and eliminated *ch* when it has
the sound of *k*, as in *christiano* and *chimera*, substituting *c* or *g* according
to cases, and eliminating the circumflex accent that had been used over
the following vowel by way of making a distinction. It also discarded
ph and *k*; and to soften pronunciation, it omitted some letters in a few
words where usage indicated this change, such as the *b* in *substancia*,
obscuro, the *n* in *transponer*, etc., and substituted an *x* for an *s* in others,
as in *extraño, extranjero*.

The 1815 edition (identical to that of 1820) added other important
reforms, such as employing *c* exclusively in combinations with the
sounds *ca, co, cu*, leaving *g* only in the combinations *que* and *qui*, in
which the *u* is mute, and hence rendering unnecessary the dieresis that
was used to distinguish words like *eloqüencia, qüestión*, and other similar
words. This novelty was a great step forward (though we do not know
whether it would have been preferable to suppress the mute *u* in *quema,
quiso*); but the idea of omitting the aspirate *x* only at the beginning or
in the middle of words such as *xarabe, xefe, exido*, and keeping it at the
end, such as *almoradux, relox*, seems inconsistent and capricious. The
worst of all was substitution of the letter *g* only before the vowels *e* and
i, and using *j* on other occasions. Why this gratuitous variety of usages?
Why not substitute *j* for the aspirate *x* before all vowels, as a letter well
known for its single value, instead of *g*, a doubtful and troublesome
letter which sometimes has one sound and other times another? The
Academy's system obviously tends toward supressing *g* even in the cases
where it is equivalent to *j*; in consequence, the new practice of writing
gerga, gícara, is a superfluous step and one that could have been avoided
by writing *jerga* and *jícara* once and for all. The other changes consisted
of omitting the circumflex accent on the words *examen, existo*, etc.,
because of the single value that the letter *x* began to assume in this
situation, and writing (with some exceptions that we do not consider
necessary) *i* instead of *y* when this letter functions as a vowel, as in
ayre, peyne.

The Academy observes that irregularity in the pronunciation of combinations and syllables with *c* and *g* and other vowels is a great obstacle
to perfecting orthography. This is why children, as well as foreigners
and especially deaf-mutes, make so many mistakes when they are learning to sound out syllables. And yet it does not correct this anomaly.
Antonio de Nebrija wanted to give the sound and function of *k* and *g*

exclusively to *c*; Gonzalo Correas attempted to give it to *k*, to the exclusion of the other two; and other writers have tried to give to *g* the less harsh sound in all cases, assigning all strong guttural pronunciations to *j*. This would avoid the use of *u* when it is mute, as in the word *querra* (*gerra*), and the accent mark called the dieresis in the other cases, such as *vergüenza* (*verguenza*). However, the Academy tells us that it has preferred, in such an important reform, to allow usage by educated persons to open the way toward authorizing it with precision and at a more favorable juncture.

This cautious approach is perhaps inseparable from a body eager to preserve its influence over public opinion. An individual is in a position to be a little more adventurous, and when his practice coincides with the Academy's progressive plan, now authorized by general consent, it cannot be said that this freedom brings about confusion. On the contrary, it prepares and speeds the time when uniform spelling, both in Spain and the American nations, will present a degree of perfection unknown in the world today.

The Academy adopted three fundamental principles for forming rules of orthography: pronunciation, constant use, and origin. Of these the first is the only essential and legitimate one; the presence of the others is a complication that only necessity can excuse. The Academy itself, which admits them, demonstrates contradiction on more than one page of its treatise. In one place it says that none of these principles is so general that it can be shown to be an invariable rule: that pronunciation does not always determine the letters with which words must be written; that usage is not common and constant in all cases; and that origin is often not followed. On another page it says that pronunciation is a principle that deserves the greatest attention, for since writing is an image of words, as these are an image of thoughts, it seems as if *letters and sounds ought to agree perfectly among themselves, and that in consequence words must be written as they are spoken and pronounced.* In one place it establishes that Spanish writing varies considerably, chiefly because of faulty habits and the effects of poor teaching or incorrect instruction in early childhood. Some letters are confused in pronunciation, such as *b* and *v*, *c* and *g* and *j* and *g*, which have the same sound. In other passages it says that it is impossible to know by pronunciation whether one spells the word *vaso* with a *b* or a *v*; and, similarly, one could write the words *vivir, vez,* with a *b.* According to the Academy, some of the words taken from other languages have preserved the features of their originals and others have ceased to have them and have taken on those of the language that adopted them; and even ancient words themselves have changed their form. It also says that often origin cannot be a general rule, especially in the present state of the language, for ease of pronunciation or the fact of use has prevailed. Lastly, it adds that correct writing presents many difficulties, because pronunciation, or knowledge of the etymology of words, do not suffice; it is also necessary to know whether "common and constant usage" is against it, for in this case (it adds) then usage "must prevail as the arbiter of languages." But these difficulties vanish in large part, and the path to be followed in spelling reform will leap to the eye, if we recall the function of writing and the aim of orthography.

The highest degree of perfection of which writing is capable, and the point toward which all reforms must lead, is based on an exact agreement between the fundamental sounds of the language and the signs or letters that are to represent them, in such a way that one sound corresponds invariably with each fundamental letter, and each letter to one sound with the same degree of invariability.

There are languages which perhaps cannot aspire to this ultimate degree of perfection in their orthography. Because they allow transitions in their sounds, and half tones, so to speak, (which simply means that they are made up of a large number of fundamental sounds), to perfect their orthography it would be necessary to adopt a large number of new letters, and to form another alphabet that would be very different from the one we have today. This is a task that must be viewed as impossible. Lacking this recourse, in those languages the values of letters have multiplied greatly, and what are called improper diphthongs have been formed; that is, complex signs representing simple sounds. This is the case of the English and French languages.

Fortunately, one of the happy features of Spanish is that it consists of a small number of elementary sounds which are quite separate and distinct. It is perhaps the only European language that has no more elementary sounds than letters. Thus, the path that spelling reform must follow in Spanish is obvious and clear: *if a sound is represented by two or more letters, the one that represents that sound only must be chosen, and must take the place of others.*

Etymology is the great source of confusion for European alphabets.

One of the most absurd things that has been introduced into the art of representing words is the rule that forces us to discover their origin in order to know how to transfer them to paper. What could be more contrary to reason than to establish as a rule for the writings of present-day peoples the pronunciation of peoples who existed two or three thousand years ago, and to expect our pronunciation to guide the spelling of a nation that will flourish a couple of thousand years in the future? For consulting etymology to find out with which letter to spell this or that word is exactly that, if we think about it carefully. And do not say that this can be verified only when the sound leaves a free choice between two or three letters that represent it. Sound judgment tells us to do away with that superfluous multiplicity of signs, leaving only one among them to merit preference thanks to its singleness of value.

And let us assume that we always know the etymology of words spelled in several different ways, so as to indicate it. Even then, the practice of going by origin would lack support. Those who see the word *philosophia* written and believe that the Greeks wrote this word in that way would be completely wrong. The Greeks denoted the sound *ph* with a single letter, from which the letter *f* perhaps derives; so that by writing in Spanish *filosofia* we are closer to the original form of this word than were the Romans, who had to adopt this form because of the different sound of their letter *f*. We can say the same of the practice of writing *Achêos, Achiles, Melchisedech*. Neither the Greeks nor the Hebrews wrote the letter *ch*, because they represented this sound with a single letter expressly intended for it. What basis in etymology, therefore, do those people have who advise writing Hebrew and Greek words in the Roman style? As for use, when it is in opposition to reason and the convenience of those who read and write, we call it abuse. Some state their opposition to the reforms so obviously suggested by the nature and aims of this art by saying that they "look ugly," "offend the eye," or are "startling." As if a single letter could seem beautiful in certain combinations and ugly in others! All these opinions, if they make any sense, only mean that the practices met by such criticisms are *new*. And what does it matter that a thing is new, if it is useful and convenient? Why must we condemn to remain in its present form something that can be improved? If useful things had always been rejected, what sort of condition would writing be in today? Instead of forming letters, we would amuse ourselves by painting hieroglyphs or knotting *quipus*.

Neither etymology nor the authority of custom should be an obstacle to the substitution of a letter which represents a sound more naturally or more generally, as long as the new practice is not in opposition to the established values of the letters or their combinations. For example, *j* is the most natural sign of the sound that begins the words *jarro, genio, giro, joya, justicia,* for this letter has no other value in Spanish. This is a circumstance that cannot be alleged for *g* or *x*. Then why can we not always represent this sound with *j*? For the ignorant, writing *genio* or *jenio* is the same thing. Only the learned will find the novelty strange, but they would approve it if they would think about how much it simplifies the art of reading and the establishment of writing. They know that the Romans wrote *genio* because they pronounced it with a hard *g*; and they will have to admit that we, having changed the sound, should also have changed the sign that represents it. But it is not too late to do so, for the substitution of *j* by *g* in such cases has nothing against it except etymology, which few people know, and the particular usage of certain words, which should bow to the more general usage of the language.

We can say the same of *z*, with regard to the sound that begins the words *zalema, cebo, cinco, zorro, zumo*. But, although *c* is in Spanish the most natural sound of the consonant that begins the words *casa, quema, quinto, copla, cuna,* this is not the reason why we believe that it can take the place of the combination *qu* when the *u* is mute, as happens before *e* and *i*; for this new value of *c* would quarrel with the value that usage has conferred on it before these two vowels. And so, writing *arranque, escilmo* instead of *arranque, esquilmo,* would inevitably produce confusion.

We think, therefore, that the best thing would be to begin by making exclusive to the letter *z* the soft sound that coincides with that of the soft *c*; and once the public (especially the semi-literate public, for which this change is contemplated) gets accustomed to giving *c* the value of *k* in every case, it would be time to substitute it for the combination *qu*, unless it might be preferred (and maybe it would be better) to completely eliminate *c*, replacing it with *g* in the hard sound and *z* in the soft sound.

Likewise, *g* is the natural sign of the sound *ga, gue gui, go, gu*; but that is no reason to replace it by the combination *gu* when the *u* is silent, for the value of *j*, which is still given to that consonant when it precedes the vowels *e* and *i* resists it. So what we need to do is to begin by never using *g* with the value of *j* in any case whatever.

Another practical reform is suppression of the letter *h* (except, of course, in the combination *ch*); that of the mute *u* that goes with *g*; substitution of *i* by *y* in every case where *y* is not a consonant; and always representing with the letters *rr* the strong sound in words like *rrazón, prórroga*, reserving the single *r* for the soft sound it has in the words *arar* and *querer*.

Another reform, though it is one of those that would have to be prepared for, would be omission of the mute *u* that follows the letter *g* before the vowels *e* and *i*.

Let us observe in passing how much the use of language has varied with respect to these letters. Old Spanish writers (with whose example we are trying to defend what they condemned, instead of carrying out the judicious reforms they had begun) had almost eliminated the letter *h* in words where it is not pronounced, writing *ombre, ora, onor*. Thus King Alfonso the Wise, who began each of his seven law codes with one of the letters that composed his name, began the fourth with the word *ome* (which by a slip of the editors, as Don Tomás Antonio Sánchez observed, was later written *home*). But then came the pedantry of the schools, which is worse than ignorance; and instead of imitating old Spanish writers and doing away with a superfluous sign, instead of consulting reason, as they did, and not the vanity of showing off their Latin, they restored *h* even in places where it had been completely forgotten.

We have already made of the letter *y* a sort of short *i*, using it as a vowel in connection with diphthongs (*ayre, peyne*) and in the conjunction *y*. Old Spanish, however, frequently used it to begin words, writing *yba, yra*; perhaps this is the reason for the practice of using it as a capital *i* in handwriting. We have to admit that this practice of our ancestors was atrocious, but what the moderns have put in its place is no better.

As for initial *rr*, we do not know why it need be condemned. Old Spanish did not duplicate any consonant at the beginning of a word, and neither do we. The letter *rr*, apparently double, really represents a sound that cannot be divided and must be looked upon as a single character, not unlike the letters *ch*, *ñ*, and *ll*. If the people who object to this innovation had lived four or five centuries ago and had put it into practice, today we would write *levar*, *lamar*, *lorar*, on the pretext of not duplicating a consonant at the beginning of a word, and our system of writing would owe a further complication to them.

Let us now present our plan of reforms to the enlightened sector of the American public, presenting them in the order of succession in which we believe it would be useful to adopt them.

FIRST PHASE

1. Replace *x* and *g* by *j* in all cases in which these letters have the guttural Arabic sound.
2. Replace *y* by *i* in all cases where *y* is a simple vowel.
3. Discard the letter *h*.
4. Use *rr* in all syllables containing the strong sound of this letter.
5. Replace the soft *c* by *z*
6. Discard mute *u* following *g*.

SECOND PHASE

7. Replace hard *c* by *q*.
8. Discard the mute *u* that accompanies *g* in some words.

Someone will surely be surprised that we do not include in these innovations the replacement of *x* by the two simple signs of the sounds that it is said to represent, writing *ecsordio*, *ecsamen*, or *eqsordio*, *eqsamen*; but we are not absolutely certain that *x* breaks down or divides exactly either in the sounds *cs*, as almost everyone believes, or in the sounds *gs*, as some (perhaps getting closer to the real pronunciation) believe. If we are to heed the evidence of our own ears, we would say that in *x* the two fundamental sounds begin to alter each other, and that the first in particular is much softer than that of the ordinary *c*, *k*, or *g*, and comes very close to the sound of *g*. It is true that many years ago *x* sounded like *cs*; but also at that time *x* sounded very much like *ds*. The *z* has softened to the point of degenerating into a sound that shows no trace of a compound; *x*, unless we are mistaken, has begun to soften in the same way. Orthography, therefore—whose aim is not to correct common pronunciation but to reflect it faithfully—ought in our opinion to preserve this letter. But this is a point on which we are happy to defer, not to the learned, but to careful observers who listen to their ears rather than to their prejudices.

We believe that when the time comes to adopt this system completely, it would be useful to reduce the number of letters in our alphabet from the twenty-seven listed by the Academy in the edition we have mentioned, to twenty-six, changing their names as follows:

A,	B,	CH,	D,	E,	F,	G,	I,	J,	L,	LL,	M,	N,
a,	be,	che,	De,	e,	fe,	gue,	i,	je,	le,	lle,	me,	ne,
Ñ,	O,	P,	Q,	R,	RR,	S,	T,	U,	V,	X,	Y,	Z.
ñe,	o,	pe,	cu,	ere,	erre,	se,	te,	u,	ve,	exe,	ye,	ze.

Thus the letters *c* and *h* would be eliminated from our language, the former because it is ambiguous and the second because it is meaningless; mute *u* and the use of the dieresis would disappear; the sounds *r* and *rr* would be represented with the necessary distinction and clarity; and moreover the consonants *g*, *x*, and *y* would always have the same value. The only room left for observing etymology and usage would be in the choice of *b* or *v*, which does not fall exactly within the purview of orthography but rather of phonology, since the latter is exclusively concerned with good pronunciation, which it is the function of the former to represent.

To make this simplification of writing facilitate as much as possible the art of reading, the names of the letters would have to be changed as we have indicated; for since they would be a guide for children learning to read, it is extremely important to have the name of each letter reflect the value it must be given in syllabic combinations. Moreover, in these names we have passed over the usual difference drawn between mute and semivowel sounds, which is quite useless and has no basis either in the nature of sounds or in our habits. We call *be, che, fe, lle*, etc. (without an initial *e*) the consonants that can stand at the beginning of a word, and only *ere* and *exe* (with an initial *e*) those that never can begin a word, nor in consequence a syllable; from which it can be deduced that, when they are found between two vowels, they form a syllable with the preceding vowel, not with the vowel that follows. Indeed, the natural separation of syllables in the words *corazón*, *arado, exordio*, is *co-ra-zón, a-ra-do, ex-or-dio*; and hence elementary readers ought not to contain the combinations *ra, re, ri, ro, ru*, or the combinations *xa xe, xi, xo, xu*, which are very difficult to pronounce because they actually do not exist in language.

We have gone on long enough, although on a point having to do with general education—and one whose aim is to facilitate and extend the art of reading in countries where it is unfortunately so rare—a certain amount of prolixity ought to be tolerated more than on any other subject. It would have been easier to present a more interesting article to our readers; but the propagation of arts, knowledge, and useful inventions, especially those most appropriate and necessary to the state of society in America, is the chief object of this journal.

The orthographic innovations that we have adopted in it are few. Replace hard *g* by *j*; *y* as a vowel by *i*; substitute *c* for *z* in words whose root is written with the first of these two letters; and place soft *r* and *x* with the preceding vowel in the division of syllables. These are all the reforms that we have dared to introduce up till now. Later we will state our thoughts about accents, capital letters, abbreviations, and punctuation marks.

We would like to believe that anyone who examines our principles without prejudice will agree that superfluous letters must be eliminated from our alphabet; that rules must be set to avoid letters that sound the same; to accept pronunciation as a general principle, and adjust common and constant usage to it without worrying about word origins. This method seems to us the simplest and most rational; and should we by any chance be mistaken, we hope that our compatriots's indulgence will pardon an error that arises solely from our desire to spread enlightenment in America. This is the only way to establish rational freedom, and with it the advantages of civic culture and public prosperity.

Orthography
(1844)

The Faculty of Humanities has set forth so brilliantly the bases of its spelling reforms that it seems a superfluous task to defend them again, were it not for the fact that we see daily that innovations of the most obvious usefulness find numerous opponents in the ranks of routine-minded persons, of whom there are many, even among those who call themselves liberal and progressive.[7] Let us therefore examine the objections that are being made to the new type of writing.

We can reply to all objections with the practice and doctrine of the Spanish Academy, the authority to which many subscribe, and which in this area is undoubtedly worthy of respect. At first glance the words *egemplo, egecución, egercicio*, written with *g* instead of the etymological *x*, must seem strange; and strange too *cuanto, elocuencia, acuoso*, with a *c*; and *baile, aire, peine*, with the Latin *i*, etc. However, the Academy did not stop there, nor did it hestitate to depart from etymology in order to simplify writing. Cannot we, then, take a few more steps along the same path, guided by the same principles and keeping in mind the same aim of orthographic simplicity? Which means, in other words, ease in the two most important arts for social life, the two most powerful instruments of civilization, reading and writing? Can we reach the point that the Academy has reached and no further? The Academy itself has been of a different opinion, and has expressly stated it. The Academy introduced certain reforms and abstained from others, which it did not deem appropriate. "There has been no lack of writers," it states in the prologue to its *Ortografía*, "who have wanted to give the letter *g* in all cases and all combinations the less harsh pronunciation that it has with *a, o,* and *u,* reserving the strong guttural sound for the *j.* This would avoid the use of a *u* which is elided and not pronounced after *g* when another vowel follows, as in *guerra, guía,* and the sign called *crema,* or the two dots placed over the *u* when it is to be pronounced, as in *agüero, vergüenza,* and others. But the Academy, weighing the advantages and disadvantages of so important a reform, has preferred to let usage by educated persons open the way toward authorizing it more accurately and at a more favorable juncture." This is the verdict of that body about the most daring of the reforms demanded by the Spanish alphabet, which our Faculty of Humanities, for its part, has not considered it appropriate to adopt. And yet the Academy allows, even encourages, introduction of this reform by following the example of educated persons.

Hence, to those who cite the Academy's authority in favor of present usage, we reply with the authority of the Academy itself. To those who oppose the innovations as strange and ugly, we say that the true beauty of an art consists in the simplicity of its procedures; that the object of writing is to depict sounds, and the more simply it does so the more beautiful will it be; that in this matter, "strange" simply means new, and if the new is simpler, easier, and consequently better than the old, it should be embraced without hesitation. In fact, we will remind those who sigh for their cherished etymologies that etymology has always been a very secondary consideration in our alphabet, and that the Spanish Academy has not taken it into consideration at all when changes have seemed appropriate. The only objection that can be made with any plausibility is the violence that we would have to do to our habits in order to practice these reforms. But the Academy encountered this same obstacle when it tried to replace *q* by *c* in so many words, the guttural strong *x* by *g,* Greek *y* by Latin *i,* and did not shrink from doing so. This is a difficulty that can be alleged more or less strongly against all innovations, a difficulty which, at the cost of a few days' bother, produces permanent advantages of a highly important kind.

It is also said that these reforms must arise from a common center, a recognized literary authority, for if this were not the case some would be adopted in one country and some in others, and even in a single country there would be many different spellings, according to the judgment or whim of writers. Writing would become a chaos, and reading, far from gaining ease, would bristle with obstacles and perplexities. But this objection cannot be made to the innovations recommended by the Faculty of Humanities. They do not alter the usual value of a single letter or combination. The person who knows how to read with the spelling that is in use today can read whatever is written using the new orthography without the slightest difficulty, for he will find no letters or combinations in it that must be pronounced differently than before. The word *general* sounds the same with *g* as *jeneral* does with *j*; *hacer*, *honor*, *humanidad* without an *h* the same as with an *h*. It is not possible to pronounce the letter *q* except with the sound of *k*, whether or not it is followed by a mute *u*. Nor need we fear that, in the progressive march of spelling simplifications, other means will be adopted than those proposed by our Faculty of Humanities. There can be no difference of opinion as to the preference for *j* rather than *g* to represent the strong guttural sound. Once we have agreed to simplify orthography, it is impossible not to accept the suitability of Latin *i* in the diphthongs *ai*, *ei*, *oi*, *ui*, wherever they occur, and in the conjunction *i*; nor would the practice of writing useless mute letters last very long. There are reforms for which different means can be employed. For example, to make the sounds of *c* and *z* each have their peculiar and exclusive sign, some would recommend always pronouncing the *c* like *k* and banning *g* from the alphabet; and others would substitute *g* or *k* for the hard *c*, writing *qama*, *qorazon*, *qútis*, *aqlamazion*, *aqróstico*, or *kama*, *korazon*, etc. But the reforms sanctioned by the Faculty are not of this kind; the means it has adopted for the purpose are all obvious, natural, and analogical; any imaginable system for simplifying the Spanish alphabet must necessarily begin with them.

The Faculty of Humanities has limited its changes to these fundamental rules:

1. To work toward perfection of the alphabet, which perfection consists, as everyone knows, of having each elementary sound be exclusively represented by a single letter.
2. To eliminate every letter that does not represent, or contribute toward representing, a sound.
3. Not to give, for the moment, a different value to any letter or

combination of letters than that commonly assigned to them today in the writing of Spanish-speaking countries.

4. Not to introduce a large number of reforms at the same time.

Now let us review each of the innovations recommended by the Faculty of Humanities; in this way the points it has agreed upon can better be appreciated.

The Academy had suggested some time ago wholly separating the uses of the Latin *i* and the Greek *y*, using the first as a vowel and the second as a consonant. For this purpose it proposed replacing the Greek letter by the Latin *i* in all the diphthongs *ay, ey, oy, uy*, in which the accent falls on the first vowel, except at the end of a word. Instead of *ayre, peyne, coyma*, as was formerly written, it introduced the practice of writing *aire, peine, coima*, but continued to write *taray, ley, voy, muy*. It does not appear that there was any basis for this strange exception. It is said that the general rule of substitution of *i* for *y* in any grave diphthong ending in *y* was about to be announced when one of its members pointed out that if the rule were generally adopted, it would be necessary to change the spelling on the stamp with which royal dispatches and provisions were signed; it read *yo el rey*, and the difficulty seemed insuperable for the academicians. It was then proposed to adopt the exception about final diphthongs. In the American republics, however, the practice of always writing those diphthongs with the vowel *i* (called the Latin *i*) is very frequent. The Faculty has merely extended this practice to the conjunction *y*, and even in this some American republics and a number of European writers have preceded it.

This reform is dictated by the first of the rules above. The vocal sound that begins the word *imajen* and that which begins the words *ya* and *yo* are very different. Therefore they must be represented with different signs in every case. In Chilean orthography only one case remained in which the consonant *y* was used instead of the vowel. The Faculty has eliminated this solitary exception; according to its system, *i* is perpetually a vowel, and *y* perpetually a consonant. The first is called *i* and the second *ye*. And this alphabetic simplification is achieved without any change in the known and ordinary values of these two letters, in agreement with Rule Three.

It would not be superfluous to observe that some persons mispronounce the consonant *y*, giving it the sound of the vowel *i* For instance, they pronounce *yacer, yugo,* as if they were written *iacer, iugo.* These persons, if they go by what their ears tell them, might think that there is an equal reason to write *iacer, iugo* and to write *Pedro i Juan;* and that, if the Faculty is to be consistent, it ought to ban the Greek *y* from the alphabet and replace it with the Latin *i* in every case. But those who argue this are basing themselves on a bad pronunciation, though one that is really not rare either in America or the Peninsula. The proper sound of our consonant *ye* combines closely with the vowel that follows it, as the letter *v* does in the words *vana, vivo.* It is close to the sound of the *g* in Italian *piange,* and of the English *j* in "joke," though if I am not mistaken it is a trifle softer.

Reply to a Subscriber

We interrupt this article to reply to the objections made to the orthography of the Faculty of Humanities in the letter from "A Subscriber" which we have just read in the *Gaceta de Comercio.*

The first objection is to the need to teach two spelling methods, the old and the new, so that the child can understand everything written in print and by hand. This is an exaggeration. The old method and the new are the same, with very small changes; and for the child to master them it will suffice, when he has become familiar with the new method, to offer him these three observations:

1. Many people, when they write, use an *h* that is meaningless, as in *hombre, hato, hilo.* Pay no attention; read as if there were no *h.*
2. There is also a habit of placing a *u* after a *g,* writing, for instance, *guema, guiso;* this *u* does not mean anything either. Read as if there were no *u.*
3. The letter *y* is often used in place of *i,* writing, for example, *Pedro y Juan, comer y beber.*

Then place in the child's hands a book written in this way, drill him in it for a couple of days, and his apprenticeship in the two methods will be complete. Note that any orthographic reform has had to cause some difficulty. When the Academy replaced *g* by *c* and *x* by *g* or *j,* was it not just as necessary then as now to make some observations to children so that they could read the innumerable books written with the etymological *g* and *x*?

The second objection concerns the difficulty of looking up words in the dictionary. This is a difficulty which can only be alleged in connection with suppression of the letter *h*, and it exists only for those adults who know something about, and have doubts about, the true meaning of a word, or about its correct pronunciation, or about its spelling. These persons will no doubt have to look up a word with an *h* and without an *h*. But is not the same thing true now? Do they not have to look up a word under both *b* and *v*; with *z*, with *c* or *s*; and also with or without *h*? Someone hears for the first time about the tree (*haya*), whose name sounds like *aya*. He probably looks for it under *a*; he does not find it, and has to look it up under *h*. The true cause of these double searches is sometimes incorrect pronunciation and at other times the use of superflows letters and letters with a dual value. The first of these cannot be avoided in any spelling system, and the second would be avoided completely by means of a rational and simple system of orthography. Let us attack the evil at its root—let us simplify the alphabet. Once the reforms were under way (as they cannot fail to be, judging from the way things are going today), they will find a place in the dictionaries; and if people pronounce well, they will never have to go from one letter to another to look up the words that they want to consult in them.

It is said that good Castilians deny that the letter *h* is unnecessary in pronunciation. We would like to hear from those good Castilians' own lips the difference in pronunciation between the word *hombre* with an *h* and *ombre* without one.

The third objection is that by eliminating the useless *h* we would not be able to find the etymology of words. That certainly is a big disadvantage for children learning to read! I return to the example of the Academy. When the Academy wrote *cual* with a *c* and *enjambre* with a *j*, was it paying any heed to etymology? And what of the infinite number of authors who, before the Academy, wrote *aver*, *avia*, *uvo*, without an *h* and with a *v*? Were these perchance unaware that this verb was derived from Latin *habere*? And who ever said that the object of writing is to preserve etymologies? The Romans wrote *habere* with an *h* because to their ears this letter had real value; to them, *abere* would not have seemed to be the true sound of the word. This is not the case in our language. When the sound is eliminated the letter must be eliminated too; and if our grandparents did not do it, that is no reason why we should not.

It is also objected that the usual way of writing gives an advantage for the study of Latin, French, Italian, etc. I again return, this time and a hundred times, to the Academy. If it is a pity that, if we write *ombre* without an *h*, the etymology of this word disappears, along with its affinity with *homo* in Latin and *homme* in French, then it was equally an error for the Academy, by writing *cuando* with a *c*, to eliminate its etymology and affinity with the Latin word *quando* and the French word *quand*. In short, the Academy should have left spelling alone, because its reforms have dealt so many blows to etymology and have placed so many difficulties in the way of learning foreign languages both living and dead. It should have kept on writing, till the end of time, *enxambre* and *execución* with an *x*, *guando* and *guanto* with a *g*. Limiting ourselves only to *h*, if the elimination of this letter takes us farther from foreign languages in some cases, it brings us closer in others and places us in harmony with them. By writing *aber* without an *h* we draw closer to the Italians and the French, who write *abere* and *avoir*. By writing *ombre, onor, orror, umanidad*, without an *h*, we are closer to the Italians, who write *uomo, onore, orrore, umanità*; the Italians have kept only two or three useless letters *h* in their modern writing. We cannot see that anything is gained with the orthography of one language to acquire knowledge of another. Some times we will find that they agree and at other times not; and this alone says that our orthography, no matter what system we use, will always be a very false guide to the orthography of Latin, French, etc. Is a Spanish word written with *b*? The corresponding word in Latin, in French, in Italian, in English, may well be written with a *v*. In Spanish we write *buitre*: the Latin word is *vultur*, the French *vautour*, the English *vulture*. When we write *pruebo* we preserve the Latin affinity, *probo*, but differ from the French *je prouve*, the Italian *io provo*, and the English *I prove*. We could amass a large number of examples of this kind. But we are told that *ombre*, without an *h*, in French is the same as Spanish *sombra*. And what is bad about that? The word that is *nombre* in Spanish is, with all its letters, *numéro* in French, and so far no one has complained about this coincidence.

There is also objection to the confusion that results from elimination of the *h*, for the word *a* can be both a preposition and a form of the verb *aber; e* can be a conjunction and a form of the same verb; *abría* can be a form of *aber* or a form of the verb *abrir; aya*, a form of *aber*, a nursemaid, or a tree. This confusion, if it can be called one, exists in spoken language, just as *aya* or *haya* is pronounced the same when we say *dudo que haya llegado la nave* as when we say *la haya es un árbol copado*, or *la niña se echó en brazos del aya*. And if it exists in the spoken language why not in the written one, which ought to be a reflection of the spoken tongue? And if it succeeds in doing this, will it not have done a good deal? But the truth is that these homonyms have never bothered anyone for an instant, for the context gives a sufficient idea of the word. *Amo* is both a noun and a verb; the same can be said of the words *ama, cambio, encuentro, corta, corte, lego, destierro, castigo, duelo, enojo, baile, danza, cena, luces, mora* (a noun, an adjective, and a verb form) and innumerable other words. And you may be sure that nobody has ever hesitated about taking one for the other. The correspondent for the *Gaceta de Comercio* will admit that to confuse the noun *ora* with the conjunction *ora*, one would have to be more than ordinarily stupid. Moreover, *hora* and *ora* were originally a single word, and either we ought to write both of them with an *h*, if we are to respect etymology, or both without an *h*, if we appreciate what the word is worth.

Lastly, now that the "Subscriber" of the *Gaceta de Comercio* is so fond of the affinities and etymologies of the letter *h*, we would like to ask him how he spells the words *teología, teocracia, apoteosis, ateo, ateísta, politeísta, panteísta, síntesis, sintético*, and a thousand others, which according to their origin ought to be spelled *theologia, theocracia*, etc. Certainly without an *h*, despite the fact that this letter is necessary in the corresponding words in Latin, French, English, and other languages. But there are so many cases in which ordinary Spanish orthography has departed from etymologies, that we are surprised that there are still sensible people so prejudiced in their favor that they place them ahead of much more important considerations. Languages never pause; and by constantly changing the forms of words in their movement, these changes must be reflected in writing, whose job it is to represent speech. To preserve useless letters out of love for etymologies seems to me like keeping debris in a new building so that we can remember the old one.

Elimination of the mute *u*, which is another of the orthographic reforms approved by the Faculty of Humanities, is an immediate result of the Second Rule: it is impossible to defend in any way the preservation of a completely useless letter.

The same cannot be said of the mute *u* which, placed between the letter *g* and the vowels *e* and *i*, makes us give to the *g* the soft sound that it has before the vowels *a, o,* or *u*. If we eliminated this mute *u* in *guerra* and *guitarra*, we would confer a new value on the combinations *ge* and *gi*, which, though very seldom used in the orthography of Chile and some other Spanish-speaking countries, retain the strong value of the *j* in most of the books that circulate among us. The Faculty has therefore thought it necessary, in agreement with the Third Rule, to tolerate the continued existence of the combinations *gue, gui,* in which the mute *u* warns that it should not be pronounced *je, ji*.

This is the most troublesome anomaly in our alphabet, because of the need it creates to mark the *u* in a particular way when it is pronounced in those combinations, as in the words *agüero, agüita*.

The punctuation mark consisting of two dots, called the *crema* or *diéresis*, was a prosodic sign intended to represent the true diaeresis; that is, the resolution of a diphthong into two syllables, as in *süave, viüda*; and it is given a different meaning when we place it on the *u* in the combinations *güe, güi*, for in these syllables the vowels *ue, ui* always form a diphthong. This dual value of the diaeresis is also troublesome. There is no question that such defects still exist in our writing, but the time has not yet come to remove them.

As for suppression of the mute *h*, we have little to add to what we said in the earlier part of our article. Those who have had in their hands Spanish editions previous to the Academy will have noted how frequently this letter was omitted at the beginning and in the middle of a word. They wrote *yo e, tú as, él a,* etc. It was very rare to find the verb *haber* written with an *h* even in the books of erudite men. Just now I have under my eyes a copy of the *Explicación* of the satires of Juvenal by Diego López, printed in Madrid in 1642, and there we read, "*no se a de usar mal de la hacienda, ni de lo que con ella se a ganado . . . Es de ombre sabio guardarla, i considerar que el ombre no solo a de querer ser rico para si, sino para sus hijos, parientes, i amigos, i principalmente para la republica, como dice Ciceron.*" Here *h* is preserved in words that were still aspirated because they had taken the place of the Latin *f*, as in *hacer, hacienda, hambre, hijo, hormiga*, etc. The Latin *h* had become a mute letter, and so words like *ombre, Omero, umedecer*, etc. were written without it. Even the aspiration into which the *f* had been changed was already very weak and had begun to disappear; and this is the reason why, in this same book, we find *ermosura, ermosos*, etc. The Academy, by reestablishing the *h* in words that were already being written without it, took a step backward. In its first efforts, it let itself be controlled by the etymological principle, which with better bases it later largely abandoned.

The reform that has been instituted on this point by the Faculty of Humanities has in its favor the example of the Italian nation, which also preserved the etymological *h* for a long time. Some scholars, observing the unsuitability of this usage, counseled eliminating that letter as useless; and we now see that the Italian alphabet has been almost entirely purged of that vice, for today, as we believe, only the four forms of the verb *avere—ho, hai, ha, hanno*—exist, to distinguish them from other words. But it would have been better to always eliminate it, for, as we have said, writing needs only to be as clear as speech. Its job is to depict speech even with its moles and imperfections; and on the other hand, there is no need to distinguish what can easily be distinguished from the context.

But, though banning the superfluous *h*, the Faculty has felt it necessary to retain it where it has a real value; that is, in the interjections *ah, oh, ha, ho*, and others. When these words are represented with the emotion that they are intended to express, they carry with them a noticeable aspiration, which sounds something like the articulation of the syllables *aj, oj, ja*, etc., though much less strong. This is the reason that the vowel just before the *h* can form a synalepha with the following vowel, as in *¡ah ingrato!, ¡oh, atroz inhumanidad!*

The *h* also sounds in the combinations *hua, hue*, as in *Huánuco, hueco*, where it has exactly the sound of the English *w* in *water, web*. However, the Faculty believed it preferable to suppress it in this case. If it had been preserved it would have represented a different sound from the one it has in interjections; consequently, it would have been an equivocal letter, being pronounced sometimes in one way and sometimes in another. Moreover, the initial articulation of *Huasco, hueste* is produced spontaneously and necessarily, in all cases where the *u* not preceded by consonants forms a diphthong with the vowel that follows. Therefore it would be no problem to omit a sign which, in similar combinations, would represent a sound that simply has to be produced because of the conformation of our vocal organs.

The Faculty would have wished that the two articulated sounds of the word *raro* could have been expressed with different signs; in other words, that when *r* is strong—as in *razón, rebelde, honra*—it could be written *rr*. But even so, it would be a defect to represent with a double letter a sound that is really indivisible. In the word *corregir* we do not duplicate the sound that the *r* has in *corazón*, as in the word *innato* we duplicate the sound of *n*. Therefore we should not represent the second articulation of *corregir* with a double *r*, but by some special sign. The same observation is applicable to *ll*. Naturally, the person who sees the word *cabello* written ought to pronounce it *cabel-lo*, as the Italians pronounce *quello, capelli, poverella*. But we shall have to resign ourselves to these and other imperfections for a long time, recognizing *ch, ll*, and *rr* as simple letters.

Returning to *rr*, the Faculty of Humanities has found it appropriate to always represent with this letter the strong sound of *r*, except at the beginning of a word, where it occurs so often that the innovation would have been burdensome, and where, in addition—since it is not possible to pronounce a single *r* in this position—speech will correct, spontaneously and even necessarily, the imperfection of writing. By limiting the reform to the *r* solely when it is initial in a word, we succeed not only in restoring to *rr* many of the sounds that *r* has usurped from it, as in *honra, Israel, Ulrica*, but also to distinguish clearly what arouses doubts and gives rise to incorrect pronunciations in the method that we follow today. How can children, or men of little education guess, in the second syllable of compound words, that *r* takes the place of *rr*, for example, in *prerogativa, prorogar*, and *cariredondo*? How can they know that after *b* it is sometimes pronounced *r* (for example *abrojo, sobrado*) and at other times *rr* (for example in *abrogar, subrogar, subrepción, obrepción*)? The reform we have mentioned removes this difficulty and takes one more step in the direction of the system of simplicity and perfect analogy toward which all alphabetic reforms must move.

The Faculty has also recommended that practice observed by many writers nowadays, that of not separating *rr*. Since this sign represents an indivisible sound, there is no more reason to divide it than there is to divide the first *l* from the second in *cabal-lo*, or the *c* from the *h* in *muc-hac-ho*. It is an old rule of orthography to separate double letters at the end of a line, as in *peren-ne, in-nato*; but to apply it to a double letter whose value is simple is going too far. What is done with *ll* should apply with equal reason to *rr*. The unnecessary latitude given to certain orthographic canons has been one of the causes of the corruption of the alphabet. It was said, for instance, that no consonant could be duplicated at the beginning of a word, and through a mistaken application of this rule *lorar, lamar*, used to be written instead of *llorar, llamar*, and we still write *rezar, reír* instead of *rrezar, rreír*.

The Faculty, anxious to simplify writing as much as possible, has also issued a general rule for the division of words at the end of a line, in a case which according to present usage offers doubts and difficulties to children. Today it is common to divide as follows the first syllables of the words *des-animar, ex-ánime, ab-orígenes, ad-aptar*, etc., in order to preserve the compositional particles with which certain words begin. If this practice were consistent, it could be believed that it ought to be respected. But there are a great many cases in which no one, or very few people, bother to separate the syllables in the way mentioned; for example, in *adorar, adornar, adolecer, anarquía, monarquía, enemistad, paralelo, paraleje, subir*, etc. In all of these, paying attention to the single composition, we ought to divide *ad-orar, ad-ornar, ad-olecer, an-arquía, mon-arquía, par-alelo, par-alaje, sub-ir*, etc. But this is not done. By constantly observing the rule not to separate compositional particles, not only children but also adults and well-educated persons would frequently make mistakes in syllabification. Knowledge of the Greek language would be necessary to distinguish the various members of many compound words. The Academy has seen the suitability of dividing *pers-picaz, cons-truir, obs-tar*, shaking off the yoke of etymology here also to better represent the genius of the Spanish language. Then why not be guided by the same principle in all cases? Undoubtedly we tend to join the consonant found between two vowels with the following vowel: we pronounce *e-ne-mis-tad, su-bir, a-dor-nar*, and so the Faculty has believed that these words should always be written like this, with no exceptions. There are only two consonants that seem to associate better with the preceding vowel: *x* and *r*. The *r* is a consonant that cannot begin a word, for the vocal organs reject it; they cannot pronounce these sounds without supporting them on a preceding vowel sound. In consequence, pronunciation appears to demand that we divide *cor-azón, natur-al*. The same thing is applicable to the *x*. However, the Faculty has preferred to make the rule universal, passing over the slight violence that we have to cause in order to divide *Ana-xágo-ras, e-xamen, co-razón, natu-ral*, in the cause of ease and simplicity.

The letter *x* gave rise to a long discussion. Some members of the Faculty wanted to eliminate this letter from the alphabet, replacing it by the combination *cs*. But the opposing opinion prevailed for a reason that we thought irrefutable. The sound *x* has become so much softened in pronunciation that it can almost be mistaken for *s*. To pronounce *ecsamen, ecsonerar*, giving *c* its true and full value, would seem an affectation and exaggeration. We pronounce, rather, *egsamen, egsonerar*, giving the *gs* combination a very soft sound which approximates that of *s*, but without being confused with it. The *x*, in a word, represents a peculiar articulation.

We have given a summary idea of the bases used by the Faculty for its orthographic innovations. Rejecting the others that were proposed by Don Domingo Faustino Sarmiento, it has done justice to his zeal for the promotion of primary education, and we have ordered included in the minutes an expression of gratitude for his interesting labors.

Prologue

IDEOLOGICAL ANALYSIS OF THE TENSES

OF THE SPANISH CONJUGATION

(1841)

After the significant work done on the analysis of the verb by Condillac, Beauzée, and other eminent philosophers, it would seem presumptuous or rash to base this part of grammatical theory on principles different from those they have indicated.[8] But examine my principles without prejudice. See if they satisfactorily explain the apparently complicated and irregular facts which the language presents in this aspect, and whether the same thing can be said of the others. And I promise to accept any decision (whatever it may be) that is pronounced with full knowledge and authority.

To tell the truth, I do not fear that my theory, if subjected to scrupulous examination, will be found baseless or incorrect; I think I see in it, at least in its fundamental principles, all the possible qualities of truth and solidity. And though I know full well how powerful are the illusions created by fancy, I cannot resist a conviction that was the result of very extensive study at another period in my life, and which has been constantly confirmed by later observations over a period of many years. What I do fear is that my readers will not have the patience to follow me in all the particulars of an analysis that is necessarily delicate and extremely detailed, and will hasten to condemn it without having understood it.

Many people will also think it not applicable to the general study of the grammar of our language. I think differently. Though I recognize that reading good writers allows certain privileged spirits to dispense with study of the rules, and though I realize that the same instinct of analogy that has created languages suffices in many cases to indicate to us the legitimate structure of sentences and the proper use of the inflections of nouns and verbs, I believe that many mistakes could be avoided, and the language of writers would be more generally correct and exact, if more attention were paid to what happens in our minds when we speak. This is an aim which, even if we do not consider its practical utility, is interesting to philosophy, for it discloses delicate mental processes that no one would imagine in the everyday use of the language.

There are few things which offer an exercise to the mind more suitable for developing its faculties, and making them more flexible and easy, than the philosophic study of language. It has been believed, quite baselessly, that apprenticeship in a language was solely a question of memory. It is not possible to construct a sentence, or to translate one language into another, without closely scrutinizing the most intimate relationships of ideas, without making a microscopic examination, so to speak, of its accidents and modifications. Nor is this kind of study as bare of attractions as those people believe who have not become familiar with such studies up to a certain point. In the subtle and fleeting analogies on which the choice of verbal forms depends (and the same could be said of some other parts of language), we find a wonderful chain of metaphysical relationships, linked together with surprising order and precision when we consider that they are owed entirely to popular usage, the true and sole maker of languages. At the outset, the meaning of the inflections of verbs presents a chaos in which everything seems arbitrary, irregular, and the result of whim. But under the light of analysis this apparent disorder is cleared away, and in its place we see a system of general laws that operate with absolute uniformity, and which are even capable of being expressed in strict formulas that combine and divide like those of algebraic language.

And this is precisely what has made me think that the value I give to the forms of the verb, insofar as they are significant of time, is the sole true value, the only one that faithfully represents the facts; that is, the different uses of verbal inflections according to the practice of good speakers. An explanation in which each fact has its particular reason, which serves only for it, and the different facts lack a common link that ties them together and makes some emerge from others; and in which, on the other hand, exceptions are in constant conflict with the rules, cannot satisfy the mind. But when all the facts are in harmony, when anomalies disappear and we perceive that variety is nothing other than unity, transformed according to constant laws, we are authorized to believe that the problem has been solved and that we possess a real *theory*: that is, an intellectual vision of the reality of things, whose truth is essentially harmonious.

Certain, therefore, that the explanation that I am going to give of a part of language that is no less difficult than interesting is supported on a firm foundation, which I have kept buried for more than thirty years; and, after a very strict revision, which has suggested to me a few illustrations and improvements, I have decided to publish it at last. I am encouraged by the hope that sooner or later there will be no lack of intelligent persons to examine it, and that they will perhaps adopt and perfect my ideas.

Once again, I entreat those who read it not to hasten to disapprove of it before they have understood it. In the first few pages objections will occur to them which they will eventually see satisfactorily resolved. At least I hope so. They will think the nomenclature strange; but if they find that it has the merit of offering a complete definition in each name, and something more than a definition, a formula, in which not only the combination but also the order of the elements faithfully portray the mental actions of which each verbal tense is a sign, I anticipate that they will deem it preferable to those adopted in our grammars.

This analysis of the tenses is especially restricted to the Spanish conjugation; but I am sure that the procedure and the principles that appear in it are applicable, with certain modifications, to other languages. I have tried to give examples of this in some of the notes that accompany the text.

Spanish Grammar

(1832)

*Quo semel est imbuta recens, seruabit odorem
testa diu . . .*

—HORACE, *EPISTLES*

[the jar will keep the fragrance it was steeped in when new]

The interest shown by the government and public of this city [Santiago] in the interesting subject of literary education leads me to hope that the following observations on the earliest, and also the most necessary but most often neglected of children's areas of study, may not seem inappropriate.[9] I refer to the study of our native language.

There are persons who regard as useless the effort employed in acquiring a knowledge of Spanish grammar, whose rules, according to them, are sufficiently learned by daily use. Were this to be said in Valladolid or Toledo, the reply might still be that the number of words and sentences in general circulation is only a small part of the language's riches; that its cultivation makes it common to all the peoples who speak it, and greatly slows the changes that time produces, in this as in all human affairs; that, in proportion to the solidity and uniformity acquired by languages, one of the most troublesome obstacles to trade among different peoples is diminished, and intercourse among different ages, so profitable for the cultivation of reason and the joys of understanding and taste, is made easier; that all highly civilized nations have cultivated their own language with special care; that Latin was studied in Rome in the age of Caesar and Cicero; that among the precious relics that have come down to us from Latin literature are a good number of grammatical and philological works; that great Caesar did not think himself above writing some of them, and found in this pleasant study a distraction from the burdens of war and factional strife; that in the most splendid century of French literature the elegant and judicious Rollin introduced cultivation of the mother tongue at the University of Paris. We could quote the well-worn phrase [by Cicero] *Haec studia adolescentiam acuunt* ... [These pursuits nourish youth ...], and, in a word, we could fall back on the authority of everything that has been written about literary education. This could be the reply, even in countries where the national language is spoken correctly, to those who condemn studying it as unnecessary and futile. What shall we say, then, to those who regard it as superfluous in America?

Others claim that a special apprenticeship in Spanish is unnecessary for young people who learn Latin, because by learning the grammar of that tongue they also learn that of their native language. This is an error that can arise only from the mistaken idea held by some people about what constitutes knowledge of the mother tongue. The person who has learned Latin much better than it is generally learned among us will know Latin, and he also will have formed a fair idea of the structure of language and of what is called general grammar. But this does not mean that he will know Spanish grammar, for each language has its particular rules, its own character, its genius, so to speak; and frequently what passes for a solecism in one language is a received idiom, and perhaps a cultivated and elegant phrase, in another. General notions of grammar are no doubt a very useful analytical means of proceeding methodically to observe the analogies that guide men in the use of speech; but to imagine that, because we have mastered this instrument, we know our native language without ever having studied it, is as if we were to say that to know the structure of an animal body, it would suffice to hold a scalpel in our hand.

Perhaps the deficiencies of the national grammars have contributed to this error. Those who have undertaken to write grammars have either confined themselves to too narrow limits, in the belief (a mistaken one in my opinion) that, to be accessible to young children, they had to content themselves with imparting a very superficial idea of the composition of language; or, if they have aspired to a complete grammar, they have adhered with excessive and superstitious servility to vague principles, imprecise terminology, and trite classifications that were outlawed by educational theory long ago. The grammar of his native language is the first subject presented to the child's intelligence, the first test of his mental faculties, his first practical course in reasoning. Hence it is essential that everything in grammar must guide his habits accurately, that nothing be vague or obscure, that he does not give a mysterious value to words that he does not understand. A theory of learning, all the more difficult and delicate because unobtrusive, must present and classify the facts (that is, the rules of speech) in such a way that by being generalized they can be reduced to the simplest possible expression.

To give an idea of what is lacking in this regard, even in the *Gramática* of the Academy, which is the one most widely used, we need only limit ourselves to a few observations. It is very far from my intention to belittle the merit of the Academy's labors; its *Diccionario* and its *Ortografía* have earned it the gratitude of all Spanish-speaking countries. And though the former work is considered incomplete, it can perhaps be presented without blushes beside other books of the same kind that are currently acceptable in England and France. Payne Knight, a worthy vote in the field of philology, believes that the Academy's *Diccionario* (the big one in six volumes, which I think was the first book produced by that body) is superior to anything now in existence along those lines. In the *Gramática* itself there are perfectly executed parts, usually those in which the Academy confines itself to unadorned exposition of facts. The radical error in this work consists of having applied to the Spanish language, without the slightest modification, the theory and classifications of the Latin language, created to demonstrate a system of signs which, though they have a certain resemblance to ours, differ from them on many essential points.

The Academy makes Spanish nouns *declinable by cases.* To do this, a somewhat new meaning had to be conferred on the word "declension." "Declension," the Academy states, "is the different way of signifying what the declinable parts of the sentence receive from union with others, whether or not they vary in ending." For example: a different way of signifying is that of this part of the sentence, *hombre* [man], when it expresses *el hombre* [the man], compared with when it says *del hombre* [of the man]. But are not the following parts of the sentence, *cerca, lejos, ahora, luego* [near, far, now, later] also a different mode of signifying when they are used by themselves, compared with what they receive in the expressions *de cerca, de lejos, desde ahora, desde luego* [from nearby, from afar, from now on, from the beginning], or, carry the matter still further, when the expression is *muy cerca, algo lejos, ahora mismo, luego al punto* [very near, rather far, right now, immediately after]. It certainly seems to me that the Academy's definition applies to these latter expressions just as much as its own example does. What motive is there, then, for saying that the noun *hombre* is declinable and that the adverbs I have listed are not? What is this mode of signifying whose varieties make up the declension? This is a mystery into which the Academy has refused to initiate us, consequently leaving in total darkness the difference between declinable and non-declinable parts.

One error leads to another, and once the Academy has established that Spanish nouns are declinable by cases only because Latin nouns are so declined, it had to establish for consistency's sake that the Spanish declension has exactly the same number and difference of cases as the Latin declension. It seems that there must have been some unknown law of the intellect, some recondite principle of philology, by which the declension of nouns in all languages had to be modeled exactly on Latin, and hence that there must be six cases, neither more nor less, and that these cases are none other than the nominative, genitive, dative, etc. Can there be anything more contrary to all educational theory than to make a universal rule of language what is merely a proper and peculiar characteristic of the Latin tongue? For surely there is no reason to attribute these six cases to the Spanish language any more than to any other of the languages spoken on earth.

But let us try to dig a little deeper into the Spanish system of declension as it is stated for us by the Academy, or rather by the editor of the *Gramática*. *De la ciudad* [of the city] is genitive when one says *el aire de la ciudad* [the air of the city], and ablative when one says *vengo de la ciudad* [I am coming from the city]. Why? Because the Romans said *urbis* to express the first and *urbe* to express the second. But do we, perchance, alter the ending of the word? We vary our way of signifying: one way denotes possession, the other the principle of movement, or what is called *terminus a quo*. According to this, the expression *de la ciudad* would be of as many different cases as there are possible different meanings. What case, then, would it be when neither possession nor principle of movement was denoted, to wit, when one says *ausente de la ciudad, se acordó de la ciudad,* or *dispuso de la ciudad* [absent from the city, he recalled the city, he made use of the city]? These expressions must be reduced to one of the cases stated. To which? To the one used in the corresponding Latin sentence. So the result is the belief that the ablative and genitive signify, in the grammar of the Spanish language, accidental qualities belonging to another language. Indeed, it would be very difficult to cite a single fact in Spanish that could be explained by this confusion of cases. Everything that needs to be explained about the matter is sufficiently explained by the Academy when it speaks of the different uses of the preposition *de.* Why erect a scaffold on which nothing is built, and which serves only to present undecipherable mysteries to a child's mind, teaching him to have a taste for vague ideas, or words that make no sense?

"Masculine gender," says the Academy, "is that which includes all male persons and animals, and other entities which, not being male, are reduced to this gender by their endings, such as *hombre, libro, papel* [man, book, paper]." This is one of those definitions that cannot impart knowledge of the thing defined, for it does not offer the mind any fixed and precise signal with which we can distinguish it from others. First, gender in grammar includes not the things signified by nouns, but the nouns themselves: "masculine" and "feminine" do not signify classes of objects, but classes of nouns. But how can we recognize masculine nouns by this definition? By their meaning? No. The definition itself gives us to understand that some masculine nouns signify objects that are neither male persons nor male animals. By the ending? Still less. We are not told which endings are masculine, nor that there is an ending which is always masculine. Add to this that there are a large number of nouns which by their ending ought to be feminine, such as *sistema, planeta, cisma* [system, planet, schism], and which nevertheless belong to the masculine gender. It is difficult to think of a more confusing, more obscure, or more useless definition. And unfortunately there are many definitions similar to this one in the *Gramática.*

However, nothing is easier than to give children an exact idea of what genders are in our language. First, they must be told that many adjectives with two endings exist in Spanish (for example, *blanco, blanca* [white]; or *bueno, buena* [good]. Then tell them immediately that among nouns, some always link up with the first ending and others with the second, and some few with either one or the other. If after this they are told that all those which always link up with the first ending are called masculine nouns, and feminine those which link up with the second, and ambiguous those which link up with either one or the other, we dare to state that they will have no difficulty in understanding it. This is, in fact, the fundamental rule that all of us follow to distinguish genders. Why do we say that nouns ending in *o* are masculine? Because we see that they are constructed with the first ending of adjectives. Why do we except from this rule the nouns *mano* [hand] and *nao* [ship]? Because we see that they are constructed with the second ending. This, then, is the fundamental rule from which all the particular rules, and their exceptions, derive. There is no other, nor need another be imparted.

Genders are simply classes into which nouns have been distributed according to the different ending of the adjectives with which they are construed. No doubt the difference of sexes was what originally gave rise to the difference in genders. But a grammar must represent not what was, but what is today. The difference of sexes that served as a basis for the gender of nouns in the early stage of languages, and which still retains this influence in the English language, serves in Latin, Greek, Spanish, and many other languages only for a few rules dependent on meaning; special and subordinate rules, such as those that make masculine in our language the names of mountains and rivers, and feminine the names of the letters.

From this simple consideration a necessary consequence follows; it is that the number of genders, based on the difference in forms that the adjective takes according to the noun to which it refers, can be neither more nor less than that of the endings of the adjectives. There may be languages in which the adjective has three or four different endings. If in them some nouns are always construed with the first ending, others with the second, and so on, there would have to be four genders in these languages. This would also lead us to the solution of the controversy that has been long discussed, whether or not there is a neuter gender in Spanish. But let us leave this subject for another occasion.

Just as the Academy unnecessarily introduces into Spanish distinctions and classifications that are peculiar to the Latin language, it also omits some that the Latin grammarians did not make because they were not necessary in the language with which they were dealing, but are necessary in our language. The three verbal forms *ha hecho, hizo, hubo hecho* [has made, made, had made] have different meanings and uses in Spanish, and in most cases cannot be replaced interchangeably by another. We say, for example, *Inglaterra se ha hecho señora del mar* [England has made herself mistress of the sea]; *Roma se hizo señora del mundo* [Rome made herself mistress of the world]; and *cuando Roma se hubo hecho señora del mundo* [when Rome had made herself mistress of the world]. This means that these three verbal forms are really three different tenses. It does not matter that all of them represent past time. The [imperfect past-tense] form *hacía* also has this meaning, and yet we consider it a different tense. Really, the only reason to join those three forms in one tense and separate them from the fourth form was that Latin had only one form for *se ha hecho, se hizo,* and *se hubo hecho,* and a different form for *se hacía.*

When the Academy explains Spanish constructions, it often does nothing but explain the corresponding Latin constructions. For example, the impersonal verb *haber,* according to the Academy, means "to exist," no doubt because in this sense the Latin verb *esse* corresponds to it.

But the truth is that the verb *haber* preserves its primitive meaning of *tener* [to have] and never denotes existence. If, when it is used impersonally, it offers this meaning, this is not because it abandons the other meaning, but because of the construction in which it is found. When we say *el mundo no tiene país más ameno* [the world has not a pleasanter country], the construction offers the idea of existence, as if we were to say *no existe país más ameno* [a pleasanter country does not exist]. And yet, no one would say that in this example the verb *tener* means "to exist." The same thing happens with the verb *haber,* except that the construction is elliptical, with the subject *mundo, universo, naturaleza* [world, universe, nature] or some similar noun unexpressed. And so, *hubo en Roma grandes oradores* [in Rome there were great orators] means the same as saying *el mundo tuvo en Roma grandes oradores* [in Rome the world had great orators].

It may seem over-literal to pause on this point. But we can explain the use of this impersonal verb through the ellipsis I have indicated, and cannot do so in any other way except by accusing the language of irregularities and whims, which appear only to those who do not wish to take the trouble to explore its analogies. Indeed, let us suppose for a moment that the verb *haber* means "to be" or "to exist," and we will encounter two anomalies, each more monstrous than the other: the verb does not agree with the thing that exists, and if this is represented by the pronouns *él, ella, ellos, ellas* [he, she, they], we will always find them in the accusative. Now, what other example does our language offer of a subject that does not agree with its verb, and which is expressed with the accusative forms *le, la, lo, las* [him, her, it, them]? On the other hand, restore the original meaning of *haber*, and everything is simple. Since the unexpressed subject is always a third person singular, and since the particular noun that joins with it is a direct object—or what our grammarians call the accusative of object—its form must be precisely that of the accusative. *¿Hay dinero? No le hay* [Is there money? There is not]. *¿Hubo fiestas? No las hubo* [Were there fiestas? There were not]. And from this it can be deduced that *haber* in the construction we are dealing with is not really impersonal, but is a verb with an unexpressed subject, for it is always singular.

It may perhaps be said that the plan adopted by the Royal Academy has the advantage of offering a child the acquisition of the Latin language, by familiarizing him in advance with its system and the peculiarities that distinguish it. To this we could reply that even if it were true, that is no reason to sacrifice to a secondary usefulness the essential and primary aim of a national grammar, which is to impart knowledge of the mother tongue, presenting it with its natural traits and features and not under alien forms; that vague ideas, incomprehensible terms, mistaken classifications, serve only to instill bad intellectual habits and to place thorns and stumbling blocks in the way of all the pupil's future efforts; and that, on the contrary, a clear and simple theory of his mother tongue is the best way to prepare the child for the acquisition, not only of Latin, but of any other language and any other type of knowledge. We insist that the study of the native language must be strictly analytical, not only because this is the plainest and shortest path, or, better still, the only path that can lead us to the stated aim, but also because, since this is the first exercise of children's mental faculties, it is the place where it is most important to offer them correct guidance.

Prologue

GRAMMAR OF THE SPANISH LANGUAGE

(1847)

Although in this grammar I would have preferred not to depart from the usual nomenclature and explanations, there are points on which I felt that the practices of the Spanish language could be represented in a more complete and exact manner.[10] Some readers will no doubt call arbitrary the alterations I have introduced on these points, or will attribute them to an exaggerated desire to say new things; the reasons that I adduce will at least prove that I have adopted them only after mature consideration. But the most negative prejudice, because of the hold that it still possesses over even quite well-educated persons, is the prejudice of those who believe that in grammar there is no harm in inadequate definitions, badly made classifications, and false concepts, if only, on the other hand, the rules of good usage are carefully set forth. However, I believe that these two things cannot be reconciled, that usage cannot be correctly and faithfully explained except by analyzing it, by uncovering the true principles that govern it. I believe that strict logic is an indispensable requisite for all teaching, and that in the first test of the awakening intellect it is most important not to let it be satisfied with mere words.

The speech of a people is an artificial system of signs, which in many respects differs from other systems of the same kind; it follows from this that each language has its own particular theory, its grammar. Hence we must not apply indiscriminately to one language the principles, terms, and analogies into which, more or less successfully, the practices of another are resolved. The very word *idiom* (in Greek, particularity or characteristic), tells us that each language has its genius, its physiognomy, its turns of phrase. The grammarian would do his office badly if, when explaining his own language, he were to limit himself to what it had in common with another, or (worse still) to assume resemblances where only differences existed—and important, radical differences at that. General grammar is one thing and the grammar of a given language another; it is one thing to compare two languages and another to consider a language as it is in itself. Are we dealing with the conjugation of the Spanish verb? We must enumerate the forms it assumes, and the meanings and uses of each form, as if there were no other language in the world but Spanish. It is a necessary position with regard to the child, who is taught the rules of the only language within his grasp, his native tongue. This is the viewpoint in which I have tried to place myself, a viewpoint in which I beg intelligent persons, to whose judgment I submit my work, to place themselves as well, laying aside most particularly any reminiscences of the Latin language.

In Spain as in other European countries, an excessive admiration for the language and literature of the Romans placed a Latin stamp on almost all productions of the mind. This was a natural tendency of men's spirits in the period when letters were being restored. Pagan mythology continued to supply the poet with images and symbols, and the Ciceronian period was the model of elocution for elegant writers. Hence it was not strange that the nomenclature and grammatical canons of our Romance tongue should be taken from Latin.

If, as Latin came to be the ideal type for grammarians, circumstances had awarded this preeminence to Greek, we would probably have had five cases in our declension instead of six, our verbs would have had not only a passive but a middle voice, and aorists and paulo-post-futures would have figured in the Spanish conjugation.

Signs of thought doubtless obey certain general laws which, derived from those laws which regulate thought itself, govern all languages and constitute a universal grammar. But if we except the resolution of thought into clauses; and the clause into subject and attribute; the existence of the noun to express objects directly; that of the verb to indicate attributes; and that of the other words that modify and determine nouns and verbs in such a way that, with a limited number of both, all possible objects, real as well as intellectual, can be designated (as well as all the attributes that we can perceive or imagine in them), then I see nothing that we are obliged to recognize as a universal law from which no language can be exempt. The number of parts of speech can be larger or smaller than it is in Latin or the Romance tongues. The verb might conceivably have genders and the noun tenses. What is more natural than the agreement of the verb with the subject? Well, in Greek it was not only allowed but customary to make the plural of neuter nouns agree with the singular form of verbs. To the intellect, two negatives must necessarily cancel each other out, and this is almost always the case in speech; but it does not alter the fact that in Spanish there are circumstances in which two negatives do not make a positive. Therefore we must not transfer lightly the effects of ideas to the accidents of words. Philosophy has erred no little in assuming that language is a faithful copy of thought; and this same exaggerated supposition has caused grammar to stray in the opposite direction. Some argued from the copy to the original, others from the original to the copy. In language, conventional and arbitrary factors include a great deal more than is commonly thought. Beliefs, whims of the imagination, and myriad casual associations cannot fail to produce an enormous discrepancy in the means that languages use to make manifest what is taking place in the soul. It is a discrepancy that becomes greater and greater the farther they depart from their common origin.

I am willing to listen patiently to the objections that may be made about what seem to be the new features of this grammar, though on careful examination it will be found that on those very points I sometimes do not innovate but restore. The idea, for example, that I present of the cases in declension is the old and genuine one, and in attributing to the infinitive the nature of a noun I am merely bringing back an idea that is perfectly set forth in Priscian: ". . . *uim nominis [rei ipsius] habet verbum infinitum . . . dico enim 'bonum est legere,' ut si dicam 'bona est lectio.'*" [The infinitive (of the action itself) has the force of a noun. I say 'To read is good' as if I should say 'Reading is good.'] On the other hand I have not wanted to depend on "authorities," for to me the ultimate authority with regard to a language is the language itself. I do not feel that I am entitled to divide what language constantly unites, nor to forcibly unite what it separates. I regard analogies with other languages as no more than accessory proofs. I accept practices as language presents them, without imaginary ellipses, without other explanations than those that illustrate usage by means of usage.

This is the logic I have followed. As for the aids from which I have tried to profit, I must cite especially the works of the Spanish Academy and the grammar of Don Vicente Salvá. I have regarded the latter book as the most abundant source of Spanish ways of speaking, and as a book which no one who aspires to speak and write his native language correctly can be excused from reading and consulting frequently. I also owe a debt to some ideas of the witty and learned Don Juan Antonio Puigblanch, in the philological material to which he refers incidentally in his *Opúsculos*. Nor would it be fair to forget [Gregorio] Garcés, whose book, even considered only as a glossary of Spanish words and phrases from the language's best period, does not in my opinion deserve the disdain with which it is treated nowadays.

After such an important work as Salvá's, it seemed to me that the only thing missing was a theory that would show the system of language in the development and use of its inflections and in the structure of its sentences, stripped of certain Latin traditions that fitted it not at all. But when I say "theory," let it not be thought that I am dealing with metaphysical speculations. Señor Salvá rightly condemns those ideological abstractions which, like those of an author whom he cites, are brought in to legitimize what usage forbids. I avoid them, not only when they contradict usage, but when they go beyond the actual practice of language. I would reduce the philosophy of grammar to representing usage by the simplest and most comprehensive formulas. To base these formulas on other intellectual procedures than those that really and truly govern usage is a luxury that grammar does not need. But the intellectual procedures that really and truly govern usage, or in other words the precise value of inflections and combinations of words, must necessarily be subject to proof; and the grammar that ignores this will not perform its function adequately. Just as the dictionary gives the meaning of roots, so grammar must declare the meaning of inflections and combinations, not only the natural and original meaning but the secondary and metaphorical meaning, whenever such inflections and combinations have entered into general use in the language. This is the area that grammatical speculations must most especially embrace, and at the same time is the boundary that confines them. If I have at any time overstepped this boundary, it has been in very short excursions, when I was trying to refute the alleged ideological bases of a doctrine or when grammatical accidents revealed some curious mental procedure. Such transgressions, however, are so rare that to call them inappropriate would be unnecessarily severe.

Some have criticized this grammar as difficult and obscure. In the schools in Santiago which have adopted it, it is obvious that its difficulty is much greater for those who, concerned about the doctrines of other grammars, do not take the trouble to read mine with attention, and scorn to familiarize themselves with its language, than for the pupils who form their first grammatical ideas with its aid.

On the other hand, there is quite a common belief that the study of a language, to the point of speaking and writing it correctly, is effortless and easy. Many points in grammar are not accessible to the intelligence of young children; hence I have thought it wise to divide my grammar into two courses, with the first of these reduced to the least difficult and most indispensable ideas and the second made extensive to those parts of language that require a somewhat better-trained mind. I have indicated these with different kinds of type and included both in a single treatise, not only to avoid repetitions but to offer to the teachers of the first course the aid of the explanations intended for the second course, should they at any time be required. I also believe that these explanations will be of some value to beginners, for as they progress, difficulties in understanding them will gradually disappear. This allows teachers to decide whether to add to the lessons of primary instruction everything that they think appropriate from the second course, according to the pupils' capabilities and progress. In the footnotes I call attention to certain nefarious practices of popular American speech so that they can be recognized and avoided, and have explained some doctrines with observations that require knowledge of other languages. Finally, in the notes at the end of the book I write at more length on some doubtful points, on which I believed that explanations which could satisfy better-educated readers would not be superfluous. In some cases it may seem that examples have accumulated rather profusely; but this has only been done when I was trying to counter the practice of writers given over to regrettable novelties, or to argue controversial points, or to explain certain procedures of the language which I thought had not been sufficiently dealt with until now.

I also believed that in a national grammar certain forms and locutions that have disappeared from present-day language ought not to be passed over, either because the poet and even the prose writer sometimes have recourse to them, or because a knowledge of them is necessary for complete understanding of the most cherished works of other periods in our language. It was also desirable to demonstrate the improper use that some writers make of them, and the erroneous concepts with which others have tried to explain them. And if it is I who have made errors, may my mistakes serve as a stimulus to more competent writers, to undertake the same labor with better success.

I do not claim to write for Spaniards. My lessons are aimed at my brothers, the inhabitants of Spanish America. I believe that the preservation of our forefathers' tongue in all possible purity is important, as a providential means of communication and a fraternal link among the various nations of Spanish origin scattered over the two continents. But what I presume to recommend to them is not a superstitious purism. The prodigious advances of all the sciences and arts, the diffusion of intellectual culture and political revolutions, daily require new signs to express new ideas; and the introduction of novel words, taken from ancient and foreign languages, no longer offends unless they are manifestly unnecessary, or unless they reveal the affectation and poor taste of those who think that by using them they are embellishing what they write. There is another and worse vice, which is to give new meanings to known words and phrases, thus multiplying the ambiguities that arise out of the variety of meanings from which all languages suffer more or less, and perhaps even more so those most often studied, owing to the almost infinite number of ideas to which a necessarily limited number of signs must be accommodated. But the greatest evil of all, and one which, if it is not controlled, will deprive us of the precious advantages of a common language, is the torrent of grammatical neologisms which inundate and render obscure much of what is written in America, and which by altering the structure of the language tend to change it into a multitude of irregular, undisciplined, and barbaric dialects; embryos of future languages which, during a long development, would reproduce in America what happened in Europe during the dark period of the corruption of Latin. Chile, Peru, Buenos Aires, Mexico, would each speak their own language, or, to express it better, a number of languages, as happens in Spain, Italy, and France, where certain provincial languages predominate but a number of others exist beside them, hampering the spread of enlightenment, the execution of laws, the administration of the State, and national unity. A language is like a living body: its vitality does not depend on the constant identity of elements, but on the regularity of the functions that those elements perform, and from which arise the form and nature that distinguish the whole.

Whether or not I exaggerate the danger, it has been the chief reason that has led me to compose this book, so superior to my powers in so many ways. Intelligent readers who honor me by reading it with some attention will observe how much care I have exercised in marking out, so to speak, the boundaries that good usage in our language respects, amid the looseness and freedom of its turns of phrase; and in pointing out the corruptions most widespread today and showing the essential difference that exists between Spanish constructions and foreign ones that resemble them up to a point, which we tend to imitate without exercising the discernment we ought to employ.

Let no one believe that, by recommending the preservation of Castilian Spanish, I intend to accuse as harmful and spurious everything peculiar to American speech. Very correct locutions exist which are considered outdated in the Peninsula, but which persist in Spanish America. Why outlaw them? If according to general practice among Americans the conjugation of some verb is more logical, why should we prefer the one that has prevailed more or less by chance in Castile? If we have formed new words from Spanish roots according to the ordinary rules of derivation that the Spanish language recognizes, and which have been used and are still being used to increase its capacity, why should we be ashamed of using them? Chile and Venezuela have as much right as Aragon and Andalusia to have their occasional divergences tolerated, when they are supported by the universal and authentic usage of educated persons. These differences are much less damaging to purity and correctness of language than are those Frenchified usages that are sprinkled today through even the most admired works of Peninsular writers.

I have set forth my principles, my plan, and my aim, and have justly recognized my obligations to those who have preceded me. I am indicating paths that have not been explored before, and it is likely that in them I have not always made the observations necessary to deduce exact general rules. Even if everything that I now propose does not seem acceptable, my ambition will be satisfied if some part of it is, and if that part contributes to the improvement of a branch of instruction which is certainly not the most brilliant of all, but is one of the most necessary.

NOTES TO PART I

1. First published in London under the title "El Repertorio Americano. Prospecto," in *El Repertorio Americano*, vol. 1 (October 1826): 1–6. It is included in Bello's *Obras Completas* [henceforth *OC*], vol. 18, pp. 199–204. Bello's project of disseminating the information that he believed useful for the new independent nations of Spanish America is discernible in earlier writings, but in this essay he provides a clear statement of the need to move from independence to cultural and political organization.

2. First published in London under the title "Alocución a la poesía" in *Biblioteca Americana*, vol. 1 (1823): 3–16, and continued in vol. 2 (October 1823): 1–12. Also in *OC*, vol. 1, pp. 43–64.

3. First published under the title "Silva americana. Agricultura de la zona tórrida," in *El Repertorio Americano*, vol. 1 (October 1826): 7–18. It is included in *OC*, vol. 1, pp. 65–74.

4. First published in the Chilean periodical *El Araucano*, No. 545, 5 February 1841. It is included in *OC*, vol. 9, pp. 349–362. In this essay, Bello demonstrated that he could move rather easily from the writing of poetry to literary criticism. His interests in literary history, developed during the London years, reveal a clear focus on the social context of language and literature, and emphasize the importance of foundational texts. The effort to relate contemporary literary developments in Spanish to its early Castilian roots was one of Bello's abiding themes. In the context of the 1840s in Chile, this essay represents a call for simplicity in literary expression, in response to the increasing adoption of European, but especially French, literary forms.

5. First published under the title "Bosquejo del oríjen i progresos del arte de escribir" in *El Repertorio Americano*, vol. 4 (August 1827): 11–26. It is included in *OC*, vol. 23, pp. 77–93. To this date, this essay has not been identified as forming a part of Bello's master philosophical work, *Filosofía del entendimiento* (1881), in which context it could be appreciated as a substantive part of Bello's larger concerns on matters of language and thought, so prevalent in that posthumously published volume. See *OC*, vol. 3, pp. 319–327. In the context in which it actually appeared, in London in 1827, the essay was consistent with the journal's stated aim of disseminating useful information to the nascent republics, in this case the recent developments in philological studies, which had made substantial progress in the first quarter of the nineteenth century. It also had a

programmatic aim, as stated in the introduction, which depicted written language as the highest expression of civilization, and which, with proper reforms to the Spanish written language, could be transferred to Spanish America.

6. First published under the title "Indicaciones sobre la conveniencia de simplificar y uniformar la ortografía en América," in *Biblioteca Americana*, vol. 1 (1823): 50–62. It was signed by Bello and his collaborator Juan García del Río. Also included in *OC*, vol. 5, pp. 71–87. The wars of independence had not yet ended in Spanish America, but the tenor of this article suggests that the authors considered independence a likely outcome. The important task ahead was to establish a language policy that would inform the construction of new nations.

7. This essay was originally published in two installments in *El Araucano*, Nos. 716 and 718, of 10 and 24 May 1844, respectively. It is included in *OC*, vol. 5, pp. 99–115. This essay is in fundamental respects similar to the 1823 article published in *Biblioteca Americana* in London. The context, however, is very different. At this time (1844), Andrés Bello was Rector of the University of Chile. The Faculty of Philosophy and Humanities, here called Facultad de Humanidades, had jurisdiction over the entire educational system, and therefore its policies had a national impact. The plan discussed and adopted is a modified form of the project presented by Domingo Faustino Sarmiento. Bello defended those ideas that were closer to his own proposals and presented them in the official government paper. Therefore, the tone of this essay, and the reply to "A Subscriber" reflect the vigorous polemics of the Chilean press in the 1840s.

8. This short piece represents the prologue to Bello's *Análisis Ideológica de los tiempos de la conjugación castellana* (Valparaíso: Imprenta de M. Rivadeneyra, 1841). It was included in *OC*, vol. 5 pp. 3–67. Bello's statement to the effect that he had kept the work "buried for more than thirty years" would place the date of writing in the Caracas period, that is, before 1810. This would demonstrate an important continuity in his grammatical ideas, but most importantly, it would seem to indicate that despite the recognition of linguistic diversity, and the influence of society on language, Bello postulated at least a certain degree of internal coherence in language and its relationship to thought. This prologue provides important background for understanding his grammatical approach.

9. This essay was originally published in *El Araucano*, No. 73, 4 February 1832. It is included in *OC*, vol. 5, pp. 175–184. Although still early in his Chilean career, Bello was clearly aware of the country's educational shortcomings. This essay represents an early statement of the need for studies of the Spanish language. On the surface, it would appear to be a critique of the emphasis on Latin, but Bello mainly meant a critique of the attempt to inform a grammar of the *Spanish* language on the basis of Latin categories. This critique dovetails with his views on orthography, but signals a more ambitious effort to develop a comprehensive Spanish grammar. This article is particularly significant in that

the concept of "national" is closely related to language, and not necessarily to a particular geographic area.

10. The first edition of the *Gramática de la lengua castellana destinada al uso de los americanos* was published in Santiago in 1847. Bello saw the publication of seven editions of his work, but numerous others have been published since the last 1864 edition (the fifth, published in 1860, is considered to be the definitive one). The *Gramática* and the version of the prologue on which this translation is based, are included in vol. 4 of *OC*. In the prologue, Bello provides an eloquent statement of the necessity of grammar for the larger aims of social unity. He also clarifies the relationship between the philosophy of grammar, and actual usage.

II

Education and History

On the Aims of Education and the Means of Promoting It

(1836)

E ducation, that exercise of early childhood which prepares human beings to play in the theater of the world the role that Fate holds in store for them, is what teaches us our duties to society as members of it, as well as our duties to ourselves if we wish to attain the highest degree of well-being of which the human condition is capable.[1] Our aim, in forming a man's heart and spirit, is to secure good things and avoid bad ones, for the individual and others like him. Hence we can think of education as the exercise of the faculties most likely to promote human happiness.

Man's peculiar characteristic is his receptivity to progressive improvement. Education, which enriches his spirit with ideas and adorns his heart with virtues, is an effective means of promoting his progress; and the more truly and rapidly he makes that progress, the more likely it is that man, the only being on the face of the globe capable of progress, will fulfill his destiny completely. If education is necessary, and if it must be perfected through reforms suggested by observation of the human heart, then it becomes a question as important as the question of whether it is necessary to promote the happiness of mankind, and to enable man to attain as fully as possible all the aims intended by his Maker at the time of his creation.

Under any type of government there is equal need to be educated, because whatever the political system of a nation may be, its individuals have duties to perform with regard to it, to their families, and to themselves. But in no nation is the obligation to protect this important branch of social prosperity greater than in republican governments. For, as reason tells us and a number of writers have observed (among them Montesquieu in particular) in no type of association is education more important than in republics. In every society, the aim of its members is the achievement of general happiness. Republican governments are simultaneously representatives and agents of the national will, and because as such they must follow the impulses of that will, they can never be exempt from directing all their strength to achievement of the great object toward which that will is moving, by rendering individuals useful both to themselves and to their fellow men through education. In addition, the representative democratic system prepares all its members to participate more or less directly in its affairs; and nations could not progress at all politically unless education were sufficiently widespread to endow each person with real knowledge of his duties and rights. Failing this, it is impossible to carry out those duties, or to endow those rights with sufficient value to make us try to preserve them.

But not all members of society need have the same education, though it is essential that all have some, for each person has a different way of contributing to the common weal. No matter how much equality is established by political institutions, there nevertheless exists in all peoples an inequality that I will not call inequality of rank (which can never exist among members of a republic, especially with regard to participation in public rights). There is, however, an inequality of condition, of needs, of style of life. Education must adjust itself to these differences in order to achieve the useful ends to which it is applied. A number of writers, among them Locke in particular, despite their interest in improving the human race, have thought of education solely as a precious gift reserved for the upper classes, if we may be permitted to so describe that group of persons who, owing to the greater gifts of Fortune or their parents' habits, engage in the scientific professions, the management of private interests, or the exercise of public office. But to deprive the less well-to-do classes of this benefit is not only an injustice, it is absurd, for all persons have an equal right to well-being and all must contribute to the general welfare. These classes, as the most numerous and the most needy, require the protection of government to instruct their youth. But because their social needs are different and their way of life has different means and different aims, they must also be given an education in harmony with this special situation. The times have long passed when intelligence was denied to the masses and the human race was divided into oppressors and oppressed.

It is very easy to think that all men are capable of an equal breadth of knowledge; but since there should only be a question of giving each man sufficient knowledge to attain the happiness he desires in his station in life, the question must be limited to the knowledge most useful for him.

It is universally recognized that one of the principles of the common weal is that there must be as few poor people as possible. Their comforts undoubtedly increase with their dedication to lucrative work; but, though that work is the source of their well-being, it is not so restrictive as to prevent the acquisition of useful knowledge and the exercise of the mind. The first years of life are the most appropriate to achieve this useful aim. Even considering the need to offer advantages to productive labor, it would be preferable for a child not to engage in them up to a certain age, until his faculties have developed completely. For man, like all animals, cannot produce all the usefulness of which he is capable if premature dedication to labor prevents him from acquiring the strength and maturity required of him. Without these qualities, that same labor would be harmful to production, to the economy, and to health, though it is a source of prosperity when undertaken after the earliest years. But if this precious period of life, during which man's arm is as yet unproductive, is used to enlighten his mind, to restrain his passions, and to inspire him with love for his work and instill habits of virtue, the occupations that will later supply all his needs for sustenance will become incomparably more useful both to society and to himself.

Of the two branches in which education can be divided—namely formation of the heart and enlightenment of the spirit—the first of these fundamental principles can only be owed to domestic education. Impressions of infancy exercise a power over all people which usually decides their habits, their inclinations, and their character. And since the period when these impressions establish their sway is precisely that period when we know no guides to conduct other than our parents, it is obvious that we owe to them this part of the exercise of our faculties, which would come too late were it delayed to the age when we were ready to receive public education. During the first periods of the regeneration of a people, and a regeneration such as we Americans have experienced, it is almost impossible to achieve perfection in guiding the human heart during childhood. There are vices in our customs; virtues are more a matter of instinct than of persuasion, and this moral situation does not permit domestic education to hold to fixed rules whose application assures success. But, if the generations are successively improved with the help of public education, it is not difficult to predict that the day will come when we can generally make a beneficent and philosophical use of parental authority.

As for public education, we need not ponder the matter very deeply to discover, as I have already said, that it must not be confined to preparing men for different kinds of literary careers and for the highest professions; for it is not only the welfare of a small portion of society that must be promoted. Placing it within the reach of all young persons, no matter what their aptitudes and type of life, encouraging them to acquire it and aiding this acquisition by a large number of establishments and uniformity of methods, are effective means of giving education an impulse that will best benefit the nation's prosperity. After our emancipation, this is one of the most important reforms. When we were educated only to obey, we lacked intellectual needs. But once elevated to a political hierarchy worthy of man's nature, we have seen those needs come into being along with our social transformation, and we observe that civilization daily broadens their scope.

At first glance it seems difficult to make public instruction sufficiently widespread to render it accessible to all classes. But what obstacles exist in any society that cannot be smoothed away by laws adjusted to the character, the personality, the needs, and the moral condition of each nation? We must also recognize that, fortunately, we live in a century in which we do not have to abandon ourselves to the inspirations of genius to reform our nations, but have examples to follow and can call solid experience to our aid.

No matter how numerous the less well-to-do class in our society may be, educating it is fortunately not a task beyond our powers. At first it may be difficult to get parents to give up their children spontaneously for the purpose of acquiring assets of whose advantages they are unaware. But are there not any number of pressures that could be applied to oblige them to make this sacrifice, which would only be considered as such until the first results began to show? After that, education would be an indispensable need, and it would be easy to fill the schools with pupils. In Prussia, thanks to such efforts, hardly a child can be found in its national territory who does not know how to read and write.

To make instruction general and at the same time uniform, nothing is more obvious and effective than the creation of teacher-training schools. By cultivating the perfection and simplicity of teaching methods in these schools, and then distributing the best-trained students throughout the Republic like so many apostles of civilization, young people everywhere would find the same means of acquiring this very important advantage, and would be prepared from an early age to engage in the kind of labor that would give them the resources to make a living. In a number of places in Europe, and more particularly in northern Germany, establishments of this kind are being promoted with very great success.

The scope of knowledge acquired in these schools, built for the impoverished classes, should go no further than what their needs require. Anything more would not only be useless but actually harmful, for besides exposing them to ideas that would not be of proven value in the course of their lives, young people would stray too far from productive labors. Well-to-do persons—who acquire instruction as a sort of luxury and engage in professions that require more study—possess other means of acquiring a broader and more careful education, in schools intended for this purpose.

As for the ideas that must be acquired by that large proportion of a people which owes its livelihood to the sweat of its brow, and which is fully worthy of the protection of governments and should be considered as one of the chief instruments of the common weal, the question presents no difficulties. The principles of our [Catholic] religion must necessarily occupy first place, for without them we could not have a standard to guide our actions, one which, by putting the brake of morality on the heart's wild impulses, enables us to perform our duties to God, to men, and to ourselves.

No matter what method we adopt, we cannot omit relations with other individuals; and since the spoken word alone is insufficient for cultivation of these relations, the ability to read and write is a necessity for all men, who without this aid would also lack the means to preserve, in safety and order, the few or many affairs in which they will engage.

How can such affairs be trusted exclusively to the weak and fallible processes of memory?

Reading and writing cannot be learned except very imperfectly if the study of grammar is not added to them. And they cannot be expected to render all their usefulness in the exercise of any profession if, content with the above subjects, we should omit arithmetic. This branch of knowledge, one of the most important in education because it is the one most constantly and frequently applied to men's activities, cannot be ignored without its lack being felt at every step in life; from the largest and most extensive mercantile speculations to the poorest and humblest branches of industry, all need its help.

Perhaps it would be too much to ask in the infancy of our nations, but it would certainly be a pleasure to lovers of our country's prosperity were we not to limit ourselves to the acquisition of these very necessary subjects and were to enrich popular education with other ideas—ideas perhaps not indispensable in the ordinary course of life, but which elevate the soul and offer the means to occupy usefully those moments free of the tasks that form our chief occupation and constitute the happiness of many moments in our existence. Among these ideas we might include, as the most advantageous, some principles of astronomy and geography, not taught in the depth of which these branches of knowledge are capable and which require knowledge of other scientific elements, but in brief compendia and in the form of axioms and information. Also a few scant notions of history that would impart some knowledge of the world in past centuries, and the chief events that have taken place since its creation. Even if these limited ideas did no more than to arouse curiosity, and encourage the love of reading to satisfy it, a positive good would have been done to the people. How many hours sinfully sacrificed to vices, or lost in idleness, could be employed in useful recreation! Perhaps these indications seem suggested by a desire that is exaggerated and impossible of achievement; but it would be very easy to convince oneself that there is no exaggeration or fantasy in this, if we consider that even in many places in India, English missionaries have given all this latitude, and more, to the education of the poorest classes.

But though these branches of instruction, because not a prime necessity, could be omitted in the early stages of our social transformation, the same must not occur with knowledge of our political duties and rights. Ruled by a popular, representative system, each person forms part of the people in whom sovereignty resides. And it is very difficult or impossible to behave correctly in this social position if we are ignorant of what we can demand of society and what society can demand of us. Hence the study of the Constitution must form an integral part of general education, not with the depth necessary to acquire full knowledge of constitutional law, but merely committing its articles to memory in order to grasp the organization of the political body to which we belong. Without this we can never perform our functions as its members, nor can we have the enthusiasm that we ought to feel about the preservation of our rights, nor will we ever see lighted that public spirit which is one of the principles of the vitality of nations.

On such an important matter, the vigilance of governments can never be too great. Promoting public establishments intended for only a small part of the people fails to promote education, for it does not suffice merely to form men who are skilled in the higher professions. We must form useful citizens, we must improve society, and this cannot be achieved without opening the area of progress to the largest part of that society. What good will it do to have orators, jurists, and statesmen, if the mass of the people live submerged in the night of ignorance and cannot cooperate, insofar as they are able, in the management of affairs, or in the expansion of wealth, or attain that well-being which the vast majority of a people deserve? Not to concentrate on the most appropriate means of educating that mass would mean not to care about our country's prosperity. We will wait in vain for the great mercantile companies, the improvements in industry, the cultivation of all branches of production, to give us rich sources of wealth if men do not dedicate themselves from their earliest years to acquiring the knowledge necessary for the profession they wish to embrace. And, stemming from the habit of keeping busy that they contracted early in life, they must be prepared not to look upon work as tedious. The impressions formed in childhood exercise an irresistible power over us, and often decide our happiness. It is difficult for anyone who has passed this beautiful period of life sunk in abandonment, who did not learn in childhood to stifle his natural inclination to idleness, and who failed to create the need to employ several hours of the day, not to regard work with horror later on, and to prefer poverty to achieving ease and comforts that he thinks too costly if the price is the sweat of his brow. With persons of this kind, can there be morality, can there be wealth, can there be prosperity?

The Study of Jurisprudence
(1835)

The constant progress observable in the capital's [Santiago] educational establishments daily offers us a reason to congratulate ourselves on the zeal of our young students, and the good direction that is being given to their natural talents, from which so much advantage will accrue if they are stimulated to spread out into a still vaster field, one more worthy of them and more appropriate to the demands of modern societies.[2]

At first sight, it appears that jurisprudence predominates unduly over the other branches of education. The number of individuals who cultivate the ecclesiastical, physical, mathematical, and medical sciences is relatively very small, and the group who apply themselves to literature and belles-lettres not large enough. It is true that, under republican institutions, there is hardly any study that can be compared in importance to that of the legal sciences. The less the power of men and the greater that of laws, there is all the more need for citizens to be familiar with them. The discussion of public affairs often demands extensive knowledge, not only in actual legislation but in the philosophy of law, in natural and international law, and in political economy (a branch that has very rightly been included in legal instruction in our country). And if there are not a certain number of members in a deliberative assembly with a full command of these sciences, and if their solid principles do not penetrate to a certain degree among the citizens of all classes, serious errors will often occur, internal and external peace will be threatened, and public opinion will not have the moderating influence that it ought to have, or perhaps will abandon itself to dangerous misconduct. We are so far from denying the importance of jurisprudence that we tend to look upon it as a necessary part of general education everywhere in the country, and all the more under a popular government. But we would not want to see it absorb everything. We could wish that the interest that we begin to see in studying our country's language and literature will not decline, and that such study will daily spread and be considered indispensable in the education of both sexes, especially among those classes which, owing to the place in society that they occupy, are destined to serve it as an ornament and an example. We could wish that the marvels of Nature, the physical economy of man, the laws of mind and heart, would find supporters among a certain number of young Chileans; and if we express the same desire in favor of those venerable sciences that concern the purity of dogma and the luster of religion, we are sure that sensible men will not accuse us of fanaticism. In fact, we would like to see the study of jurisprudence itself broadened and ennobled, to see the young lawyer extend his interests beyond the narrow and obscure circuit of legal practice. We would like to see him deepen the philosophical principles of this sublime science, and contemplate it in its relationship with the eternal bases of justice and general usefulness, and not to forget to temper its severity, making it pleasanter by the assiduous cultivation of philosophy and the humanities, without which there has never been an eminent jurist. Fortunately, the organization of this branch of knowledge in the *Instituto Nacional* [National Institute of Secondary Education] already possesses all the elements necessary to attain this object.

Latin and Roman Law

(1834)

All the arguments that are made against study of the Latin language, and which *El Valdiviano Federal* has reproduced at length in its last issue, can be reduced to only one: that the time spent on Latin can be employed in acquiring other, more useful knowledge.[3] This argument might have some force for us if we could see that foreign languages were being cultivated among us at the same rate as Latin is disappearing; if instead of Vergil or Quintus Curtius the young were reading Milton, Robertson, Racine, or Sismondi, and if the classes devoted to the natural sciences had a reasonable number of students in them. But this is not the case; Latin is disappearing, and we see nothing that replaces it. We also observe that persons who excel in modern knowledge are usually the same persons who have studied Latin, and that this was what should naturally have happened. The enumeration we are about to make of the usefulness of studying that language will serve as a reply to those who wish to see it forgotten and banned.

First, it is difficult to speak Spanish correctly if one does not possess its mother tongue, from which almost all its words and phrases derive, because it is so similar both in vocabulary and spirit. What causes the incorrect usage of a multitude of words that is so common among us, and the solecisms so often committed both in speech and in writing? It will be said, and correctly, that they come from not studying Spanish; but we must add that one of the things that makes the study of Spanish easier, and leads us most quickly and surely to the legitimate use of its words and sentences, is knowledge of the Latin tongue. It is a mistake to believe that correct Spanish is learned solely by studying the grammar of the Academy, or any other grammar.

In the second place, nothing enhances the acquisition of foreign languages more than previous knowledge of Latin. I am not referring to that superficial acquisition which consists of translating some easy book, and of following without effort a conversation about familiar subjects. Such an acquisition is no doubt worth something, and it is much rarer than one might think. But if we consider languages as one among many other means of achieving intellectual culture, which is the aspect under which *El Valdiviano* views them, we must go further: we must possess them in a way that lets us form an adequate idea of the value of their signs, and the different modifications and nuances that their connections and conditions impart to thought. Lacking this, it is not possible to follow the thread of a philosophical discussion or to understand the steps in analysis of abstract objects; and much less is it possible to perceive the value of works of genius, in which it can be said that the mode of expression is everything. For those who do not possess foreign languages to this degree, the compositions of Racine, La Fontaine, and Bossuet, or of Milton, Pope, and Byron (to say nothing of writers like Shakespeare and Montaigne), lose all their color and beauty. Such persons will understand the meaning in general terms, but will not grasp the spirit that informs masterworks of art, a taste for which demands total immersion on the part of the young people who cultivate them. To reach this point, we believe that the habit of philological analysis formed by the study of ancient languages is extremely useful. It is a master key that leads into the most difficult and abstruse features of other languages. If we discover the identity of those persons who best understand the French or English languages, and who are most capable of translating them correctly into our own, we will see that hardly one in a hundred of them has not had the preparation of which we speak.

In the third place, Latin is of supreme importance for the cultivation of belles-lettres, not only because without this means of expression it is impossible, or at least extremely difficult, to acquire modern foreign languages to the level that would enable us to perceive the merit of what has been written in them, but also because of the incomparable value of the immortal compositions of Latin orators, poets, and historians. We would like to have *El Valdiviano* tell us if it believes that the idea of reading Vergil and Cicero easily is of no value, or if it knows of some translated version that represents with reasonable fidelity the beauties of style and feeling in these and other Latin writers. Europe imbibed good taste in those works, and with the renaissance of Greek and Latin letters a new era dawned. Philosophy shook off the chains that had burdened human reason up to that time, and the sludge of Scholasticism disappeared from the sciences. Love of freedom increased with that resuscitated literature, whose inspirations are so dynamic in the productions of ancient eloquence. Everything changed. The same thing will happen among us. Given the auspicious natural gifts of Chilean youth, how much can we not expect of them, if they are not deluded by that spirit of literary vandalism which clips the wings of the noblest aspirations of genius; which, by gratifying sloth, tries to perpetuate barbarity, and condemns as outdated and archaic precisely the studies that pulled Europe out of archaism, and polished and civilized her?

In the fourth place, Latin is the language of the religion that we profess. Everyone who is capable of studying it is obliged to do so, if he is a Catholic, and if he is not content to hear the Church's prayers and sublime canticles without understanding them, and most particularly if he wishes to be instructed solidly in her doctrine and discipline.

In the fifth place, hardly any science exists that does not gain a great deal from knowledge of the ancient languages, for almost all their nomenclature is Latin or Greek. However, we do not believe that the *Instituto [Nacional]* requires previous knowledge of Latin of anyone in order to attend classes in mathematics or the natural sciences. This requisite is demanded of students who study the ecclesiastical sciences, and *El Valdiviano* itself recognizes that for them it is indispensable. It is also a requirement for legal studies, because Roman jurisprudence is considered to be one of the necessary ones and because many writers of glossaries and treatises on our system of law have written in Latin. And it is required for philosophy, for everyone who enters into that course of study does so with the intention of going on to the ecclesiastical and legal sciences.

But *El Valdiviano* believes that the study of Roman law is superfluous, and that it is harmful to read the writers of glossaries and treatises. As for Roman law, we believe that its importance to us and even to most modern nations is not regarded from its true perspective. We believe that even the clearest and most methodical legislation needs commentaries, for the hardest task is not to understand laws (and it is no easy matter to understand ours), but to become imbued with their spirit and know how to apply them correctly. These are very delicate operations in which, because it is easy for the keenest intellect to go astray, it will never be superfluous to call to its aid the intelligence of those who have shed light on this difficult area of human knowledge. The jurist must apply the laws to every aspect of life, and an exact classification of all of them is therefore necessary for him; and as the number of laws is always infinitely less than the number of cases (and these vary infinitely among themselves), without a thread to lead him through this intricate labyrinth he is in danger of stumbling and getting lost at every step. Now, Roman law, source of the Spanish legislation that governs us, is the law's best commentary. All of our commentators and glossarists have studied it; they have recourse to it to elucidate obscure points, to restrict one decision, to broaden another, and to establish a proper harmony among them all. Those who regard it as a foreign body of law are themselves strangers to our law.

In the writers of treatises there is no doubt a plethora of distinctions and subtleties; but all sciences have such excess, and that of zoology is neither more useful nor more innocent when it counts the hues that shimmer on a butterfly's wing, or that of botany when it describes the most insignificant features of a plant that is good for nothing. Nor will this be a reason to call zoology and botany useless sciences. The most useful and necessary things can be carried to excess, but that is not a good excuse for proscribing them.

If there is one nation that could dispense with studying Roman law and consulting treatises, it might be France, which not long ago reduced its laws to a complete, methodical body adapted to the intelligence of all. These are qualities at the farthest possible remove from the tangled and obscure chaos of Spanish legislation; and yet Roman law is eagerly cultivated in France, is illustrated with new commentaries, and the national codes are also glossed and commented upon.

But it is said that Justinian was a tyrannical prince, and that consequently, like good republicans, we must consign to the flames everything that comes to us from such an impure source. Let us do the same, then, with the *Siete Partidas*, which are a copy of the Roman

Pandects, and with that multitude of compilations and decrees laid down by the Ferdinands, Philips, and Charleses at a time when the monarchs of Castile were no less despotic and arbitrary than the emperors of the East. But we need not do either one thing or the other. The constitutional form of a state may be detestable and its civil laws excellent. Roman laws have passed the test of time; they have been tried in the crucible of philosophy, and have been found to agree with the principles of equity and strict reason. Let us distinguish public law from private law. No one studies the former, which is bad, in the Pandects; but the Romans' private law is good, it is ours, and there is scarcely anything in it that needs to be simplified or improved. Those same emperors who horrify *El Valdiviano* so much made important reforms in it. These reforms have made it much better than the iron code of the Roman republic, and most of the cultured nations of Europe have adopted it.

Moreover, Roman law is necessary to canon law and to international law; if we possess the noble curiosity to explore the institutions and laws of other nations, and to consult their books of jurisprudence in an effort to utilize the large amount of material they contain that is good and applicable to ourselves, we must familiarize ourselves with Roman law, whose principles and language are those of Germany, Italy, France, Holland, and part of Great Britain.

Address Delivered at the Inauguration of the University of Chile,

17 September 1843

His Excellency the Patron of the University
Ladies and Gentlemen:

The university council has asked me to express, in the faculty's name, our profound appreciation for the distinctions and trust with which the supreme government has been so good as to honor us.[4] I must also transmit the university's gratitude for the kind remarks with which the Minister of Public Instruction has alluded to its members. As for myself, I know all too well that I owe those distinctions and that trust much less to my aptitudes and energies than to my longstanding devotion (this is the only quality I can claim without being presumptuous), my longstanding devotion, I repeat, to the spread of enlightenment and sound principles, and the strenuous dedication with which I have pursued certain branches of study, never interrupted at any time in my life and never abandoned even in the midst of very important tasks. I feel the weight of that trust, I know the scope of the obligations that it imposes, and I understand the magnitude of the efforts it demands. This responsibility would be overwhelming were it to fall upon a single individual or a different order of intelligence, one much better prepared than mine has been. But I am encouraged by the cooperation of my distinguished colleagues on the council and the entire faculty of the university.

Fortunately for me, the law has decreed that guidance of the university's studies must be the common task of the faculty. With the assistance of the council, with the enlightened and patriotic activity of the different schools, and under the government's auspices, under the influence of freedom, which is the living spirit of Chilean institutions, I can confidently expect that this precious stream of knowledge and talent that is already in the university's possession will increase and spread swiftly, to the benefit of religion, morals, and freedom itself, as well as material interests.

Ladies and gentlemen, the university would not be worthy to occupy a place among our social institutions if (as some dim echoes of old oratory murmur) the cultivation of science and letters could be viewed as dangerous from a moral or political point of view. Morality (which I consider inseparable from religion) is the very life of society; freedom is the stimulus that imparts healthy vigor and productive activity to social institutions. Whatever sullies the purity of morality, whatever hampers the orderly but free development of man's faculties both individually and collectively, and even whatever exercises them uselessly, must be denied a part in the state's organization by a wise government. But in this century, in Chile—in this gathering, which I regard as a solemn homage to the importance of intellectual culture—in this gathering, which by a very significant coincidence is the first ceremony to take place today in celebration of the glorious date of our national holiday, the anniversary of Chilean freedom, I do not feel called upon to defend science and letters against the sophistries of the eloquent philosopher of Geneva [Jeau Jacques Rousseau]. Nor do I need to defend them against the fears of pusillanimous spirits who, with their eyes fixed on the reefs that have caused many a rash sailor to come to grief, do not want reason ever to unfurl her sails. They would willingly condemn her to eternal inertia, which is more harmful to the causes they defend than the abuse of knowledge would be. Not to refute what has been refuted a thousand times, but to illustrate the connection that exists between the sentiments just expressed by the minister of public instruction and those with which the university is imbued, allow me to add to the honorable minister's words some general ideas about the moral and political influence of science and letters, about the mission of literary institutions, and about the special tasks to which, in my opinion, our university faculties are called in the present state of the Chilean nation.

Ladies and gentlemen, you know that all truths touch one another, from those which guide the orbit of the planets in the vastness of space, which determine the marvelous agencies on which life and movement depend in the universe of matter, which compose the structure of animals, of plants, of the inorganic mass beneath our feet, which reveal intimate phenomena of the soul in the mysterious theater of consciousness, to the truths that express the actions and reactions of political power, those that form the immovable foundations of morality, even those that determine the precise conditions for development of industry and those that lead and nourish the arts. Achievements along all lines attract each other, become linked together, urge each other on. And when I say "achievements along all lines" I certainly include those that are most important to the happiness of mankind, namely achievements in the moral and political sphere. What accounts for this progress of civilization, this yearning for social betterment, this thirst for freedom? If we wish to find out, let us compare Europe and our fortunate America with the sullen empires of Asia, where the iron scepter of despotism presses on necks already bowed by ignorance, or with the African hordes, where man—scarcely better than the brutes—is like them an article of trade for his own brethren? Who first struck the sparks of civil liberty in enslaved Europe? Was it not letters? Was not the intellectual heritage of Greece and Rome reclaimed, after a long dark age, by the human spirit? It was there indeed that the vast political movement began which has restored their freeborn status to so many enslaved races. This movement, propagated in all possible ways and continually accelerated by the printing press and by letters, whose surges are in some places fast and in others slow but everywhere necessary and inevitable, will at last sweep away all the obstacles placed in its path and will cover the surface of the globe. All truths touch one another, and I extend this statement to religious dogma, to theological truth. Those who imagine that there can be a secret antipathy between religion and letters slander either one or the other, I do not know which. Indeed, I believe that a close connection exists, must exist, between positive revelation and that other universal revelation that speaks to all men in the book of nature. If diseased minds have abused their knowledge to impugn dogma, what does that prove, except the condition of all human affairs? If human reason is feeble, if it stumbles and falls, then it must be provided even more urgently with adequate food and solid support. For this curiosity, this noble daring of the mind that causes it to confront the secrets of nature and the enigmas of the future, cannot be extinguished without simultaneously rendering the mind incapable of everything great, insensible to everything beautiful, generous, sublime, and holy, without poisoning the springs of morality, without making religion itself ugly and vile. I have said that all truths touch one another and even so, I do not think I have said enough. All human faculties form a system, in which there can be no regularity and harmony without the contribution of each. Not a single fiber (if I may express it thus) of the soul can be paralyzed without weakening the others.

Science and letters, apart from this social value, apart from the varnish of amenity and elegance that they give to human societies and which we must also count among their benefits, possess an intrinsic merit of their own insofar as they increase the pleasures and joys of the individual who cultivates and loves them. They are exquisite pleasures, untouched by the turbulence of the senses; they are pure joys, in which the soul does not say to herself:

> Medio de fonte leporum surgit amari aliquid, quod in ipsis floribus angit.
> Lucretius
>
> [From amid the spring of delight a whiff of something bitter rises pushing up amid the beauty of the flowers.]

The sciences and literature bear within themselves the reward for the labors and vigils spent on them. I am not referring to the glory that lights the great scientific discoveries or the aureole of immortality that crowns works of genius. Few are permitted to hope for these. I am referring to pleasures more or less lofty, more or less intense, that are common to all ranks in the republic of letters. For the intellect, as for other human faculties, activity is in itself a pleasure: one that, as the Scottish philosopher [Thomas Brown] has said, shakes out of us that inertia to which we would otherwise succumb, to our own detriment as well as society's. Every path that science opens to the cultivated intellect displays enchanting vistas; each new aspect discovered in the ideal type of beauty makes the human heart tremble with delight, if it has been trained to admire and feel beauty. In the retreat of meditation the cultivated intellect hears the thousand voices of nature's chorus; myriad strange visions flit about the solitary lamp that lights its vigils. For intellect alone, the order of nature unfolds on an immense scale; for it alone, creation clothes herself in all her magnificence, all her splendid garments. But letters and science, while they give delicious play to intellect and imagination, also elevate moral character. They weaken the power of sensual seduction and strip of their terrors most of the vicissitudes of fortune. Except for the humble and contented resignation of the religious soul, they are the best preparation for the moment of death. They bring comfort to the sickbed, to the exile's place of refuge, to the prison, to the scaffold. On the eve of drinking the hemlock, Socrates illumined his cell with the most sublime speculations on the future of human destinies that have been left to us by pagan antiquity. Dante composed his *Divina Commedia* in exile. [Antoine Laurent] Lavoisier asked his executioners for a short reprieve to finish an important investigation. [André] Chénier wrote his last verses while awaiting death within instants, leaving them unfinished when he went to the scaffold:

> *Comme un dernier rayon, comme un dernier zéphyre*
> *anime le fin d'un beau jour*
> *au pied de l'échafaud j'essaie encor ma lyre.*

> [As a last ray, as a last breeze
> stirs the end of a beautiful day,
> at the scaffold's foot I test my lyre.]

Such are the compensations of letters; such are their consolations. I myself, though I follow their most favored adorers from afar, have been enabled to share their benefits and taste their joys. Letters adorned the morning of my life with joyous bursts of light and still retain some glimmerings in my soul, like a flower that lends beauty to ruins. Letters have done still more for me; they have sustained me in my long pilgrimage and guided my steps to this soil of freedom and peace, this adoptive country that has offered me such benevolent hospitality.

Another point of view exists, in which perhaps we wrestle with specious concerns. Are universities, are literary bodies, the proper instruments for the diffusion of learning? I can hardly imagine how this question can be asked in an age which is so peculiarly an age of association and representation; in an age where societies for agriculture, trade, industry, and charity abound everywhere, in the age of representative governments. Europe and the United States of America, our models in so many respects, will provide the answer to that question.

If the diffusion of knowledge is one of the most important functions of letters (for without it they will merely offer a few points of light among dense clouds of darkness), than the bodies chiefly responsible for the rapidity of literary communication confer essential benefits both on learning and on mankind. No sooner has a new truth sprung up in the mind of an individual than the whole republic of letters appropriates it. The scholars of Germany, of France, of the United States, recognize its value, its consequences, and its applications. In this propagation of knowledge each of the academies, the universities, forms a reservoir where all scientific acquisitions tend to accumulate continually; and it is from these centers that they most easily spill over into the different classes of society. The University of Chile has been established with this special aim in mind. If it is true to the intent of the legislation that has reorganized it, if it responds to the desires of our government, the university will be an eminently expansive and disseminative body.

Others claim that the encouragement given to scientific instruction ought to be given instead to primary education. Certainly, I am one of those who consider general instruction—the education of the people— as one of the most important and privileged aims to which a government can turn its attention. This is a primary and urgent need, the basis of all solid progress, the indispensable foundation of republican institutions. But for this very reason, I believe that the development of literary and scientific education is both necessary and urgent. Nowhere has the elementary instruction demanded by the working classes, who constitute the larger part of mankind, become general except in places where science and letters have previously flourished. I am not saying that the cultivation of letters and science necessarily brings in its train the spread of elementary education, though it is undeniable that science and letters have a natural tendency to spread when artificial causes do not prevent them from doing so. What I am saying is that the first is an indispensable condition of the second; that where the first condition does not exist it is impossible for the other to be carried out properly, whatever the efforts of government. The diffusion of knowledge involves one or more hearths from which light is emitted and spread; and this light, expanding little by little through the intervening spaces, will at last seep into the furthest levels of society. Making education universal requires a large number of carefully trained teachers, and the skills of these, the ultimate distributors of knowledge, are in themselves more or less distant emanations of the great scientific and literary depositories. Good teachers, good books, good methods, and good guidance of education are necessarily the work of a very advanced intellectual culture. Literary and scientific instruction is the source from which elementary teaching is nourished and brought to life, just as, in a well-organized society, the wealth of the class most favored by fortune is the wellspring from which flows the sustenance of the working classes and the people's welfare. But in reorganizing the university the law has not been content to trust only in knowledge's natural tendency to spread, for in our day the printing press represents a power and mobility unknown before. It has closely joined the two kinds of education; it has given one sector of the university faculty the special task of supervising primary instruction, of observing its movement, of aiding its propagation, of contributing to its progress. Above all, encouragement of the nation's religious and moral instruction is a duty that each member of the university assumes by the mere fact of belonging to it.

The legislation that has reestablished the old university on new foundations, adjusted to the present state of civilization and the needs of Chile, indicates the great aims to which this faculty must be dedicated. The minister, our vice-patron, has also stated the aims that presided over the reorganization of the university, the goals proposed for it by the legislators, and the hopes that it is called upon to fulfill. He has expressed these ideas so well that, were I to continue along the same lines, I could make only an idle commentary on his address. However, I shall add a few brief observations which I believe have their importance.

Encouragement of the ecclesiastical sciences, whose aim is to educate worthy ministers of religion and ultimately to provide an adequate religious and moral education to the population of the republic, is the first and most important of these objectives. But there is another aspect under which we must regard the university's dedication to the cause of morality and religion. While cultivation of the ecclesiastical sciences is important for the functioning of the sacerdotal ministry, it is also important to disseminate an adequate knowledge of the dogma and annals of the Christian faith among all the youth who participate in literary and scientific education. I do not think it necessary to prove that this must be an integral part of general education, indispensable for any profession and even for any man who aspires to occupy more than the humblest place in society.

The broadest field, and the one most susceptible of useful applications, opens before the schools of law and political science. You have heard it said that practical usefulness, positive results, social improvements, are what the government chiefly expects from the university; they are what must chiefly justify its efforts to the country. Heirs to the legislation of Spain, we must purge it of the blots that it acquired under the evil influence of despotism. We must sweep away the inconsistencies that mar a work to which so many centuries, so many alternately dominating interests, so many contradictory inspirations, have contributed. We have to adjust it, restore it to republican institutions. And what purpose can be more important, or grander, than the formation and perfecting of our basic laws, the swift and impartial administration of justice, the protection of our rights, the integrity of our commercial transactions, the peace of the domestic hearth? The university, I daresay, will not subscribe to the prejudice that condemns the study of Roman law as useless or harmful; on the contrary, I believe that it will give new stimulus to that study, and will establish it on broader bases. The university will probably view such study as the best apprenticeship in juridical and forensic logic. On this point, let us hear the testimony of a man who certainly cannot be accused of partiality to ancient doctrines, a man who has probably gone to extremes in his enthusiasm for popular emancipation and democratic leveling. "Science stamps its seal on the law; its logic establishes the principles, formulates the axioms, deduces the consequences, and adduces boundless ramifications from the idea of what is just, by reflecting it. From this point of view, Roman law has no equal: some of its principles may be disputed, but its method, its logic, its scientific system, have made it and keep it superior to all other bodies of law. Its texts are master works of juridical style; its method is that of geometry applied in all strictness to moral thought." This is what [Jean Louis Eugène] Lerminier affirms, and before him Leibniz had said, *"In iurisprudentia regnant [Romani]."*

Dixi saepius post scripta geometrarum nihil extare quod vi ac subtilitate cum Romanorum iurisconsultorum scriptis comparari possit; tantum nervi inest, tantum profunditatis." [The Romans dominate in jurisprudence. I have said very often that there is nothing, after the writings of the geometricians, that can be compared for force and subtlety with the writings of the Roman jurisconsults; there is so much vigor, so much depth].

The university will also study the special features of Chilean society from an economic viewpoint, which presents problems that are no less vast and no less difficult. The university will develop the field of statistics, will examine the results of Chilean statistical figures, and will read in their numbers the expression of our material interests. For in this as in other branches of study, the university is entirely Chilean: if it borrows from Europe the deductions of science, it does so to apply them to Chile. All the paths that the work of its faculty and students must follow converge on one center—our country.

Following the same procedure, medicine will investigate the peculiar modifications that confer upon Chilean man his climate, his customs, and his nutrition. It will dictate the rules of private and public hygiene. It will spare no effort to extract from epidemics the secret of their germination and devastating activity; and, insofar as possible, it will encourage widespread knowledge of simple means of preserving and restoring health. Shall I now enumerate the positive uses of the mathematical and physical sciences, their applications to a nascent industry which has only a few simple, rude arts in operation, an industry that does not have clear procedures, that has no machines and none of the commonest tools? Shall I enumerate the applications of those sciences to a land crisscrossed by veins of metal, a soil fertile in vegetable wealth and foodstuffs, a soil on which science has scarcely bestowed a passing glance?

But, while I favor encouraging practical applications, I am far from believing that the university should adopt the unworthy slogan of *cui bono*? Nor should it fail to appreciate the full knowledge of nature in all its different departments, in all its true value. First of all because, to guide practice adequately, intellect must rise to the highest summit of science, to the appreciation of its general formulas. Undoubtedly the university will not confuse practical applications with the manipulations of a blind empiricism. And secondly, as I said before, cultivation of the contemplative intelligence which tears the veil from the secrets of the physical and moral universe is a positive result in itself, and of the greatest importance. On this point, so as not to repeat myself, I shall quote the words of an English scholar who has honored me with his friendship. Doctor [Neil] Arnott says:

> It has been a prejudice that persons thus instructed in general laws, have their attention too much divided, and can know nothing perfectly. The very reverse, however, is true; for general knowledge renders all particular knowledge more clear and precise . . . The laws of philosophy can be compared to keys that give admission to the most delightful gardens that fancy can picture; or to a magic power, which removes a veil from the face of the universe, and discloses endless charms which ignorance sees not. The informed man, in the world, may be said to be always surrounded by what is known and friendly to him, while the ignorant man is as one in a land of strangers and enemies . . . he who, through general laws, studies the *Book of Nature*, converts the great universe into the material of a sublime history which tells of God, and which may worthily occupy his attention to the end of his days.

Ladies and gentlemen, I shall go on to that literary department which possesses in a peculiar and eminent degree the quality of polishing manners; which refines language, rendering it a faithful, beautiful, and transparent vehicle for ideas; which, through the study of other languages both living and dead, puts us in touch with antiquity and with the freest and most civilized nations of our time; which makes us hear, not through the imperfect medium of translations (which are always and inevitably flawed), but alive and sonorous and vibrant, the accents of foreign erudition and eloquence. It is the department which, through its contemplation of ideal beauty and its reflection in works of genius, purifies taste and makes daring flights of fancy harmonize with the inalienable rights of reason; which, at the same time as it initiates the soul into arduous studies (necessary accompaniments to beautiful literature and indispensable preparations for all the sciences and indeed all the paths of life), forms the primary discipline of the intellectual and moral being, teaches the eternal laws of intelligence in order to guide and affirm its progress, and explores the deep folds of the heart to preserve it from lamentable error and establish on solid foundations the rights and duties of man. Enumerating these different aims, ladies and gentlemen, means presenting to you the university's program, as I understand it, in the philosophy and humanities section. Among those aims, I believe that the study of our language is of the utmost importance. I will never argue for the exaggerated purism that condemns everything new in language; on the contrary, I believe that the multitude of new ideas that daily pass from literary intercourse into general circulation demands new words for its expression. Shall we find in the writings of Cervantes and Fray Luis de Granada (nay, I need not go so far back in time), shall we find in the writings of [Tomás de] Iriarte and [Leandro Fernández de] Moratín adequate means, lucid signs, to express the common ideas that drift nowadays over reasonably well-educated minds, to express social thought? New institutions, new laws, new customs, their substance and forms everywhere varied in our eyes, versus old words, old phraseology! This, in addition to being a useless attempt—for it would quarrel with the first object of language, which is the clear and easy transmission of thought—would be totally impossible to achieve. But language can be broadened, it can be enriched, and can accommodate itself to all the demands of society and even to those of fashion, which exercises an undeniable influence on literature without adulterating it, without undermining its constructions, without doing violence to its genius. Is the language of Chateaubriand and Villemain different from that of Pascal and Racine, perchance? And does not the language of the first two writers perfectly express the social thought of present-day France, so different from the France of Louis XIV? Furthermore, were we to allow that kind of bombast to spread, were we to embrace all the whims of extravagant neologisms, our America would soon reproduce the confusion of languages, dialects, and jargon, the Babel-like chaos of the Middle Ages, and ten nations would lose one of their most precious instruments for communication and trade.

The university will encourage not only the study of languages but that of foreign literatures. Yet I do not know whether I am deceiving myself. The opinion of those who believe that we must receive the synthetic results of European enlightenment, neglecting the examination of its bases, exempting ourselves from the use of analytical methods (the only way to acquire true knowledge), will not find many votes in the university. Respecting the opinions of others as I do, and demanding only the right to discuss them, I must confess that for the purpose of nourishing the intellect, educating it, and making it think for itself, it would be just as inappropriate to accept the moral and political conclusions of Herder, for example, without the study of ancient and modern history, as it would be to adopt Euclid's theorems without the previous intellectual labor of demonstrating them. Ladies and gentlemen, I believe that Herder is one of the writers who have most usefully served humanity: he has given history all its dignity by demonstrating in it the designs of Providence and the destinies to which the human race is called on this earth. But Herder himself did not try to supplant the knowledge of events, but to illustrate them, to explain them; nor can his doctrine be appreciated except through prior historical studies. Replacing that knowledge by deductions and formulas would be like giving our youths a skeleton instead of a living representation of social man; it would be like giving them a collection of aphorisms instead of placing before their eyes the ever-changing, instructive, colorful, panoramic view of institutions, customs, and revolutions of great nations and great individuals. It would mean depriving human experience of the salutary power of advice at precisely the age when it is most receptive to lasting impressions. It would mean depriving the poet of an inexhaustible vein of images and colors. And I believe that what I am saying about history must be applied to all other branches of knowledge. Thus intellect finds itself obliged to undeniably long yet pleasant studies. For nothing makes teaching more insipid than abstractions, and nothing makes it more easy and agreeable than the method which, by furnishing the memory, simultaneously exercises the mind and exalts the imagination. Reasoning must engender the theorem; examples etch the lessons deeply.

In the course of this very rapid review, ladies and gentlemen, how could I fail to mention, albeit briefly, the most enchanting of literary vocations, the aroma of literature, the Corinthian capital, so to speak, of cultivated society? Above all, how could I fail to mention the sudden excitement that has caused to appear on our horizon that constellation of youthful minds who cultivate poetry with such ardor? I will speak candidly: there are errors in their verses, and things in them that a severe and censorious mind condemns. But correctness is the result of study and years. Who can expect it from those who, in a moment of exaltation that is at once poetic and patriotic, have burst into this new arena, determined to prove that a divine fire, of which they thought themselves deprived by unjust prejudice, also burns in Chilean hearts? Brilliant examples, and not limited to the sex which until now has cultivated letters almost exclusively among us, had already shown this. Now they have refuted that prejudice again. And I do not know whether my judgment has been misled by a partial predisposition toward the efforts of youthful intelligences. I say what I feel: I find in these works undeniable sparks of real talent, and in a few of them even true poetic genius. In some of these works I find rich and original imagination, felicitously daring expressions, and (something that seems possible only by dint of long practice) a harmonious and fluid versification that intentionally seeks out difficulties in order to wrestle with them, and emerges triumphant from this bold test. To encourage our young poets, perhaps the university will say, "If you do not want your name to be confined between the Andes and the Pacific Ocean, too narrow an area for the ample aspirations of talent; if you want coming generations to read you, then study well, beginning with the study of your native language. Do more than this: write about subjects that are worthy of your country and posterity. Abandon the bland tones of Anacreon's and Sappho's lyres; nineteenth-century poetry has a higher mission. Let moral feeling throb in your works. Let each of you say to himself, as he takes up the pen, 'I, a priest of the Muses, sing for pure and innocent souls.' [*Musarum sacerdos, virginibus puerisque canto.* (Horace)]

And has not our young republic already presented you with magnificent themes? Celebrate its great days; weave garlands for its heroes, consecrate the shroud of the country's martyrs." The university will also remind the young of that piece of advice from a great mentor of our times. Goethe said, "Art must be the measuring stick of imagination, and must transform it into poetry."

Art! Some who hear this word, even though taken from Goethe's own lips, will place me among the supporters of the conventional rules which for long usurped the name of art. I solemnly protest against such a view, and do not believe that my past actions justify it. I do not find art in the sterile precepts of a school, in the inexorable unities, in the bronze wall raised between different styles and genres, in the chains that some, invoking the names of Aristotle and Horace, have tried to place upon the poet, attributing to them things that they never thought of. But I do believe that there is an art based on the impalpable, ethereal relationships of ideal beauty, relationships that are delicate but accessible to the keen gaze of the properly trained genius. I believe that an art exists that is a guide to the imagination, even in its most impetuous transports. Without that art I believe that imagination, instead of including in its works the type of ideal beauty, will produce aborted sphinxes, enigmatic and monstrous creations. This is my literary profession of faith. Freedom in everything. But in orgies of the imagination I do not see freedom; I see instead licentious intoxication.

As a counterweight—on the one hand, to the servile docility that receives everything without examining it; and on the other to the unbounded license that rebels against the authority of reason and against the purest and noblest instincts of the human heart—freedom will undoubtedly be the university's theme in all its different departments.

But I must not abuse your patience any longer. The subject is a vast one; to review it superficially is all that has been possible for me. I regret not having occupied more worthily the attention of the estimable audience that I see around me, and thank you for the indulgence with which you have so graciously heard me.

Address Delivered at the Opening
of the Colegio Santo Tomás,
4 August 1848

Ladies and Gentlemen:

The speakers who preceded me have presented such a clear picture of the nature and aims of this new educational establishment that I feel it unnecessary to occupy much of your attention on the subject.[5] But it would not be fair to pass over a feature which characterizes it, and which seems important to me: the total absence of any concern for profit. This noble disinterestedness on the part of a religious community, whose lack of funds even for its ordinary expenses is public knowledge, is highly meritorious. And I have no doubt that you will judge correctly the spontaneous guarantee that is being offered to the public in this regard, through a periodic statement of income and gifts to the establishment. Reduced to such easily determined details as the low tuition rates offered to students on the one hand, the salaries of professors from outside the community, teaching materials, and the maintenance of the building's comfort and cleanliness on the other, we can all judge of the accuracy of this periodic report. It will bear constant witness to the pure motives and useful aims with which the plan has been conceived, and which must be carried out in order to assure the public's support.

The venerable prelates of this house and the reverend Director of Studies have two objects in mind: improving the teaching imparted here to those who embrace religious studies; and contributing to general education. You can imagine how important both these aims are. But can they be completely reconciled? I am convinced that they can. The branches of preparatory education are the same for the young man who, by embracing the monastic life, aspires to fulfill the arduous duties it imposes, as for the youth who is trying to acquire that common body of knowledge so indispensable today for all the pursuits of life.

Just as the missionary who spreads the seeds of the divine word in the jungles of a savage tribe must learn the language of his unlettered flock, speak to their rude understanding and move their hearts, enter the depths of their souls and plant the fertile seed from which will sprout correct ideas and pure feelings, and must be thoroughly aware of their customs, their beliefs, their concerns; just so must one who proclaims the evangelical doctrine in a civilized country place himself on the level of the minds toward which he is aiming his instructions and warnings. If he did not possess the knowledge that today forms the basis of intellectual culture, he would debase his holy mission. He must be well acquainted with geography, history, literature, and philosophy, as well as those ideas about the exact and natural sciences of which even persons of mediocre education can scarcely afford to be ignorant. He must speak the language of educated people, and clothe whatever he says and writes in the urbane and decorous language that society requires. I am not saying that he must succumb to the frivolous demands of fashion. His dignity will not allow this; and good taste itself, which always requires perfect agreement between substance and external accidents, will counsel him to try to make himself attractive without ceasing to be modest, simple, grave, and solemn. What is the cause, ladies and gentlemen, of the pro-religious and Catholic resurgence that is observable in European society? You may be sure that the literature, philosophy, and scientific knowledge of a considerable number of the clergy have played no small part in this fortunate revolution.

And if it is necessary to teach humane letters in convents of the regular clergy, why should the doors be closed to those who wish to learn about them simply to be able to carry out their social duties usefully in ordinary life? Our population is growing; the institutions of learning open to secular students scarcely have room for the youth that is being taught in them. Preparatory classes—those of most interest to the community in general—have two serious defects. When they are free, they are very crowded, and the excess number of students over-whelms the professors and is deleterious to teaching. When they are not free, the tuition paid in them makes them inaccessible to a large proportion of those who, if they were better taught and distributed all over the nation, would contribute to its improvement. They would be a credit to it, and would constantly render broader, more real, more intimately appreciated and felt, the benefits of our political institutions, and thus these institutions would receive all the development, all the perfection that they hope for. For in democratic governments even more than in others, the spread of political rights is intimately linked to the spread of this indispensable secondary education. The need for primary schools is undeniable, but they are no more than a means for acquiring useful knowledge. Ideas must be imparted, wholesome ideas disseminated, the mind developed as well as the heart. It is not so much a question of easing the apprenticeship of professional ministries as of making general that kind of education which in other countries forms part of primary instruction and is so rudimentary in ours. It is vitally necessary to multiply the schools that broaden and vivify general edu-cation. The present tendency in human affairs is to generalize more and more, until the whole of humankind is included within its circle.

Some will exclaim, "Dream, chimera, utopia!" Ladies and gentlemen, I have a profound faith in social perfectibility. I do not understand it without cultivation of moral feelings, nor is it intelligible for me without cultivation of the intellect. The dismal prejudice that looks upon the ignorance and degradation in which most of humanity now lies as a necessary inheritance must be far from our thoughts. Fulfillment of our vows is still far away; perhaps it will never be realized in all its aspects. But it is the end toward which we must all move and must try to reach, insofar as our efforts permit.

> *Est quodam tenus, si non datur ultra.*
> (HORACE, *EPISTLES*)

> [It is something to have made some advance, even if one is not allowed to go further.]

This is a sacred right of peoples, all the more important because more necessary to the appropriate exercise of other rights. And hence it is an obligation that cannot be forgotten governments, by the classes favored by fortune, by literary institutions, and—let me also add—by religious institutions. The venerable prelates of this school and the reverend Director of Studies have understood this.

Ladies and gentlemen, the history of humane letters attests to a fact that everyone knows, a fact so commonly acknowledged that the speakers whose brilliant speeches you have just heard have not needed to emphasize it. But why should I too not recall something that writers of all nations and all beliefs have recognized as an important service of the religious orders to the cause of civilization and humanity? It was they who sheltered literature when it was dying, when the successive waves of northern hordes submerged the degraded Greek and Roman culture; the cloisters saw the dawn of the happy days that witnessed the restoration of letters. From the solitary hearth that had served them as a refuge, they spread over the face of the earth; and not only did they recover their ancient sway, but broadened it with new conquests. They polished the rude peoples who had tried to extinguish them, and scattered their reborn light over a new world, the world that we inhabit. With the Cross, the sacred symbol of regenerate humanity—with the standard of peace and charity that the sons of Dominic, of Francis, of Augustine, and of Pedro Nolasco brought to our America—sacred letters arrived in majestic procession: the language of Cicero, Lactantius, and Jerome; the philosophy of Aristotle; the jurisprudence of Spain. A legion of historians, combining with the vividness of their narration the ingenuousness and candor that are the sign of primitive literatures, lauded the deeds of our ancestors on this soil that they colonized. The sound of sublime poetry was heard in the midst of the conquering hosts, and in this uttermost southern region, a Spanish soldier wrote on the bark of trees the noblest of Spanish epics. Later came natural and exact sciences, the renewed philosophy of the Enlightenment, and the cultivation of foreign languages. That precious plant, though stripped of its green leaves, maintained a trace of life in the cloister during the dark winter of the Middle Ages and has grown and been enriched, filling the world.

And could the cloisters be closed to the brilliant descendants of those sciences which, threatened by complete extinction, frightened and weeping, took refuge there, preserved their greatest works there, and reemerged from their narrow confines confident, active, and fruitful? Or could they disdain to bring them, as recompense for their old hospitality, part of the rich results in which they glory today? Of course not. The solemn retreat of the cloisters, which invites philosophical meditation, has no quarrel with studies that purify the heart by elevating the mind. Rather, that retreat is appropriate to give humane letters a purer luster, which they have not always been able to maintain in the present world's mingling of interests and passions. The study of a varied literature is equally appropriate to give to the religious orders' peculiar studies the breadth and sophistication that they lack. This is the dual task to which, I believe, those who direct instruction in religious schools are called; it is also the dual object of the establishment whose inauguration we are witnessing today.

Let us then salute it joyfully, with the enthusiasm that it deserves. Let us cherish the hope that its efforts—and, I may add with truth and justice, the sacrifices of the worthy prelates who have conceived its idea, have accepted it and promoted it—will not be fruitless. The influence of the reverend Director of Studies is so well known to everyone that I do not think it necessary to offend his modesty by speaking of it. I will only say that the thought has been his, and the activity and persistence with which he has brought it into being are also his. His love for letters, his cultivated intelligence, aided by teachers of recognized merit, makes success certain.

Let us congratulate this house for possessing such a worthy member, and the reverend Director of Studies for having been able to count on the cooperation of learned and pious prelates, zealous like him for the honor of their community and no less desirous of contributing to public service, which in this case is completely in harmony with the aims of their holy school. I agree whole-heartedly with the prayer with which he ended his speech. May Heaven bless this newborn establishment, and may it prosper to the benefit of religion and of our fatherland!

Report on the Progress
of Public Instruction
for the Five-Year Period
1844–1848
(1848)

His Excellency:
Ladies and Gentlemen:

I am performing the duty expected of me by Article 24 of the Rules for the Council of the University.[6] In accordance with it, I shall draw your attention to four points: the present state of public instruction; an enumeration of the improvements that have been introduced into it; their results; and the obstacles that have been placed in its way, together with a summary of events closely connected with public instruction and a list of the members of the university who have died and who had distinguished themselves by their efforts on its behalf. I shall try to be brief and to flesh out these indications to the best of my ability.

The first three are so closely linked together that, for the sake of brevity and clarity of expression, I think it best not to separate them.

As for the first, I have little to add to the beautifully clear picture presented to the two Chambers by the minister [of Public Instruction], Vice-patron of the university, in his report of 11 September of this year. Beginning with primary instruction, comparison of our present situation with that of other civilized nations is dismal. Using as a basis the total number of persons who receive such instruction throughout the Republic, according to the figures that accompany this report, and adding to it the numbers for the province of Chiloé according to the very incomplete bulletin that exists in the offices of the Faculty of Humanities; adding to this an estimate of the numbers for the department of Concepción which could not be included in that report, and taking into account the inevitable lack of data with regard to other areas and even the province of Santiago, as well as the considerable number of very small schools that have escaped observation, and individuals of both sexes who are taught at home, I believe that we can fix the number of persons who receive the first seeds of mental culture at one in forty-five inhabitants. From these figures we may deduce that primary education reaches barely one-sixth of those eligible to receive it.

We must recognize that, of all the countries which enjoy a more or less advanced degree of civilization, none presents as many difficulties for extending primary education as does Chile. In many of our rural areas the inhabitants do not form compact nuclei of a certain size, like the hamlets and small villages of Europe and other countries in America. The traveler often searches in vain for these small groups of families to appear, and in places where he expected to find one of them, he can see only a broad stretch of land dotted with scattered houses that are very far apart, with almost no communication among them. How many of the people who live in this way can send their children to a school which, in addition, is a long distance away from most of them? The number of those who do avail themselves of the primary instruction offered them by the State and the municipalities bears no relationship either to the number of schools or the costs invested in them. The same families who, if concentrated in a town, might furnish thirty or forty pupils, barely contribute a small fraction of this number. In order to offer this aid to their children, even families who live at a reasonable distance have to submit to losing most of the not insignificant help that the children can provide, even at an early age, in daily chores and domestic tasks. Hence most families are reluctant to send them, or let them attend school only during the times of year when their help is least necessary. Therefore not only is school attendance limited, it is often interrupted. And so the precious seed that the government sows, at no little expense, can be described without exaggeration as yielding less than half of the harvest that it should.

The Faculty of Humanities has dedicated its efforts with unflagging zeal to the task entrusted to it, in the field of primary education, by the Basic Law of the University. The Faculty has paid special attention to the Normal School, to which our worthy Dean makes frequent visits of inspection, either unannounced or as a member of committees from the Faculty of Humanities. I am happy to be able to tell you that in the course of these visits he has observed that conditions there have gradually improved, thanks to the interest taken in it by our government and to the intelligence and assiduous activity of its very admirable director. Recently the plan of studies has been revised by the Faculty and by the Council, and has been approved by the government. At present it includes (in addition to reading, writing, and arithmetic) Spanish grammar, line drawing, cosmography, physical and descriptive geography, dogma and Christian ethics, fundamentals of the Faith, sacred and profane history, and singing. Its facilities are fairly comfortable, and will be entirely so when the building is finished, as it soon will be. Establishment of a boarding facility has rewarded the hopes placed in it. Strict discipline guarantees the students' good moral conduct. The students have practice teaching in an annex, and the proximity of the Farm Normal School has seemed a good means of imparting to future teachers some elementary knowledge of the theory and practice of agriculture, which, when later carried to the provinces, cannot fail to influence the progress of this useful industry that is of such great importance to Chile. Finally, to this extensive and varied instruction, lasting for three years, are added practical ideas of surveying, vaccination, French, and a few other subjects according to the director's judgment, which the students, especially the most advanced among them, study in the hours left free from their ordinary occupations.

The Faculty of Humanities, not content with supervising the Normal School and guiding its progress, and with inspecting the other schools in Santiago, has devoted itself to the revision of texts, readers, and programs. It has done still more; it has broadened the scope of its interest to include everything relating to primary instruction everywhere in the republic.

One member of the Faculty of Humanities—who has made primary education a special object of study, and to whom our government assigned the task of observing the organization of this branch of education in the most advanced nations of Europe and America—has recently returned. He will soon present the result of his demanding researches to the government, to the University, and to the public. I think it is fair to say, from the sample he has offered to the Faculty of

Humanities at one of its sessions, at which the Minister of Public Instruction was present and which I also had the honor to attend, that Don Domingo Faustino Sarmiento has collected a large amount of valuable data that can usefully be applied to our country, with the modifications required by circumstances. No material concerning primary instruction has been overlooked by our traveler; and the part of it that he excerpted from his voluminous manuscript, an enumeration of the means employed in other nations to defray the necessarily high costs of extensive primary instruction, open to all classes and in the truest sense popular, is not the least important part for us.

It would be useless for us to call upon the experience of other countries for a complete plan, adaptable to all of the Chilean territory, owing to the special circumstances that largely characterize it, and which I have already mentioned. But I can imagine that, in some towns and perhaps even in whole districts, it will not be difficult to adapt at least partially some of the systems that have passed the test of time in Europe and the United States of America, with results that have exceeded all expectations. Let me add that in this as in other aims, nothing would be less desirable than to aspire to that rigid uniformity which some people think of as perfection. Were we to submit to the same standard towns that abound in everything necessary to organize a good plan of primary instruction and towns that not only lack all those means but even the desire for improvement, we would defraud the former of what they have the right to expect and simultaneously do harm to the others. For these, Santiago, Valparaíso, Talca, Copiapó, and other well-organized cities in the Republic would represent models to be imitated and elements to be utilized.

I cannot end this picture of the condition, and the hopes, of primary education without offering the recognition they deserve to the brothers and nuns of the Sacred Heart. Dedicated through their order to this charitable ministry, they offer free education to a large number of children of both sexes, besides contributing to secondary education in separate establishments with suitable buldings constructed at their own expense, and with an intelligent system in which the ethical formation of the students is a special concern.

Preparatory and higher education present a most favorable picture, and in this aspect the accuracy of the statistics is much more trustworthy. The total is 3,400 students, a proportion of one in every 350 inhabitants. This proportion does not seem excessive in a country where the constitutional regime draws a large number of persons to the exercise of important functions, not only in the literary professions but also in the legislature, in municipal service, public offices, and the administration of justice, and in which the group of landowners and well-to-do persons grows proportionately larger every day.

As for secondary education, I would like to call your attention to something that I consider a lack. In schools for girls, women are given a type of general instruction suitable for all the circumstances of life, no doubt more or less complete but not considered as preparation for other studies. This is not true of youth of the male sex. Generally speaking, those who enter our secondary institutions are thinking of the acquisition of higher knowledge, necessary for the exercise of a particular profession: the law in most cases, the ecclesiastical, medical, or commercial professions, or that of surveyors or engineers in others. But very few attend classes with the sole aim of giving their minds that indispensable cultivation which, in an advanced society, is necessary to every individual who does not belong to the lowest classes. What supplies this lack to some degree is the large number of those who, having begun a literary career during their preparatory studies, leave it behind and carry into their second-level jobs that stream of enlightenment that they have been able to acquire during their unsuccessful attempt. And what is the use of time spent on certain studies that serve only to achieve higher and more important ones? What is the use, for example, of the two or three years spent in acquiring Latin, which do not suffice even to understand that language? Obviously, an equal amount of time and effort spent on general studies would have been more useful for them and for society in general. If this general instruction were considered indispensable for all those who do not live from mechanical work though without looking forward to a literary profession, we would not see so frequently persons from other classes who, having received no more intellectual cultivation than elementary letters or who have spent a considerable part of their precious youth in secondary instruction, cannot appear politely in social intercourse, for they degrade it; nor can they exercise adequately the rights of a citizen and the duties to which they are called in the service of communities or in administration of the lower forms of justice. But the root of the evil does not lie in the organization of secondary studies as much as in the widespread prejudice that sees them as only a pathway to professional studies. Very few enter our secondary schools without this aspiration to professional occupations. A process is begun in which it is given to few to reach the goal they desire; and the inevitable result is the loss of a great deal of time and work, and the accumulation of a disproportionate number of students in certain classes that are only relatively useful, in which the excessive number of students exhausts the professor and does harm to teaching. What procedure can we find to lessen this evil? If there were a complete separation between preparatory teaching properly speaking and the general instruction to which we refer, if classes and courses were set up separately for both groups, it is probable that the latter would be looked on with scorn, and that youths would rush en masse to the former as enthusiastically as they do now. In the *Instituto Nacional*, the first step has been taken to fill the void that I have indicated; but in this matter, the result to which we aspire can only be the work of time. The superabundance of would-be lawyers will make their emoluments smaller, and as the number of incentives diminishes and the number of frustrated hopes for this difficult career grows larger, other professional careers will attract more students and general knowledge will be desired for its own sake.

These improvements in the establishments supported by the nation have had a favorable influence on private schools; and the need to make them substantially conform with the texts and programs of the official *Instituto* has had a good deal to do with this, for the latter is the place where students must be examined and passed if their studies are to avail them for the professional careers.

This privilege of taking examinations that qualify students for university-level studies has not been given to the Military Academy and the Seminary, except with regard to students educated in those establishments. The same privilege has been extended, with some additional restrictions, to the high schools of La Serena, San Felipe, Cauquenes, and Talca, which would find it difficult to prosper without this measure because the advantage of taking examinations valid for university-level studies, which the *Instituto* in Santiago enjoys, diverts too many youths from the provinces to the capital. However, the University Council is convinced that the privilege of the *Instituto*, which is a very heavy burden for its professors, must be maintained with the smallest possible number of exceptions. This is true because, as long as examinations are given there with due solemnity and severity, they will continue to exercise a beneficent influence on all other levels of education. Its progress and its improvements will be transmitted to them, and, without recourse to direct intervention, all the desired uniformity of teaching will occur.

Secondary and higher instruction at the *Instituto* includes the following branches: catechism, sacred history, and fundamentals of the Faith, in sequence; Spanish grammar and Spanish metrics; Latin and Greek (which so far has very few students); French; English; natural and landscape drawing (besides line drawing, which is taught to young artisans); arithmetic, algebra, and geometry for students of the humanities; geography and cosmography; general principles of literature; Latin literature; survey of the history of literature; fairly complete courses in profane history, philosophy, natural law, political economy, theory of legislation, Roman and national law, canon law, and international law; all branches of pure mathematics up to advanced and descriptive geometry; topography and geodetics; experimental physics, chemistry applied to mineralogy and medicine; botany applied to medicine; anatomy, physiology, and pathology; and clinical medicine. A number of these branches of knowledge are taught in two-year courses; and for those of Spanish grammar, Latin, history, and mathematics, there are quite a large number of classes.

The separation of the two kinds of instruction, preparatory and higher, decreed by the national government and already on the point of being put into practice, is a measure likely to produce the best results on both levels, and will provide the necessary development of the university faculty by involving it directly on the latter level. This is an essential mission for the universities. But our university is not a mere copy of the old corporations that bear this title in European nations. The chief idea for its creation is in our fundamental charter, which calls for the institution of a higher body of instruction charged with inspection of teaching on a national scale, as well as its guidance under the authority of the government. This supervisory capacity is what the law has deposited in the University Council; and whether it rests on a single authority, or, as has seemed more appropriate, on a collegial one, it is obvious that it could exist without the university. But the Basic Law's intention was to join to the supervision of national education a body which, divided into five sections, would dedicate its attention not only to teaching but to cultivation of the different courses of study, even including primary education. The separation that I have just mentioned is aimed at making the first of these duties—teaching—effective. Thus the university will be a teaching body, and according to the provisions of the Supreme Decree, will be such a body in a way that I believe includes two aims: that of guiding teaching in the direction of morality and public usefulness; and that of granting university professors the independence and freedom consonant with their exalted mission.

But we must not forget that our Basic Law, inspired—in my opinion—by the sanest and most liberal ideas, has charged the University not only with instruction, but with the cultivation of literature and the sciences. It has tried to make it both a university and an academy, and has intended it to contribute to the increase and development of scientific studies. The University must not be a passive instrument, devoted solely to the transmission of knowledge acquired in more developed nations, but must work, like the literary bodies of other nations, to swell the stream of common knowledge. This aim, which honors the government and the legislature that promulgated it, appears very frequently in the Basic Law. Is there an element of presumption here, of inappropriateness, of exceeding our grasp, as some have said? Shall we still be condemned to servilely repeat the lessons of European science, not daring to disagree with them or illustrate them with local applications, to give them the stamp of our nationality? Were we to do this we would be unfaithful to the spirit of that same European science, and would offer it a superstitious worship which science itself condemns. Science itself prescribes examination, close and frequent observation, free discussion, conscientious conviction. It is true that there are branches of science in which we should be content to listen for the present, to give a vote of confidence to branches in which our present state of understanding, for lack of resources, can only accept the results of foreign experience and study. But this is not true of all branches of literature and science. There are areas that require local investigation. Chilean history, for example: where can it be written better than in Chile? Is it not our task at least to collect materials, collate them, and purify them? And as for what has been accomplished already in this single branch of knowledge, under the university's aegis, the historical memoirs that appear annually, the work done by a distinguished member of the University on the history of the Chilean Church, the work published by another distinguished member on the history of the Chilean constitution: do not these works give us a glimpse of all that can and should be expected of us, in a branch of study that is peculiarly ours? There are few sciences that need no adaptation to ourselves, to our physical nature, our social circumstances, in order to be well taught. If we seek the hygiene and pathology of Chilean man in European textbooks, we will not study to what extent the organization of the human body is changed by the accidents of Chilean climate and Chilean customs. Could so necessary a study be done elsewhere than in Chile? In Chile a vast field of exploration for medicine lies open, a field until now almost untouched, but which will very soon cease to be so. The areas of physical education, health, life, health services, and population growth will be deeply involved in its cultivation. Natural history, physics, and chemistry are beginning to be studied in our secondary schools. As for the first of these sciences, which even for the acquisition of elementary ideas consists almost totally in observation, it is a question of observing, not the species that European textbooks tell us about, but Chilean species, the tree that grows in our forests, the flower that blooms in our valleys and on our mountain slopes, the arrangement and distribution of minerals in the soil that we walk upon and in the enormous mountain ranges that enclose them, the animals that live in our thickets, in our fields and rivers, and in the sea that bathes our shores. Hence, even the textbooks of natural history need to be modified in order to be useful to instruction in Chile, and that modification must be carried out by intelligent observers. And after we have taken this step and supplied the necessary instruction, should we not take another, enriching science with the knowledge of new entities and new phenomena of living creation and the inorganic world, increasing the catalogues of species, enlightening and correcting the knowledge of foreign specialists, which have been collected in large part during superficial trips to our country? The Old World wants the collaboration of the New in this respect. Not only does it want such cooperation; it promotes and demands it. Has not much been done along these lines by English-speaking Americans? Even in the Spanish provinces of America and under the colonial yoke, examples of this important collaboration have occurred: the name of [Francisco José de] Caldas, of [New] Granada, who never visited Europe, and that of [Juan Ignacio] Molina, who acquired in Chile the expertise to which he owed his reputation, have an honored place in the lists of observers who have enhanced and enriched science. Can we not be capable, in the nineteenth century, of doing what the Spanish Jesuit José de Acosta did in the sixteenth? His *Historia natural y moral de las Indias*, fruit of his personal observations, is still consulted by European naturalists. And if we are capable of doing it, will we condemn as inappropriate the existence of a body to promote and direct this cultivation of the sciences? What I have said can be applied to mineralogy, geology, meteor theory, heat theory, and magnetic theory; the basis of all these studies is observation, local observation, daily observation, observation of natural agents at every season all over the surface of the globe. European science asks us for data. Will we not even have enough enthusiasm and diligence to collect them? Shall not the American republics play a greater role in the general progress of science? Shall they not participate in the common works of human understanding to a greater degree than African tribes, or the islands of Oceania? I could go on talking about these matters for a long time, and could give them new impetus by applying them to politics, to moral man, to poetry, and to all kinds of literary composition. For either it is false that literature is a reflection of a nation's life, or we have to admit that each nation, among those not submerged in savagery, must be reflected in a literature of its own, and must impress that literature with its forms. But I think that what I have said suffices to establish the idea that the dual task imposed on the university by the Basic Law is not a monstrous or premature concept, and that we can and must work at both these tasks to our own advantage as well as to the common advantage of the sciences.

The Faculty of Humanities, which has early begun to distinguish itself among the other faculties in the University, has understood this. The Faculty of Medicine and that of Physical Sciences have entered the contest enthusiastically. To help them, the government has recently increased the inadequate number of individuals who compose each faculty. Corresponding members, named by both faculties and by the Council, will join their work, making observations and collecting data in the provinces and even in foreign countries. The two faculties will have frequent meetings, as does the Faculty of Humanities, which merits praise for having offered the first example. Students who wish to attend will be admitted to these meetings, and the results obtained, results that will be particularly concerned with local aims, will be announced to the public.

I now return, gentlemen, to the subject of teaching, which is indisputably the primary charge laid on the University; and at the same time I intend to remind you of what has been done with regard to cultivation of the intellect, something that is not as insignificant as some people think. I have congratulated myself, along with you, for the improvements observable in preparatory and scientific instruction; and I am happy to say that on this point the foremost and chief part is owed to the intelligence, concentration, and zeal of the excellent professors at the *Instituto Nacional,* because all progress made by it is also acquired by the other literary establishments of our republic, for which it serves as a model.

There is another matter—a more personal matter, if that is possible—and it will be the last. Having been reelected by almost unanimous vote by this illustrious body to occupy first place in the list of three candidates for the vacant rectorate, and having been reelected by the largest university gathering that has taken place up to now, I want to take this first opportunity to offer to the university a public testimony of my profound gratitude. I must also offer it to the most excellent Patron of the university, who has graciously confirmed the university's vote. I must also offer gratitude to the Minister of Public Instruction, who has been kind enough to speak to both houses of the Legislature about my reelection in such flattering terms for me. But the best proof of my gratitude will be the consecration of my weak efforts to the service of the Chilean nation, which has so constantly supported me, the university, and student youth, in whom (I have said it many times and am happy to repeat it) I have sincere confidence. The nation, which does so much for that youth, which expects so much of it, to whose organization it must place the last touches, will not see its hopes frustrated. To contribute to this happy outcome is the mission of the university in the sphere of its functions. As for the part in this mission that refers to me, I regret not being able to offer more than enthusiasm and labor. You may count on them as long as life and strength remain to me.

Commentary on "Investigations on the Social Influence of the Spanish Conquest and Colonial Regime in Chile" by José Victorino Lastarria

(1844)

To praise this composition, its abundant ideas, its philosophical excellence, its lucid order, and the vigorous, colorful, and generally correct style in which it is written, would merely add our feeble voice to that of the educated public, which sees in it a brilliant sample of what Señor Lastarria's talents and knowledge promise to our country and to the University of which he is a member.[7] Señor Lastarria has reached a height in his investigations from which he judges not only the events and people that are his special province, but the different systems that strive for dominance nowadays in the science of history. Confronting difficult metaphysical questions connected with the laws of moral order, he disputes general principles that for many years were an article of faith, and which we see reproduced by eminent writers of our day.

> Says Señor Lastarria: man has so effective a part in his fate that neither his good or ill fortune, in most cases, are anything but a necessary result of his operations; that is, his freedom. Man thinks independently, and his

ideas are always the origin and basis of his own will, so that his spontaneous acts merely promote and hasten the development of the natural
causes destined to produce either his happiness and perfection, or his
complete decay.... History is the oracle that God employs to reveal his
wisdom to the world, to advise peoples and show them how to attain a
happy future. If you think of history only as a simple account of past
events, your heart feels constrained and skepticism takes over your mind,
for then you can see nothing but a picture of miseries and disasters. Freedom and justice are in perpetual battle with despotism and iniquity, and
almost always succumb to their adversaries' repeated blows; the most powerful and flourishing empires are shaken to their foundations, and from
one instant to another immense ruins that astound the generations are
seen in the place that those empires formerly occupied, attesting to the
weakness and constant shifts in the affairs of men. Man wanders everywhere presiding over destruction, shedding his blood and tears in torrents.
It seems that he is running after an unknown good which he cannot attain
without devouring his own brothers' entrails, and inevitably perishing
himself under the devastating axe that rises and falls ceaselessly against
everything that surrounds him. But how differently does history reveal
itself to us if we think of it as the science of events! Then philosophy
shows us, amid this interminable series of vicissitudes, in which man progresses by trampling on man, and hurtles into abysses that he has dug
with his own hands, a profound wisdom that the experience of centuries
has confirmed, a wisdom whose counsels are infallible because they rest
on the sacrosanct precepts of the law to which Omnipotent God adjusted
the organization of that moral universe. The nations must penetrate into
that august sanctuary with the torch of philosophy, to learn there the
experience that must guide them. Bid them flee, along with the men who
guide their destinies by that blind confidence in fatality which would draw
them away from reason, cutting off at the root the faculties with which
their very nature has endowed them in order to achieve their happiness!
The human race has in its own essence the capacity for perfection; it
possesses the elements of its own good fortune, and only it has been given
the ability to guide itself and promote its development, for the laws of its
organization form a key that only man can touch and cause to produce
harmonious sounds.

This sad and desperate dogma of fatalism, against which Señor Lastarria protests, underlies a great deal of current speculation about the
destiny of the human race on earth. Acknowledging man's freedom, he

regards history as a science from which we can extract wholesome lessons that can guide the progress of governments and peoples.

What the author later says about his reasons for selecting his subject may arouse doubts about the appropriateness of the program indicated in the university's Basic Law concerning reports [*Memorias*] to be delivered before this body in the solemn meeting of September:

"I confess that I would have preferred to offer you the description of one of those heroic events or brilliant episodes that our history tells us about, to make your hearts swell with the enthusiasm of glory or admiration as I spoke to you of the wisdom of Colocolo, the prudence and strength of Caupolicán, the skill and daring of Lautaro, the swiftness and courage of Painenancu. But what real advantage would we have gained from these flattering memories? What social utility would we achieve by calling attention to only one of the separate members of a great body, the analysis of which must be complete? I could also, and no doubt more easily, have spoken about the important events of our glorious revolution; but I have been constrained, I admit, by the fear of not being completely impartial in my researches. I can see that, because the heroes of those brilliant actions and the witnesses of their deeds are still alive, even the simplest facts that we possess about the important events in the unfolding of that sublime epic are constantly contested and contradicted. And I dare not pronounce a judgment that condemns the testimony of one side and sanctifies that of the other, arousing passions that are in the last moments of their existence. In that case my comments would be, if not offensive, at least tiresome and fruitless, and hence I do not think that I have sufficient instruction and other gifts, lacking in a young man, to rise to the heights necessary to judge events that I have not seen and have had no means of studying philosophically. Because our revolution is still in process, we are not prepared to construct its philosophic history. But we are engaged in the task of discussing and accumulating data, in order to transmit them, along with our opinion and the result of our critical studies, to another generation which will possess the true historical criterion and the necessary impartiality to judge them.

These reflections, expressed with noble modesty, could serve as an example to younger writers than Señor Lastarria. They suggest, as we have said, some doubts as to whether the authors of these annual reports can confine themselves to the program of the Basic Law without encountering serious difficulties. No doubt it is hard for the present generation to judge impartially the events and persons of our revolution; and moreover, it is almost impossible to do so even impartially and truthfully without arousing denials, without pressing the alarm button of sleeping passions, which it would be desirable to extinguish. But without these subjects, whose very sensitivity is a powerful stimulus to addressing them; if authors draw back for fear of walking, as Horace puts it in his *Odes, per ignes suppositos cineri doloso*, [. . . through fires set beneath deceptive ash] on what historical discourse relating to Chile can they exercise their pens? Señor Lastarria has anticipated them in a discourse entirely devoid of this risk. By disentangling the antecedents of the revolution, he has traced a picture of such vast dimensions, and has colored its different parts so vigorously, that he seems to have left little or nothing for those who will explore this area in the future. The material, after all, is very abundant. Even without the variety conferred on a single subject by the different viewpoints from which it can be regarded, the different intellectual qualities and the opposing opinions of writers, there still remain many partial subjects, small ones if you will, compared with the grandiose subject of the 1844 report. But this does not render them unworthy of attention; perhaps for that very reason they are capable of those lively colors—that individual delineation—which brings the past to mind at the same time as it furnishes a delicious pleasure to the imagination. What is lost in the breadth of perspective is gained by the clarity and liveliness of the details. The domestic customs of a bygone age, the founding of one city, the vicissitudes and disasters of another, the history of our agriculture, our commerce, our mines, the proper appreciation of this or that part of our colonial past, can furnish material for many and interesting researches. There is no lack of materials to consult, if they are sought intelligently and patiently in private collections, in archives, and in trustworthy traditions, and we must hasten to publish them before they become completely obscure and forgotten. Even the war between the Spanish colonists and the indigenous tribes would yield many pictures full of animation and interest. History is not useful solely for the large and comprehensive lessons of its combined results. Specialties, periods, places, individuals, have peculiar attractions and also contain valuable lessons. If the writer who sums up the whole life of a people is like the astronomer who traces out the centuries-old laws to which great masses are subject in their movements, the writer who gives us the life of a city, of a man, is like the physiologist or physicist, who shows us the mechanism, in a given body, of the material agencies that determine its forms and movements and mark its features, the attitudes that distinguish it. We cannot judge of a vast epic unless we see the position, the correspondence, of all its parts. But this is not the only, or perhaps even the most useful, job of history; the life of a [Simon] Bolívar or a [Antonio José] Sucre is a drama in which all the passions, all the resources of the human heart come into play, and confer a higher interest on self-communion and individuality.

If we confine ourselves to the Chilean revolution and the danger of factionalism, there are a large number of events in it where this obstacle can be overcome. For we do not think worthy of consideration the fear of wounding someone's pride or reducing to its proper limits some exaggerated boast. There are events like the occupation of Rancagua, for example, with its scenes of savagery and atrocity, which history must not forget; like the battle of Chacabuco and the curious and colorful events leading up to it, and with the sudden change in the luck of both winners and losers; like the battle of Maipú, with its anxiety as to the outcome, its shifting episodes, and its joyous triumph; and like so many others to which only the generation contemporary with those events can impart the liveliness, the freshness, the dramatic movement without which historical accounts are mere abstract generalizations or pale jottings. The history that fascinates us is the history of its contemporaries, and more than any others the history that has been written by the actors themselves in the events narrated in it. And after all, this is (with the lowering of tone prescribed by strict criticism, taking into account the historian's emotions) the most authentic history, the most worthy of belief. Can Plutarch be compared with Thucydides? [Antonio de] Solís with Bernal Díaz del Castillo? Does not Xenophon, in his account of the Retreat of the Ten Thousand, combine the interest of a novel with the merit of history? Nor are contemporary or hand-written memoirs as devoid of useful instruction as Señor Lastarria appears to think. Have not Caesar's *Commentaries* been the favorite book of the great commanders? If contemporary memoirs provoke objections, so much the better. Our descendants can extract the truth from contradictory accounts, and reduce everything to its true value. If history is not written by contemporaries, then future generations will have to write it by following adulterated oral traditions (for nothing deforms and falsifies as quickly as oral tradition), newspaper articles, impassioned speeches by political parties, the product of first impressions, and arid official documents whose veracity is frequently suspect. History says *uaticinare de ossibus istis* [prophesy about these bones—Ezechiel 37:4] to the writer who has before him only the skeletons of events; and the writer, if he wishes to give us a real picture and not a fleshless account, will have to compromise truth by extracting from his imagination and from fallible conjectures, what his insubstantial materials do not provide.

But let us return to Señor Lastarria's report, and discover with him the influence of Spanish arms and laws in Chile. Chapter One, in which he deals with the conquest and with the prolonged struggle between the Chilean colonists and the indomitable offspring of Arauco, is written with the brisk energy that the material requires. It would be difficult to give along general lines a fuller idea of those rancorous hostilities which, transmitted by fathers to sons and from generation to generation, smolder to this day beneath the appearance of a peace that is really a truce. Except for a sentence or two more appropriate to oratorical exaggeration than to historical evenhandedness, we cannot see that there is much reason to describe as exaggerated and impassioned the description that he makes in this chapter of the conquistadors' cruelty. It is a duty of history to tell the facts as they were, and we must not soften them simply because they do not seem to do honor to the memory of Chile's founders. Injustice, atrocity, treachery in war, have not been committed by Spaniards alone, but by all races in all centuries; and if even among very similar Christian nations, and during periods of civilization and culture, war has assumed and still assumes this quality of savage and inhumane cruelty, which destroys and sheds blood for the sheer pleasure of destroying and shedding blood, what is so strange about the murderous battles and harsh consequences of victory between peoples in whom everything—customs, religion, language, physical traits, color—was different, everything was repugnant and hostile? The vassals of Isabella, Charles I, and Philip II were subjects of the premier nation of Europe; Spain's chivalric spirit, the splendor of its court, its magnificent and honorable noble class, the skill of its captains, the adroitness of its ambassadors and ministers, the courage of its soldiers, its daring enterprises, its vast discoveries and conquests, made Spaniards the target for detraction because they were the object of envy. The records of that century present us with horrible scenes on every side. The Spaniards abused their power and oppressed and affronted humankind. Not impudently, as Señor Lastarria says, because they did not need to be impudent to do what everyone else was doing, with no limit except that of their own strength, but with the same concern for humanity, the same respect for the rights of men, that powerful states have always displayed in their relations with weak ones, and of which we have seen too many examples even in these days of morality and civilization.

If we compare the practical ideas of international jurisprudence in modern times with those of the Middle Ages and the ancient peoples, we will find a great deal of resemblance at bottom, under not very great differences as to means and forms. "But the attempt to bind nations by mere moral sanctions," says a writer [Henry Wheaton] of our day, is to fetter giants with cobwebs.

> To the greatest of human restraints, the fear of a hereafter, they are insensible. Nations, *qua* nations, have no existence beyond the grave. Their life in this world, indeed, is of indefinite duration; but experience does not justify the belief that national crimes, except those crimes of which one part of a nation is guilty towards another, are always, or even usually, punished. The principal states of continental Europe—France, Russia, Austria, and Prussia—have grown from small beginnings to powerful and flourishing monarchies, by centuries of ambition, injustice, violence, and fraud. The crimes which gave Wales to England, Alsace and Franche Compté to France, and Silesia to Prussia, were rewarded by an increase of wealth, power, and security. Again, nations are not restrained by fear of the loss of honour; for honour, in the sense in which that word is applied to individuals, does not apply to them . . . Never has the foreign policy of France been more faithless, more rapacious, or more cruel than in the reign of Louis XIV . . . At no time was France more admired, and even courted. At no time were Frenchmen more welcome in every court, and in every private circle. What are often called injuries to the honour of a nation, are injuries to its vanity. The qualities of which nations are most vain, are force and boldness. They know that, so far as they are supposed to possess these qualities, they are themselves unlikely to be injured, and may injure others with impunity.

Thus, in the great masses of people that we call nations, the savage state of brutal force has not come to an end. Apparent homage is offered to justice, using the trite commonplaces of security, dignity, protection of national interests, and others that are equally vague. These are premises from which, using only moderate skill, all the imaginable consequences can be extracted. The horrors of war have been partially mitigated, but not because there is more respect for humanity; rather, because material interests are better calculated, and as a consequence of the very perfection that the art of destruction has achieved. It would be insane to make slaves of the losers if more can be gained by making them tributaries and forced producers of the victor's industry. Aggressors have become merchants, but merchants who have the scale of Brennus on the counter: *Vae victis*. Nowadays we do not colonize by killing the indigenous inhabitants. Why kill them, if it suffices to shove them from forest to forest and plain to plain? Destitution and hunger will complete the task of destruction in the long run, noiselessly and without fuss. In the bosom of each social family, customs are improving and becoming purer; freedom and justice, those inseparable companions, are extending their sway more and more. But in the relationships of race to race and people to people the savage state endures, underneath hypocritical outward appearances, with all its primitive injustice and rapacity.

We do not accuse any single nation, but man's nature. The weak call for justice, but give them power and they will be as unjust as their oppressors.

II

The picture that Señor Lastarria gives us of the vices and abuses of Spain's colonial regime is based largely on documents of irreproachable authenticity and veracity: laws, ordinances, histories, the *Memorias secretas* of Don Jorge Juan and Don Antonio de Ulloa. But many distorting nuances have blurred the picture; there is something that disclaims the impartiality recommended by the law, and which is not incompatible with the energetic tone of reproof with which the historian, advocate for the rights of humanity and interpreter of moral feelings, must pronounce his judgment on the corrupting institutions. Spain sacrificed to the dominant idea of perpetuating the colonies' dependence not only the colonies' interests, but her own as well; and, in order to keep them dependent and submissive, she made herself poor and weak. American treasure flooded the world, while the mother country's treasury was exhausted and its industry left in its infancy. The colonies—which for other countries have been a means of stimulating population and the arts—for Spain were a cause of depopulation and backwardness. Neither industrial life nor wealth were attained, except in some markets that served as intermediaries between the two hemispheres, where the accumulated wealth of monopoly maintained them above the level of the general poverty: oases scattered at long intervals in a vast desert. But let us be fair; it was not a *ferocious* tyranny. It kept the arts in chains, clipped the wings of thought, even plugged the springs of agricultural fertility, but its policy was one of restrictions and privations, not torture or blood. Penal laws were administered loosely. In punishing acts of sedition it was not extraordinarily severe; it was what despotism has always been and no more, at least with respect to the Spanish race, up to the period of general uprising which ended with emancipation of the American dominions. The despotism of the Roman emperors was the model for Spanish government in America. The same amiable inefficiency of the supreme authority, the same praetorian arbitrariness, the same tendency to consider the throne's rights divine, the same indifference to industry, the same unawareness of the great principles that vivify and nourish human associations, the same judicial organization, the same fiscal privileges; but in addition to these odious resemblances there are others of several different kinds. The civilizing mission which moves from east to west, like the sun, and of which Rome was the most powerful agent in the ancient world, was exercised by Spain on a western world that was farther away and vaster. No doubt the elements of that civilization were fated to combine with others that improved it, just as in Europe the civilization of Rome was modified and improved by foreign influences. Perhaps we are mistaken, but we certainly believe that none of the nations which sprang from the ruins of the Empire preserved a more pronounced stamp of the Roman genius than did Spain. The language itself is the one that best retains the character of the language spoken by those who ruled the world. Even in material things, the Spanish colonial administration had some Roman and imperial elements. America owes to Spanish rule everything great and splendid in her public buildings. We confess it with shame: we have barely been able even to preserve the buildings that were constructed under the viceroys and captains-general. And keep in mind that Crown income was liberally spent on their construction, and there was no imposition of taxes and forced labor such as Rome employed, exhausting its provincial subjects to pay for its highways, aqueducts, amphitheaters, baths, and bridges.

Nor, to be truthful, do we find entirely correct the explanation of the historical phenomenon that Señor Lastarria examines at the beginning of his Chapter Three. We do not believe that the history of universal legislation "clearly shows us that the laws adopted by human societies have always been inspired by their respective customs, and have been an expression, a true formula, of the habits and feelings of peoples." Nor do we believe that the only exception to this phenomenon is to be found in colonized countries, and more specifically in the Spanish colonies of America. We believe that there has always been a reciprocal action between laws and customs; that customs influence laws and laws customs. How could all the influences of some peoples upon others be explained in any other way? Have not conquest, and the laws imposed by the victors on the vanquished, often been either a means of civilization or a cause of retrogression and barbarity? Laws must be aimed precisely at the satisfaction of needs, of local instincts, provided that the legislator has felt them within himself from the cradle; even were he able to control them, he would have to accommodate to those instincts the arrangements that he promulgates in order to make them acceptable and effective. But outside forces often either modify customs, and, following these, laws; or they alter laws and in consequence customs. The ideas of one people are incorporated into the ideas of another, and as both lose their purity, what was at first a mixture of discordant parts gradually becomes a homogeneous whole. It will in many ways resemble its divergent origins, and from certain points of view will also present new forms. From the collision of different ideas a result will appear that will be more or less close to one of the motive forces, according to the intensity with which these operate and the circumstances that respectively favor them. Certainly laws, by altering customs and assimilating them, are eventually the expression and formula of custom; but then that formula precedes the assimililation instead of being a consequence of it. When two races mingle, the idea of the immigrant race will prevail over that of the native race depending on its comparative numbers, its moral vigor, and its more or less high degree of civilization. The northern barbarians imparted a new temper to the degraded inhabitants of the Roman provinces, and in return received many of Rome's social forms; gradually, the religion, language, and laws of Rome replaced those of the proud and fierce conquerors. But it can also happen that the disparity between the elements that come together is so great that an invincible repugnance does not allow them to penetrate each other and produce a real mixture. The races may mingle, and they may mutually reject each others' ideas. In just this way did the Arabs and Spaniards present two types of antipathetic civilization in western Europe. With the exception of certain material and purely external details, nothing Arabic ever took root in Spain; religion, laws, the genius of the language, of the arts, of literature, took little or nothing from the Mohammedan conquerors. Arabic culture was always an exotic plant amid the triple Iberian-Roman-Gothic mixture that occupied the Iberian Peninsula. One of the two elements had to expel or smother the other. The struggle lasted for eight centuries, and the Strait of Hercules was once more crossed by the vanquished and proscribed civilization of Islam, fated everywhere to abandon the field forever to the weapons of the West and the Cross. In America, on the other hand, the sentence of destruction has been pronounced over the native people. The indigenous races are disappearing, and in the long run will be lost among the colonies of transatlantic peoples, leaving no more traces than a few words that have crept into the newly brought languages, and scattered monuments where curious travelers will ask in vain the name and description of the civilizations that brought them into being.

In colonies that remain under the control of the mother country—in the populations of the founding, immigrant race—the mother country's spirit necessarily pervades its distant emanations, and its laws are received docilely even when they are in disagreement with local interests. When the time comes that those local interests feel strong enough to dispute primacy, it is not really two different ideas or two types of civilization that enter the fray, but two sets of aspirations to power, two athletes who fight with the same weapons and for a common prize. This was the nature of the Spanish-American revolution, considered in its spontaneous development. For it is necessary to distinguish two elements in it, political independence and civil liberty. In our revolution freedom was a foreign ally which fought under the banner of independence, and which even after the victory has had to make considerable efforts to become consolidated and established. The work of the warriors is finished, but that of the lawmakers will not be finished until there is a more complete penetration of the idea being imitated, the idea brought from outside, in the hard and tenacious Iberian materials.

This is the way we conceive of the moral law on which Señor Lastarria is so intent. Our explanation of it may seem too obvious, too simple. But it is the correct summary of the facts insofar as we can understand them. Spain's American colonies are no exception, but rather a confirmation, of the general rules to which such phenomena are subject.

We also feel a great deal of repugnance about agreeing that the Chilean people (and we can say the same of the other Spanish-American countries) were so "profoundly debased," reduced to a condition of such "complete annihilation," so stripped of "any social virtue," as Señor Lastarria would have us believe. The Spanish-American revolution contradicts his statements. Never has a country that has been profoundly debased, completely annihilated, stripped of all virtuous feeling, been capable of carrying out the great deeds that inspired the campaigns of our patriots, the heroic acts of abnegation, the sacrifices of every kind, with which Chile and other American countries won their political emancipation. And anyone who observes from a philosophical viewpoint the history of our battle with the mother country will easily recognize that what caused us to prevail was precisely the Iberian element. The native Spanish persistence collided with itself in the inborn persistence of Spain's children. The instinct of fatherland revealed its existence to American hearts and reproduced the feats of Numancia and Zaragoza. The captains and veteran legions of transatlantic Iberia were conquered and humiliated by the leaders and improvised armies of that other young Iberia which, abjuring the very name, preserved the indomitable spirit of ancient Iberia in the defense of its homes. Therefore it seems incorrect to us to say that the Spanish system "smothered before their birth the inspirations of honor and fatherland, of emulation and all the generous sentiments that give birth to civic virtues." There were no republican elements, for Spain had not been able to create them; its laws undoubtedly gave souls a completely opposite direction. But in the depths of those souls there were seeds of magnanimity, of heroism, of high-minded and generous independence; and though customs were simple and modest in Chile, there was something more in those customs than the stupid brainlessness of slavery. This is true to such an extent that Señor Lastarria himself has found it necessary to restrict his descriptions, speaking of "at least," "to all outward appearance," and "ostensibly." But they lose almost all their force when limited in this way. A system that has degraded and debased only in appearance has not really debased and degraded.

We are talking about the facts as they are in themselves and are not trying to investigate the causes. It is an article of faith for us that despotism degrades and demoralizes; and if, either in Europe or America, it has not been able to bastardize the race, to choke off over the course of three centuries the wellspring of generous feelings (for without them the moral phenomena of Spain and Spanish America in our day cannot be explained), causes must necessarily have coexisted that worked against such a pernicious influence. Is there a peculiar complexion in races, an indestructible idiosyncrasy, so to speak? And now that the Spanish race has mingled with other races in America, would it not be possible to explain, up to a point, the diversities presented by the character of men and the revolution in the different American provinces by the diversity of the mixture? Here is a problem that deserves to be solved analytically, and on which we cannot pause, because we lack the necessary data and because we have already exceeded the limits that we set when we began this article.

For the same reason we must pass over several interesting chapters in the *Memoria* in which we encounter doubts and difficulties about fully accepting the ideas of its enlightened and philosophic author. But we cannot resist contemplating with him, for a moment, the spectacle of the Chilean revolution offered in his Chapter Eight.

Señor Lastarria grasped to a considerable degree, though he sometimes seems to forget it, the dual nature, previously indicated, of the Spanish-American revolution. The Americans were much better prepared for emancipation than for the freedom of the domestic hearth. Two movements took place at the same time: one was spontaeneous, the other imitative and exotic. Each was often an obstacle instead of a help to the other. The external principle produced progress; the native element dictatorships. No one loved freedom more sincerely than General Bolívar, but the nature of things held him in thrall, as it did everyone. Independence was necessary for freedom, and the champion of independence was and had to be a dictator. Hence the apparent and necessary contradictions of his acts. Bolívar triumphed, dictatorships triumphed in Spain; governments and congresses still battle the customs of Spain's descendants, the habits formed under the influence of Spanish laws. It is a war of vicissitudes in which ground is lost and gained, a silent war in which the enemy has powerful helpers among ourselves. The scepter was wrenched away from the monarch, but not from the Spanish spirit; our legislatures obey, without realizing it, ideas inherited from the Goths. The administrative ordinances of the Charleses and Philips are the laws of our country. Even our warriors, clinging to a special right [the military *fuero*] that is opposed to the principle of equality before the law, the cornerstone of free governments, reveal the domination of the ideas of that same Spain whose flags they trampled under foot. Says Señor Lastarria:

> The despotism of the kings fell, and the despotism of the past remained erect and with all its vigor, for that is what had to happen as a result of past circumstances. The fathers of the country and the warriors of independence acted in the sphere of their power . . . ; and when the power of despotism dissipated along with the smoke of the last victory, the cannon of Chiloé announced to the world that the revolution of political independence had ended. And then the war began against the powerful spirit with which the colonial system had imbued our society.

Señor Lastarria triumphantly answers those who censure the American revolution, those who have called it ill-timed, criticizing its inevitable disorders and errors. Its evils were the necessary result of the condition we were in; no matter at what time the insurrection had broken out they would have been the same or greater, and perhaps success would have been less certain. We had to choose between seizing the first opportunity or prolonging our servitude for centuries. If we had not received the education that predisposed us for the enjoyment of freedom, we could not hope for it from Spain; we had to educate ourselves, no matter how costly the attempt. We had to put an end to a guardianship three centuries long, which in all that time had not been able to prepare the emancipation of a great people.

"All the servile people of Europe," says [J. C. L. Simonde de] Sismondi, quoted by Señor Lastarria,

who are still very numerous, have shouted for joy when they saw the cause
of freedom dishonored by those who call themselves it defenders. Reactionary writers, admitting our principles for a moment in order to twist
them against us, and agreeing that political institutions ought to be judged
according to their tendency to produce the welfare and perfection of all
their citizens, tried to make us believe that there was more happiness and
perfection in Prussia, Denmark, and even in Austria, than that produced
by the vaunted institutions of South America, of Spain and Portugal, and
even of France and England.

"Sismondi makes us see," (this time Lastarria is speaking)

that this cry, so insulting to humanity, has only a false appearance of
truth, because the disasters brought about by attempts at freedom in new
nations must not be judged by the exaggerated descriptions of the supporters of despotism without taking into account the greater, and a thousand times more degrading, disasters caused by the system of absolutism.

We cannot better end this long discourse than to quote again, along
with Señor Lastarria, the eloquent warnings of that brave champion
and wise counselor of peoples [Sismondi]:

After having repeated to servile men that they have no right to triumph
over liberal men; that all their errors, all their misfortunes do not render
their efforts less than just and generous, nor do they convince that the
system they intend to destroy is not shameful and culpable, and that
servitude is not always the worst of misfortunes, the greatest of degra-
dations. We will also agree that the promoters of new ideas have committed fundamental errors, and that, by recognizing the evil that they were
trying to destroy, they have formed false ideas of the good that they
wished to achieve. They have thought that they were discovering principles when they possessed only paradoxes. That social science on which
the happiness of humanity depends demands new studies, more serious
and profound ones. It demands that philosophical doubt replace assertions
and empirical axioms. It demands evocation of the spirit of the universe
in order to discover the linkage of causes and effects, for experience everywhere presents difficulties to be conquered and problems to be solved.

Commentary on "Historical Sketch [Bosquejo histórico] of the Constitution of the Government of Chile during the First Period of the Revolution, 1810 to 1814" by Don José Victorino Lastarria

(1848)

This work has received a prize in the university competition of 1847, and its author is well known for other literary productions which place him among the most distinguished and hard-working members of the University and the *Instituto Nacional*.[8] The present work is no less interesting than other works of history that have cast light on the history of Chile ever since the reorganization of the University in 1843, and that Señor Lastarria himself initiated with his "Investigations on the social influence of the conquest and the Spanish colonial system in Chile," an account presented to the University on its solemn anniversary in 1844.

The *Bosquejo* is preceded by a speech, intended to serve as a prologue, by Don Jacinto Chacón, a professor of history at the *Instituto Nacional*, and a Report by Don Antonio Varas and Don Antonio García Reyes, members of the university commission charged with examining and judging the work. These two pieces of writing contain two very different opinions of it, and present the *Bosquejo* to us under two opposing viewpoints; but both are quite flattering to the author. For our part, we agree with the Report. Though it does not try to fly to the loftiest regions of metaphysical history, it does describe Señor Lastarria's work with great good sense and impartiality, and at the same time offers clear and exact ideas about the true mission of history and the way of cultivating it that will bring about the best results.

"The Commission feels inclined to wish that works be written, before all else, that are chiefly designed to tell the facts clearly;" it believes that "the theory that illustrates those facts will immediately appear, treading firmly on known ground." We profess the same wish, and think it sufficiently justified by the considerations with which the Prologue begins. Señor Chacón has recognized that "the formation of constitutional history, which is simply the progressive development of the kind of principles on which society rests, could not have appeared until after the science of history, passing through all its successive steps from the simple chronicler to the philosopher who discovers humankind's laws of rotation, had reached its ultimate development." By accepting these ideas (though we do so only with certain reservations that we will express later), we can assume that in Chile, as in Europe, historical studies must follow the same path, from the chronicle that gives us a list of events to the philosophy that concentrates and summarizes them, and to constitutional history, which is, according to Señor Chacón's way of thinking, the ultimate expression of that philosophy. What, then, is the basis of the disdain with which the distinguished author of the Prologue has regarded the Commissioners' wishes? Do they wish for anything else than the realization in Chile of the progressive development of history sketched out in the first few lines of the Prologue? There is something inconsistent here, or at least obscure; and the inconsistency or obscurity increases rapidly when those lines are compared with later assertions. If it were necessary for constitutional history to appear after historical science had progressed, step by step, from the chronicle to the most sublime philosophy, to the history of the constitution, which is the last step, how is it possible for *the political historian to study in the school of the constitutional historian, and in that school to learn to understand events, before beginning to recount them?* How can it be first *to establish the principles and then their consequences, or the facts, against the opinion of the University's commission?* Despite all our respect

it is assumed that Chileans know either through tradition or previous writings? The author does not distance himself from the facts, from individual characteristics. On the contrary, he describes them insofar as they are necessary to his object; and this, in our opinion, is what makes the work more instructive. Perhaps, because its antecedents are not sufficiently proved, the fidelity of the picture is not wholly guaranteed, just as the Commission states. But it seems unquestionable to us that there is more in the *Bosquejo* than principles and generalities, and that it is properly speaking a political history, though a rapid and summary one. This has also been the opinion of Señor Lastarria. The title of the work indicates it, the execution is in harmony with the design. And that is why there is a certain shade of contradiction between the Prologue and the *Bosquejo*, relative to the nature of constitutional history and the field that it embraces. According to the Prologue, it is the ultimate summary, the quintessence, so to speak, of all positive history. Señor Lastarria, on the other hand, thinks of it only as a special history, as the history of society in one of its most important aspects. Let us listen to what he says:

> A distinguished writer has said that today we are entering the century of constitutions; that the peoples in modern history who do not possess a social contract are struggling to obtain one, or at least want one. This truth, prominent in the picture of events that forms the life of the present century, leads us to consider as *an essential part* of a people's history the history of its political constitution, all the more in America, whose nations have been born in a constitutional regime, have fought for it, have torn their own entrails for it, are developing in it, and will not live or be consolidated except under its protection.

In fact, the history of a country's constitution is like that of its religion, its commerce, its industry, its letters: an integrating element, entirely indivisible, within which national history operates. It is an element that must be studied separately, like each of the others, in order to better understand its antecedents, its local genius, its influences, and the future that awaits it.

Observe, too, that Señor Lastarria is dealing only with written political constitutions, which often are not emanations of society's *heart*, for a dominant party usually writes them, or they are engendered in the solitude of the study of a man who does not even represent a party; an exceptional intelligence, who puts into his work his political ideas, his speculations, his prejudices, his utopias. We would not have to go very far to find examples of this.

One thought occurs to us. Señor Chacón identifies the constitution of a people not only with its institutions, but with its ideas, beliefs, and customs. The constitutions of the Spanish-American states have been made in the image and likeness of the Anglo-American constitutions. Would it not follow from this that the ideas, beliefs, and customs of a Chilean, a Peruvian, or a Mexican share the ideas, beliefs, and customs of the inhabitants of New York or Pennsylvania? And is it not true that instead of similarities, there are decided contrasts between the character, the genius, and the *heart* of those societies and ours?

Perhaps the contradictions and inaccuracies that we have noted are only apparent, and consist only in the fact that we do not perfectly understand the meaning of some of Señor Chacón's expressions. We fear it all the more because of the high concept we have of his capacity and his vast studies. If this is the case, we would like to have our mistaken judgments corrected. Especially, would we wish that there be no attempt to sanction, with the doctrine of the Prologue, the mode of thought of those who, limiting themselves to general results, try to reduce the science of history to a sterile and superficial empiricism. For in our humble opinion, the historian who learns only general, aphoristic principles second or third hand, clothed in brilliant metaphors, is just as empirical as the one who contents himself with the outside of things, failing to grasp their spirit, failing to perceive their connections. In every class of studies, it is necessary to change the opinions of others into convictions of one's own. Only in this way can a science be learned. Only in this way can Chilean youth take over the stream of knowledge offered it by cultivated Europe and become capable of contributing to it some day, of enriching it and making it more beautiful. We are convinced that Señor Chacón has guided his studies in no other direction, and almost flatter ourselves that, in the ideas that we have just expressed, he as well as ourselves are in agreement.

The Craft of History
(1848)

Joining example to doctrine, almost all the most distinguished contemporary historians [Thierry, Sismondi, Barante] have given the world instructive and interesting histories, which represent perhaps the ripest fruits of modern literature.[9] All of them agree on the importance of facts and consider exposition of living social drama as the substance and soul of history. Our authority is worth very little (no matter how much Señor Chacón, a biased judge in these matters, has tried to exaggerate it). That is why we had to confer authority on sound doctrines by citing illustrious names. In the passages we have chosen (the first that have come to hand) it is easy to see that what Señor Chacón calls a well-traveled road is the only road for history—as he himself has intimated in the first lines of his Prologue—and that only through the facts about a people individualized, alive, and complete can we gain access to the philosophy of history of that people.

We must distinguish between two kinds of philosophy of history. One of them is simply the science of humanity in general, the science of moral and social laws, independent of local and temporal influences, and as necessary manifestations of man's intimate nature. The other is, comparatively speaking, a concrete science, which deduces from the facts of a race, a people, or a period, the peculiar spirit of that race, people, or period, just as we deduce the genius, the nature of an individual, from the facts about him. This allows us to see an idea that develops progressively in each man or people, assuming different forms which leave their mark on the country and the period; an idea which, when it reaches its final development with its forms exhausted, its destiny accomplished, yields to another idea that will pass through the same stages and will also perish some day. Just so does man the individual constantly change his desires and aspirations from the cradle to the grave, at every age developing new instincts that attract him to new objects.

The general philosophy of history, the science of humanity, is the same in every place and every time. The progress made in it by one people aids all people; they enter the common stream over which all peoples have solid control. It resembles the theory of attraction or of light in the natural sciences; the laws of physics and chemistry operated in the same way in the antediluvian world as they do today in ours. They operate the same in Japan as in Europe, and the physical and chemical discoveries of England and France enter the common stream of all the nations on the globe. But the general philosophy of history cannot lead us to the particular philosophy of the history of a people, in which a large number of agencies and diverse influences overlap with the essential laws of humanity and modify the features of the different peoples, just as laws that overlap with those of physical nature modify the physical aspect of the different countries. Without direct observation, what would be the use of all the science of the Europeans to tell them about the distribution of our mountains, valleys, and streams, the forms of our Chilean vegetation, the facial features of the Araucanian or the Pehuenche Indians? Doubtless very little. We must say the same of the general laws of humanity. To try to deduce the history of a people from them would be like a European geometrician trying, with the sole aid of Euclid's theorems, to draw a map of Chile from his study.

This is the concept of the philosophy of history held by Victor Cousin, the philosopher who has best grasped the importance, the elements, and the scope of the philosophy of history. According to him, it is the philosophy of the human spirit applied to history. Therefore it presupposes history, and does so to such a degree that that philosophy must be proved and guaranteed by history, so that we may be sure that it is the exact expression of human nature and not a false system which, if imposed on history, adulterates it. This philosophy must study everything; it must examine the spirit of a people in their climate, their laws, their religion, their industry, their artistic productions, their wars, their letters, and their sciences. And how can such a philosophy do this if history does not spread before it all the facts about those people, all the forms they have successively assumed in each of the functions of intellectual and moral life?

If the philosophy of history must study each of the elements in a people, then is it not obvious that the history of that people must already be in existence, and must represent that people completely, if possible, represent them alive and active? We blush to have to stress such an obvious truth.

Señor Chacón is correct in stating that the scientific world is a unit. The advances made in the scientific field by each nation and each man belong to the heritage of humanity. But we must understand one another. European philosophical works do not give us the philosophy of history of Chile. We Chileans must shape ours by the only legitimate route, which is that of synthetic induction. This does not mean that we regard as useless the knowledge of what Europeans have done in the course of their history, even when we are dealing only with ours. The philosophy of European history will always provide a model, a guide, and a method for us. It smooths the way, but does not excuse us from following it.

Our young friend will allow us to tell him that there is more poetry than logic in the comparisons he insists on making to buttress some of the ideas in the Prologue. "What would be thought," he says, "of a sage who says that Chile ought not to take advantage of the European system of railroads, because Chile needs to follow the path of discovery from the simple cart to the railroad? What would be thought of a sage who said that Chile ought not to avail itself of the excellence of European dramatic art, because it must begin the path of this art, as Europe did, with crude 'mysteries'? . . . What would be thought of a sage who said that Chile must not take advantage of the discoveries and progress of European machinery, but would have to begin, as in Europe, with the rough homespun cloth and hand-knitted stockings of our grandparents?" The truth is that these same statements, with slight modifications, would not seem at all absurd. In all matters there really is a certain path that must be followed, though more or less speedily. No nation needs to produce a Watt in order to have railroads, but it still would have to begin, let us not say with a highway, but with the narrow path that leads from one hut to another. Would Señor Chacón take the railroad to our colony on the Straits? Would he locate a lace factory, or a silk mill, in Araucania? And would he have to go very far to find towns where the medieval mysteries would be better received than the tragedies of Racine or the dramas of Victor Hugo? But comparisons do not consist in this. Those that Señor Chacón uses do not suit the matters with which he deals. A machine can be brought from Europe to Chile and can produce the same effects in Chile as in Europe. But the philosophy of the history of France—for example, the explanation of the individual manifestations of the French people at different periods in their history—lacks meaning when applied to the successive events in the Chilean people's existence. The only thing it can do for us is to give an accurate direction to our labors when, as we consider Chilean facts in all their circumstances and details, we attempt to uncover their inner spirit, the various ideas, and the successive metamorphoses of each idea, in different periods of Chilean history. If this were not so, Señor Lastarria, who according to the prologue wishes to give us the philosophy of our history, would have assumed a superfluous task.

In another article we will continue to develop these ideas and demonstrate that the *Bosquejo histórico* is, as its title suggests, a strictly historical work, though it is true that on some points and qualifications, the testimony of facts would be desirable. But I cannot lay down my pen without replying to the serious charge made against the Commission, accusing it of exclusivism and intolerance because it believed that, in the study and cultivation of Chilean history, a clarification of the facts was the place to begin. If this opinion, expressed in the modest form of a hope, is an act of intolerance, we can bid farewell to literary criticism. Villemain wanted Robertson, instead of describing the facts in general terms, to individualize and describe them. We protest against the depiction of this desire as an act of exclusivism. What more could have been said if the Commission, instead of giving the *Bosquejo histórico* its just due—as Señor Chacón himself confesses—and awarding it the prize, had assumed inquisitorial powers and banned the reading of it? The same freedom that one writer has to produce whatever his intelligence and his conscience dictate, another writer also has to examine and criticize him, according to his honest knowledge and understanding.

It must be said that although Señor Chacón had set out, at the beginning of his first article, to settle the question (which, in our opinion, was perfectly clear), it seems instead that he has wrenched it out of context. The Commission, after having given well-merited praise to the *Bosquejo histórico*, says that it lacks sufficient information to accept the author's opinion on the character and leanings of the parties involved in the Chilean revolution. It quite rightly believes that, in the absence of a picture in which events, persons, and all the material details of history appear in rough form, merely tracing general outlines has the defect of allowing scope for many theories, and of partially disfiguring the truth; a defect, it added, of all works that do not provide the whole background that the author has used to form his judgments. And the commission is inclined to wish that studies intended to make the facts clear must be undertaken first of all. "The theory that illustrates those facts will soon appear, treading firmly over familiar ground."

Therefore it is not a question of knowing whether the *ad probandum* method, as Señor Chacón calls it, is good or bad in itself, or whether the *ad narrandum* method is preferable to the other in absolute terms. It is only a question of knowing whether the *ad probandum* method, or, to express it more clearly, the method that investigates the inner spirit of a people's deeds, the idea that they express, the future toward which they are aimed, is appropriate in relation to the present state of the history of independent Chile. It is a history that has not yet been written, for so far only a few essays have been published, and they are far from constituting a whole, or even exhausting the subjects that they cover. With which of the two methods should we begin to write our history? With the one that provides the antecedents or the one that deduces the consequences? With the one that clarifies the facts, or the one that comments on them and summarizes them? The Commission believed that it should be the first method. Did it or did it not have a basis for this belief? This, and no other, is the question that had to be settled. Each of the two methods has its place, each is good at the proper time, and there are also times when, according to the writer's judgment or skill, either one or the other ought to be used. The question is purely one of order, of relative appropriateness.

Once this is established, it is easy to see that the quotation from [Amable Guillaume Prosper Brugière] Barante, which Señor Chacón considers decisive, does not touch upon the point under discussion. In the presence of the great historical works of his contemporaries, Barante says that no one direction is exclusive, no one method obligatory. We say the same, agreeing with Barante's approach. When the public is in possession of a large mass of documents and histories, then the historian who undertakes a new work on the basis of those documents can well adopt either the method of philosophical linkage, as Guizot has done in his *Histoire de la civilisation*, or Augustin Thierry's method of colorful narrative in his *Histoire de la conquête de l'Angleterre par les Normands*. But when the history of a country does not exist except in incomplete and scattered documents, in vague traditions that must be weighed and judged, the narrative method is indispensable. Let anyone who denies this cite a single general or particular history that has not begun in this way. But there is more: Barante himself, within the approach he has chosen, does not hide his preference for the philosophy that springs almost spontaneously from facts, told in all their details and native colors, to the philosophy that is presented as a theory or a system *ex profeso*, which always results in a certain fear that history may involuntarily be twisted in order to adjust it to a preconstituted idea which, according to Cousin's expression, may adulterate it. Let my readers examine Barante's preface to his *Histoire des ducs de Bourgogne*, and particularly the history itself, which is an admirable weaving together of original materials without the slightest philosophical pretension.

We do not mean to say that there is or should be an absolute separation between the two methods, which we might call narrative or philosophical. What happens is that the philosophy contained in the former is enclosed in the narrative and rarely appears directly, while in the second it is the chief consideration, to which the facts are subordinated. These facts are not touched upon or explained except to the degree that they show the linkage of cause and effect, their spirit and tendencies. Between the two methods there can be an infinite number of nuances, examples of which it would not be difficult to find in modern historians.

The Commission's judgment is not exclusive, nor is its preference absolute. We need only read its report to be convinced that the arguments adduced by the author of the Prologue lead nowhere; they contest what no one has said or even thought. The Commission has not issued a judgment on any question that divides opinion in the literary world, as he supposes. It has felt inclined to wish that we could be given the premises before arriving at the consequences, the text before the commentaries, the details before they are condensed into generalities. It is impossible to state more modestly a judgment more in consonance with the experience of the scientific world and the doctrine of the famous authors who have written precisely about historical science. And we will say more: given that the point was questionable, the Commission, by declaring itself in favor of one of the opposing opinions, would merely have exercised a right which the laws of the literary republic give to everyone. Is it not allowable for everyone who wants to make use of his intellect to choose, between two opposing ideas, the one that seems to him most reasonable and well-founded? And is that man a champion of literary freedom who forces us to withhold judgment on any doubtful question, and to express no other ideas than those that bear the imprimatur of universal approval?

Señor Chacón offers us a review of the origin and progress of history in Europe beginning with the Crusades. It is a gratuitous review for the subject with which he is dealing, and not an entirely correct one. He begins with Froissart, and places him at the head of the list of chroniclers "who in the twelfth and thirteenth centuries mingled history and fable, the ballads of Charlemagne and King Arthur, with the deeds of chivalry." Señor Chacón forgets that [Jean] Froissart flourished in the fourteenth century, and seems unaware that the ballads of Charlemagne and King Arthur had begun to contaminate history well before the First Crusade. Judging from this review, it could be believed that during the early period of the French language (which, properly speaking, is not "the language of the troubadours") there were no accurate historians, no eyewitnesses, like [Geoffroi de] Villehardouin and [Jean Sire de] Joinville, of the events of the crusades. However that may be, Señor Chacón passes before our eyes a procession of chroniclers, historians, and philosophers of history that begins with Froissart and ends with [Henry] Hallam. "And are we expected to go backward?" he asks us. "Are we expected to close our eyes to the light that comes to us from Europe, fail to utilize the progress that European civilization has made in historical science, as we do in the other arts and sciences that come to us? Or must we tread the same path, from the chronicle to the philosophy of history?"

It is not hard to reply to these questions. A person who has barely placed his feet on a path can hardly go backward. We are not asking to have the chronicles of France rewritten: how can the history of Chile go backward when it has not been written? Once it is written, philosophy will come to give us an idea of each character and each historical event (ours, of course), "treading firmly over familiar ground." Do we have to go and seek our history in Froissart, or [Philippe de Commines], or [Philippe de] Mézières or Sismondi? The real backward movement would consist in beginning where the Europeans have left off.

To assume that "we are expected to close our eyes to the light that comes to us from Europe" is pure oratory. Nobody has thought of doing that. What is expected is that we open our eyes wide to it, and not believe that we can find something in it that is not there nor can be there. Yes, let us read, let us study European histories; let us observe very closely the particular spectacle that each of them develops and summarizes; let us accept the examples and lessons they contain, which is perhaps the aspect of them that we least consider. Let us also use them as a model and guide for our historical labors. Can we find Chile, with all its accidents, its characteristic features, in such books? Those accidents and those features are just what the historian of Chile must describe, whichever of the two methods he may adopt. Open the finest works written by the method of philosophy of history. Do they give us the philosophy of the history of humanity? The Chilean nation is not mankind in the abstract—it is mankind under certain special forms, as special as the mountains, valleys, and rivers of Chile, its plants and animals, the races to which its inhabitants belong, the moral and political circumstances in which our society has been born and now develops. Do those works give us the philosophy of the history of one people, one period? Of England under the Norman conquest, Spain under Moorish domination, France during its memorable revolution? Nothing could be more interesting or more instructive. But let us not forget that the Chilean man of the Independence—the man who is the subject of our history and our peculiar philosophy—is not a Frenchman or an Anglo-Saxon or a Norman, or a Goth or an Arab. He has his own spirit, his own features, and his own peculiar instincts.

We must confess that we have found inconsistency or obscurity in certain passages of the Prologue. Truthfully, the key with which Señor Chacón has tried to resolve these passages in his "first article" has occurred to us. But the idea appeared too contrary to common sense for us to attribute it to him. The fact is that even now we do not dare to credit him with it, and prefer to believe that (undoubtedly our fault) we have not quite understood him.

We beg our readers' pardon. We have prolonged somewhat tiresomely the defense of a truth, of an obvious principle, that for many is a trivial one. But we wanted to speak to young people. Our young men have taken up the study of history eagerly; we have recently seen brilliant proofs of their progress in this field, and we could wish that they fully understand the true mission of history in order to study it successfully. Above all, we would like to warn them of excessive servility toward the science of civilized Europe.

There is a kind of fatality that subjugates emergent nations to those that have preceded it. Greece took over Rome; Rome and Greece took over the modern nations of Europe at the time when letters were restored there; and nowadays we are influenced more than we ought to be by Europe, although, at the same time as we take advantage of its knowledge, we should imitate it in independence of thought. It was not very long ago that European poets went back to pagan history in search of images, and invoked muses in whom neither they nor anyone else believed; a spurned lover would send up devout prayers to Venus to make her soften the heart of his beloved. This was a kind of poetic solidarity similar to that which Señor Chacón seems to want in his history.

Moreover, we must not assign too much value to philosophic terms, generalizations which say little or nothing in themselves to the person who has not looked on living nature in the paintings of history and, if possible, in the ancient and original historians. We are not talking here about our history, but about all history. Young Chileans! Learn to judge for yourselves! Aspire to freedom of thought. Drink of the sources, at least those closest to us. The very language of the original historians— their ideas, even their prejudices and their fabulous legends—are a part of history, and not the least instructive and reliable part. For example, do you want to know what the discovery and conquest of America was like? Read Columbus's diary, the letters of Pedro de Valdivia, those of

Hernán Cortés. Bernal Díaz will tell you much more than [Antonio de] Solís and [William] Robertson. Interrogate every civilization in its works; demand guarantees of every historian. That is the primary philosophy that we must learn from Europe.

Our civilization also will be judged by its works, and if it is seen to servilely copy European civilization even in matters where this is not applicable, what judgment will be formed of us by a Michelet, or a Guizot of the future? They will say that America has not yet shaken off her chains, that she follows in our footsteps with bandaged eyes, that in her works there is no sense of independent thought, nothing original, nothing characteristic. She apes the forms of our philosophy and does not take over its spirit. Her civilization is an exotic plant that has not yet absorbed all the sap of the land that sustains it.

One further observation, and we will have finished. What is called the philosophy of history is a science still in its infancy. Were we to judge it by the standards of Cousin, it has scarcely taken the first steps in its long journey. It is still a fluctuating science; the conviction of one century is anathema to the following century; the thinkers of the nineteenth century have rejected those of the eighteenth. The ideas of the loftiest of them, Montesquieu, are no longer accepted without restrictions. Have we reached the end? Posterity will give the answer. It is still an arena where parties struggle. Which of them will win out definitively? Knowledge, like Nature, feeds on ruins, and while systems are born and grow and wither and die, it will rise again, fresh and flourishing on its ashes, and will preserve eternal youth.

NOTES TO PART TWO

1. First published in two installments in *El Araucano*, Nos. 208 (29 July 1836) and 309 (5 August 1836). Is is included in *OC*, vol. 22, pp. 657–667. This essay provides the rationale for universal education, with emphasis on its practical as well as moral aspects, that would occupy Bello for the rest of his life in Chile.

2. First published as an untitled editorial in *El Araucano*, No. 278, 31 December 1835. It is included in *OC*, vol. 18, pp. 3–5. Bello received a law degree from the University of San Felipe in 1836, but as indicated in this article, he had both concerns about the narrow practice of the law and great expectations for the field in informing and strengthening national republican institutions.

3. First published in *El Araucano*, No. 184, 21 March 1834. It is included in *OC*, vol. 8, pp. 489–494. Bello's defense of Latin in this article would appear

to contradict his views on Latin and Spanish grammar, but his principal contention in his grammatical works was the problematic practice of transferring the grammatical categories of one language in order to understand the workings of another. Latin, as a language with deep roots in a variety of humanistic fields, and especially Roman law, is defended here from the attacks of the liberal paper *El Valdiviano Federal*. Hence the polemical style, which Bello used in his press articles, but which was moderate by the standards of a highly contentious Chilean press during the period.

4. Published in *Anales de la Universidad de Chile*, vol. 1 (1843–44): 139–152. It is included in *OC*, vol. 21, pp. 2–28. The creation of the University of Chile involved closing the colonial, church-run University of San Felipe. Bello, who was asked to design the university's statutes and preside as Rector, crafted an inaugural speech that, while consistent with his educational and philosophical views, was also designed to dispel any concerns about a possible conflict between church and state.

5. First published in *La Revista Católica*, No. 165, 15 September 1848. It is included in *OC*, vol. 21, pp. 22–28. As this essay demonstrates, Bello was convinced that there was no incompatibility between the educational aims of church and state. Both could benefit from the contributions of the other. Still, it is clear that Bello supported more openness on the part of the clergy to the social and cultural needs of secular society.

6. This quinquennial report was read before the faculty of the University of Chile on 29 October, 1848. It is included in *OC*, vol. 21, pp. 28–81. A comprehensive report on the state of Chilean education and the activities of the various faculties of the University of Chile, the detailed text has been edited for this collection in order to highlight Bello's central educational ideas. One part that has been omitted includes a homage to members of the University rules died during the period, including his son Francisco. In addition to emphasizing the supervisory role of the University, and the key role of the *Instituto Nacional* as the teaching arm of the institution, Bello elaborates on his view of the need to develop Chilean research in the humanities and sciences.

7. First published in *El Araucano*, Nos. 742 and 743, of 8 and 15 November 1844, respectively. It is included in *OC*, vol. 23, pp. 155–173. The University of Chile was mandated by law to develop the field of Chilean history. A report, or *Memoria*, on a historical subject was to be presented annually to the faculty. Bello commissioned the first of these *Memorias* to José Victorino Lastarria, who was a member of the Faculty of Philosophy and Humanities. The original title of Lastarria's essay was "Investigaciones sobre la influencia social de la conquista i del sistema colonial de los españoles en Chile." Bello produced this comment, the first of a series of other comments on history, in order to define the purposes of the *Memorias*, in particular, and of the craft of history more generally.

8. First published in *El Araucano*, No. 909, 7 January 1848. It is included in *OC*, vol. 23, pp. 221–227. Bello directed this essay to the prologue of Lastarria's work rather than its text because the historiographical assumptions that he wished to contest were clearly stated in the former. Bello continued to defend a notion of history based on research and documentation rather than "philosophical" interpretation. This essay provides an important link to his definitive ideas on the subject, which he presented in subsequent months in 1848.

9. First published in the form of two articles in *El Araucano*, Nos. 912 and 913 of 28 January and 4 February 1848. They were included in *OC*, vol. 23 under the titles "Modo de escribir la historia," (pp. 231–242) and "Modo de estudiar la historia," (pp. 245–252), following the format of the first Chilean edition (vol. 7, published in 1884). They are, however, sufficiently related to merge in one article. For the purposes of this collection, long quotations from various European historians have been omitted, as they illustrate, but do not alter, the substance of the articles. Bello continued to discuss some of the ideas on history which he presented in his previous rebuttal to Jacinto Chacón, but this time in the context of Chacón's own articles of rebuttal in several issues of *El Progreso*, between January and February, 1848.

III

Government, Law, and International Relations

Letter to Servando Teresa de Mier
(1821)

15 November 1821
London

My dear Mier,

Two nights ago I received your letter of the seventh of last month, which has given me the pleasure that you can easily imagine; I too have had no lack of misfortunes, the most terrible that can afflict a sensitive heart, as mine unfortunately is; but in any case I have had the consolation of not lacking resources with which to live.[1] A man from Havana who has been in London for some time, and who has just left for Tampico in an English ship carrying a steam engine for draining certain mines in Mexico, has given me a good deal of news about you; though to tell the truth, I did not give much credit to them, for the person in question does not have among his vices too much addiction to the truth. His name is Don Mariano Medina, and he told me that he sailed from Veracruz to Havana with you.

Here, as you can imagine, the latest news from Mexico has caused quite a sensation. Everyone has the most favorable possible notion of the advantages and resources of that part of America, and right now all the merchants are making guesses about it. I don't know what to say about the government, because it continues to maintain its usual reserve, though I am and have always been of the opinion that our compatriots have no reason to complain of it, and that its conduct has been very different from the conduct observed by that Machiavellian government which is, of all nations both ancient and modern, most odious in my eyes. It is true that England, like the other great European powers, would be glad to see monarchical ideas prevail in our countries. I do not say that this feeling is dictated by philanthropic ideas. I am well acquainted with the spirit of the cabinets on this side of the ocean, and have never believed that justice and humanity weigh very much on statesmen's scales. But I will say that on this point the interests of European governments coincide with those of the American peoples; that monarchy (limited, of course) is the only government suitable for us, and that I regard as particularly unfortunate those countries which, because of their circumstances, cannot consider this type of government. What a misfortune that Venezuela, after such a glorious fight, a fight which in virtues and heroism can be compared with any of the most famous battles recorded in history, and which leaves a long way behind the struggle of the fortunate North Americans; what a misfortune, I repeat, that for lack of a regular government (for the republican type of government will never be so among us) the country continues to be the theater of a civil war, even after we have nothing to fear from the Spaniards!

But let us leave this subject aside and deal with your personal affairs. Mrs. Moore is alive; fate, or rather Providence, has repaid her beneficence, giving her husband a brilliant inheritance of a hundred and fifty thousand pounds sterling. She has received letters from you, and I suppose has answered them, for she has told me that she greatly appreciated the testimony of your gratitude that you have given her. [José María] Blanco [White] is ill, as always, though as good and as pleasant as always; but we rarely have the good fortune of seeing him in London.

No news of your books. Only the devil could have put into your head the idea of sending 750 copies of a single book (whatever it was) to Buenos Aires, which of all the countries in America is undoubtedly the most ignorant and where people read least. Fifty copies would have been too many, and I am sure that no more than twenty have been sold. It is a great pity that some of them didn't stay in London, for at the moment there has been a demand for them, and in these circumstances they would have sold very well. I will write to Capdevila and Manuel Pinto asking them to send me a hundred, and if I succeed in selling them here, I will send the money to wherever you tell me. But

I think it necessary for you to write to those men authorizing this request that I mean to make of them.

[Antonio José de] Irisarri, a representative of Chile, is here; he esteems you greatly and will write to you. Give us news about things in Mexico and the Cortes in Madrid, for we are in the dark here about the ideas and intrigues of the court and the Peninsular legislature.

It would be a very good idea if you would set about writing a complete history of the Mexican revolution, incorporating into it a recasting of the first one you published in London. But if you do, it would be well to leave out certain rhetorical passages that are not compatible with the impartiality of history, as you know better than anyone. It is merely a question of preserving the memory of events; that alone is enough to heap the enemies of our cause with infamy, and all the more certainly the more just and impartial the historian is. Remember that you are speaking to posterity, not with the [Juan López] Canceladas and other journalists of the same stripe, whose ephemeral productions will return to the bars where their authors learned their manners, there to contain *thus et odores, et piper, et quidquid chartis amicitur ineptis.* [incense and spices and pepper and whatever is wrapped in useless pages.—Horace, *Epistles*]

But I am afraid that I am a voice crying in the wilderness, and that your blood is too hot to follow this advice. In that case, don't think about writing the history.

One who is and will always be your true friend,

United States A[ndrés]. Bello
Dr. Mier
Care of Manuel Torres, Esq.
Philadelphia

American Politics

(1832)

In previous issues we have presented to the readers of *El Araucano* a long extract from the message sent by the President to the Congress of the United States of America.[2] It would be difficult to publish a more instructive and more curious document. For us, the politics of the United States is a subject of great importance, owing to the influence that it must necessarily exercise on the fate of the new American nations and the weight that the example of that powerful country will always have in questions of international law.

Those who see only the surface of things explain the rapid progress of the North Americans by the single word "federation," as if this were the first federation that had ever been seen, or the only one that exists in the world, or as if all federations had produced similar results. Any free constitution would have prospered equally in peoples as prepared for it as were the North Americans, and favored by the same natural circumstances. And the most perfect federation would have accomplished little or nothing without the spirit that imbued that budding society, a spirit that grew and thrived in the shadow of monarchical institutions, not because they were monarchical but because they were free, and because in them the inviolability of the law was fortunately combined with guarantees of individual freedom.

If in the new American states emancipation has not produced that rapid progress, to find the cause we need only compare the political education of the Spanish colonies, aimed exclusively at perpetuating their childhood, with the system adopted by Great Britain in its northern establishments, each of which was a free republic with a perfect representative government. What did these governments do to become independent but erect the dome of the magnificent structure that their forefathers had left them? We had to begin by tearing down, and we are still, and will be for some time, engaged in this preparatory task. But anyone who examines with impartial eyes what we have done, despite so many difficulties, will see that important steps have been taken in all the American republics; that amid great political errors, great things have been done; and that a struggle has been carried on with incredible sacrifices and with no outside help, in which our adversary counted on our habits as aids to himself. The fact is that these lose ground daily, that public opinion is becoming informed, that the time has come at last when our governments, if they aspire to permanence, will have to rely on this supreme regulator of social destinies. And (which in our opinion is a sure sign of the success that will crown our efforts) the *beau idéal* of visionary politicians and the architects of utopias will have lost all its prestige.

Monarchies in America

(1835)

The coronation of General [Antonio López de] Santa Anna as Emperor of Mexico (about which we know only what was published in *El Mercurio de Valparaíso*) is not an event that ought to cause satisfaction to the friends of order and liberal institutions.[3] For a long time we have observed with extreme skepticism the theoretical speculations of constitutional politicians; we judge the merit of a constitution by the effective and practical benefits enjoyed by the people under its aegis. And we do not believe that the monarchical system, considered in itself and apart from local circumstances, is incompatible with the existence of the social guarantees meant to protect individuals against the assaults of power. But monarchy is a prestigious form of government; its antiquity and the transmission of a recognized right inherited by a long series of generations are its indispensable elements, and without them it is, in the eyes of a people, an ephemeral creation that can be overthrown as easily as it was erected, and is at the mercy of every popular whim. The time for monarchies has passed in America. When Mexico made the first attempt at a constitution of this kind, it did so in much more favorable circumstances for its entire success; and yet [Augustín de] Iturbide's work was too weak to resist the attacks of the democratic spirit. Will Santa Anna be more fortunate?

On Relations with Spain
(1835–44)

1

Judging by the latest news from Europe and private communications that have reached our hands, we do not see that recognition of South American independence, announced as one of the first matters on which the successors of [Francisco] Cea Bermúdez were going to concentrate, has taken a single step forward in Madrid during the new administration.[4]

In the debates in the Cortes stemming from the treasury's financial straits, some members have taken notice of the former American colonies, proposing that they be adjudicated a proportional part of the Spanish debt, and that if the governments of England and France wanted their subjects to be paid, they should use their influence to carry out this distribution. The ministers of the queen regent, proceeding with the mysterious reserve that they have adopted from the outset in everything concerning America, have either abstained from answering these suggestions or have given only evasive answers.

For some time now, the conduct of the Spanish ministers has seemed most unlikely to inspire confidence. Reading between the lines of parliamentary and diplomatic formulas, it seems apparent that Spain is willing to renounce her imaginary rights, but that in exchange she expects important concessions which amount to more than mere stipulations of friendship and trade. If these do not involve political combinations threatening to the institutions and interests of the new republics, why so much circumspection and secrecy? Why has not a single word been pronounced on the American question either in the queen's speech to the Cortes or in ministerial memoranda? Why such repugnance toward the frank explanations requested by some members of the parliament? Why that veil of mystery over the long evening sessions which the Spanish cabinet, according to what [Francisco] Martínez de la Rosa has told the Cortes, was holding to discuss the matter? And what is so difficult and complicated about it, why does it give so much trouble to the queen's ministers? The American governments have explained themselves about this matter with a frankness that does them honor, declaring in no uncertain terms what they are asking and what they are willing to concede. This is an extremely simple negotiation which, if a desire exists to handle it in good faith and in the true interests of both parties, should not leave anything for diplomacy to do but a bit of editing and the exercise of pure etiquette.

2

For some time now *El Valdiviano [Federal]* has engaged in the dull task of commenting on our articles, but in an extremely flattering way for the editors, since its charges are so futile, its interpretations so violent, its arguments so vague and intricate, that it simply seems that, for lack of material on which to exercise criticism, it invents, like its prototype the ingenious knight of La Mancha, the monsters and giants toward which it aims its lance.

"*El Araucano,*" it states, "seems to be more a partisan of Spain than a true son of America, when it laments, as it does, the fact that Cea Bermúdez's successors have not taken a step to recognize America."

Readers who are kind enough to glance at the editorial article in our No. 232, to which *El Valdiviano* refers, will observe the candor with which it attributes "laments" to us, when there is not a word or a sentence or any other thing in it resembling a lament. In that article we limited ourselves to expressing reasons for distrust of the secretive and mysterious behavior of the Spanish administration on a subject which, in our opinion, requires nothing more than good faith and frankness; and all the perspicacity of *El Valdiviano* (which sometimes manages to see things that do not exist) was needed to find the slightest touch of partiality for Spain in that article.

But let us admit for the sake of argument that we did indeed lament the conduct of the Spanish administration. Cannot a good American want peace with Spain and deplore the ridiculous prejudices that hold it back? *El Valdiviano* has said itself, in one of its lucid intervals, that "no enemy should be despised as impotent, and that at a time when we thought we were completely secure after the glorious victory of Maipú, a wretched sergeant who had miraculously escaped death succeeded in setting the whole province of Concepción aflame and throwing the entire republic into a state of alarm." There would be nothing strange about the fact that a true friend of humanity and America would regret an enemy's error which, both to his detriment and ours, prolonged a state of mutual insecurity and danger.

El Valdiviano claims that we are partisans of Spain, for in speaking of the intentions expressed in the Cortes to burden America with part of the Spanish debt and requesting the influence of two powerful nations for the purpose, we have not mentioned such a presumption, leaving room for this silence to be interpreted as tacit acceptance. But did we not express our opinion on this matter some time ago? And has not the Foreign Minister's memorandum been printed in the columns of *El Araucano*, in which one of the bases established for the expected peace negotiations with Spain is that Chile refuses any kind of pecuniary concession? Is this not the very thing to which we alluded in our No. 232, contrasting the open and explicit declarations of the American governments with the secrecy and evasions of the Spanish cabinet? Why more explanations about something that is so well known, and about which we are all in agreement? We were not concerned that sensible and unprejudiced readers would interpret the second paragraph as a tacit approval, for such approval is not there. As for other kinds of readers, any explanation would have been superfluous. If this door were closed, they would have slipped out by another. Truth is indivisible, and there are an infinite number of ways to rave.

El Valdiviano defends its opinion of our "tacit approval" because we said that the Americans have explained themselves on the matter with a frankness that does them honor, declaring in no uncertain terms what they are asking and what they are willing to concede. It does not like the sound of the verb "ask." In its imagination it sees the Spanish ministers full of rosy hopes because the Americans are "asking" for something. It even hears the words they speak to each other in the cabinet, conspiring to sell us what we are "asking" at the highest possible price.

El Valdiviano could have spared itself these elaborate political interpretations if it had consulted the dictionary of the Spanish language, where it would have seen that not only can one ask a favor and ask for alms, but one can ask in justice, ask a price for what is given, and by asking can claim, demand, and exact. It might also have reflected that favors are not asked for in no uncertain terms, and that this way of asking is more typical of claiming an act of justice with weapons in one's hand than of requesting a favor.

Recognition of our independence will not be a "favor" by Spain, but it will be a good thing for America because peace is a good thing, and because peace will expand our trade, placing us in relationships either with Spain herself or with other countries who have declined to trade with us as long as we lacked a title which, they believe, is necessary to legitimize our political existence.

Nor would it have been a bad idea for *El Valdiviano*, before attacking our article, to consult precedents. Chile has not asked anything of Spain. As far as we know she has not initiated any kind of negotiations with that power. Up to the present her agents in foreign countries have not even received instructions for dealing with the Spanish ministers. The conduct of those agents, undoubtedly in agreement with the spirit of their government, has been prudent and circumspect to the highest degree. In short, Chile has simply declared to her allied republics, and through the press to the entire world, what she demands of Spain in case the negotiations come to pass, and what she is willing to concede. She demands recognition of her independence under the established form of government, and is ready to concede reciprocally beneficial commercial stipulations; but she refuses pecuniary concessions in the strongest possible terms. Chile and other American governments have expressed themselves to this effect, and this is the frankness that we have praised in them. If the Spanish government had done as much on its side, any negotiations that we might institute with it would be "extremely simple, and would not leave diplomacy anything to do but a bit of editing and the exercise of pure etiquette."

3

We bring to our readers' attention the debate that took place on 9 December of last year [1834] during the session of the Spanish Chamber of Deputies, on recognition of the new American states; and we can do no less than to applaud the conciliatory tone with which the ministers have expressed themselves, though we wish that they a been a trifle franker, and—just as they showed themselves ready to perform an action demanded not only by humanity and justice but by Spain's own interests—that they had stated the conditions under which the queen's ministers propose to carry it out.

In confirmation of the arrangements that Spain seems willing to make, we can add that the president of the United States of America has informed the president of Chile, through its chargé d'affaires in Santiago, that the [U.S.] minister in Madrid has been officially notified that the Spanish government was ready to receive the duly authorized agents of the new republics, and to deal with them on the subject of recognition of their independence.

It appears that the time has come for the new states to reply to this invitation, authorizing diplomatic agents who, provided with instructions already agreed upon with their respective congresses, will initiate this important discussion with the Spanish government. There may be some who believe that, in imitation of the Spaniards, we ought to feel that it is indecorous and degrading to send plenipotentiaries instead of receiving them. But if one of the belligerent parties must take the first step, we believe that there is no impartial judge who would not decide this question of etiquette in favor of Spain.

Some of the observations made by the Spanish ministers strike us as not quite exact, and we think that they should be rejected.

"The present Government," said the Spanish Secretary of the Treasury, "does not intend to take steps that it considers dishonorable, not forgetting that it controlled those countries not long ago, that they owe Spain their civilization, and that Spain, though it does not refuse to deal with them, realizes that it is much stronger than their governments." Spain undoubtedly has the means to do us harm; but she does not have the power to do us harm from which the smallest good may come to her, which does not turn back upon her, even though it be no

more than increasing her financial difficulties and depriving her, perhaps forever, of the advantages she could gain from trade with us. If
the Spanish administration is governed by the principles of common
sense, what good is the superiority of resources that she brags about?
Will she sacrifice the nation's real interests to an insensate pride?

We are not unaware of the benefits the Americas owe to Spain, but
we will not include in those benefits the colonial system that she established. Her codes of law, says the Minister of Justice, if compared
with those that have prevailed until now in the colonies of England
and France, give witness that the legislation of the Indies was superior
to that of all other nations. If the wisdom of a colonial legislation were
judged by the choice of means adopted to perpetrate the colonies' state
of tutelage, that superiority might be true; but in other respects, what
comparison can possibly be made between the Spanish colonial regime
and that of the English colonies? In those colonies there were provincial
legislatures, juries, and free press. In our colonies, what was there?

4

We possess only a manuscript copy of the petition we are printing,
addressed to the Queen Regent of Spain, and do not know with cer-
tainty whether it was approved by the Spanish Chamber of Deputies
and in consequence presented to the queen as an expression of that
body's opinion, or whether it simply represents the private vote of the
individuals who are its signatories. We incline toward the first interpretation, and are going to address it.

The Spanish government cannot accede to this petition by the deputies without abandoning the attempt, to which it is bound in our
opinion, to enter into negotiations with the Americans on the basis of
their independence, and without aborting these negotiations at a very
early stage. The petition shows a certain desire to leave dangling the
Spanish crown's claims on the emancipated provinces, as well as certain
hopes of union that give it an insidious tone, very different from the
tone of frankness and good faith that appears in the verbal explanations
of Martínez de la Rosa and in some of his written communications.
The American plenipotentiaries, if this was the Spanish cabinet's intention, will no doubt hasten to destroy this crude illusion. The negotiations would dissipate like smoke at the slightest appearance of

odious claims. Our very interest in peace obliges us to administer a new and decisive rebuff to the visionaries who think that peace is possible under any plan but absolute political separation; for this is the only way to establish friendly and fraternal relations, which can be based solely on mutual confidence.

In this petition there is mention of influence and counsels, internal discussions, changes of government, and so on. Those who like rumors have a large field here over which to spread themselves. We gladly leave them to this innocuous pastime. No glosses are necessary to make everyone see all that is ill-timed, not to call it something worse, about this attempt to guide the political careers of other peoples by those who have done nothing, up till now, but make a shambles of their own. Of all the internal confrontations that have taken place in America, which of them can be compared with the bloody, brutal fight that is now devastating a considerable portion of the Peninsula? We hope that the queen's ministers have formed a less erroneous idea of the present state of the Americas, and will have the good sense to reject a plan which, under whatever name and under whatever colors it is presented, can deceive no one, and will serve only to offer fresh fuel to mistrust and hatred, further postponing the durable, beneficent, and truly fraternal agreement that is the object of all our hopes.

5

We now know officially that the Mexican Federation has named a plenipotentiary to deal with Spain on recognition of its independence. Venezuela has done so some time ago; and though it revoked the mission of General [Mariano] Montilla, we know that it did this only to replace him with General [Carlos] Soublette, a man well known for his prolonged and relevant services to the cause of the revolution. The Peruvian government has recently named a plenipotentiary for the same purpose. Bolivia has conferred the same charge on Señor [Casimiro] Olañeta, its representative to the French government. Letters recently received from Montevideo tell us that Uruguay was also hastening to take part in these negotiations by sending a commissioner to Spain, and it is probable that the other parts of America will adopt similar conduct. This step has seemed so natural and opportune that the President of the United States [Andrew Jackson], after having taken a great interest in accelerating the process, has spontaneously offered to our government the support and good offices of the American Legation in Madrid.

There are some among us who doubt the appropriateness and advisability of this measure; but the reasons on which they support their opinion do not seem very convincing to us. It is not a question of making peace with Spain at any price, but of starting the negotiations with her that she has invited us to make, and from which peace may or may not result, depending on the conditions that she proposes. If these conditions were such that our honor or interest would not allow us to accept them, no one would think of purchasing peace at this price without being a traitor to his country.

Spain wishes to put an end to the war. She has declared this to the world. She assures us that she will exclude no basis for peace, and the language of her government's official organs has clearly given us to understand that recognition of our independence and sovereignty is a concession that they have already granted and resolved. Since this is the state of things, we have no hesitation in saying that a government that could cast these indications aside without examining them would assume the greatest of responsibilities before God and humanity. War is a mode of existence which not only brings in its train great evils for the warring parties, it also disturbs the order of the universal society of peoples, imposing onerous obligations on them and hindering their mutual commerce and correspondence. War, says [Emmerich de] Vattel, is such a terrible scourge that justice alone, together with a certain type of necessity, can warrant it, render it praiseworthy, or place it beyond the reach of censure.

Listening to our enemy does not force us to receive his proposals as law and place our fate in his hands. Let us arm ourselves with mistrust; let us take all possible precautions for our security. But let us hear him at least; the counsels of prudence are no bar to the humanity and courtesy which, even when exercising the baneful right of war, distinguish civilized peoples from barbarians and make victory even more glorious.

Will some say that we cannot count on Spain's good faith, and hence should not engage in fruitless negotiations? Even if we believed this we would gain a great deal by giving the world proof of our peaceful intentions, and by making the responsibility for the odiousness of a rash war fall on our enemy.

Will some say that the moment is not opportune? Spain does not retain an inch of territory on the American continent; and while she nourishes civil discord in her bosom, and her attention is concentrated on the arduous task of establishing institutions that arouse the open or concealed hostility of the ruling classes, peace and order reign in all the new republics, the bases of their political organization are firmly established, and differences of opinion concern only points of secondary importance. Spain needs external peace more than we do. Above all, victory has left us masters of the field. There cannot be a more opportune moment to deal with an enemy.

Will some say that any agreement we make with the liberal government in Spain might not be recognized by the pretender [to the throne], if he should triumph in the end? The possibility is unlikely, but let us entertain it. The pact celebrated with Isabel II's government would always give us a very valuable claim in the eyes of all the nations that have recognized her as the sovereign of Spain, and above all we would be in the same situation as we are now: the negotiations would have been fruitless, but we would not have lost anything.

Will some say that Spain ought to send agents to America, and not America hers to Spain? Let us respect the feelings that make some persons feel as they do, but we repeat that in this question of etiquette any impartial judge would pronounce in favor of Spain. War has not destroyed the natural relationships that we have with this power; from the moment when Spain sheathed her sword, we owe her consideration, and even her misfortunes make her worthy of respect in our eyes. Indeed, she had already taken the first step, publicly inviting us to deal without excluding any basis for agreement. What shame is there in our taking the second step? In circumstances very different from the present ones, it was not considered indecorous to send commissioners to Europe with full powers to negotiate with the Spanish government. Then, at a time when a large part of America was still occupied by enemy troops, and when we had not heard from Spanish lips any language but pride and threats, this measure could have been looked upon as motivated by a timid policy. Today there is not the slightest reason to believe this. Our plenipotentiaries can present themselves before the throne of our former tyrants with their heads held high, upholding a cause in which the prestige of victory is added to its irrefutable justice.

6

El Filopolita jeers at the plan to send a mission to Spain as one of those absurd and frivolous ideas worthy only of occupying the attention of children. The reasons it employs, after they have been sifted and separated from rhetorical exaggerations and everything else that is simply chaff as far as reason is concerned—except as it tries to divert and dazzle—can be reduced to only one: we are in fact independent. Recognition by Spain does not confer on us any title of legitimacy that would make enjoyment of our independence more tranquil and secure.

But is it true that this recognition would not produce real benefits? Without it, would our flag be received in all the ports of Europe? Have we established communications even with the Holy See? It is true that the nations that we most need, or who can have most influence on our affairs, have recognized us. But what a recognition! What treaties have the Americans made with some of them! We do not think it certain that, as *El Filopolita* says, we occupy a place in the political hierarchy comparable to that of the other peoples of the earth who call themselves nations. The United States of America is perhaps the only power that has recognized us truly and cordially; and yet, even the United States of America needs to recognize, ostensibly at least, (and in this case what is ostensible is what is real) Spain's rights of sovereignty. The United States, which would probably resist any ambitious claim on the Americas by other powers, would be a mere spectator if Spain attempted it. England and France would, in their turn, do the same. As for the courts of "passive obedience and divine right," there are clear indications that they would be something more than spectators, if they could, and that they would favor Spain, as they have sometimes done, with something more effective than good wishes. *El Filopolita* will not deny that every nation, without a single exception, still recognizes Spain as sovereign of the Americas, and that in consequence, in everything concerning Spain, we are outside the protection of international law. If *El Filopolita* believes that such a state of affairs is not dangerous, and that Spain's impotence is eternal, that she can do nothing either by herself or aided by other nations; that the new American republics inspire more sympathy than Spain in the monarchical courts of Europe, which in a sense owe their existence to her; if it believes that in this era of revolutions and vicissitudes the day will never arrive when Spain's claims, either in her hands or those of some nation more powerful than she, will become a dangerous tool against independence, or against America's present institutions: if it believes this, it believes that we lack nothing, and that the legation to Spain is pure diplomatic ceremony without any real value.

Spain has no means of subjugating us, says *El Filopolita*. It is true; but she does have the means to harass us. An immense and underpopulated coastline offers an infinite number of vulnerable points. Would it be impossible for Spain to take over some of them, not to keep them or subjugate them but to use them as security in order to obtain more favorable conditions from us than we are ready to concede to her now? *El Valdiviano* has said very sensibly that there is no such thing as a weak enemy. Not to make peace with ours, when we can negotiate it without humiliation, and to run the risk of having to buy it back later with sacrifices (as certain states in America have sometimes been willing to do), would seem to us, in a government whose fidelity to our country we were sure of, to be the height of folly. This is a matter in which every eventuality must be prepared for, and in which it is impossible to err through an excess of precaution. The fate of the present generation and future generations is involved in it. And what do we risk, after all, by dealing with the enemy? Absolutely nothing. If we make an honorable peace with him, we will improve our prospects; if not, at least we will have given proof of our peaceful intentions, and we will remain as we were before.

Actual possession and legal possession are one and the same in politics; that in this world force makes a mockery of laws, and laws without power are useless, are dicta on which many very clever things can be said in a satirical and declamatory style. However, injustice, even in the present-day course of human affairs, is the exception. Justice is the general rule because it is the necessary condition of societies. And when we say justice, we understand the justice that is clothed in those forms and rites which, in international as well as civil law, are indispensable to their authenticity and external effects. Even first-class powers base themselves on forms and rites. Are we strong enough to disdain them?

If the distinction between fact and law is one of those Scholastic quibbles which "the progress of civilization and the enlightened ideas of the century" have relegated to imaginary spaces, we proclaim our ignorance without a blush. Our excuse is the opinion of all the jurists and writers on the law, and the example of the nations that have been in our situation. Holland did not think recognition by Spain superfluous. She went to a great deal of trouble to obtain it, and was not satisfied with anything less than the Spanish monarch's solemn renunciation in the first article of the Treaty of Münster. She was so insistent on it that, as [Johannes von] Müller says (and *El Filopolita* knows very well what kind of a historian Müller is), "as soon as she succeeded in being recognized by Spain as an independent republic, believing that she no longer had any reason to continue the war, she made a separate peace with that power, in which her ally France had no part." And keep in mind Holland's role in the world at that time. She was the foremost naval power and the close ally of the Protestant states and the House of Bourbon. Her flag fluttered on every sea and was known and respected even by the most barbarous and remote nations. She had rich establishments in both the East and West Indies. Indeed, her power was superior to that of Spain herself. And yet she did not consider herself degraded by receiving from Spain the recognition of a sovereignty that she had enjoyed in fact for nearly a century.

The United States of America did not think of recognition by Great Britain as an idle formality or a degradation. The American commissioners encountered some difficulties on this point, even when England had already agreed to peace, and yet they insisted on this recognition as an indispensable condition; and such was the eagerness with which they received it that—fearing some obstacle on account of the claims of France, their ally—they concealed the preliminaries of peace from the French until the treaties were signed, disobeying the instructions of Congress. One of these American commissioners was [Benjamin] Franklin; and surely we will not include him among the number of the timid who pay attention to unimportant details.

These cases, to which we could add others which we need not recall because they are more recent, show (unless we are mistaken) that what *El Filopolita* calls a useless formula is in fact current coin, which has value in the conferences and protocols of European diplomacy. And we cannot deny that old Europe, with all her outworn prejudices and feudal and peripatetic traits, has weight on the world's scale.

In view of the surprise that the legation to Spain has caused *El Filopolita*, it would appear that this was an occurrence peculiar to Chile, and that the other American republics had not thought this step honorable, appropriate, and very natural. It is true that there was much declamation in Colombia against the mission to Spain, and that a good deal of noise was made there about "Spain's impotence," and "*de facto* possession," and "victory," and "Goths." The senate did not approve General Montilla's mission and revoked the powers of that illustrious patriot; but it did so only to replace him hastily with another plenipotentiary.

Hence we cannot see anything extravagant or unusual or ill-timed about the Chilean government's conduct. If it is distinguished by anything, it is by the liberality with which, even though it could have taken this step unilaterally, it consulted with the legislature and has made the bases of negotiation open to all.

7

We think that *El Filopolita* writes in good faith, and do not hesitate to believe it when it assures us that the only motives that have guided its pen have been the public good and the praiseworthy desire to have the question of the legation to Spain decided with full knowledge of its background. But if this is the case, as we think it is, should not *El Filopolita* refrain from using expressions that distort the question, and seem deliberately chosen to give an incorrect idea of the central matter, and to present it in an unfavorable way? To "entreat" is to obtain a favor that has been requested by begging for it, and no one is going to beg Spain for anything. She has demonstrated the first desires for peace; she is really the one who has taken the first step. To approach her, to test the sincerity of her cabinet, to arrange an honorable peace with her, like the peace which crowned Holland's independence and that of the British colonies, or, if she still cherishes illusions, to disabuse her of them: is this what *El Filopolita* called "entreating" recognition, and what it has previously described as "humiliating ourselves"?

The instability of Queen Cristina's government is offered as an objection. It would be well founded if we were risking anything on our side. If, for instance, we were to purchase our independence with a million or two million pesos, there would be some reason to say, "Let us wait until there is a solid government in Spain; let us not make a costly sacrifice until we are sure it will produce the desired result. If the Infante Don Carlos wins, we will have lost that money, and Queen

Cristina's recognition will be inexistent and null." But in the present case, what value does such an objection have? Is there any rule of prudence or honor that prevents us from taking a step in which one hypothesis can have a good result and the opposite hypothesis can do us no harm at all? Honor does not bar us from taking it, and prudence demands that we take it.

"But such recognition," says *El Filopolita*, "would be indecorous, because European diplomacy would think it offered by force of circumstances." We do not know what the theory of European diplomacy is, but we do know what its practice has always been: to shrewdly spy out the circumstances and skillfully take advantage of them to achieve its ends, even when the credentials of reason and justice that favor our cause are absent. Besides, what country asks Spain to choose between recognizing us or perishing? In our opinion, Spain is fully free to adopt the position she wishes. By recognizing us, she will enjoy our trade; by denying recognition, she will keep on existing as she has existed these past twenty years. Why should not this be as good a time as any other to deal with Spain, without doing violence to the chivalric generosity that *El Filopolita* recommends to us?

The language of Martínez de la Rosa and the other ministers, during the debates in the Cortes, has been in our opinion sufficiently clear. Recognition of independence has been mentioned in a way that leaves no room for twisting the facts. In the letter to Señor [José] Gestal of Montevideo (which can be considered as addressed to the governments of America), the president of the Council says very clearly that they are not thinking of excluding any basis for negotiation. The government of the United States, which has very good ways of knowing what is going on, and of probing the Spanish cabinet's political plans, has understood that this is the case. The ministers of the American republics in Paris and London have formed the same idea. Is this not sufficient to excuse the government from any charge of indiscretion? We do not censure the skepticism of *El Filopolita*. Let it doubt and welcome. Neither do we have a blind faith in European diplomacy. What we do say is that, even considering the outcome of the negotiations as doubtful, there is no reason to reject them. If they are successful we win; if they are not, we do not lose. On the contrary, we will put a better face on our cause. For the enemy will have given further proof of his stubbornness and injustice, and we, by dealing with him decorously and courteously, will deserve the appreciation even of *El Filopolita*, and of every man who is able to distinguish between modest dignity and plebeian haughtiness, between true patriotism and that other false and simulated patriotism whose badge is boastfulness and bluster.

We will not insist further on what we said in our article about Spain's weakness. Conquest is not the only object of hostility. A province, a town, a desert island, are prizes of great value in war, even when there is no thought of permanent occupation. The fortune of arms would always be in our favor; we have no doubt of that. But, in good politics or in good ethics, can we throw away the chance for an honorable peace, for the hope of a victory, no matter how brilliant?

Let us return to the advisability and opportuneness of the negotiations, a point on which, unfortunately, our liberal and enlightened adversary does not think as we do. *El Filopolita* insists that recognition by Spain is a pure formula; but it does not take the trouble to answer the questions we posed on a previous occasion, proving that something which produces real and practical results is not pure formula, and is something that nations more powerful than we are, with more means of defending themselves and of offending their former mother countries, have thought of as important and necessary. Undoubtedly the primary consideration is to have justice on our side. But this is not enough; the triumph of our cause consists in having that justice recognized by all. And it cannot be recognized without Spain's recognition, for in the external forum of the other powers Spain is the rightful sovereign, and still as free to do whatever she is able and wishes to do with us without anyone's having the right to prevent her, as she was before the American insurrection. This is the true state of things; and those who believe that England, France, and the United States recognize us as they recognize Switzerland or Portugal, for example, are very much mistaken.

The difference between *de facto* and *de jure*, and between internal justice and recognized justice, is really of greater importance in international relations than in relations between citizen and citizen. The reason for this is obvious. In the civil order of things, the person who has right on his side resorts to a tribunal which protects him in the enjoyment of his rights. But in the universal society of which nations are members, there is no higher authority that adjudicates disputes; and right, once recognized, does not expire except when its owner abandons it.

El Filopolita doubts that Spain is ready to recognize us and comments on the weakest part of the ministers' declarations, ignoring the rest. As for the letter to Don José Gestal, it certainly does not have the authority of an official document. It does not commit the Spanish cabinet to anything; but it does disclose the cabinet's thoughts and personally compromises its prime minister. Martínez de la Rosa would certainly put a stain on his reputation as a minister or a man of honor if, after negotiations were opened, he were to say, "The queen's cabinet excludes the basis of independence."

We are in agreement about the possibility that this minister, as well as the others, may not remain in the cabinet, or that they may change their minds, or that they may propose unacceptable conditions, or that Don Carlos may win, etc. But on the other hand, let the opposite possibilities be admitted. If the first happens we lose nothing; if the second, we win. What does prudence recommend? We fear we are annoying our readers by repeating the same thing so many times. But has an answer been forthcoming even once?

8

We are extremely pleased to be able to offer to our readers the memorandum of Señor [José María] Calatrava and the report of the special commission of the Cortes on recognition of the Spanish-American republics, because of the spirit of nobility and liberalism which these documents reveal on the part of the Spanish government and its representatives. We will be all the more pleased to announce, as soon as possible, confirmation of the news (for at the moment it is not official) that the Congress has approved the article proposed in the report.

This moment could not fail to arrive. The voice of reason, of justice, and especially of Spanish interests inevitably had to be heard sooner or later among the policy makers who guide the destinies of that nation. Why prolong a harmful and obstinate lack of communication? Why continue a war without a battlefield and without armed enemies? Why insist on claims that were impossible to attain? Why defer a reconciliation that would be all the less advantageous for the Peninsula the later it occurred? Religious belief, language, legislation, customs—all invited it. But the last two of these links, which become weaker every day owing to the innovations taking place in America in this respect, will necessarily diminish the advantages that the Spaniards could promise themselves in their relations with peoples who had formerly belonged to the same family. Happily, the cabinet in Madrid has given us today, by its liberal policy, a proof that it is convinced of this truth; and not only does it renounce any claim with regard to recognition, but is determined, as can be inferred from Señor Calatrava's explanation, to present the Spanish nation in its relations with its former colonies in exactly the same way as any other of the powers that deal with them. This conduct—which removes all the obstacles that have been placed to our peace and harmony with Spain, and which will permanently build relationships that include even links of blood—undoubtedly does great honor to María Cristina's government.

9

We have inserted into our columns a communication in which General [José Manuel] Borgoño, Plenipotentiary Minister of the Republic [if Chile] at the court of Madrid, advises our government that he has signed with Her Majesty's Minister of State a treaty of peace and friendship between Chile and Spain. General Borgoño tells us in no uncertain terms that the instructions of this government have been followed in the stipulations of the treaty; and we know that these instructions were in strict agreement with the bases set in advance by the National Congress for negotiations with Spain. In substance these were aimed at the explicit and solemn recognition of Chile's independence, with no onerous conditions for the republic. Since we believe, as we cannot do less than believe, that the treaty has been negotiated on these terms, we look upon it as a highly praiseworthy event, and congratulate ourselves on the happy ending of a matter which, up to a few days ago, was considered a desperate one according to the terms that our Minister of Foreign Relations used when referring to it, in the memorandum that he presented to the two Chambers.

We are in fact at peace with Spain; a spirit of cordial fraternity has begun to breathe in the communications of our two countries. The citizens of our republic have been welcomed in the Peninsula with affectionate hospitality, and Spaniards resident in Chile have realized that, from the moment when the fortunes of war decided the struggle between our former country and its colonies, the affections inspired by common factors of origin, religion, customs, and laws recovered their former influence, and, to express it still better, were revived in a stronger and more intimate form; for cordial friendship can exist only between peoples who recognize each other as equals. Independence has made us what we could not have been without it, the Spaniards' true brothers. But present circumstances offer us a special reason for congratulation. Spain, to which we now open our arms, is not the decrepit monarchy whose weakness we shared; it is not the tyrannical and superstitious power that ignored the rights of peoples, and whose only principles in politics were the divine right and absolute power of kings. It is a young Spain, militant like us in the cause of freedom and progress, and facing the same dangers, the same needs, and the same interests as ourselves.

American Congress

(1844)

1

We do not find convincing the objections to the plan for a congress that would represent all the new states on this continent and would discuss and regulate their common international interests.[5] We will admit at the outset that there was a time when those objections bore some weight with us. We looked upon the idea as a beautiful utopia, sterile of practical consequences for our America. Today we are of a different opinion. Let us suppose that the undertaking will not produce all the results that we anticipate. If some are achieved, this alone would justify it; and the points to which the planned congress ought to give its attention are so many, and of such importance, that the least of them would compensate for the small costs and effort necessary to bring together and organize this body. But let us imagine that the plenipotentiaries spend their time in uselesss discussions, and that they adjourn without having established a single beneficent institution, without settling a single stable and advantageous basis for action. What would we have lost? The expenses of a mission that would perhaps have been necessary for other reasons. Chile, for instance, in any case must have a representative in Lima. Bolivia, Ecuador, and New Granada are in the same situation. The other states have less interest in this diplomatic exchange with the southern republics, but it is undeniable that all of them need to approach one another, observe one another, and communicate with one another. The experience of each can serve the others; the mutual contact of nations, even were they more strange to one another, even were they linked by less strong ties, has always been one of the ways to extend and circulate civilization and enlightenment. Until now the different parts of America have been too separate from one another. Their common interests invite them to association, and nothing that can contribute to this great end is unworthy of consideration by governments, statesmen, and friends of humanity. For us, even a common language is a precious heritage that we must not squander. Were we to add to this link the tie of similar institutions, a legislation that recognizes substantially the same principles, a uniform international law, the cooperation of all the states in preserving peace and administering justice in each (of course, with the well-known and necessary restrictions having to do with individual security), would this not be an order of things worthy in every way, for the sake of which we would attempt much more difficult and costly means of achieving it than those required by the meeting of a congress of plenipotentiaries?

It is believed possible that "some points of American international law might be sanctioned," and this sanction is placed among "matters of pure form." Would recognition of the immunity of the flag, or of neutral property, or extradition of criminals who have committed horrible crimes, or forgery, or fraudulent bankruptcy—would those be matters of pure form? Would the establishment of general rules be pure form? Would rules to help litigants in one state acquire proofs in another, to assure that sentences in the official courts of Chile would be carried out in New Granada [Colombia] or Mexico, to establish the rights of succession of Mexicans or New Granadans to inheritances in Chile, and vice versa; that in the case of rival claims, spread over two or more territories, competence and method of procedure would be defined in the most equitable and impartial way for all concerned? These are some of the points of international law on which it would not be very difficult to agree; and certainly, decisions that may be made about them do not seem to us to be such insignificant things that they deserve to be called "pure form."

The Minister of Foreign Relations has indicated in his Memorandum the internal navigation of the great rivers that bathe several different states. One need only cast a glance at a map of South America to see to what degree Providence has wished to ease the trade of its peoples and make them all a society of brothers. The family alliance which must unite all the nations that occupy its immense regions is stamped on our continent. But we do not regard this vast aquatic system as an exclusive possession, as solely a way of uniting Americans; opened to every trading nation on the globe, it would offer an increase in the fortunes of the entire human race, facilitating immigration and with it the populating of broad spaces that abound in precious products and are now either totally deserted or only occasionally occupied by savage tribes. With population would come the pacification and civilization of those same tribes, and with them trade, industry, and wealth for all.

The only weighty objections refer to political relations with European powers; and we are not far from agreeing that it would be dangerous to establish a basis for armed intervention in disputes that might arise between any of the confederated states and any of the great European powers. Not only would we regard it as dangerous, but also as unattainable. At the same time, however, we believe that the confederation could usefully employ other means than that of open force: mediation, for example. And we believe in the efficacy of those measures without relying on anything but the self-interest of the European powers. All strong nations have abused and will continue to abuse their power; there is no congress in the world that can offer effective resistance to a law whose origin lies in man's moral constitution. But at least it is undeniable that the votes expressed by any combination of nations whose good will is not entirely indifferent to those who speculate about them and regard them as a market, will always count for more than the isolated vote of one country. Let us encourage, insofar as possible, the feelings that ought to unite us; once these are expressed, the hope that they can be considered at least up to a point, and that they will not be stirred up lightly, is not so illusory. Trade has done more to improve international relations than all other causes put together. Trade is calculating by definition, and the better it calculates its material interests, the more openly it will regard them as dependent on the cultivation of friendship and peace.

In our government's view, the congress must not interfere with the inner workings of any state. In a war between different states it could intervene as an arbiter or mediator. And for its regulations to have general sanction, it would not be necessary to resort to arms. Punitive measures could very well perform this function, as for example suspension of commercial and war rights of the rebel state, insofar as they related to the other members of the confederation. To form an exact idea of the advisability of the project, it must be considered within the limits established quite clearly by our Foreign Minister in his Memorandum. Stating the obstacles that would be produced if these limits were overstepped does not mean refuting the project, but rather supporting it.

The fact that most of the American states do not as yet possess settled institutions is no obstacle. They do have *de facto* governments, they draw up obligatory treaties; they can, in consequence, join together. If one of them is unfortunately in a condition of complete disorganization, what prevents the others from getting together and settling their common interests without it? For Chile to preserve her neutrality and avoid aiding any of the political parties that are making war in another state, to prevent *émigrés* from abusing the hospitality they are being given in her territory by organizing armed expeditions in Chile against some of the governments with which we are at peace, she needs only to act as she has done up till now, without becoming a criminal in the eyes of a congress in case the political *émigrés* might have escaped the government's vigilance. But would it not be desirable, if Chile's conduct is based on sound principles, to have other governments adopt them, and to make them obligatory for all? If Chile violated a rule once she had established it, she certainly would be a criminal before the congress; that is, she would be responsible for her acts, just as any nation that has infringed its promises is responsible to those with whom it has signed them. There would be nothing new in this, unless it might be said that we ought not to sign any treaty simply to avoid the responsibility of observing it. But even so we would have natural obligations to fulfill—abstract, vague obligations—to which only pacts can give a precise form. Every nation is responsible for its conduct toward other nations, and one of the great benefits that we could promise ourselves from a federation would be precisely this: determining that natural responsibility and replacing general theories with practical and concrete rules.

The congress, some say, will bring the aid of force to all *de facto* governments and to all tyrants; it will expel the *émigrés*; it will ban them from legitimate use of the press. Does this not amount to believing that the congress will not know its mission? Does this not mean attributing to it principles and bases very different from those that the Minister has indicated? Does it not mean presupposing a different congress from the one that is envisaged? If these presuppositions were found to be true, there would be no congress, for Chile and the other governments who think as we do would refuse to join an immoral alliance from which nothing good could be expected. The congress can cooperate for peace and external order without becoming the instrument of persecutions and rancor; and if the mere possibility of abuse were a reason, we would have to destroy all institutions, for there is not one that could not be abused if one of them harbored sinister intentions, undermined constitutional guarantees, and flagrantly defied public opinion.

2

After considering the objections that have been made to the idea of an American congress in the abstract, let us briefly examine those being raised against the plan sketched out in the Foreign Minister's Memorandum.

The title of "confederation" has seemed strange to one correspondent of *El Progreso*, for a very strange reason: because it was the title of the German Confederation of the Goths. But it was also the title of the Anfictionic Confederation, the Aquean Confederation, and the Helvetic Confederation; or rather, it was not the title of any confederation in particular, for it is an appellative noun, generally denoting an association of states for any particular end, and can apply to any imaginable association of states, good or bad, meaning one thing or another according to the adjective attached to it. Just because an association of Goths or Vandals wanted to call itself a confederation, cannot an association that is neither Gothic nor Vandal give itself the same name? And what name should it give itself to avoid incurring a similar problem? "Alliance" and "league" are words no less free of the stigma of having been connected at various times with the Inquisition and the monarchy. Nor can we understand why a confederation necessarily has to be one of absolute and not popular governments; a confederation, alliance, or league is a society of sovereign states, and where the people are sovereign the government confederates in their name, just as it contracts and stipulates in their name in every pact between two nations. "Confederation," says the correspondent of *El Progreso*, "is not possible among governments that are still nothing and peoples which are everything, at least by the power of the mob and of anarchy." We do not understand what is meant by this. Is he trying to say that it is impossible for the governments of the new republics to confederate or join, or to form an alliance or union for some special object, by representing their respective nations? This would be like saying that the American congress, whatever the objects it may deal with, is impossible either *de facto* or *de jure*; that it is the opposite of what the author of the articles on this subject published in *El Progreso* seems to believe. After all, there is no reason to suppose that the title of the proposed league has to be the one that sounds so bad in the correspondent's ears. Our Minister has employed it, and has no choice but to continue to employ it provisionally, until that society of nations gives itself a name.

He has not liked the plan for the congress because it aims "to settle domestic affairs with puerile meticulousness before settling the more important ones that result from contact with the world, and which are frequently disturbed by that very contact." We would like to know what important points these are, so superior in importance to those mentioned in the Memorandum, and beg the correspondent of *El Progreso* to be so kind as to tell us what they are. Do not the rights of peace and war, of belligerents and neutrals, of refuge and asylum, of navigation on the great rivers that cross, or form the borders, of different states, arise from contact with the world? Do not the border police pertain directly to contact with the world? Are not the property and family rights that the citizen of one state can possess in the territory of another state things on which the legislations of the different states are not only in contact but in conflict, and which can be, and often are, disturbed by that same contact and conflict? Chile, like each of the other states, can undoubtedly settle some (not all) of these points by her own laws, and that is why the writer of the article thought of them as material for domestic legislation. But what Chile can do at home does not suffice: Chile wants the rules that she applies to citizens of other nations in her territory to be applied to Chilean citizens in the territory of those other nations, or, if her rules are not sufficiently just and liberal, wants others to be promulgated so that there can be fraternal reciprocity among all the countries. This is an object not covered by civil legislation, and must be settled precisely by international pacts. Absolutely speaking, each state can establish the border police that it thinks best; but to how many disputes, how many complaints, can the rules that she establishes give rise, and justly give rise? And how to avoid those disputes, unless the nations come to agreements to settle them? So true is it that what the correspondent of *El Progreso* calls the objects of civil legislation also belong to international relations (or, to use his phrase, contact with the world) that there is scarcely one of them that is not found today even in elementary works of international law.

We repeat that we do not see points of importance greater than those pointed out in the Memorandum of Foreign Relations. We cannot understand what other great questions can result from contact with the world. We ask him to enlighten us on this matter. In a club, perhaps, the fine points of a loftier and more transcendental policy can be discussed; and so it might be that the writer of the article considers the American assembly as a club on a grand scale. When we are told what some of those points are, we will see if they are the kind that can usefully be discussed in a congress of plenipotentiaries.

Moreover, where does the correspondent of *El Progreso* get the idea that it is a question of settling the points mentioned with "puerile meticulousness"? What is there in the Minister's language that justifies such a concept? The Minister merely gives us a catalogue of topics, indicating the need to subject them to precise rules. Rules must necessarily be set down; the object of the congress can be nothing but that. But why meticulous and puerile? The European powers have subjected the navigation of their great rivers to certain regulations. Are the clauses that they contain, with the aim of protecting the navigation and trade of all nations and placing obstacles to the arbitrary behavior of each, insofar as it may injure the others, a matter of puerile meticulousness?

But the writer's scorn for the matters mentioned by the Minister on the grounds that they are merely domestic suddenly changes to horror, for they seem to him to be fraught with discord, and likely to cause horrible convulsions on a ground that he feels shaking everywhere under his feet. There is no correlation between these two charges. The writer of the article clearly recognizes that the things he referred to a short time ago as domestic are now transcendental questions, the kind that arise from contact with the world, the kind in which dreadful explosions are produced because of that very contact. And he is right about this, but not about the consequence that he deduces from this principle.

Because of the very delicacy of these questions, the natural susceptibility of the states on those points, it is desirable to work toward preventing collisions and explosions by means of prearranged general rules; rules agreed upon at a time when things can be seen coolly, without the irritating circumstances that always accompany real events. What a congress of plenipotentiaries does is the same as what ten or twelve people do who have complicated affairs in which their interests are mutually involved: they sign a contract in which they foresee, insofar as prudence can, occasions for dispute and the conflicts of rival claims. And they set rules in advance to settle them in the way that they think most equitable. This, which common sense dictates to individuals, is prescribed to states by that same common sense; for it is certain that if these agreements are left to the time when the partners have begun to contend and quarrel about some given object, and when after their passions are aroused they are least likely to hear the counsels of reason and justice, a friendly agreement will be infinitely more difficult.

The correspondent of *El Progreso* has emphasized the point of refuge and asylum, and does not think it worthy of an American congress "to busy itself with a practice, of a right if you will, which until now has not been granted by all civilized nations as a routine matter, but only through particular agreements according to the degree of fraternal relations that reign among the signatories." First (supposing that he is speaking of the right of extradition or expulsion, insofar as it is closely related to asylum), that practice, or that right, is in fact granted by custom by all civilized peoples. No doubt there are differences in the methods of applying it, but in substance they are the same. In the second place, something that is worthy of two or three states that make particular agreements cannot be unworthy of a congress of states, unless he is saying that what is suitable for two or three persons in private is not suitable for a group of ten or twelve. In the third place, the right of extradition has to do with each state in its relations with all the others, not only to those with which it is most closely linked. It is important to the administration of justice in Chile, for example, that the right of extradition and the rules of equity and humanity that must restrict it be recognized in New Granada and Mexico, and if possible in China and Japan, as well as in Peru and Bolivia. In the fourth place, it is much better for an arrangement of this kind to be made among ten or twelve states at one time, rather than in separate binary combinations between the same states, for in this way a not inconsiderable object is attained: uniformity, which assists in the knowledge and observance of every law. In the fifth place, what stronger brotherly relations can be imagined than those that link the new American states? When has there existed in the world a group of nations that more truly forms a family? The correspondent of *El Progreso* believes that this principle must be modified according to the nature of each state. There will always be a common ground on which changes can devolve; and this common ground can be decided upon in a congress, leaving to each two states the opportunity to make those additions or restrictions that the circumstances require.

Civilized nations recognize a common international law, which they observe in their general relations; but this does not mean that they lack the freedom to restrict or add to that general law in the pacts they make with one nation or another. Thus, the obstacle that overwhelms the correspondent of *El Progreso* in this regard is entirely illusory. We say the same of his fear that international jurisprudence will extend to so-called political crimes or misdeeds, which often will not be crimes except in the territory of tyrants. What astonishes us is the idea that it can be thought possible that the Chilean government might want to extend the right of extradition to such crimes; what we do believe is that our government is not so liberal that it would consider compatible with its obligations toward other states the freedom of certain abuses of the right of asylum, which have more than once caused ill-fated clashes. The writer of the article, however, even without knowing what agreements will be made on this point by the American plenipotentiaries, imagines with horror the "chain of scaffolds" which that agreement would "make necessary from one end of the country to the other." Pure oratory. The question here is the persecution of terrible crimes, punishment of which is the desire of all associations of beings who are human in more than name; and we cannot see that to deprive such crimes of one of the ways that most often allows them to be committed with impunity can be a bad thing for humankind.

Border police, and the promptness and safety of the mails, are regarded as matters to be handled internally. The author of the article has not thought about all the international questions that can arise from the crossing of frontiers, nor has he considered the connection of this matter to that of the pursuit of criminals on foreign soil, and other matters concerning the administration of justice. As for the mails, we would like to have him tell us if it is not in the common interest of the new states that the mail of the citizens of each country reaches its destination with all the promptness and safety that the protection of the law, and the authorities of the countries through which it must pass, can give it. New Granada and Venezuela have made a pact exclusively for this purpose, and their example is worthy of imitation by the other republics.

The correspondent of *El Progreso* is mistaken in believing that an attempt is being made to provoke controversies about borders or controversies of any other kind. What is being attempted, if such controversies arise, is to submit them to arbitration by the congress before angry answers begin to fly, or before rash actions occur. He is also mistaken in believing that the creation of new armies is being implied. "Means of repression" is not the same as "armies."

After this the writer of the article goes on to indicate the "transcendental" points to which the assembly of plenipotentiaries must give its preferential attention, leaving aside as less important those enunciated by our Minister. The writer of the article proposes six, and two of them coincide with some of those mentioned in the Memorandum of Foreign Relations, which are condemned en masse because they did not arise from contact with the world, nor did they run any risk of being disturbed by that same contact.

First, the correspondent of *El Progreso* wants the assembly to sanction "the absolute right of all the American republics, in cases where they are not linked by preceding treaties, to legislate in accordance with their own interests and even their whims." We suppose that it is tacitly admitted, in the cases where our interests collide with outside interests, that there are natural laws in addition to treaties which impose duties on us vis-à-vis other nations and humankind as a whole. These duties are no less sacred, no less to be respected, than those which have their origin in agreements. But the absolute right that he indicates is, with those two restrictions, both express and tacit, one of those elementary axioms that does not need the sanction of any congress. And if it is considered necessary for the American plenipotentiaries to declare and promulgate it, why not do the same with other equally important natural laws? Is there anyone who really believes that such declarations and promulgations lead to some practical result? That principle has often been violated and trampled upon, it is true; but the same people who infringe it, and at the very moment of infringement, not only recognize but perhaps invoke it. It is like all general principles; it is vague, an abstract generality which with very little mental effort can be interpreted, twisted, and evaded. Civilized nations, when they try to insure their rights by pacts, do not do so by setting forth incontrovertible axioms, but rather, practical rules that are very clear, very precise, and very detailed.

Second the writer of the article wants the assembly to establish the rights of the new states' neutral flag. If he wants the assembly to aspire to recognition of those rights by the powers of the Old World, he is asking the impossible. The Old World will laugh at this quixotic claim, and the United States will laugh loudest. All that the new republics can do is to establish a special right among themselves, imitating what the great republic of the North, a model of wisdom and sanity, has done in its pacts with them.

Third the writer also recognizes the advisability of an agreement on navigation of the great rivers. But it seems that he wants to make their use exclusive to the American nations. Our opinion would be to open them to the world, and we believe that this is the opinion of the Chilean government. But on this point our government can express no more than theoretical judgment and impartial counsel. The states that have rivers are those who must decide: Chile only wants the rights and obligations of the interested parties clearly defined.

Fourth, the writer wants to make a kind of republican propaganda statement out of the assembly. The object is irreproachable, but the means do not seem appropriate to us; and the correspondent of *El Progreso* appears to agree with us when he calls this aim "almost exotic, if North America does not agree." We would like to know what kind of propaganda the assembly would use. We know of only one: the kind the United States has employed with such success. Let us have wisdom, let us have order, let us have an intelligent and active democracy, let us prosper, and our example will spread. If, on the other hand, we continue to give the world a bad example by ambitious aspirations and revolts, if we are heard to stammer theories while we lack commerce, arts, national income, primary schools; in short, if we are seen as stationary if not retrograde in the race of civilization and industrial prosperity, as is the case in most of our republics, then the reasoning and homilies of all the congresses in the world will not win us a single proselyte. We will discredit republican institutions, and tarnish the luster imparted to them by the great work of the Washingtons and the Franklins.

The aims indicated by the Minister all tend to the propaganda of practical lessons, which we look upon as the only effective kind. But there are other aims tending toward the same end which do not enter into the sphere of pacts and confederations. The international policy of the new states will be sterile if rational and progressive and civilizing institutions do not emerge within each of them.

"Offensive or defensive alliances, sometimes general and sometimes reduced in scale according to geographic affinities," is the fifth of the aims enumerated by the correspondent of *El Progreso*, who is forgetting here the arguments with which it attacked the point of refuge and asylum, and of the increase in the size of armies that it seemed to perceive in the idea of the "repressive measures" necessary to sanction the assembly's agreements. Special alliances must grow out of particular negotiations. A general offensive and defensive alliance requires a scale of forces and mobility which our America will not achieve for a long time. Imagine Chile and Bolivia sending their contingents of troops and warships to a Mexico invaded by a French army or blockaded by a British squadron. Only one war is possible between the new and old institutions: that of its positive effects. Only one general alliance is possible among the new states: that of acting together for an end that is common, just, great, and beneficent.

The correspondent of *El Progreso*, who waxes indignant about the Assembly of Plenipotentiaries getting bogged down in puerile and meticulous arrangements, such as property and family rights, navigation of the great rivers, and the other bagatelles indicated in the Minister's Memorandum, finds it lacking in the grave and arduous problem of *ceremony* in the new states, which is the sixth and last of the "transcendental" points in his summary. We can assure him that neither this matter nor others of equal importance have been forgotten; but they did not seem important enough to be mentioned beside the others.

We recognize the American spirit, the love of freedom and humanity that shines in every line of the articles that we are refuting; but really, do they contain the good sense and logic that their author has been unable to find in the plan that he criticizes?

Letter to Antonio Leocadio Guzmán
(1864)

24 September 1864,
My dear sir, and compatriot: Santiago

The news you give me of your return to Lima after an absence of ten years has afforded me the greatest pleasure and fills me with gratitude for the affectionate regards that accompany it.[6] It has made me remember your last letter, and has also brought to mind the curious articles that arrived with it, and of which I promptly made the best use possible, distributing them among various people and corporations, as I told you in my reply.

Among those articles was one that was particularly pleasing to me: a bag of coffee from El Helechal, which for some years belonged to me and my brothers and sisters, and which during the War of Independence passed into other hands.

I have seen General [Francisco] Iriarte several times, and need hardly tell you the value of the recommendation that you gave me for that gentleman, no less than his fine personal qualities.

I have read rapidly, though with all possible attention, the important documents that you have been good enough to include in your letter, and up to the last-dated one I have found only the preliminary steps that the organization of the Congress required, and in which (allow me to tell you so) your patriotic and truly American zeal shines forth and does you much honor. As for the concept and spirit of the undertaking, I must tell you that I do not find them sufficiently clear and well defined. Perhaps I ought to have thought the documents through at a little more leisure before expressing this opinion; but you will be indulgent, and pardon any slip or haste on my part, for I have had them in my hands for only three days. Add to this the limited amount of time I have available for serious matters, owing to the numerous privations to which my state of health has reduced me, and which General Iriarte has witnessed as well.

I have said that I cannot see with sufficient clarity the thoughts and spirit of the planned, and already initiated, Congress of Plenipotentiaries. To me, this expression means a meeting of ministers who join together to sign one or more treaties on certain matters, and which after they are discussed and agreed upon will produce all their effects in the future, after which the members will consider the job done and will retire. A meeting of three, four, five, or any other number of plenipotentiaries is, in substance, the same as a meeting of only two who negotiate any sort of treaty. In both cases the complete agreement of the negotiators, the legitimacy and adequacy of their powers, and the ratification of their respective governments are required.

This doctrine, which I believe to be founded on incontrovertible principles of public law, nevertheless admits of some restrictions. It could be stipulated, for instance, that ratification would not be necessary, and that the signature of the contracting parties would from the outset possess all the effects of a solemn treaty. It could also be stipulated that the plenipotentiaries themselves be enabled to meet again, to discuss and agree upon points about which they would have received instructions. But all this could be established in any kind of treaty, which for that very reason would not cease to constitute one or more international pacts.

It would be another thing altogether if there were an effort to set up a permanent congress to give real unity to different nationalities, with questions decided not by unanimity but by a majority vote. I think you would agree that this would mean forming a Federation, like that of the United States of America, and even more strictly like that of the United States of New Colombia. Each of the participating states would divest itself of a larger or smaller part of its own sovereignty in order to deposit that part in a common center, which would of course be a foreign authority, for a body composed of representatives of different nations would be a foreign authority for all of them; and its decisions would have equal force on all of them, even against the will of a nation that might be in the minority.

Now, what government will be allowed to act against the Constitution that has brought it into being, and which it has sworn to transmit, untouched and whole, to the legitimate government that follows it? Would it not be acting against its most essential duties if it "conspired" with other governments to establish an order of things that would be in open opposition to the fundamental laws of its country? Could the government of Chile, for example, confer on its plenipotentiary the ability to reduce Chilean sovereignty, divesting his country of a greater or lesser share of that sovereignty in order to deposit it somewhere else? If he lacked such an ability, how could he delegate it? Only through one of the means that have been foreseen to alter the constitution of the state, that is, a Constituent Congress, would it be possible to accomplish such a transformation. And you will observe that we are not dealing here with an unimportant diminution of national sovereignty, for it appears that in the plan of the projected action, it is intended to confer on the Congress of Plenipotentiaries the absolute decision on questions as important as those of peace and war, borders, international mediation and transactions, etc. So vast and grandiose a plan could only acquire a certain amount of solidity by the free acquiescence of the participating countries, observed over a period of several years and demonstrated in positive events. This is not to mention the obstacles, division of interests, foreign influences—maybe corrupt ones—and other things that would disturb the functioning of this great machine, and that would assail it and cause it to fail even though it had some shade of legitimacy.

Among the documents that you send me, I have read your Memorandum with the greatest satisfaction; in it you list with great precision and wisdom the various subjects for negotiation on which the Congress of Plenipotentiaries might work. All but one of them would tend toward producing a sort of union among the South American republics which, without infringing their respective constitutions, would help to ease reciprocal communication, conjoin their interests, propagate enlightenment among them, and define their public law. After so much crowing about union, what has been done along all these lines? In some cases there seem to have been efforts to the contrary.

The exception to which I refer has to do with the library. I do not think it necessary, because I do not believe it necessary for the plenipotentiaries to reside in the same place. They would meet only when there were matters to discuss and not otherwise, and each of the participating states would undertake to acquire the necessary books and documents to bring itself up to date on common interests and its relations with other states. This would undoubtedly increase the costs a great deal, but it would have the advantage of making more accessible to everyone the knowledge that governments and people could extract from these collections; to which we might add that the great collection existing in the capital of the Federal Congress would not relieve the need for other similar collections for the use of the government and people in each of the confederated nations.

There is one thing that I fail to find in the interesting notes in your Memorandum, namely the rules relative to Private International Law, a special branch of knowledge which today forms a most interesting area of international jurisprudence, and which in the broad field that it includes contains some of the materials indicated in the Memorandum's notes, and various other materials of no less importance.

The well-known writings of [Joseph] Story, *Commentaries on the Conflict of Laws*, [Jean Jacques Gaspard] Foelix, *Private International Law*, and the fourth volume of [Sir Robert] Phillimore, *Commentaries*, have contributed a great deal toward establishing the principles of this branch of knowledge in the most important nations.

Submitting this long rhapsody to your opinion, for you to let me know in all frankness how you feel about it, I repeat the expression of my friendly feelings and respectful consideration, and remain your very affectionate

Servant and compatriot,
Andrés Bello

Principles of International Law

(1864)

General Concepts

1

International Law, or Law of Nations, is the collection of laws or general rules of conduct that nations or states must observe among themselves for their security and common well-being.[7]

2

Every law presupposes an authority from which it emanates. Since nations do not depend on one another, the laws or rules to which their reciprocal conduct must be subjected can only be dictated to them by reason, which, in the light of experience and in consultation with the common good, deduces them from the chain of causes and effects that we perceive in the physical and moral order of the universe. The Supreme Being, who has established these causes and effects, who has endowed man with an irresistible bent toward the good, or happiness, and does not allow us to sacrifice the happiness of others to our own, is in consequence the true author of these laws, and reason merely interprets them. International law, or *jus gentium*, then, is simply natural law, which, applied to nations, considers the human race, scattered over the face of the earth, as a great society of which each nation is a member, and in which some nations have toward the others the same primary duties that individuals of the human species have among themselves. Hence we must look upon nations as so many moral persons.

3

Every law presupposes a *sanction*, that is, a penalty that falls upon those who transgress it, and by means of which the common good, of which the penalty is a guarantee, is made a necessary condition of individual good.

Natural law has as many different sanctions as there are kinds of evils that can befall us as the result of a voluntary act, and which are not compensated for by any good that may come from that same act ("good" being understood as any feeling of happiness or pleasure, and "evil" any opposite feeling). These evils are produced either without human intervention and only as a result of the physical laws that govern the material universe, or they consist of the internal pain we feel when we witness the sufferings of others, or they come to us through aversion, anger, or scorn for other men. Hence the sanction that we can call *physical*, the *sympathetic* sanction, the sanction of *human justice*, or the *social* sanction. This last, in civil society, is exercised and regularized in large part by positive laws and the administration of justice.

But there are two other sanctions which consecrate, if we can employ this word, the ones previously mentioned and confer all its dignity on the law of nature, placing it under the tutelage of divinity and our own conscience. The sanction of *conscience*, or the *moral* sanction, is the penalty which, in any heart that is not totally depraved, accompanies the testimony that the soul gives to itself of the irregularity of its acts; and the *religious* sanction consists in the punishments with which offended divinity threatens those who violate its laws.

The sanction of human justice is that which operates between nations and within each nation, in the most general, constant, and effective way. But it influences much more vigorously and regularly in the conduct observed between individuals than in the mutual relations of peoples or of supreme powers. In a fairly well-organized civil state, the power of society employed against breakers of the law is superior to that of any individual, no matter how powerful he may be. But nations have not set up an authority which, armed with the strength of all, would be capable of making powerful states obey even those rules of natural equity that are recognized as most essential to common security.

Nor can we say that the particular self-interest of each nation leads it to cooperate with the others to punish acts of inhumanity or injustice. States, like individuals, usually make decisions out of immediate and momentary motives that work powerfully on their passions, and fail to hear the reasons presented to them from a distance, in a speculative and abstract way. A nation formidable for its power insults a weaker state. The other nations, mindful of their own security, ought to band together to punish the insult. But, by adopting this conduct, they would then have to submit to all the calamities and contingencies of war in order to avoid a peril that is uncertain and distant. Thus we see that each nation, when some injury is committed, regards with indifference, or at best with a lukewarm and short-lived indignation, the wrongs perpetrated on others.

Moreover, to obtain reparation, a league of states would be necessary; it would be a hotbed of disputes and quarrels that would often worsen evils rather than cure them.

However, this is no reason to believe that the opinions of men, their praise or scorn, their love or hatred, lack any influence on the conduct of states. There are circumstances that confer strength, even in politics, on this great motive force of human actions. The first is intellectual culture, which spreads wholesome moral ideas and constantly tends toward cementing the relationship of peoples on the basis of justice, which is that of their true self-interest. The second is the growth of industry and trade, which makes individuals appreciate security and mutual confidence more and more. The third is the resemblance of institutions: all history testifies to the fact that nations who are ruled by similar dogmas, customs, and laws sympathize more warmly with each other, and submit to more equitable laws in their dealings with one another. The fourth and last is equality, or what can take its place, a balance of interests and strengths. A state that fears none of the others owing to its excessive superiority can employ fear and compulsion to make them serve its ends; but if it is surrounded by equals it will be obliged out of self-interest to cultivate their good will and merit their approval and confidence.

The operation of these causes becomes perfectly clear in the history of modern nations. If those of Europe and America form a family of states, which recognizes a common law infinitely more liberal than anything that has borne this name in antiquity and in the rest of the globe, they owe it to the establishment of Christianity and the progress of civilization and culture, accelerated by the printing press, the spirit of trade that has come to be one of the chief regulators of politics, and the system of actions and reactions which, in the bosom of that great family as in the bosom of each state, unceasingly struggles against preponderance of any kind.

4

The word *derecho* in Spanish has two meanings. In the first (which is the one we have been using up to now) it means a collection, system, or body of laws; in the second, it means a right, the ability to demand that another person execute, omit, or tolerate some action, an ability whose object is the real or imaginary benefit of the person who exists in it. In this sense it always presupposes in the other person a correlative obligation to execute, omit, or tolerate some action, for it is obvious that we cannot have the ability to demand either a positive or negative service if the need to give it does not exist somewhere.

Rights (and consequently obligations) are either perfect or imperfect. *Perfect* right, also called *external*, is the one we can exert by using force if necessary. In a state of nature this is individual force; and in civil society it is the public force with which the administration of justice is armed. *Imperfect* or *merely internal* right is that which cannot be carried out without the consent of the person receiving it.

This difference consists in how more or less specific are the laws on which rights and obligations depend. Acts of beneficence are obligatory, but only in certain circumstances and under certain conditions, and the person who performs them is the one who has to decide whether each case that occurs is included in the rule or not; for if it were general and absolute, it would produce more harm than good to people. We must, for example, help the poor, but not all of them, nor on all occasions, nor with everything that they ask of us; and the determination of these points belongs exclusively to us. If the situation were different the right of property, subject to continuous demands, would lose much of its value or might not even exist.

The result of this is that, though the moral necessity that constitutes the obligation always exists in the conscience, there are many obligations which, subjected to the judgment of the person who is to observe it, are in consequence subjected to their will as far as external effects are concerned. An individual (or a nation) who neglects these obligations is undoubtedly doing the wrong thing, and exposes himself not only to the disapproval of divinity and his own conscience, but the censure and aversion of men. Yet that is no reason for the person who was sinned against to resort to force to make his right effective, for in matters which owing to their natural indeterminateness do not admit of a precise rule, whatever was done to correct the will would destroy the independence of judgment to which, out of the interests of humankind itself, obligations of this type must be subjected.

To say that a service that is requested of us is an immperfect obligation is the same as saying that demanding it by force would mean violating our freedom and doing us an injury.

The law of nations, or the collection of international laws or rules, is called *internal* when it applies only to conscience and determines what conscience orders, permits, or bans; and *external* when it determines the obligations whose performance can be demanded by force. And from what I have said, it obviously follows that a nation can be obliged to offer a service according to internal law at the same time it has the ability to refuse it according to external law. A nation, for example, is obliged by its own conscience to open its seaports to the trade of other nations as long as no harm comes to it from this action, but usefulness and advantage instead. But if for reasons either good or bad it decides to ban all foreign trade, the other nations with whom it had not agreed to permit such trade would have to submit to its decision. And if they resorted to violence or threats to compel that nation to allow trade, they would do it a serious wrong.

5

The *natural, universal, common, primitive,* or *primary* law of nations is the law whose only basis is reason or natural equity, and *voluntary, special, conventional, positive,* or *secondary* the law formed by conventions either tacit or expressed, and whose strength is derived directly from reason, which prescribes to the nations the inviolability of pacts as a rule of supreme importance.

The universal law of nations can produce all kinds of obligations. Insofar as it produces perfect obligations, it is usually called *necessary.*

Positive law of nations always authorizes the use of force to carry out the obligations that it prescribes. Sometimes, as well as being positive, it is natural and necessary, for it does not need an agreement to produce external obligations. At other times it is natural and voluntary because, without the agreement, it would obligate only in conscience, and at other times it is entirely arbitrary because it derives all its strength from the pact.

Consuetudinary law is the law that arises from custom; that is, what is practiced between two or more nations on some matter. A custom, if it refers to indifferent things or to things that the natural law neither mandates nor prohibits, obligates only those nations who have wished to observe it; and this obligation has its origin in a tacit contract in which, by the very fact that we have adopted a practice, it seems that we are bound to be ruled by it. In consequence consuetudinary law is part of conventional or positive law. But there is no reason to suppose that, by adopting a custom, we have bound ourselves irrevocably to observing it. Thus we can compare the obligations of consuetudinary law to those that arise from those pacts in which each party reserves the ability to end them when it wishes, giving notice to the other long enough in advance not to cause it harm.

Although primitive law is by its nature immutable because it is founded on constant relationships of order and justice, it can vary greatly in its applications owing to the different circumstances in which human societies often find themselves. Moreover, it can be better known and interpreted in one age than in another; and that is why, in connection with this as with other branches of knowledge, undoubted advances have been made in modern times. Finally, there are conventions and customs which are illegitimate in the light of conscience but which nevertheless produce external effects, for the independence of each state would be an illusion if the others took upon themselves the ability to call them to account and invalidate their pacts.

The law introduced by pacts and by custom is to the primitive law of nations what the civil code of each nation is to the precepts and prohibitions of natural law. Hence it renders specific and regularizes that which in natural law was vague and required fixed rules. For example, it dictated the fact that nations might have authorized persons through whom they could communicate, and that these persons would be given complete security in performing their duties; but it left open the form of their credentials and the scope of their immunities, points which, if left unsettled, would lead to disputes and fraud. This determination could be made in a number of ways, and it was necessary to settle some things by express or tacit conventions, as in fact has been done.

Unfortunately many cases remain in which, owing to the vagueness of natural laws, specific rules are needed that can serve to avoid or solve controversies. Prescription offers us an example. Civil laws have defined with considerable precision the natural title of ownership that undisturbed possession can give over a period of time; but in the law of nations there is still no rule that determines the length of time and other circumstances that are required to make possession prevail over any other claim.

In a family of nations, such as that formed today by the Christian peoples, when one of these rules that correct the necessary imperfection of natural laws is established, the nation that departs from it without justification would act against the general good. Therefore it is exceedingly important to know those rules.

Conventional law can also be thought of under another aspect: it stands in the same relationship to primitive law as do pacts by individuals in relation to the laws and statutes of each people. It forms alliances, smooths over differences, legalizes transfers, and regulates trade; in fact, it creates a large number of special obligations that modify common law, but that are valid only between the contracting parties and in consequence do not involve the science of law except as a simple historical document.

In a word, if on the one hand custom is based, as we have seen, on a tacit convention, on the other hand all conventions, no matter how express they may be, lose all their force and really do not exist except when continued observance—that is, custom—confirms and sanctions them. Thus, *consuetudinary* law and *positive* law of nations are expressions which have, from this point of view, the same breadth and significance.

In modern times a new branch of international jurisprudence has been introduced, or rather recognized and developed, under the name of *private international law*. It includes those questions in which there seems to be a collision or conflict between the laws of two different states, when those laws concern the person or possessions of an individual who is found to be in relation to both. Thus, a foreigner can sometimes feel obliged on the one hand to perform the obligations imposed on him by his own country, and on the other hand to perform those prescribed by his country of residence. Hence the division of international law into public and private, the former (*jus inter gentes*) referring to the general rights and obligations of states among themselves, and the latter to the special questions that I have just mentioned, and in which reasons of common usefulness advise a transaction between two legislations through a sort of courtesy or mutual respect.

It has often happened that certain practices which in their origin were purely benevolent have been raised, through pacts or custom, to the category of perfect obligations. There are others that today are regarded as mere courtesy (*comitas juris gentium*, in the language of the Roman jurists), which present a great deal of variety depending on the laws and institutions of the different states.

Lastly, the expressions *European, Germanic, Spanish*, and other similar words are added to the term international law when there is a question of designating the changes that it receives in its practical applications, according to the customs and institutions of the respective countries.

6

The modern nations of Europe have recognized international law as part of their national jurisprudence. "By those statutes," says Sir William Blackstone, "that have been made from time to time in England to reinforce this universal law and facilitate its performance, new rules have not been introduced, but the old fundamental constitutions of the realm have merely been declared and explained, for without these it would cease to be a member of civilized society." Chancellor [Charles] Talbot declared that the law of nations, in all its breadth, was part of British laws. The state tribunals of the United States have expressed a similar doctrine.

There is no doubt that the law of nations is part of national jurisprudence in a given nation and a given period. But it must not be inferred from this that the British statutes have been limited to reforming and facilitating primary law, and to explaining the old fundamental constitutions of the realm without introducing new rules. This is in open contradiction to the facts. Talbot's doctrine, and that of the US courts, must be understood in the same sense.

The legislation of one state cannot alter the law of nations in such a way that the changes are obligatory for the subjects of other states; and the rules established by reason or by mutual consent are the only ones that can serve to settle the differences between sovereign entities.

7

An obligatory code of laws in which are set down all the precepts and prohibitions of international law, whether natural or established, does not exist, and it hardly seems possible that it could exist. This gives rise to a large number of uncertainties and doubts, which sometimes entail a risk to peace among sovereign states.

To make up for the lack of this code, the rules of international law must be explored and illustrated by the following means:

1. Pacts or conventions. We have already pointed out that pacts frequently do not offer declarations of principle or general rules; in consequence, they can rarely be cited in this regard. But when the participants recognize a rule as generally obligatory, they confer upon it not only a respectable authority but a true standard of law, to which they themselves must adhere in their mutual conduct as well as with other states. Apart from this, among civilized nations, when in a large number of pacts a uniform rule is stipulated on some point, we have reason to infer that it is dictated to all nations by reason, at least in the circumstances of the political world at the time.

2. Proclamations and manifestoes addressed by one state to others, and diplomatic correspondence on various points of the law of nations.

3. Marine ordinances and regulations insofar as they testify to the practices of the different nations in matters of navigation and commerce. When the codes of the great powers are all in agreement, they constitute a tribunal whose jurisdiction it would be difficult to escape.

4. The sentences of criminal courts. In England and the United States numerous collections of these sentences are published. The judges who have most distinguished themselves by the justice and wisdom of their decisions have been: in England, Sir William Scott, later known as Baron Stowell (we will mention him under both names and not pay attention to chronological exactitude, which we do not always have at hand); and in the United States, Henry Wheaton and the great jurist [Joseph] Story.

5. What the ancient world has left us on this matter, especially the doctrines brought together in the writings and great collections of Roman jurists. Their luminous doctrines on what they called *jus gentium* deserved, and will always deserve, the attention and study of all who cultivate knowledge.

From the period of the Renaissance, a system of mutual laws, founded chiefly on Roman jurisprudence, began to be introduced in Europe, applied to the questions that presented themselves one after another. But the Spaniard Francisco Suárez (1548–1617) was the first writer who in modern times succeeded in offering pure and solid ideas of natural and international law in his treatise *De legibus ac Deo legislatore*.

A short time later Hugo Grotius (1583–1646) assumed the task of making into a special and independent branch of knowledge all the doctrines issued up to his time, completing and illustrating this summary with admirable wisdom and soundness. In his immortal treatise *De Jure Belli et Pacis* he recognizes the dual distinction of international law; that is, a natural and immutable law and a voluntary law of all, or of the chief, nations. There is a moral flavor in his writings that assures them of permanent acceptance.

Later, two different tendencies emerged. One of them, taking natural law as its starting point, postulates an innate rational law, or one inherent in man's nature; this law cannot be evaded either by individuals or by human associations. The other has been defended warmly by a number of writers who absolutely deny the existence of a true law, obligatory in itself and independent of human will. For according to them, there are no other laws than those which are promulgated by the material power of rulers, clothed as they are in a divine mission of domination. This was what was taught by the Englishman [Thomas] Hobbes (1588–1679), among others.

Natural ideas of justice have also been considered as the basis of the law by Samuel von Pufendorf (1631–1694), in his *Jus Naturae et Gentium.*

But most of the writers preferred the comfortable and practical path traced out by Grotius; and at the same time as they conceded absolute authority to positive laws, they admitted the natural law of individuals and nations as a direct, or at least subsidiary, source of the former. Many philosophers taught and wrote in this vein, among them Johann Christian von Wolf (1679–1764) who on fundamental points followed the principles of Grotius, and shortly afterward Emmerich de Vattel, of Swiss origin (1714–1767), who embraced von Wolf's system almost completely; and thanks to his elegant and practical—though somewhat superficial and diffuse—style, entered the libraries of lawmakers alongside Grotius's book. T. Rutherford, J. J. Burlamaqui, and Gérald de Rayneval deserve mention along with him.

The partisans of practical historic law, enthusiastic adversaries of Pufendorf, split in their turn into two parties: those who adhered to pure positive law, founded solely on treaties and conventions, and that of those writers who, regarding the will of nations as their only source, found it not only in international manifestations but in the necessity of things, and in the position and mutual relations of states, whose presumed will thus imposes rules on persons and things and engenders general precepts of justice.

The chief supporters of pure positive law, who emphasized tradition and history, were: Cornelis van Bynkershoek (1673–1743), *Quaestiones juris publici*; Gaspar de Real (*Ciencia del gobierno*, published in 1764), and almost the whole new school of writers who, after Kant had discarded natural law, established the positive will of nations as the only basis for international law. Georg Friedrich von Martens (1756–1821) wrote in this spirit; he was an indefatigable writer, author of various doctrinal treatises and voluminous collections. The 1831 edition of his *Précis du droit des gens modernes de l'Europe* is of great interest for the notes with which it was enriched by Pinheiro Ferreira, who pronounced himself energetically against this school. After them came Friedrich Saalfeld (Göttingen, 1809), Heinrich Schmalz (1760–1831), Johann Ludwig Kluber (1762–1835), and others. All these deny the existence of a natural or philosophical law, except to the degree that it influences the writing of positive laws. But the same cannot be said of Henry Wheaton, who, though he placed himself on the side of the positivists, certainly did not close his ears to equity and high-minded considerations of universal justice; his *Elements of International Law* and his *History of the Progress* of this law are classic works which cannot be studied too much.

We venture to make the same recommendation about Phillimore's *Commentaries* and [A. G.] Heffter's *Public International Law in Europe*; we have mentioned them in the preliminary note to this edition, and have chiefly used them as material for this article.

Nor would it be fair to close this list of sources by passing over the *Commentaries on American Law*, by James Kent, the *Règles internationales de la mer*, by J. H. Ortolan (Paris, 1845), the *Researches on International Law* by James Reddie (Edinburgh, 1844–1845, and its second and augmented edition, Glasgow, 1851) and *Des Droits et des devoirs des nations neutres* by L. B. Hautefeuille (Paris, 1858).

Although on many points the doctrine of the principal writers is not uniform, there is a very strong presumption of the soundness of their maxims when they are in agreement; and no civilized power will disdain them unless it has the arrogance to go against the judgment of humankind; though, to tell the truth, there has been no dearth of examples of this in the last few centuries, and even in our day and in the most cultivated part of Europe.

On the Nation and the Sovereign

1

The nation or state is a society of individuals which has as its object the preservation and happiness of its members, which is governed by the positive laws that have emanated from itself, and which has control of a certain amount of territory.

2

Since individuals are by nature equal, the groups of persons who compose universal society are also equal. Even the weakest republic enjoys the same rights and is subject to the same obligations as the most powerful empire.

Since a nation can rarely do something for itself—that is, through the individuals who compose it acting en masse—it is necessary for a person or group of persons to exist who are charged with administering the community's interests and with representing that community to foreign nations. This person or group of persons is the *sovereign*. The *independence* of a nation consists in not receiving laws from another nation, and its *sovereignty* in the existence of a supreme authority that directs and represents it.

3

The power and authority of sovereignty is derived from the nation, if not by a positive institution, at least by its tacit recognition and obedience. The nation can transfer it from one hand to another, alter its form, and constitute it as it wishes. Hence the nation is, *originally*, the sovereign. But it is more usual to give this name to the head or body which, independently of any other person or corporation, if not of the community as a whole, regulates the exercise of all the constituted authorities and dispenses laws to all *citizens*; that is, all the members of the association. It follows from this that the legislative power is *actually* and *essentially* the sovereign.

Legislative power, the power that actually exercises sovereignty, is usually constituted in several ways: in one person, as in absolute monarchies; in a senate of nobles and holders of property, as in aristocracies; in one or more chambers, of which at least one is composed of deputies of the people, as in pure or mixed democracies; in an assembly composed of all the citizens who have the right to vote, as in the ancient republics; in the prince or in one or more chambers, as in constitutional monarchies, which, depending on the number and composition of the chambers, can have elements of aristocracy, democracy, or both.

In some constitutional monarchies it is assumed that the royal sanction is what imparts the force and vigor of the laws to the decisions of the legislative assemblies; this is a legal fiction, for the prince has the title, though not the power, of sovereign.

4

The part of sovereignty that must chiefly be considered in international law is the part that represents the nation outside its boundaries, or the part with the ability to contract in the country's name with foreign nations. Treaties are laws that are binding on the subjects of each of the contracting sovereignties; but it is possible that the authority which makes these kinds of laws, and the authority from which laws pertaining to internal administration proceed, may not be precisely the same. In absolute monarchies, they are; in constitutional monarchies and in republics they are usually different. Thus in England, the prince, who concurs with the peers and the commons in the formation of internal laws, directs foreign relations alone, and makes definite agreements with foreign powers. To adopt the language of some writers, the sovereignty that regulates internal affairs can be called *immanent*, while that which represents the nation in its relations with other states is *transient*.

It is important to determine exactly the person or body in which this second kind of sovereignty resides according to the constitution of the state, for pacts drawn up with any other authority would be null and void.

It is also important for the acts of this sovereignty not to overstep the capabilities provided for it by the constitution, for every contract that exceeds them would also be subject to nullity.

However, we must observe that the constitution of a state is not a fixed and immovable thing, but rather suffers (as the history of almost all countries attests) violent swings at times which pull it from one extreme to the other, or at other times slow and progressive alterations that make it assume different forms over the course of time. Hence it would often be difficult for nations to determine what the legitimate organ of external representation is in each of them, and to what point their powers extend according to the laws currently in force; and so the best rule that foreign states can rely upon in this area is apparent possession of the authority with which they are dealing, and the nation's acquiescence to its acts.

5

The special quality that renders the nation a true political body, a *person* who acts directly with others of the same kind under the authority of international law, is the power to govern itself, which makes it independent and sovereign. In this regard, transient sovereignty is no less essential than immanent sovereignty; if a nation lacked the first of these, it would not enjoy true personality in international law.

Hence every nation which governs itself under any form whatsoever, and which has the ability to communicate directly with other nations, is in their eyes an independent and sovereign state. We must include in this number even states that are linked to another more powerful state by an unequal alliance, in which the more powerful state is given more honor in exchange for the aid it gives to the weaker state; those who pay tribute to another state; feudatories, who recognize certain obligations of service, fidelity, and courtesy to an overlord; and federated states, who have set up a common and permanent authority for the administration of certain interests but who have not renounced, through a pact of alliance, tribute, federation, or fief the power to guide their internal affairs and to deal directly with foreign nations. The states of the United States of America have renounced this last power, and hence—though they are independent and sovereign in other respects—they are not sovereign under international law.

Two or more different states can be ruled coincidentally by the same prince, as was seen not very long ago in Great Britain and Hanover: then its union was called *personal*. But, when by the identical quality of the law of succession that rules them they are inseparably linked, this union is called *real*, and then it can be said that their reciprocal independence disappears with regard to the other nations. This has happened with Austria, Bohemia, Hungary, and until recently the kingdom of Lombard Veneto. States which, when they are incorporated into others, lose the power to deal directly with the other nations (though on the other hand they are administered internally with total independence), are called *semi-sovereign* in present-day classifications.

Hordes or migratory tribes who occupy no particular country, and all associations formed to accomplish immoral ends, such as piracy, do not come into the category of nations even though they have a fixed place of abode and declare themselves states or independent peoples. But even if a nation is guilty of the violation of international rights, or commits an act of piracy, that is not sufficient reason to consider it as stripped of the nature of a state.

power that exists actually depends on other nations

6

↖ The independence and sovereignty of a nation is a fact in the eyes of other nations; and from this fact naturally arises the right to communicate with them on the basis of equality and good relations. Therefore, if a new state appears as the result of the colonization of a recently discovered country, or of the dismemberment of an old state, the other states need only discover whether the new association is in fact independent and has established an authority that rules its members, represents them, and up to a point is responsible for their conduct to the world. And if this is the case, they cannot in justice refuse to recognize it as a member of the society of nations.

In the case of violent separation from an old nation, where one or more provinces that comprised it established themselves as independent states, it has been claimed that other nations were obliged to respect the rights of the original nation, regarding the separated provinces as rebellious and refusing to deal with them. While the conflict between the two parties lasts, there is no doubt that a foreign nation may embrace the cause of the mother country against the provinces if it finds this course of action just and appropriate, just as it can support the provinces against the mother country in the opposite case. But once the new state or states are in possession of power, no principle forbids the other states to recognize them as states, for in this regard they are merely recognizing a fact and remaining neutral in a foreign controversy. The united provinces of the Low Countries had shaken off Spain's yoke before the end of the sixteenth century, but Spain did not renounce her rights over them until the Peace of Westphalia in 1648;

and the other nations did not wait for this renunciation to establish direct relations, and even close alliances, with the new state. The same thing happened in the interval between 1640, when Portugal declared itself independent of Spain, and 1668, when Spain recognized that independence.

But such conduct on the part of other nations is not only lawful but necessary, for, as Mr. Canning explained in his note of 25 March 1825 to Señor Ríos, the Spanish minister at the court in London, justifying the recognition of the new American states by Great Britain, he said that "all political communities are responsible to other political communities for their conduct; that is, they are bound to perform the ordinary international duties, and to afford redress for any violation of the rights of others by their citizens and subjects. Now, either the Mother Country must have continued responsible for acts over which it could no longer exercise the shadow of a control, or the inhabitants of those countries, whose independent political existence was, in fact, established, but to whom the acknowledgement of that Independence was denied, must have been placed in a situation in which they were either wholly irresponsible for all their actions, or were to be visited, for such of those actions as might furnish ground of complaint to other nations, with the punishment due to pirates and outlaws. If the former of these alternatives, the total irresponsibility of unrecognized States, be too absurd to be maintained, and if the latter, the treatment of their inhabitants as pirates and outlaws, be too monstrous to be applied, for an indefinite length of time, to a large portion of the habitable globe, no other choice remained for Great Britain, or for any country having intercourse with the Spanish American Provinces, but to recognize in due time their political existence as States, and thus to bring them within the pale of those rights and duties, which civilized nations are bound mutually to respect and are entitled reciprocally to claim from each other."

To the example of the restoration of the Bourbons to the French throne after a long series of years and revolutions, an example alleged by the Spanish minister to prove the unextinguishable right of legitimate sovereigns, Mr. Canning replied victoriously that

> every Power in Europe, and specifically Spain amongst the foremost, not only acknowledged the several successive Governments *de facto* by which

the House of Bourbon was first expelled from the throne of France, and afterwards kept, for near a quarter of a century, out of possession of it, but contracted alliances with them all—and above all . . . the Government of Bonaparte, against whom not any principle of respect for the rights of legitimate monarchy, but his own ungovernable ambition, finally brought combined Europe into the field . . . It cannot be denied that in 1796 and 1797 Great Britain opened a negotiation for peace with the Directory of France . . . that in 1801 she made peace with the Consulate; that, if in 1806 she did not conclude a treaty with Bonaparte, Emperor of France, the negotiation was broken off merely on a question of terms; and that, if, from 1808 to 1814, she steadily refused to listen to any overtures from France, she did so, declaredly and notoriously, on account of Spain alone, whom Bonaparte pertinaciously refused to admit as party to the negotiation.

Mr. Canning adds that in 1814 Great Britain was not far from making peace with Napoleon "if he had not been unreasonable in his demands; and Spain cannot be ignorant that, even after Bonaparte was set aside, there was a question amont the Allies of the possible expediency of placing some other than a Bourbon on the Throne of France."

7

It follows from the independence and sovereignty of nations that no one of them is permitted to dictate to another the form of government, religion, or administration it must adopt, nor call it to account for anything that happens among its citizens or between the government and its subjects. The intervention of Russia, Prussia, and Austria in Poland's internal affairs, and the right that they subsequently arrogated to themselves of dismembering her and at last extinguishing her political existence, has generally been regarded as an outrageous abuse of power. During the course of the French Revolution a number of examples occurred of this kind of violation of the rights of independent nations to exist as seemed best to them. Examples of this were the invasion of France by Prussian arms in 1792, and France's declared hostility in subsequent stages of its revolution to the monarchical states. A decree of the Convention, issued on 19 November 1792, promised France's aid to all peoples who wished to regain their freedom, and ordered the generals of its armies to help all those who had been, or in the future would be, troubled in the cause of freedom. This decree was printed and translated into all languages. Another was the invasion of Naples by Austria in 1821, and that of Spain by France in 1823, under the pretext of smothering a dangerous spirit of political innovation. Public opinion expressed itself against this type of intervention as iniquitous and criminal.

There is no doubt that each nation has the right to provide for its own preservation and to take security measures against any danger. But that danger must be great, manifest, and imminent before it is licit for us to demand by force that another state alter its institutions in our favor. It was in this sense that Great Britain informed the courts of Europe in 1821 (at the time when the measures announced by the so-called Holy Alliance against the new institutions of Spain, Portugal, and Naples, and of the general principles that it was trying to lay down for the allies' future conduct in these cases) that no government was more ready than the British government to uphold the right of any state to *intervene*, when its immediate security or its essential interests were seriously compromised by the domestic acts of other states, but that the use of this right could only be justified by the most absolute necessity, and must be ruled and limited by it; that, in consequence, it was not possible to apply it generally and indiscriminately to all revolutionary movements; that this right was an exception to general principles, and hence could arise only from the circumstances of the case; and that it was extremely dangerous to make the exception into a rule and to incorporate it as such into the institutions of international law. Great Britain further stated that the principles serving as a basis for this rule would sanction a too frequent and extensive intervention in the internal affairs of other states, that allied courts cannot place such an extraordinary capability on existing pacts, nor can it be attributed to some new diplomatic agreement among them, without assuming a supremacy that cannot be reconciled with the rights of sovereignty of the other states and with the general interest, and without setting up an oppressive federative system which, in addition to being ineffective, would bring the most disastrous consequences.

Therefore, limitation of the prince's powers, the rights of the reigning family, the order of succession to the throne in monarchical states, are points that each nation can establish and settle as and when it finds this convenient, and the other states cannot properly criticize them for this or employ any other means than persuasion and advice, and even these with moderation and respect. If a nation places restrictions on the power of the monarch, if it deposes him, if it treats him as a criminal, expelling him from its territory, or perhaps condemns him to the ultimate punishment; if it excludes from the succession an individual, a branch of a family, or all of the reigning family, foreign powers have no business to intervene in the matter, and must regard such acts as those of an independent authority which judges and acts in matters of its own exclusive competence. It is true that the nation that performs such acts without very grave and legitimate reasons would be acting in the most criminal and injudicious way; but after all, if it errs it is responsible to no one but God for its actions as long as it does not infringe the perfect rights of the other states. And it does not infringe them in this matter, for it is unthinkable that, as long as it preserves its independence and sovereignty, it can renounce the right to set up and arrange its domestic affairs in the way that it considers best.

France exercised these rights of sovereignty in the revolution that overthrew the primogenital branch of the Bourbons and raised the Orleans branch in its place. It acted in the same manner in 1848, proclaiming the republic, and shortly after that restored the Empire in the person of Napoleon III. The other great powers, after a more or less brief waiting period, recognized these changes as having been made by legitimate authority.

An intervention whose cause, or pretext, is the danger of revolutionary contagion has almost always been harmful, short-lived in its effects, and rarely exempt from dangerous consequences. There are other types of intervention. One of the most frequent is an intervention that occurs as the result of a *guarantee* issued by a foreign power, either to assure the inviolability of a treaty or the permanence of a constitution or goverment in another country.

Let us suppose that two princes had promised to maintain each other in possession of the throne: This pact would be applied in cases where a third power might try to interfere with either of the parties in possession of the throne; but it would be monstrous to think of this as a personal league of these two against their respective peoples. The right of patrimonial property that some princes think they have over their people is looked upon nowadays as illusory by the best-known writers. Private patrimony exists for the good of its owner, but the institution of civil society has not had as its object the prince's good, but rather that of its associates.

It follows from what I have said that first, in cases of disputed succession, the nation is the natural judge among the contending factions; and second, that the renunciation of his rights to the throne made by a member of the reigning family, for himself and his descendants, is not valid in the case of the latter unless the nation confirms it. Those who are called to the throne by a fundamental law that determines the order of succession receive this right not from their ancestors, but immediately from the nation. Hence, in Spain it was believed necessary for the renunciations of the Infantas Ana and María Teresa of Austria, married respectively to Louis XIII and Louis XIV of France, to receive the form of laws drawn up in the Cortes; and indeed they were given this form in the laws of Madrid of 1618 and 1662. This means that the descendants of those two princesses would have been legally excluded from the succession to the crown of Spain, if national acceptance had not revalidated their rights in the person of Philip V of Bourbon.

It also follows from what I have said that, when a sovereign cedes a province or district, no matter how small, to another monarch, the power of the grantor can only stem from the assent of the part being ceded, which, owing to its separation from the whole to which it belonged, acquires an independent national existence. It is allowable, therefore, for it to resist the new incorporation if it believes it to be contrary to justice and its own interests. What is called a grant in this case is a simple renunciation.

The need to prevent the bloodshed occasioned by a prolonged and destructive civil war in another state has also often been alleged as a legitimate cause for intervention. This kind of intervention, based on the general interests of humanity, has occurred frequently in our times, but never, perhaps, without other reasons of more importance; such as, for example, the danger that continuation of the conflict would bring to other states, or the right to accede to the request of one of the contending sides.

Phillimore says that this reason for intervention can be defended as accessory to others; but as a substantive and sole justification of this right it can scarcely be admitted into the international code, for it manifestly lends itself to many abuses and tends toward violation of vital principles, such as the abuses that arose from the various partitions of

Poland. This is a precedent that has been cited and imitated many times by transgressors of international law.

The need to end the shedding of blood was one of the chief reasons alleged for intervention in the affairs of Turkey and her Greek subjects in 1827; but it was not the only reason, though perhaps if it had been, the war's long duration and the atrocities committed in it would have sufficed to justify the interference of the Christian nations, if such reasons could ever have done so.

Another motive for intervention is the one that results, in a civil war, from the request of both sides; and in this case its legitimacy is uncontestable. But it is less legitimate when it has been evoked by only one of the contenders. However, it cannot be argued that such intervention is contrary to consuetudinary law even then, for we have seen it sanctioned many times by the practice of nations, from the time when (to seek no further examples) Queen Elizabeth of England lent aid to the Low Countries against Spain, up to the time when Russia joined forces with Austria to crush the Hungarian insurgents.

An isolated movement does not suffice to justify the intervention of which we are speaking; there must be a certain proportion of forces and the final result must appear doubtful up to a point, after the struggle has lasted for some time.

Another frequent motive for intervention has been religious affinity. It can happen that a state wishes to extend its protection to coreligionists who are subjects of another state that professes a different faith.

Apart from the interventions of Elizabeth of England, Cromwell, and even Charles II in favor of foreign Protestants, in 1690 Great Britain and Holland intervened in the affairs of Savoy and obtained free practice of their religion for Sardinian Protestants.

Intervention can take place without international law having anything to complain about, if it is limited to negotiations, stipulations, or conditions that have been imposed in a peace treaty, after a war that has had other aims.

Some writers argue that, in the case of a persecution that extends to large groups of people owing to their religious beliefs, an armed intervention could be tolerated in order to stem bloodshed and put an end to internal hostilities.

But Martens's observation must be kept in mind:

All the wars for which religion has served as a motive or pretext have showed, first, that religion has never been the only motive for war; second, that when political stimuli have been in agreement with religious interests, the powers have effectively upheld the cause of their religion; third, that religious zeal has always given way to political interest; fourth, that more than once the nations have entered headlong, because of ambitious views, into a course of conduct completely opposed to the interests of their religion.

The doctrine that we have stated does not change when the object of the intervention is to protect the Christian subjects of a Muslim or infidel nation; but in this case there is a much broader field for application of the exceptional principle of interference.

Ever since establishment of the Turks in Europe, the Christian powers have tried to exercise, and have gradually succeeded in exercising, jurisdiction over their own subjects residing in Turkey and other infidel nations, through consuls. Moreover, subjects of Christian powers have been granted various privileges for visiting the holy places in Palestine and for protection of the religious practice of the Latin churches and the Christian religion in general.

There is another source of intervention which, with the aim of maintaining peace, has given rise to frequent disagreements and war in order to assure the balance or *equilibrium* of power between two different states, so that no power can be allowed to extend its control and increase its forces to the point of threatening the freedom of the others. When properly understood this doctrine does not imply a pedantic adherence to the existing equilibrium, because it must not be forgotten that any independent state has the right to extend its territory, population, wealth, and power by all legitimate means. Even an increase in its naval and military forces has generally been recognized as an unquestionable right of sovereignty. When its army places the security of other states in jeopardy, it is not difficult to remind them of precise limits, and there would certainly be a basis for demanding this. But when there is only a fear of eventual danger, the same reason does not exist, though the questions that can be raised on this point would belong to the realm of politics rather than international law.

8

Lastly, a nation always remains the same moral person, whatever changes it undergoes in the organization of its supreme powers and the succession of its princes. It loses none of its rights; its obligations of all kinds with respect to the other nations are not lessened or weakened. The body politic stays the same as it was, though it may appear under another form or have a different organ of communication.

Restored princes have sometimes tried to evade fulfillment of the obligations contracted by the governments that have preceded them by describing these as usurpers and as such incapable of binding the nation by their acts. But this excuse is inadmissible. During the Restoration, France posed this objection for a long time against the United States of America, which was claiming heavy indemnities for American properties illegally seized in the previous period; but in the end she had to abandon it. "Must we," said the Duc de Broglie, Minister of Foreign Affairs to the Chamber of Deputies during the session of 31 March 1834, "must we, as the government of the Restoration had done, or rather as it had timidly tried to do, allege the irresponsibility of a new government by the procedures of the old one? Such a shameful subterfuge was unworthy of us."

This is the general principle, though subject to limitations which we will indicate below.

Among the obligations of sovereign states, it has seemed to us that we ought to mention those contracted by them in the form of loans from foreign subjects, and which have been so frequent during the present century, with the creditors usually being English subjects.

The protection of its subjects is an unquestionable right of every sovereign state, when they have been damaged in their persons or their interests by the government of another, and especially in the case when their pecuniary credits have not been satisfied, resulting from contracts made with the foreign sovereign or his legally authorized agents. The same applies to indemnities owed pursuant to an injury inflicted by the foreign sovereign or by persons acting legally in his name.

Loans contracted for the service of a state, and the debts created in the administration of public affairs, are contracts in strict law, obligatory for the entire nation. No one can excuse the nation from paying those debts. Whether the money that was loaned was spent to the advantage of the nation or irresponsibly squandered has nothing to do with the loaner. He has entrusted his money to the nation and the nation must return it to him. So much the worse for that nation if it has placed the management of its interests in evil hands.

The basis of the circular which Viscount Palmerston, then Minister of Foreign Affairs of Great Britain, sent to British representatives abroad, was this important rule. In the circular he tells them that it is discretional for the British government to deal or not to deal with this matter in diplomatic negotiations, but that there was absolutely no doubt about the perfect right of every government to deal, by diplomatic means, with every reasonable claim of any of its subjects against a foreign government, or to request reparation of any offense that might be dealt it from the same government; that England would always have the means to obtain justice, but that it was a question of convenience and not of power; and that, in consequence, no foreign country should expect that Great Britain would permanently fail to react against the offense, or that, in case it made its right effective, the British government would not have ample means of procuring justice; that successive British administrations had been, until then, very far from wishing that a country's capital should be invested in loans to foreign governments, that perhaps they could not or did not wish to pay the interest agreed upon, and that hence the British government had believed that its best policy had been, up till then, not to raise such claims to the level of international problems; that, as the British government believed, the losses of those who had placed rash confidence in the good faith of its debtors would be a good lesson for others, and would prevent the making of those loans except to honorable and solvent countries; but that, all the same, it could happen that the losses reached such magnitude that the lesson would be too costly, and that in that case the government would be obliged to begin diplomatic negotiations.

Martens's rule appears to be correct; that is, the foreign creditor can only ask to be placed on the same level as the state's other creditors. It can happen, as Martens himself observes, that the debtor state adopts such fraudulent and criminal fiscal measures, and with such a manifest intention of frustrating claims, that the creditor's government may feel authorized to resort to other measures and even to war itself; as could happen, for instance, with the adulteration of minted or paper money, or absolute refusal to recognize debts contracted on the basis of national public faith. However, in case of extraordinary need, it would not be fair to deprive a nation of the ability to adopt temporary fiscal measures relating to paper money, but under these two conditions: that the real value that was promised be paid, and that in the meantime the foreign creditor be treated under the same conditions as the domestic creditor.

Even when a state is divided into two or more states, neither its rights nor its obligations undergo any change, and they must be either enjoyed or paid together, or be divided among the new states by common consent if division is possible.

Reforms to the Constitution

(1833)

The great convention has now finished the reform of the Constitution of 1828, and we believe that if its efforts do not satisfy the desires of everyone, it will at least be conceded that the system of administration has been much improved.[8] The chief defects that could be observed in the formation of laws, the vacancy of the presidency of the republic, the assembling of the Senate, and the organization of the internal regime have been corrected. Everything that can be altered in the course of time has been suppressed, leaving it at the disposition of special laws that vary according to circumstances, and only what can be considered as permanent within the variability of the human condition has been retained. The powers of the President of the Republic have been sufficiently strengthened to allow him to act well, placing under his authority all the secondary positions that he needs to preserve order throughout the nation; and to prevent the abuse to which this might give rise, a council of state has been created which, at the same time as it provides him with advice, acts as sentinel of public and individual rights. The chapter entitled "Public Law in Chile" merits particular attention, for its articles accurately disclose the liberal principles that rule the members of the great convention. Their chief task has been to combine a vigorous government with the complete enjoyment of well-ordered freedom; that is, to give the government strength to defend itself against attacks of insubordination produced by the excesses of democracy, and to give both to the nation and to individuals resources to preserve them from despotism. Everything useless in the charter [of 1828] has been suppressed; and when the provincial assemblies were considered in this regard (for their chief features can be performed better by the municipalities, which are closer to the interests of the people), they were in consequence abolished.

On examination of the reformed code of laws to which the National Congress has just solemnly sworn, one's attention is drawn to the chief alterations that it has received. It does not contain those invitations to frenzy that license allowed, to the detriment of justice and the curtailment of true freedom. There are no theories inapplicable to our country's circumstances, but rather, clear and unequivocal rules for administering the public interest. The reformers' aim has been to assure permanent general prosperity by establishing a solid administration, one which can simultaneously perform its duties with ease and at the same time is prevented from impugning the rights of Chileans. If we remember the terms of the Constitution of 1828—infractions of which caused great unrest in the Republic in 1829 owing to their vague and indeterminate character—we can only applaud the way in which the reformers have forever closed the path along which ill-intentioned persons were leading the people's actions, at the time when the citizens were settling their political fate.

Restriction of the right of suffrage is a formidable barrier set up against those who, in the elections, made public opinion the agent of their secret aspirations. This precious faculty has been given only to those who know how to appreciate it, and who are incapable of putting it up for sale. With the change made on this point to the electoral law by the Congress of Plenipotentiaries, the happiest of results was achieved, and the Great Convention took advantage of this good lesson and wisely enacted the limitations that are observable in the reform.

In the formation of the laws there were cases where nothing could be done after a bill was rejected. The legislative body had to veer between the reefs of uncertainty, or try to proceed either without rules or only by the rule that the body itself might lay down. There was the danger of ruinous laws being passed because there were no firm arrangements; but this precipice has been completely avoided because, according to the measures laid down by the Great Convention to enact these laws, a majority that wins the respect of public opinion must be obtained. Owing to these measures, intrigue can have no influence nor can personal interest exercise its sway.

The chief infraction of the Constitution of 1828 that caused the unrest leading to the popular movement of 1829 were Articles 72 and 73, and, no doubt to avoid another similar situation, the Great Convention has eliminated the post of Vice-President of the Republic. In addition to this reason, it surely considered the evils that can result from a future succession established in advance. If misguided electors were to nominate an ambitious citizen as Vice-President of the Republic, how many maneuvers might he not put into play to provide a vacancy in which he could use the supreme power to achieve the object of his passions? The chair of chief magistrate of the Republic of Chile was in danger of sinking into an abyss of conspiracies or secret intrigues. As is very possible, leaders of two opposing parties could be elected President and Vice-President of the Republic; and in that case, would one of them allow the other to lead peacefully? In view of the human condition and the confrontation of parties that the democratic system allows, a case as ill-fated as this could have occurred, brought about by the fundamental charter that ruled us. It was also rather a ridiculous thing to have a citizen, designated by law to perform the functions of Vice-President with no other badge of office than the title, and lacking any distinction to command the respect of his countrymen.

The Constitution of 1828 tried to establish a government; but the men in charge of it were not given the means to fulfill their chief obligations during the periods of unpredictabilty and threat that are so frequent. This is especially true when the repeated lessons of popular unrest have taught men to be as discreet in their actions as they are careful to avoid the judicial formulas, dictated for special cases, to which the supreme chief was limited. These very serious deficiencies have been corrected by the reform, and if fears exist that the powers conceded to the President of the Republic can be abused, these vanish when we consider the creation of the Council of State, whose purpose is to serve the government as a severe censor of its operations, a bulwark of laws, and defender of the rights of the citizen and the public. Among the powers conceded to the President of the Republic, a dike has been constructed against the stream of party unrest; and in the creation of the Council of State, and the breadth given to the guarantees, a huge temple to internal freedom has been erected. The Great Convention has wisely tried to restrain the efforts of despotism and to quench the ardor of an immoderate freedom, whose impact would necessarily result in terrifying anarchy.

The rules established by the Constitution of 1828 for organizing courts of justice were exposed to changes which the variation of circumstances will probably make necessary in the future. Judging from the progress made by population and trade, the way in which the courts were set up did not suffice for the administration of justice; and certainly even greater reasons to reform them will appear in the future. The Constitution ought to contain only general principles for the application of justice, and for establishing judicial guarantees and the responsibilities of judges; but the mechanics of courts and tribunals, their organization, must be reserved to particular laws, as has been done.

As for the internal government adopted by the Constitution of 1828, though there is no difference in the types of employees, the way in which they were appointed rendered invalid or unimportant the authority of the nation's chief magistrate. With intendants elected by assemblies, and governors of departments by municipal councils, there was a lack of that successive and continued organization by which the head of the republic could make effective the responsibility of all the administration's agents. Formerly they were isolated functionaries who could abandon themselves to all kinds of misconduct, based on the fact that they could not be fired by their superiors. But now that the reform has established that they can be both nominated and fired by the President of the Republic, they must be more conscientious in performing their duties and must have very few means of shirking them.

The provincial assemblies, created at that time as a means of calming the remnants of the federal fever that nearly devoured us [in the 1820s], have been suppressed, for there is no longer any need to preserve bodies whose chief task, other than being in recess, was that of serving as a basis for revolutions. To elect them, voters were divided into two or more parties, which sowed rancor among the citizens; and as this rancor continued to increase from election to election, the people remained in a disastrous state of struggle which ended only when the defeated party either bowed to the whims of the winner or became its victim. The sessions lasted for only three months of each year; they had been assigned municipal functions that required assiduous attention, and in consequence those functions were neglected because of the short period to which their meetings were restricted. By the terms of the reformed constitution these functions have been transferred to the municipal councils, and the power to propose intendants and judges has been consigned to the civil servants on whom these powers naturally devolve. The previous system had the bad feature of arousing the provinces to the point of combustion every time there was a vacancy, and the result was that the governing of a province was given to an official who did not enjoy the confidence of the supreme chief. It meant also that the administration of local justice was entrusted to a lawyer who had no other qualifications for it than his influence and his relationships with members of the assembly. In the new chapter on "Administration and Internal Regime", there is merely an enumeration of the individuals who must take charge of it, reserving expressly for a particular law the distribution of the functions of each. This is doubtless for the reason that these functions can change with time and adjust to the different customs of the provinces. In our opinion, the organization of the government of Chile established by the reformed constitution is the most satisfactory that can be desired, and if time uncovers errors that must be corrected, the method to be followed with all the caution necessary for a work of this kind is arranged for in a separate chapter.

As for citizens' rights, we believe that they are sufficiently set forth in the chapters on "Public Law in Chile" and "Guarantees of Security and Ownership." In these clauses are found everything that could be desired to defend individual freedom against the attacks of power, and property against the invasions of poor administration of justice. No one can be imprisoned except in the cases prescribed by the law, and when the law is infringed the reformed Constitution provides a simple means of limiting the damage and disciplining the violator. In our opinion the work that we have analyzed, though not complete, is at least better than the one that served it as a model, and it enjoys a recommendation that merits acceptance by all our compatriots. It has been drawn up with all the freedom that can be imagined in a deliberative body. No foreign influence, no private interest have been the object of its discussions. And further—and it is necessary to say this—the President of the Republic [Joaquín Prieto] has taken special care to distance himself from any act that might have even the appearance of influencing the members of the Convention; and when he did intervene, it was to ask to have the article concerning reelection to his post suppressed. In this he did not receive satisfaction, for the Convention, ever mindful of the country's fortunes, believed that it was most unjust to deprive a people of the advantages of continuing in the government a citizen who over a period of five years had completely merited their confidence in him. The arguments made against this powerful reasoning were considered as very frivolous, and as originating in that timidity which, while attempting greater security, only succeeds in undermining it.

Finally, to the observations here expressed we can only add that we do not find any clauses in the reform that are a danger to freedom, opening secret paths or private plans to enchain it. And, on the other hand, we have found the rules for preserving and supporting it successfully established, and obstacles placed on the paths where abuses might take root. If the aim of a constitution is to determine the conditions of the social pact, we believe that we have achieved this for the present; and if not, time will disclose the defects of the reformed constitution, and they will be corrected in conformity with its own rules.

Observance of the Laws

(1836)

We can only applaud the zeal with which our administration is working to draw up laws, some of which the Constitution of the Republic has envisaged, and others that are no less necessary to establish and secure public order, to protect and preserve the rights of individuals, and to maintain in the best possible condition the administration of justice, without which there is neither freedom nor any social good.[9] But can we say that when we have secured these laws, with all the perfection of which human works are capable, we will have everything necessary to attain the great aims that those same laws propose? This is the most interesting question, one with which we have intended to deal ever since we began our observations on the regulation of justice, and to which we now expressly turn our attention.

Laws alone cannot provide for the happiness of a people in the absence of the love, respect, and all the considerations that the individuals of a nation must profess toward such laws. Without the firm and stern actions of the magistrates whose task it is to see that they are carried out, laws are merely a vain illusion, and far from being useful would preferably not exist, for as disdain for them grows and becomes general, it destroys every principle of morality and decreases the last hopes of improvement. In that case there could be no assurance that other laws, passed to make the abandoned laws obeyed, would have any better luck than the previous ones. Therefore, the work of ordering society and securing all the good things that we seek in it, has to be accomplished with the concerted action of the laws, the magistrates, and all the individuals in society itself. Each person who obeys the precepts of the law does all that he ought to do in the service of his country. He who pays no attention to them does as much as he can to ruin that country, which perhaps he thinks that he loves. If laws are not obeyed, if each person infringes them as he pleases; if the only rule of action in society is the rule of each individual in it, at that very point society disappears, a bottomless chaos of disorder yawns, and safety. Property and honor lose all their support. And everything necessary and pleasant on the face of the earth is destroyed.

Exaggerated ideas of freedom are diametrically opposed to the truths and clear principles that we have just set forth; they cause unthinking men to consider this precious gift as what must properly be called license, and it is the greatest enemy of national freedom. For this latter freedom is precisely the ability to exercise all just and honest actions, to use our assets legitimately, to communicate our feelings without moral offense, and—in short—to live in such a way that, by preserving free use of all our faculties, we do not disturb others in the exercise of theirs. If this were not so, freedom simply could not survive; if some had license to do whatever they pleased, this license would have to be absolute, and then others would not be able to do what they wanted to do. If the murderer who attacks the peaceful citizen has freedom to kill him, the citizen has no security for his life. By exercising license for what is unlawful we directly attack the freedom of others, and thus threaten the very bases of the social order. An inevitable result comes from what I have said: so great is our need for the law to moderate actions, to mark out the limits that freedom can reach, that by restraining the injuries that can be done to freedom by its abuse, we permit the true enjoyment of freedom by the individuals who form society in order to achieve it. If we want freedom as it can exist on earth, we must love subjection to the law; if we scorn laws, we must be enemies of freedom. With what right, with what reason, does the man who sees his property taken away complain, if he himself has taken the liberty of wresting property from others? What considerations of honor can the immoral man demand when he does not disdain any means of taking advantage of others? Can there be greater injustice than a readiness to trample on the rights of others, and trying to have one's own rights religiously observed? Praising justice when it takes place in someone else's house, and detesting and cursing it when one feels it in one's own, is an unpardonable sin, but it is what we most frequently observe, a result of the human heart's weakness and corruption. For that very reason it is something that must always be combated with principles of the opposite kind, for a lack of reflection on them is perhaps the most abundant source of the vices that we observe in this regard.

If the law, and obedience to the law, are so necessary, it can truly be said that these constitute man's true homeland, and the source of all the good things that he can hope for in order to be happy. Certainly the soil on which we were born is not necessarily our homeland, nor is the land where we have chosen to spend our lives. Nor are we ourselves that homeland, for we are not sufficient for all our needs, nor can we think of the people who live with us as lawless, for in that case they would be our greatest enemies. Therefore, our true homeland is that rule of conduct indicated by the rights, obligations, and functions that we have and that we owe each other; it is that rule which establishes public and private order, which strengthens, secures, an imparts all their vigor to the relationships that unite us, and forms that body of association of rational beings in which we find the only good, the only desirable things in our country. Therefore that rule is our true homeland, and that rule is the law, without which everything disappears. After this, can anyone pretend love of country without love of laws? Discuss all you like; form great plans for useful establishments; find courage to fight against the enemies of the state and resolution to face risky undertakings. If love of the laws is lacking, all this is nothing; the foundations of the building you wish to erect are undermined, for without observance of the laws, all advantages are pure illusion.

Everything that we have said cannot be considered as pure theory; all of it must be turned into practice, for what is practiced makes the good of nations, and what is omitted causes their ruin. Observance of the laws necessarily leads to the improvement of those very laws, for it makes their defects visible, their lacks noted, their suitability or lack of adaptability known. Observance of the laws restrains men; it strips away all harmful distraction, leads them to knowledge of their own interests, and places them in possession of a truth which has so much influence on order, considered under any aspect:namely, that the best way of ensuring the respect of one's own rights is to care religiously about the rights of others.

If we recall the ancient nations, if we then look at modern nations—and chiefly those contemporary to ours—we become convinced that love for their institutions and careful observance of them have been, at every period, the sole principle of their prosperity and power, just as all of them fell from their grandeur for the opposite reasons. We shall see those nations, who have prospered not so much from their good laws as from appreciation of them and the consequent severity of their customs; at the same time, we can observe their decadence when their laws became more perfect but were observed less. Rome, by respecting and carrying out laws that approached perfection, opened the way toward becoming ruler of the world. But Rome herself, with laws that were more perfect, destroyed her power when, at a time when virtues were beginning to decay, men ceased to observe the laws. Sparta, with laws that in a sense seemed to deny nature, remained glorious for more than seven centuries while she observed them, but she opened the door to her ruin at the very time when she thought she could loosen the rigor of her institutions a little. Spain did not have as many, or as good, laws at a time when, because she observed them strictly, she produced men capable of heroic undertakings which raised her to the highest rank of power; and, with laws that in themselves were good, we have seen her decay for no other reason than non-observance of her laws, which was inevitably followed by wrong actions that caused the destruction of a monarchy that was so far-flung and so powerful. What other source is there for the disturbances that have racked France, if not the unobservance of her laws? And what but observance, respect, love for her institutions, has preserved England unmoved in the midst of political oscillations, happy amid the misfortunes so common in other nations, and growing greater amid the ruins that have been so abundant in this age of ours?

If observance of the laws is so important that the happiness of nations depends wholly on it, then all the consideration of the government and the citizens must focus on it. But it must be general, strict, and careful, for without these qualities it has no hope of surviving. The observance of laws must be general, and this general quality must be understood under two really important respects; one which regards persons, who must observe, and the other aimed at the things in respect of which observance is prescribed. For if there are persons who evade obeying the law, and this is allowed to happen; or if infractions are committed respecting things, and these are hidden, the spirit of observance falls away, scandals multiply, the people become familiar with disobedience, and disdain for the law is sometimes looked upon coolly and sometimes even with pleasure.

If observance of the laws is so necessary that society cannot survive without it, this places a strict obligation on each of society's individuals to do whatever he is supposed to do. And there are no titles, no considerations sufficient to relieve them of this obligation, from the supreme authority to the most junior official, either whether we are considering the general administration of a republic or the power of administering justice, from the master of the richest fortune to the humblest person. The law's power ranges from the man found at the summit of honors and distinctions down to the most obscure inhabitant, and all are equal before it because the measuring stick of justice and equity that measures everyone is the same, and essential variations cannot be allowed, no matter how different the condition of persons.

The same persons charged with giving the laws, the supreme government which must sanction them, are bound in the exercise of their high functions to laws that they cannot transgress. For, even if a legal disposition can be swept away, while it lasts it must be respected by no one more than those who, if they infringed the laws, would undermine the very bases on which their authority rests. One Roman emperor who thought himself above the law said, "Though we are not bound to the laws, we live with them." This is a sentiment worthy of being retained in memory, and demonstrates the necessity that even rulers of despotic governments have to possess laws, to respect them, and to carry them out, because nothing less than their political existence is at stake. How much greater must this necessity be in regular governments, from which everything that involves proceeding out of whim must be far removed? The law, therefore, must be the inspiration of legislators and governments; the law must be what informs the activities of all those in charge of such sublime functions, for they lose all their splendor, value, and influence at the moment when the law ceases to be their guide.

Subjection to the laws is still more important in those charged with administering justice. The individuals in whom this great confidence of nations is deposited cannot be separated from the law in performing their offices. And no matter how powerful the private reasons that tempt them to stretch the law, or depart a very little from its letter, all those reasons must be silenced. No other voices can be heard in the sanctuary of justice than those which, pronounced by reason before specific cases arise, give judges sure rules of conduct, rules that in no case could be related to the choice of a will subject to variations and displacements. Often a law may seem unjust to a judge: he can believe that it is a rash one; he can find his opinion buttressed by doctrines that seem to him to be worthy of respect; and it may be that his idea is not mistaken. Yet he cannot act against that law, nor can he ignore it, for if judges were able to do so, decisions would no longer be ruled by law but by the magistrates' private opinions. Judges who are well aware of the gravity of their office and its true attributes are for this reason very careful to examine legal pronouncements, to give them their true value, and to disdain all perverse interpretations, all doctrine that is not in true agreement with them. And these judges are the ones who best fulfill the great responsibilities connected with the tremendous task of deciding the fortunes, life, and honor of their fellow men.

It seems unnecessary to say that, since the judge is so bound to the law that he cannot separate himself from it, no matter how useful and just the reasons that oppose it may seem to him, this same obligation must make him ignore persons when there is a question of applying the laws. We have said that it seems useless to pause over this obvious point, because the essence of a judge's office resides in it; but we mention it because we believe that we can extract from this principle very important consequences in favor of magistrates, of the manner in which they must proceed in performing their office, and the acceptance and good will with which their decisions must be received. For, if it is so well known that a judge cannot depart from the law out of respect for persons, nothing is so frequent as wishing to incline laws and judges toward persons, and sometimes discharging upon judges the effects of an unfounded anger because, though they heard the precepts of the laws, they did not listen to the importunate cries of individuals.

If, we repeat, the judge is the slave of the law, if he has no power over it, if nothing is so opposed to his office as the consideration of persons, it follows that nothing can be so wicked as trying to influence judges by means that are not the ones established and justified by the law. We do not wish to dignify by mentioning them the means which at first sight assault reason and decency, such as bribery, gifts, and various services. Other means are employed which, for the very reason that they are more decent, are more difficult to refuse, easier to produce an effect, and more likely—for the same reason—to arouse the gravest and most reasonable doubts. Frequently, in addition to the lawyer entrusted with the defense in a lawsuit, both the person involved and the lawyer seek out another sort of protection for the case, consisting of private recommendations in order to obtain victory through them; and sometimes more effort is spent on this defense, which we might call clandestine, than on the one made through the workings of public justice. Unfortunately, usage has made this type of recourse so frequent that litigants do not hesitate to use it, even though some persons may be reluctant to accept it. Nor do judges draw attention to the offense as they ought to do. This procedure involves the dignity of their office and of their persons, linked to the responsibility of carrying out their office as best they can.

Every time that the influence of one person is interposed to secure from another person a favor that results in the success of some judicial process, there must be consideration of what the circumstances of that influence have been, whether it can have some rational reason to take over the performance of this office. What is going to be asked of the judge? If leniency, it is not within the scope of his powers; if justice, the person has no power over this, nor is he asking in the way he ought to ask, nor can the judge hear him except in the way established by the law. For this purpose, the procedures of his office suffice; and to add to them the power of mediation and the value of influence is simply a very great insult to the person of the judge himself, inferring that the reasons that move him are more powerful than the sacred duties that he has assumed by accepting the post and swearing to act faithfully and legally in the exercise of his office.

If extraordinary efforts—that is, if the different tricks in which litigants sometimes indulge outside the courtroom to incline the judges' favor toward them were constantly rebuffed—judges would find it easier to exercise their office, and lawsuits would be less troublesome because fewer steps would have to be taken; but, once recommendations and private conferences come into the picture, all those who have an interest in such matters are forced to abuse these tricks even though they find them repugnant. For they see their adversaries practicing them and believe, not without reason, that if they omit them they place the success of their endeavors in jeopardy. This is the reason why magistrates, convinced of the importance of the administration in their charge, must declare constant war on this unfortunate custom, and must omit no means of making it clear that their role in society is to give to each person what he deserves in strict accordance with the laws, which cannot change, no matter what respects and considerations are introduced into the affair. Conduct upheld in this way by magistrates is in our opinion the only effective lesson that will make the public understand the importance of this noble office, and will cause all the acts that emanate from its exercise to attain the degree of acceptance that they deserve. It is one way to avoid the complaints and personal resentments that are often heard against magistrates even for the justest acts, much to the disgust of right-thinking men. This comes about for no other reason than the belief that magistrates can act according to their personal preferences.

If in the application of the laws there is no room for partiality toward persons, nothing can be so unacceptable as the possibility that laws, other things being equal, can have all their effect on some individuals and not on others. Such a disparity of treatment strips the laws of all the respect that is owed to them, and opens the speediest way to total unobservance. After the law has decided what must be done, no one has any rational reason to be exempt from its demands. The application of the law is often harsh, especially in criminal cases; but the merit of the person whose job it is to apply the law consists precisely in this. This is the sacrifice that he has sworn to make to justice; and the man who does not think that he has strength enough to constantly restrain even his dearest affections, when the law demands it, ought not to occupy a place in the magistracy for a single moment.

Nothing is more characteristic of man's condition than the vicious propensity to escape from the law that limits his absolute freedom and reduces his activities to terms of reason and justice; hence, in nothing is he as productive as in thinking up reasons to relieve himself of the consequences of departing from what is just and honest. The states of euphoria or despair, of wealth or poverty, are pretexts to which men often resort, to believe themselves free of the law's prohibitions or punishments; and the authority who moderates the actions of individuals must take the greatest care that no one seizes on these pretexts or uses them to justify their infractions. Not to do so would necessarily result in the worst consequences: the example of those who are located on a higher level is a rule for the lower levels, who, taking refuge in the haven of tolerance that they share with the others, thus escape prohibitions and punishments, and make the provisions of the law useless and its holy empire a vain simulacrum. Therefore authority must always be ready to resist the exaggerated claims of the rich; and, because poverty and indigence also have their seductive powers (and perhaps even more dangerous seductions, for they involve in their favor the noblest and most disinterested sentiments of the human heart), it is also necessary to avoid having these pure and generous feelings turn into criminal weakness, thus distorting the staff of justice. The decisions of the magistracy must not, even from the most plausible motives, depart one jot from the standard traced for them by the laws, for they cannot do so without introducing into the judicial order a principle of arbitrariness, which will not always be guided by equally excusable impulses, and which, increasing by degrees, will eventually undermine it all. This has always opened the way to corruption and abuse.

Civil Code

PRESENTATION OF THE BILL TO
THE CONGRESS

(1855)

M any of the most civilized modern nations have felt the need to codify their laws.[10] It can be said that this is a periodic necessity in societies. No matter how complete and perfect a body of legislation is deemed to be, the change of customs, the progress of civilization itself, political change, immigration of new ideas that are the precursor of new institutions, scientific discoveries and their application to the arts and to practical life, the abuses introduced by bad faith, which abound in stratagems to evade legal precautions, constantly bring about circumstances that are added to the previous ones, interpreting them, expanding them, changing them, revoking them, until at last it becomes necessary to recast this confused mass of differing, incoherent, and contradictory elements, conferring consistency and harmony upon them and relating them to the social order.

Attempts of this kind made in the course of the last century, and their generally fortunate results, have inspired us to undertake a similar piece of work, with the advantage of being able to make use of the works of other nations' knowledge and experience. As you know, the work was begun some years ago. When the bill was finally presented, I submitted it to examination by a commission of learned magistrates and jurists which has dedicated to this work a zeal and assiduity so great that I do not know if any other examples can be found among us.

You will realize that from the outset we did not want merely to copy any portion of other modern codes. We had to make use of them without losing sight of our country's peculiar circumstances. But, where these circumstances did not present real obstacles, we did not hesitate to introduce useful innovations. I will make a brief survey of the most important and far-reaching of these.

Following the example of almost all modern codes of law, we have stripped custom of the force of law.

Time is an element of so much importance in juridical relationships, and has given rise to so many differences of opinion in the decisions of judges and the doctrines of jurists, that it has not seemed superfluous to set uniform rules (which at first sight may seem over-detailed) to determine the precise point where the rights and obligations that figure in this area arise and where they cease.

* * *

[THERE ARE FOUR sections in the proposed Civil Code]:

Personal Status

Absolute rules, or in other words presumptions against which no proof is accepted, have been established concerning birth and death of persons, as in almost all modern codes. On the presumption of death after a long absence, to which this bill gives the name of "disappearance," thus distinguishing two very different juridical states, our legal bodies feel the need of precise and complete instructions. We have tried to fill this void by copying the legislation of other countries, but with substantial differences. In general, we have lessened the time of provisional possession of the assets of the person who has disappeared. Provisional possessions are an obstacle to the circulation and improvement of assets, and should last only the time necessary to reasonably protect the private rights that may be in conflict with society's general interests. On the other hand, the ease and rapidity of communications between distant countries has increased enormously in our day, and what has increased in the same proportion is the probability that a person of whom no news has been received by his family and business relationships has either ceased to exist or has voluntarily broken the links that held him to his previous home. Though admitting the fallibility of legal presumptions in extraordinary circumstances, we have tried to provide in some way for these extremely rare cases.

A promise of marriage mutually accepted is in this code something wholly subject to the honor and conscience of each of the parties, and produces no obligation whatever in the eyes of civil law.

Ecclesiastical authority retains the right of decision on the validity of matrimony, and impediments to the contraction of matrimony are recognized as those declared as such by the Catholic Church. A marriage that is valid in the eyes of the Church is also valid in civil law, though this does not mean that the temporal power exceeds its rational limits when it denies the civil recognition of a marriage that it believes to have pernicious social and domestic consequences, even though the ecclesiastical authority may have permitted it for considerations of a different nature, relaxing, despite misgivings, its ordinary rules in exceptional circumstances.

Although preserving marital authority in the person of the husband [*potestad marital*], there has been an attempt to prevent its abuses, and women's status has been improved in many respects. Though dowry privileges are eliminated, and the old classification of dowry and non-dowry assets nullified, following the tendency of Spanish jurisprudence, if the legal mortgage of the married woman follows the same path as the other mortgages of its kind (for according to the present bill it ceases to exist and will reach the limit to which the legislature's provisions have tended ever since 1845), to compensate for this the benefit of separation of property has been organized and extended to favor women. The odious inequality between the two spouses in the civil effects of divorce has been lessened, and property acquired during marriage has been regularized; effective guarantees have been given to the preservation of a woman's real property in the hands of her husband.

The status of children is legitimate, natural, or simply illegitimate. As for children illegitimately conceived in a true or putative marriage, the present bill does not differ substantially from that established in other legislations, including ours. As for children legitimized by marriage following conception (the only type of legitimation admitted by the bill), the system adopted combines the rules of Roman law, canon law, and the French Civil Code. In Roman law, a written document was demanded of a man who married his concubine in order to legitimize the children he had had with her; not to make the marriage valid, for this was contracted by simple consent, but to establish that the concubine entered the category of legitimate wife; and if children existed, which of them were being legitimized. This is the doctrine of the most famous interpreters of Roman law. From this it is inferred that legitimation was voluntary on the part of the parents, and did not extend to all the children a man had had with a concubine, but only to those whom the father wished to legitimize. It was also voluntary on the children's part, for without their consent *alieni juris* could not be performed; nor did a child need to associate himself with a father who was perhaps a man of bad reputation and perverse habits. These two principles—legitimation granted by public document and legitimation voluntarily offered and accepted—have been adopted in the bill, with the exception of only two cases: a child conceived before the marriage and born within it, and the natural child, that is, the illegitimate child who has previously been recognized formally and voluntarily by its father or mother. In these two cases they are legitimized *ipso jure* by subsequent marriage.

The status of legitimate child is one of the most important that civil law has created. Then how can it be left to the mercy of testimonial proofs, which are so easy to forge, if not during the parents' lifetimes at least after their deaths? Will the law penetrate into the shadows of these clandestine connections, and confer on them the right to constitute all by themselves the presumption of paternity, which is the privilege of matrimony? Can a carnal, vague, uncertain relationship in which nothing guarantees the fidelity of a woman who has already degraded herself, be a principle of legitimacy, even though the father's opinion does not corroborate it? And supposing that the man believes that the illegitimate child is his, would he be forced to legitimize a son or daughter of bad habits, and would he be placed in the position of either not marrying or introducing a source of immorality and depravity into his family? And would the child, on his part, participate against his will in a debased union, and place the administration of his property in the hands of a dissolute man? Canon law relaxed the principles of Roman law on this point; but the temporal power is the one which must prescribe the necessary conditions for the enjoyment of civil rights.

The code of the *Siete Partidas* confers legitimation *ipso jure*, but only to the child of a concubine, to the natural child. With this detail the present bill is in agreement.

It is an inescapable consequence of the above mentioned principles that legitimation be announced and formally accepted. As for the time when it is offered, the French and other modern codes of law have been followed, but less strictly. No great force has been found in the objections that were at first offered against drawing up an instrument in which husband and wife admit their own failings. This is a sacrifice demanded by the social order, the just expiation of a fault. On the other hand, granting legitimation says nothing that does not reveal much more eloquently the presence of legitimized children in the father's family. Above all, an authentic act covering all claims of the rights and reciprocal obligations of both legitimized and legitimizers has seemed to be supremely necessary. The existence of pre-established documents is an object that has not been lost from sight in other parts of civil legislation, as the best means of preventing controversies and analyzing them.

The voluntary recognition of children born outside marriage has been subjected to similar formalities, and in this case they assume the legal denomination of natural children, and acquire important rights.

As for illegitimate children who do not obtain this spontaneous recognition from their father or mother, they are granted no other right than to request support, and to obtain this the only proof they must have is the father's admission. This is a harsh condition at first sight, but it is justified by the experience of all countries, ours included. The French code and other modern codes of law have been still more severe, for they have absolutely prohibited the investigation of paternity. Nor has there been a prohibition, except in rare cases, of the investigation of maternity by ordinary means, though there are very compelling reasons for treating mother and father in the same way, as expressed by a famous jurist—president of the commission that prepared the Spanish Civil Code—with a great deal of truth, good sense, and sound philosophy.

Majority, fixed at the age of twenty-five, emancipates the child from his family by means of the law. This alone would improve his condition among us, for as you know, according to Roman and Spanish law, there is no single age limit to this state of dependency. Various modern codes have abbreviated considerably the length of parental authority; but—though on this point it has not seemed appropriate to imitate them—in compensation this law has been made much less restrictive and onerous, simultaneously giving effective stimulus to study and industriousness during the early periods in life. Everything that the son acquires in the exercise of a profession, from a job, from any industry, is exempt from the usufruct that the law concedes to the father over the son's property; and in this respect the son is given a true and almost independent personality, which is of course extended to younger emancipated children as long as they remain under guardianship.

The different kinds of guardianship have been carefully defined, as well as the causes that nullify or excuse the exercise of such charges, their administrative features, their duties, their emoluments, and their responsibilities.

Property

As to ownership, use, and enjoyment of property, novelties have been introduced that will lead to important and beneficial results. According to the bill I now present to you, the tradition of ownership of real estate and the other property rights established in it—except those of right of way—must be inscribed in a register similar to that now existing for mortgages and liens, which will be joined with it. Indeed, it is a question of a new fusion of the mortgage regime, associating two objects which are intimately connected, or which—to express it better—are included each in the other, in order to give complete publicity to mortgages and to expose to public view the status of fortunes that consist of possession of land.

As for the former, it can be said that we have merely carried to their logical conclusion the laws of 31 October 1845 and 25 October 1854, giving their true name to the order of things created by the second of these. By Article 15 of this law, special mortgages take precedence over legal ones of any date, which, mutually excluding each other according to the dates of their causes, take precedence only over unofficial credits. Ever since the time, in our country, when the legal mortgage did not prevent the debtor from disposing of any part of his property, or from using it against third creditors, it actually ceased to be a pledge, and consequently ceased to be a mortgage. The only thing that to some degree justified this title was the circumstance that it coincided with special mortgages. Once this prerogative was abolished by the above mentioned Article 15, the name was completely inapplicable. Hence it has seemed best to eliminate it. This bill does not recognize any kind of mortgage but the one formerly called "special," and now simply "mortgage." Moreover, those who enjoyed the benefit of the legal mortgage are exactly in the same situation in which the law of 25 October placed them.

As for bringing to public view the status of land ownership, the simplest procedure was to make obligatory the inscription of all transfers of real estate, including its hereditary transmission, its adjudications, and concessions of property rights. Those of predial right of way were excepted because they did not seem of sufficient importance.

The transference and transmission of ownership, the establishment of all property rights, with those of right of way excepted as I have said, require a tradition; and the only form of tradition that corresponds to these acts is their inscription in the permanent register. As long as inscription is not made, a contract may be perfect, may produce obligations and rights between parties, but it does not transfer ownership or any property right, nor does it have any existence with respect to a third party. The inscription is what gives real, effective possession. And as long as it is not canceled, the person who has not inscribed his title does not possess it; he is a mere holder of it. As the permanent register is open to everyone, there can be no more public, more solemn, more indisputable possession than inscription. In some legislations inscription is a guarantee not only of possession but of ownership. But to carry things to this point, it would have been necessary to force every proprietor, every receiver of usufruct, every user of real estate, to be inscribed after previously establishing the reality and value of their titles. Clearly it was not possible to obtain this result except by compulsive means, which would produce multiple and troublesome judicial procedures, and in many cases contradictory, costly, and lengthy lawsuits. By not giving the permanent registry any character other than that of simple tradition, the possession that it confers leaves intact the rights of the true proprietor, which could be eliminated only by legal prescription. But since not only acts between living persons, but also hereditary transmissions are subject—in the case of real estate—to the solemn act of inscription, all the properties referred to, if they do not belong to juridical persons, at the end of a certain number of years will be registered and sheltered from any attack. Inscription will then be an invincible title of ownership, thus obtaining the result that others wished to attain on the spot, but without the need to use disagreeable measures that would produce a serious upheaval in all landed property.

The benefits that would accrue to this order of things are obvious: the manifest and indisputable possession of real estate, rapidly progressing toward a time when "registration," "possession," and "property," will be identical terms; the territorial property of the entire republic in full public view, in a situation that would simultaneously represent its successive mutations, responsibilities, and divisions; mortgages established on a firm basis; territorial credit invigorated and capable of being mobilized.

The institution that I have just described is similar to the one which has existed for some time in various states in Germany, and which other civilized nations are presently trying to imitate. Its good effects have been widely demonstrated by experience.

Concerning possession, it has been thought useful to adopt a less unwieldy and ambiguous nomenclature than the one used at present. All possession is essentially characterized by the reality or appearance of ownership. The only possessor of a property is the person who holds it as his own, either actually in his power or in the power of another who recognizes him as its owner. Since *de facto* property-holding can be varied, the man who is not the possessor of ownership can be the possessor of a right of usufruct, of use, of habitation, of a right of inheritance, of a right of security or mortgage, or of right of way. The holder of usufruct does not possess the thing he uses; that is, he does not have either real or ostensible ownership of it. He possesses only the usufruct of it, which is a real right and in consequence susceptible of possession. But the renter of a property possesses nothing; he enjoys nothing more than a mandate for preservation of the rights that the contract conferred on him. He who possesses in the name of another is only a representative of the real possessor, nor does he possess more than simple tenancy. Hence the terms "civil possession" and "natural possession" are not to be found in the bill that I submit to you; the words "possession" and "tenancy" are words of opposite meaning in it. Possession is in one's own name; tenancy in the name of another. But possession can be regular or irregular: the former is acquired without violence or clandestinity, with legal title and good faith; the second lacks some or all of these requisites. All possession is protected by the law, but only regular possession places its possessor on the road to acquisitive prescription. This is the system of my bill; its definition indicates precise limits to each of the two species of possession, with both of them preserving the generic nature which consists in the investiture of a real right.

Among the various divisions of ownership, particular attention has been paid to the one which limits it by a condition that, if confirmed, makes it pass to another person, who acquires it finally and absolutely. Usufruct and fiduciary ownership, the property which upon fulfillment of a certain condition expires in one person to be born in another, are, therefore, two contrasting juridical states. In one, termination is necessary; in the other, it is eventual. The former presupposes two actual coexistent rights, but the second only one, for if on the one hand it implies the exercise of a right, then on the other it offers only a simple expectation, which can vanish without leaving any trace of its existence. This is the establishment of fideicommissum. Though there is little or nothing original in the bill, at least it has tried to define the two juridical states in such a way that they will not be confused, to give clear rules of interpretation for the arrangements that establish them, and to enumerate their various and peculiar effects.

Therefore fideicommissum substitution is preserved in this bill, though abolished in many modern codes of law. An offshoot of the law of property has been recognized in it, for every proprietor seems to have this right in order to impose on his liberalities whatever limitations and conditions he wishes. But, once this principle is admitted in all its scope, it would conflict with the public interest and would sometimes either be an obstacle to the circulation of property or would weaken that care in preserving and improving it that has its most powerful stimulus in the expectation of perpetual enjoyment of something without conditions, without responsibilities, and with the ability to transfer it freely between living persons and on the occasion of death. Fideicommissum is admitted, therefore, but gradual substitutions are prohibited even when they are not perpetual, except under the form of a lien in which, consequently, everything relative to the order of succession in entailments has been included. In the lien itself, the special features that make it prejudicial and odious have been weakened.

It is a fundamental rule in this bill to prohibit two or more usufructs or successive fideicommissums; for both of these hinder circulation and dilute the spirit of preservation and improvement, which each give life and movement to industry. An additional rule tending to the same result limits the duration of suspensive and resolutory conditions, which in general are considered expired if they are not exercised during a 30-year period.

In the interesting matter of rights of way, the French Civil Code has been followed almost step by step. For the legal right of way of an aqueduct, we have used as a model the civil code of Sardinia; it is the only one, I believe, among known codes that has sanctioned the same principle as our memorable decree of 18 November 1819, which has brought into cultivation so much land that nature seemed to have condemned to perpetual sterility. But on this point—as on everything having to do with the use and enjoyment of water—this bill, like the code that guided it, has limited itself to little more than establishing bases, reserving details for special ordinances which probably cannot be the same for different localities.

Inheritance

Intestate succession is the point on which the bill departs furthest from existing models. The right of representation does not enter in, except in the legitimate descendants of the person in question, nor in any other descendants but the dead person's children or brothers and sisters, either legitimate or natural, with representation descending to all degrees and with no penalty attached to the circumstance that the person in question had no rights to transmit; it is sufficient that for any reason he has not participated in the inheritance.

The fate of the surviving spouse, and of natural children, has been considerably improved. The surviving spouse who lacks the necessary funds for sustenance has been assured a considerable portion of the dead person's estate, just as is done in the legislation now in existence, but creating equal conditions for widow or widower; if this has sometimes been observed in the past, it was done only by an unjustified interpretation of Roman and Spanish law. In addition to the obligatory assignment of funds, which prevails even over testamentary arrangements and is measured by the legitim of the legitimate children if they exist, the spouse is given by law a part of the intestate succession when there are no legitimate descendants; everything, when there are no survivors from previous generations, nor legitimate siblings, nor natural children of the dead person. Natural children collectively, as well as the spouse, enjoy equal rights in intestate succession.

The inability to inherit mutually by those who have committed the sin of a wicked and punishable union does not descend to the innocent offspring of that criminal connection; and the rights of collaterals in intestate succession extend only to the sixth degree.

As for the legitimate portions that the law allows to heirs, and additional bequests, half of what would have been inherited by each of the legitimate heirs, or heirs to whom the law allows inheritance in the case of *ab intestato*, form their legitim, which can be considerably augmented but not diminished or encumbered in any way. Any person may dispose freely of half of his estate if he has no legitimate descendants who succeed him personally or by representation; if this is not the case, he can distribute only one-fourth of his property with absolute freedom. The remaining fourth must be used for additional bequests; that is, in favor of one or more of his legitimate descendants, as he wishes. Additionally, each person has during his life the ability to make use of his assets as he wishes. Only in extreme cases does the law intervene, imputing to the half or fourth that can be disposed of freely, the excess of what has been given *inter vivos*, and revoking it if necessary.

This has been an attempt to reconcile the right of ownership with the obligation to provide for the well-being of those whom a person has brought into being, or from whom their being has been received. Those other restrictions have been omitted whose aim was to assure the portion allowed by the law and to prevent, in the distribution of assets, the inequalities that might be committed by parents out of capricious favoritism, even when these did not truly defraud any of the legitimate heirs.

More than the law, the parents' good judgment and natural feelings have been considered. When the former goes astray or the latter are lacking, the voice of the law is powerless and its recommendations are very easy to evade; and the sphere in which they can be extended is very narrow. What power has the law, in testamentary matters and donations, against habitual dissipation or vain ostentation, which endangers the future of families? What can the law do against the accidents of gambling, which secretly devour estates? The bill has been limited to restricting the enormous excesses of an indiscreet liberality, which, even though it is not the thing most to be feared by the just hopes of legitimate heirs, is the only thing that civil law can achieve without exceeding its rational limits, without invading the sanctuary of domestic affections, without laying down inquisitorial practices which would be difficult to carry out and would be ineffectual in the end.

In determining hereditary quotas, when the dispositions of the will contain numerical difficulties, the rules of Roman law and the code of the *Partidas* have substantially been followed, with a single exception. It may be surprising that the rules of the bill are conceived in arithmetical formulas. The writer of the *Partidas* does not lay down explicit rules. The judge must deduce them from the examples that are presented to him; this is a generalization more appropriate to the law than to man. Once this rule's necessity was admitted, there were only two ways to go about it: a phraseology that indicated vaguely the arithmetical procedure; or the use of strict formulas which would lead to the resolution of each problem as quickly as possible. This last procedure has seemed to be the one least exposed to inexactitude and errors; and since nowadays arithmetic is a universal branch of primary education, a person who has received any education whatsoever, even of the most common and ordinary kind, will understand its peculiar terms.

Contracts and Obligations

As for contracts and quasi-contracts, there is very little that does not have its source in present-day legislation, which applies to most of them, or in the authority of a modern law code, especially the French code, or in the doctrine of the most eminent jurists. We have kept the practices of our country firmly in mind in some contracts, such as rental contracts, whose special circumstances seem to demand peculiar arrangements. The transfer of ownership in real estate is not completed except by means of a public instrument, nor is it official until it is inscribed in the official registry, which, as I said before, is the sole form of transfer in this class of property. On nullity and recission of contracts and other voluntary acts that constitute rights, we have closely followed the French code, aided by its skillful commentators. The greatest novelty you will find in this section is abolition of the privilege of minors and other natural and juridical persons assimilated to them, to be restored *in integrum* against their acts and contracts. Such a privilege has been regarded not only as extremely damaging to credit, but contrary to the true interests of the privileged persons themselves. With it, as a wise jurist of our day has said, all contracts are broken, all obligations invalidated, and the most legitimate rights disappear. "This restitution," he adds, "is an inexhaustible hotbed of unjust lawsuits, and an easy pretext for making a jest of good faith in contracts. . . ." All the restrictions that have been tried are not sufficient to overcome its most serious obstacle: namely, that it renders useless some contracts that follow all legal procedures, leaves ownership uncertain, and places obstacles to transactions with orphans, who have no less need than others to make contracts for the preservation and enhancement of their interests. What the French code has to say about this matter—in the codes of the Two Sicilies, Sardinia, and others—is much more in agreement with justice, and even more favorable to the minors under tutelage themselves. According to these codes, the contract drawn up with a minor without the consent of his guardian is not null *ipso jure*, though it can be rescinded; but the contract drawn up with all the solemnities of the law is subject to the same conditions as those drawn up by adult persons. The jurist [François] Jaubert, in explaining the reasons for this arrangement, said, "It is indispensable to insure completely the rights of those who deal with minors, by observing the formalities of the law; and if this precaution were not necessary, it would at least be useful owing to the stubborn prejudice that exists against persons under guardianship, believing, and rightly, that contracting with them offers no security."

In the section entitled "On the Proof of Obligations," the existence of a sworn written statement is necessary for every contract involving anything that exceeds a certain amount of money, but the scope for admission of other kinds of proofs is much broader than in other legislations, especially those of France and Portugal, countries in which this requirement of the proof of witnesses is very old, and has produced beneficial effects. I need hardly mention the ease with which, through sworn verbal declarations, the most legitimate rights can be impugned and discarded. In interior towns the existence is known of a perfidious class of men who make a living off prostitution of the oath. The contents of this bill may seem somewhat timid from this point of view, but we have tried hard not to place obstacles to the ease of transactions, and have believed that it was more prudent to wait until another period of time when, after the use of the sworn written statement has become general, the admissibility of verbal proof can easily be restricted to narrower limits.

Various kinds of liens (except for the life lien) have been reduced to only one, and hence are subject to identical rules, among which we need only take note of those which make the lien divisible together with the real property that they affect; and the one which, having to do with real property whose value considerably exceeds that of the taxed sums, permits reducing its value to a certain part, exonerating the rest from any responsibility. But at the same time the interests of lienors have been taken into account, placing a limit on the division which, if continued indefinitely, would make collection of interest payments too difficult and expensive, and which after several generations would convert them into an infinite number of tiny fractions. If by this means the taxing of capital subject to lien would be discouraged, a great good would have been achieved indirectly. The life lien, which by its nature is of short duration, does not offer the same difficulties as the others; it is the only one in this bill which does not admit of redemption, reduction, or division.

In business society contracts, it has been decided to follow the example of nations which, owing to extensive commerce, are well acquainted with the true demands of credit. Members of a business society, according to the present bill, are responsible for the total value of the obligations contracted in its name. At the same time, there has been an attempt to subject the business society to precise rules in its administration, and in the partners' obligations both among themselves and with respect to third parties. The same specification and clarity has been requested in proxies, in building contracts, and in surety bonds.

Among lawful agreements, antichresis [a contract by which a creditor enjoys the products of a mortgaged property by applying them to payment of the debt] has been allowed. Innocent in itself, useful for credit and sometimes palliated, it can now be presented without disguise under the sanction of the law. As a general rule, the code of the *Partidas* and the French Civil Code have been the two guiding lights that we have kept most constantly in view. Where they differ, we have chosen what seemed most adaptable and convenient. The arrangement of preference of credits has been very much simplified, and increase in credit has been the dominant consideration. Concurrent creditors are divided into five categories: those who enjoy a general of privilege; those who enjoy a special privilege over movable property; holders of mortgages; minors, married women, and other persons whose assets are administered by legal representatives; and chirographers. A number of general and special privileges have been abolished, and among them all those that devolve upon real property. It is hardly necessary to state that preferential credits do not survive in this bill either in the form of conventional mortages or in public documents. The work that was begun by the laws of 1845 and 1854 has been completed.

Innovations no less favorable to the security of possessions and of credit will be found in the article entitled "Of Prescription." Prescription of thirty continuous years wipes out all credits, all privileges, all real actions. Every personal obligation that has ceased to be required during the same period of time will lapse. But this exception must always be requested by the person who intends to enjoy its benefits; judges cannot supply it.

I shall finish with some general observations.

In this bill, public and private instruments (which one famous modern writer has called "preconstituted proofs" [*prvebas preconstituides*]) are made obligatory for certain acts and contracts which the law does not require today. To this number belong legitimation by subsequent marriage and the recognition of natural children, of which I have already spoken; definition of guardianship and pupilage in all cases; assumption by the wife or recovery by the husband of administration of the conjugal society; and acceptance or repudiation of all inheritance. It prescribes the drawing up of a solemn inventory in the case of the father who, while administering assets for a child, marries again and requires as a previous condition the inventory of hereditary assets, when the heir proposes not to contract the responsibility of such an inventory until agreement about the value of what he inherits. Either a public or a private deed is required for every conventional obligation over a certain amount. All change of property and all establishment of rights of property are subject to the solemnity of a public instrument, without which instrument they do not produce civil obligations, even among the contracting parties themselves; and the credit that is enjoyed by a fourth degree of preference in insolvency proceedings cannot be obtained except when established in the same manner, barring only actions for indemnification of damages on account of bad administration by legal representatives.

The usefulness of this type of proof is obvious in order to prevent contests and claims; to protect the interests of minors and other persons without detriment to the credit in whose increase these same persons are interested, as are all persons; and to prevent frauds that may be hatched under cover of their privileges.

As for the method and plan that have been followed in this code, I will observe that it could have been made less voluminous, omitting either the examples that often accompany abstract rules or the corollaries derived from them, and which are certainly unnecessary to the experienced eyes of magistrates and jurists. But in my opinion we have been correct in preferring the opposite method, imitating in this the wise legislator of the *Siete Partidas*. Specific examples place before our eyes the true meaning and spirit of a law in its applications; corollaries demonstrate what is contained in it, which may escape less perspicacious eyes. Brevity, in this regard, has seemed to be a secondary consideration.

The current bill is presented to you after having been discussed at length and modified by a select commission that was greatly concerned about accuracy and highly deserving of the public's confidence. The discussion of a work of this kind in the legislative chambers would postpone its promulgation for a very long time, when it is already an imperious necessity; and after all, the legislature could not confer upon it the unity, the agreement, the harmony, that are its essential characteristics. I do not presume to offer a perfect work in these respects; no such work has as yet come from the hand of man. But I do not fear to pronounce judgment by announcing that, through adoption of the present bill, a large part of the difficulties that for the moment obstruct the administration of civil justice will disappear. A large number of lawsuits will be cut off at the root, and the judicial arm will gain all the more confidence and veneration when the agreement of its decisions with legal precepts becomes patent. Practice will no doubt uncover defects in the execution of this arduous undertaking; but the legislature can easily correct them once they are properly understood, as has been done in other countries, and even in France itself—the country to which the most famous of law codes is owed, and the one that has been the model for so many others.

One indispensable addition remains to be made, a law of transition that will facilitate observance of the Code. That the law should not have a retroactive effect is a principle that the Code itself sanctions, and which seems as obvious as it is just. But its application is not so easy. Many cases may be presented in which application of that rule would give rise to a difference of opinion, as has been seen in all the countries where one body of laws has been replaced by another. It is necessary to distinguish mere expectations from acquired rights, and forms from substance.

I believe I have said enough to recommend to your wisdom and patriotism the adoption of the present bill regarding the Civil Code, which I propose to you jointly with the Council of State.

Government and Society

(1843)

Nothing is easier than to criticize a government by accusing it not only of all the bad things that exist, but all the good things that do not; this second theme is a vast one, susceptible to oratorical exaggerations so facile and brilliant that few writers have sufficient discipline not to let their pens run freely, even at the expense of reason and justice.[11] What defense can our government make against the magnificent catalogue of everything we lack? Decrees and regulations are called routine and meaningless because they do not have the magic power to confer as rapid a movement on social life as we see in other nations, whose material and moral advantages, as everyone admits, are far beyond comparison with ours. Yes, the catalogue of what we lack is immense, and the comparison of our social situation with that of more privileged nations offers us little motive for pride. But reason and justice demand that, to attribute this difference to the government, we would have to find out: first, to what extent government is responsible for it, and what specific measures, in the opinion of the critics, would produce the instant metamorphosis they yearn for; and second, to what extent these marvels of public spirit and industry are owed to the economic measures of governments in those fortunate countries that they present to us as models.

It is an fact that social activity, rapid movement of industry, and accelerated increase in prosperity, have not been the work of government in those countries, nor have they been owed except in very small part to administrative procedures. The chief agent in the production of these phenomena is the public spirit of those countries' inhabitants, favored by particular circumstances. Among these are: race (as some people believe); a very old moral and political education that has had time to put down deep roots in customs; geographical location, abundance of natural products endlessly desired by other nations and easily exchanged for the products of foreign industry; and internal transportation systems provided on a large scale by nature herself. In one place there exist virgin soil with immense possibilities for expansion and colonization, vast and fertile stretches of territory, bathed in all directions by voluminous and navigable rivers, and a torrent of European immigration brought there first by necessity and later by custom. In other places there are an ancient culture, flourishing arts and sciences, and capital accumulated over centuries. Do the new American republics have these means within their grasp? Is it possible for them to change the profound and mysterious effects of organic action, which, according to some, make the Anglo-Saxon fiber so different from that of the Celt or the Iberian? Is it possible for them to change customs in an instant? Is it within their power to create, where they do not exist, those colossal instruments of greatness to which the United States owe their rapid progress, or those precious crops that in a few years have multiplied the wealth of Cuba ten times over? Shall we say to the mountains, be moved, and to the turbulent rivers, lend your waters to internal navigation? Even if we had all that power in our hands, we would have to perform a new miracle by bringing our coasts closer to the world's great markets. If we compare in good faith what the Chilean nation has achieved along all lines by the means that Heaven has placed at her disposal, with the gifts that nature has lavished on other nations, we will find no reason to humiliate her. For on this point the government and the nation have a joint task. It is useless to regard national prosperity as the exclusive province of the government. Everywhere, prosperity has been the collective work of society; and if we cannot blame society for what it does not do without taking its material elements into account, much less can we blame the government without simultaneously taking into account matter and spirit, customs, laws, and moral and political antecedents. To do otherwise would be a manifest injustice. Let everyone say what we lack, and welcome; repeating it will never be out of place. But let us explore the causes of that lack and then point out means of correcting it; then, examination of the social accomplishments of other countries will be both instructive and abundant in practical results.

What the government can promise to its voters is a fervent desire to merit public approval, an assiduous attention to the community's interests, and a firm resolution to find its inspirations in those interests and not in the atmosphere of partisan politics. Imbued with these sentiments, it will always welcome the suggestions of the press as long as they are founded on reasonable and just principles of politics and economics. Never has the government been more ready to listen to the press than when, served by enlightened writers and zealous advocates for humanity and the people, it is seen as ready to fulfill its highest and most beautiful mission: that of proposing and discussing useful innovations and simultaneously preparing for them. But clear and definite advice is needed, not airy speculations. Golden dreams and theatrical concepts are no match for the severe and inflexible laws of matter and spirit, laws that place quite narrow limits on human legislators' sphere of action.

We have to see things as they are. Government cannot act without the agreement of the nation; and even the meeting of all the political powers cannot control material accidents. To change moral phenomena it must do so by means of laws, which influence customs all the more slowly the more necessary it is to depend on them in order to be effective. The progress of our republic will not be like that of Homer's gods. But who ever said that all republics, or even most of them, have progressed like that? In our opinion, social progress has been more rapid where a fortunate combination of circumstances has favored it. Because of those circumstances the North American states progress rapidly; because of them, New Holland and Cuba, which are not republics, also progress. If those natural and moral circumstances develop prodigiously under the influence of democratic freedom, it is not impossible that their action may sometimes be so powerful that even the hobbles of colonial servitude will not slow them down. And the confluence of those circumstances is so necessary that without them freedom itself, the most active and influential of political influences, will operate in a relatively slow and feeble way on material developments.

Each nation has its features, its aptitudes, its method of moving forward; each nation is destined to pass more or less swiftly through certain social phases. And no matter how great and beneficent the influence of some nations on others, it will never be possible for one of them to blot out its peculiar character and adopt a foreign model; and, we insist, this would not be suitable even if it were possible. Humankind, as one man who best understood the democratic spirit has said, does not repeat itself. Freedom develops industry in modern societies, to be sure; but this development, in order to be as rapid in one country as in another, must be based on equally favorable circumstances. Freedom is only one of a number of social forces, and supposing this force to be equal in two given nations does not mean that it will produce equal effects in its combination with other forces, which, either in parallel or in antagonism, must necessarily come together in it.

Hence freedom is not as exclusive as some believe. It allies itself with all national characteristics and betters them without changing their nature; it allies itself with all the predispositions of the mind and gives them vigor and daring. It gives wings to the industrial spirit wherever it can be found and cultivates industry where industry does not exist. But it is not in the nature of freedom to act except with the two great elements of all human actions: nature and time. Administrative measures can undoubtedly either retard or accelerate movement. But we must not exaggerate freedom's power. There are moral obstacles that it should not face head-on. There are natural accidents that it cannot change. Those who accuse freedom of being inert or timid will do the public a great favor by pointing out the route it ought to follow in its progress. Above all, do not forget that it is under the influence of popular institutions that customs can least be disregarded, and that abstractly useful and civilizing, progressive measures—adopted without concern for the circumstances—can be very harmful to us and can involve us in endless evils and calamities.

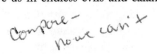

Letter to Manuel Ancízar[12]
(1856)

11 October 1856
Señor Don Manuel Ancízar
Santiago
My very dear friend:

I have inadvertently written "Don," forgetting that the word is considered rude and offensive *piarum currium* in Bogotá. Wouldn't it be a good idea to omit "Señor" too, which means the same, and is still more insulting than "Don"?

Dear friend, I can't get used to being deprived of the spiritual nourishment that you so freely dispensed to me in your conversation. Just now I am living, or rather vegetating, in the most abject prose, except when I am in the company of our mutual friend General [Francisco Antonio] Pinto and another survivor or two of the eighteenth century. It is only rarely that young people nowadays have your tolerance for the musty ideas that form most of the furnishings of my brain, at least in political matters; though to tell the truth, in those ideas I belong to no political party, and what I do profess (in my heart of hearts) is skepticism. Don't think that this means I am in opposition to new things; but I do demand for them the credentials of experience and guarantees of *social order*, which for me means *security, peace, mutual tolerance*, and *material well-being*, with a moderate dose of *freedom*. If material well-being (as I believe) is not the aim but the barometer of civilization, then Chile has no reason to be discontented with itself. Some have laughed at our telegraphs and railroads. I myself fell into the error of thinking them premature. But the truth is that today the telegraph is a real necessity between Santiago and Valparaíso, that other telegraph lines are being considered, and that the Atacama railroad is quite useful. Other lines are planned, work progresses on the southern railroad, and the part already built between Valparaíso and Santiago helps itself and the other lines with the not inconsiderable revenues that it produces. Would you believe that more than four hundred carriages of all sizes and shapes circulate in Santiago for the exclusive comfort of its citizens? I am experiencing this and can hardly believe it. There is not a single street where large and magnificent buildings are not going up.

On the same day that I received your welcome letter, I went to the Ministry of Foreign Relations, which is no longer under the charge of Don Antonio Varas but of Don Francisco Javier Ovalle. Señor Varas has retired from public life with empty pockets, but with immense popularity. The new ministry continues to be imbued with the same spirit. So, I went to the Ministry of Foreign Relations and spoke to Señor Ovalle about sending four copies of the *Civil Code*, and about the appointment of Don Manuel Cordovéz to the consulate in Bogotá. The first errand was accepted without difficulty. The second will be taken under advisement, and I am convinced that it will have the result you want. I will spare no effort to promote it.

I believe that the new Code has few things that will seem acceptable to the patriots of Bogotá. In the matter of marriages and divorces we have made no progress, nor was progress possible. Instead the Code was made somewhat statutory, to render the spirit and application of its rules better understood. What will perhaps be judged more indulgently there is the abolition of restitutions *in integrum*, and establishment of territorial property and mortgages and other real rights.

I have received many printed materials of various stripes from Bogotá, and was already sure that I owed most of them to your kindness. *El Tiempo* is received here very regularly, and General Pinto reads it with great interest.

Tell me, my dear friend, of the progress made by the topographical expedition of [Agustín] Codazzi; it is a subject that interests me very much. I would like to know whether the botanical and astronomical seeds sowed by the famous [Jose Francisco] Caldas, so tragically lost to us, are preserved in Bogotá.

I don't want to prolong the pain that your eyes will suffer when you read these scrawled lines, those of a septuagenarian in whom the flame of life begins to gutter; but until its last spark he will preserve in his heart the memory of Ancízar, his good friend and true patriot.

Affectionately yours,
A[ndrés]. Bello

[PS.] My wife sends you most affectionate greetings. Josefina has married.

NOTES TO PART III

1. This letter never reached its intended destination, having been intercepted and sent to the authorities in Gran Colombia. Pedro Gual, the Minister of Foreign Relations, instructed the representative in London, José Rafael Revenga, to keep his distance from Bello. This letter provided the basis for the belief, echoed long after the matter had been cleared up that Bello was a monarchist. The text of the letter is in *OC*, vol. 25, pp. 114–117.

2. First published in *El Araucano*, No. 83, 14 April 1832. It is included in *OC*, vol. 18, pp. 83–84. Bello makes reference to Andrew Jackson's message to the US Congress in December 1831, but the central concern of the article is the relationship between political structures and nation building. Bello was reluctant to reject monarchy, which had different legacies in North and Spanish America. He was equally reluctant to advocate a political model that had proved successful in the United States, but which would not necessarily have the same results in Spanish America.

3. First published in *El Araucano*, No. 270, 6 November 1835. It is included in *OC*, vol. 18, p. 93. Although Bello once again showed his reluctance to reject monarchy as a political system, here he provided his strongest statement to the effect that "the time for monarchies has passed in America."

4. The following series of articles was published in *El Araucano*. They have been edited for the purposes of this collection, and arranged in sequence following a different format from *OC*, which published them under two general titles, "Reconocimiento de las repúblicas hispanoamericanas por la España," in vol. 10, pp. 545–561, and "Reconocimiento de la independencia suramericana por España," in vol. 11, pp. 295–321. Sections 1–4 were published in *El Araucano*, Nos. 232 (20 February 1835); 235 (13 March 1835); 239 (3 April 1835), and 253 (10 July 1853). Sections 5–7 appeared in *El Araucano* Nos. 252 (3 July 1835); 257 (7 August 1835); 258 (14 August 1835), and 259 (21 August 1835). Sections 8 and 9

appeared in the same periodical in Nos. 342 (25 March 1837) and 734 (13 September 1844). Bello was Vice-Minister (*Oficial Mayor*) in the Ministry of Foreign Relations. His views, therefore, reflect government policy and must be credited with the successful outcome of 1844.

5. First published in *El Araucano*, Nos. 742 and 743, of 8 and 15 November 1844, respectively. It is included in *OC*, vol. 10, pp. 641–656. Bello's views in this essay grow out of his concerns about international law. Although the proposal for a Latin American congress did not succeed, for the very reasons stated in the letter by Bello to Antonio Leocadio Guzmán that follows this selection, the proposal reflected Chilean government views, and included items and issues that gave substance to Chile's foreign policy. Bello articulated that policy and defended it in the press, as was his custom.

6. First published in Miguel Luis Amunátegui, *Vida de Don Andrés Bello* (Santiago: Imprenta Pedro G. Ramírez, 1882), pp. 376–78. It is included in *OC*, vol. 26, pp. 448–453. Guzmán, a fellow Venezuelan, had a distinguished political career in their native land. Bello's letter, written in the twilight of his life, is significant in that it acknowledges the problems of creating a viable Latin American congress, and implicitly recognizes the enormous weight of nationalism in the region.

7. The *Principios de derecho de jentes* was first published in Santiago in 1832. Bello supervised two other editions under the title of *Principios de derecho internacional* in 1844 and 1864, the latter being the most complete. The text of the two chapters included in this section is extracted from the 1864 edition, which is included in *OC*, vol. 10, pp. 13–49. A comparison of the various editions shows that the central points remain essentially the same. This would place Bello's ideas on international law as among the first in Latin America in the post-independence period. Of particular relevance to the subject of nation building are the sections on the sovereignty of recently independent states (b–6), and the matter of debt (b–8), which Bello considered fundamental for the credibility of the new nations.

8. First published in three untitled parts in *El Araucano*, Nos. 140 (17 May 1833), 141 (25 May 1833), and 142 (1 June 1833). It is included in *OC*, vol. 18, pp. 85–92 under the title "Reformas a la constitución." The 1833 Constitution, which replaced that of 1828 and remained in effect with modifications until 1925, has been widely regarded as the pillar sustaining Chile's political stability during the nineteenth century. Bello commented favorably on it, and he may well have had a hand in writing it.

9. First published in three untitled articles in *El Araucano*, Nos. 307 (27 July 1836); 311 (19 August 1836), and 312 (26 August 1836). It is included in *OC*, vol. 18, pp. 50–65. Bello's reflections on the law must be placed in the context of his emphasis on internal order. Just as the nation required a constitutional

framework to guide political development, a firmly established judicial system was necessary to guide individual conduct. Only observance of the law could keep the entire system balanced. Bello devoted considerable attention to defining legislation for both individual and social activity.

10. The following proposal for the adoption of the Civil Code was made by President Manuel Montt to the Chilean Congress on 22 November 1855, but it was prepared by Andrés Bello, who was also the author of both the project and the finished product. The Civil Code was promulgated [into law] in December 1855, and went into effect on January 1, 1857. More than twenty years in the making, the Civil Code had the participation of other law makers, but it was essentially the product of Bello's knowledge and writing. It is included in its entirety, with valuable commentary, in vols. 14, 15 and 16 of *OC*.

11. First published in *El Araucano*, No. 647, 13 January 1843. It is included in *OC*, vol. 18, pp. 179–185. A long quotation has been edited from the original, but it does not alter the main purpose of this article: that social virtues and favorable geographic and economic conditions, more than abstract political models, are important contributors to the progress of nations.

12. Letter included in *OC*, vol. 26, pp. 337–339. Manuel Ancízar was a Colombian writer, educator and politician who represented his country in Chile in the 1850s. In this lighthearted letter, Bello summarized his political beliefs and embraced the changes experienced by Chile during his lifetime.